DATE DUE

JL 28 2005			
AUG 15 '05			
SEP 03 2005			
JAN 24 2006			
JUL 05 2011			
FEB 28 2012			
JAN 31 2015			
GAYLORD			PRINTED IN U.S.A.

DISCARDED
DISCARDED

JOSEPHINE COUNTY   6/05
LIBRARY SYSTEM
GRANTS PASS, OREGON

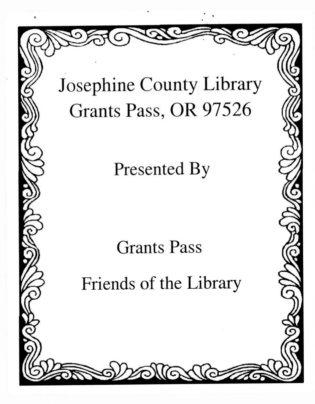

Josephine County Library
Grants Pass, OR 97526

Presented By

Grants Pass

Friends of the Library

FASHION VICTIM

FASHION VICTIM

a novel

Sam Baker

ballantine books new york

Josephine County Library
Grants Pass, Oregon

Fashion Victim is a work of fiction. Names, characters, places, and incidents are the products of the author's imagination or are used fictitiously. Any resemblance to actual events, locales, or persons, living or dead, is entirely coincidental.

A Ballantine Book
Published by The Random House Publishing Group

Copyright © 2005 by Sam Baker

All rights reserved under International and Pan-American Copyright Conventions. Published in the United States by Ballantine Books, an imprint of The Random House Publishing Group, a division of Random House, Inc., New York.

Ballantine and colophon are registered trademarks of Random House, Inc.

www.ballantinebooks.com

LIBRARY OF CONGRESS CATALOGING-IN-PUBLICATION DATA

Baker, Sam, 1966–
Fashion victim : a novel / Sam Baker.—1st ed.
p. cm.
ISBN 0-345-47587-9
1. Women journalists—Fiction.   2. London (England)—Fiction.
3. New York (N.Y.)—Fiction.   4. Paris (France)—Fiction.
5. Fashion shows—Fiction.   I. Title.

PR6102.A574F37 2005
823'.92—dc22   2004055400

Manufactured in the United States of America

2   4   6   8   9   7   5   3   1

First Edition: June 2005

Text design by Laurie Jewell

For Jon

acknowledgments

I owe a huge debt of gratitude to countless people, in no particular order . . . Jonny Geller, truly an agent with vision (or should that be blind faith?); Jane Wood, genius editor with excellent taste in croissants; Doug Kean, who answered every stupid question I asked without even gritting his teeth; and the American team, Emma Parry and Allison Dickens.

Nancy Brady, Clare Grogan, and Catherine Turner for alcohol, sanity (of sorts), and excellent accessories. Oonagh Brennan, partner-in-crime and fellow sufferer of "the fashion feeling"; Laura Bacharach—unsurpassed in the art of blagging; Shelly Vella for her limitless fashion knowledge, Jane Alexander and Shelley Marks for helping me out of "someone stole my title" hell. Ali Harris, a woman who genuinely knows how to keep a secret.

Julian Vogel, first among many, whose economy-class seat allocations gave me the view from the back row essential to write this novel. Kate White, who has been beyond generous with her time, advice, and friendship. Staff at the Red Flame Diner and Algonquin Hotel. And, almost finally, Marc Jacobs, genius and fashion designer, who doesn't know me from Adam but whose Autumn/Winter 2003 show unwittingly gave me the inspiration for Annie Anderson's first outing.

And, absolutely finally, to Jon Courtenay Grimwood, for just about everything and the rest, but the words *patience* and *saint* spring to mind.

Part One

chapter one

"What I don't understand is why?"

Annie Anderson took a deep breath and began to reply. "Well, the thing is, Mum—"

"You get bored too easily, that's your trouble."

Same conversation, same chance of coming out on top.

"Mum! I'm not *bored*—"

"Why can't you just stay put? You've hardly been there for five minutes and now you're chucking it all in to work on one of those magazines that make women anorexic."

The horror with which her mother said this made Annie wince.

"And what about money?" her mother continued, barely pausing for breath. "You always said magazines paid less than newspapers."

"They're paying me the same. Not a penny difference." It was Annie's first truthful comment since her mother called. Staring at the scruffy woman who stared back from the rain-spattered office window, Annie scowled; her short dark curls looked like she'd just gotten out of bed, and not in a good way.

"So why are you leaving, if they're not even paying you more?"

Too late Annie realized that a bigger salary might have given her mother a reason for accepting the change. Damn it, why hadn't that occurred to her ten seconds earlier? Holding the phone away from her ear, Annie began to count slowly: *one . . . two . . . three . . . four . . . five . . . six . . .*

"Annie," came the voice. "Are you there?"

Annie forced a smile onto her face in the hope it would carry through to her voice. "Mum," she said patiently. "This is a great opportunity. And you know I always wanted to work on a glossy. *Handbag* is really well respected and I'll get to travel all over the world. New York, Paris, Milan . . . Just think, I'll see all those amazing cities and it won't cost me a penny. Anyway, you're always saying how much you worry about me being lonely since Nick left, now you won't have to. Maybe I'll find a good-looking Italian . . ."

It wasn't hard to interpret the silence swirling down the telephone line. Annie had played the wrong card and she knew it. She could almost see her mother's face, tight-lipped with disapproval as she sat at the kitchen table, six o'clock news playing in the background, one eye on Dad's tea bubbling on the cooker, the other focused inward on the mess her younger daughter was making of her life.

Disturbed only by the distant murmur of Trevor McDonald, Annie decided to quit while she wasn't ahead and took advantage of the lull.

"Got to go," she said hurriedly. "Can't be late for my own leaving do. Call you Sunday."

Annie pressed the button to kill the call before her mother could object and slumped back in her swivel chair, tossing the mobile onto her now empty desk. Without the usual wad of newspapers, Post-it notes, and random cuttings to block its fall, her Nokia bounced away, landing on the industrial gray carpet in the middle of the five desks that made up the *Post*'s investigations department.

Everyone knew the end of January was a lousy time to change jobs, the worst. Right up there in the Top Ten things everybody knows. It's inevitably borne out of the post-Christmas blues, and Annie's festive season had been enough to give anyone those.

Oh, there were countless reasons why she was doing the wrong thing.

And Annie had heard them all over the past month. Heaving herself out of her chair, Annie trawled around to the other side of the desk to retrieve her mobile. Everything ached, from her brain downward, with the exhaustion of having to listen to other people's opinions—about her life in general, about resigning from the *Post* in particular. Except everyone was wrong, because Annie wasn't leaving; Ken had talked her out of that. She was taking the easy option, going undercover on a soft job.

Ken's idea, their secret.

Crouched by her phone in the half darkness, Annie was randomly punching buttons in an attempt to resurrect its ominously blank screen when a voice from behind almost made her drop the thing again.

"What the hell are you doing here, Anderson? Everybody's waiting for you down at The Swan."

Her boss, news editor Ken Greenhouse, leaned against a filing cabinet, shirtsleeves rolled up, tie half undone, his heavy eyes troubled. "Sure you want to go through with this *Handbag* thing?"

As she checked that her mobile was working, Annie nodded. "Yes," she said, glancing up. "You know why."

The Yorkshireman shrugged. "You couldn't have saved Irina, you know."

"Then I shouldn't have started," said Annie, pushing away the memory of a teenage girl, large eyes dark and haunted, devoid of trust. "Saving her was the whole point, surely?" They were talking about Annie's last story, and not for the first time.

Ken allowed himself a small sigh, deciding not to go there. Instead he summoned a half smile. "Get a move on, love," he said.

"Five minutes," said Annie. "Let me put my face on."

"Five minutes." Collecting his jacket from the back of his chair, Ken Greenhouse strode across the office, stopping off briefly at the night editor's desk as he passed. At the lift he turned and glanced back to where Annie stood.

"Anderson!" he yelled, showing her the spread fingers of one hand. "The Swan. In five."

Annie nodded and watched him thin to nothing as the lift doors closed.

Her face would have to wait, she decided. That glimpse of her reflection in the office window had already confirmed that her pale skin and eyes rimmed gray from lack of sleep needed more than a simple touch-of-mascara-and-dash-of-lippy repair job. And she could always do it in the pub loo, use it as an opportunity to escape.

Not that it would make a blind bit of difference. Annie without makeup looked much the same as Annie with, except for the bright red lips; a shortish woman in her late twenties, not bad looking but for the scowl and a mouth she'd learned the hard way to keep in check.

Annie's PC blinked reproachfully as she clicked on SHUT DOWN. Its dark screen and her desk, empty save for several years of coffee rings, brought home the enormity of her decision.

She'd always had a desk at the *Post,* always known she wanted to come back. But this time was different, and besides, she had to be seen to resign. She could hardly expect to be welcomed with open arms at *Handbag* if there was any suggestion she was still working for the *Post.*

Aware that she'd undoubtedly exceeded her five minutes, Annie grabbed her coat from the stand behind her desk and made herself turn slowly, taking in the entire floor. It was half empty at that time of night. Sky News was playing in the background and Derek, the *Post*'s night editor, was giving some junior hack hell for whatever he had or hadn't done. No change there then.

Rain was sheeting against plate glass as Annie stepped into the foyer. Was it worth bothering with an umbrella? She decided against—her coat already bore the signs of a hard winter, and her reflection in the window upstairs had reminded her there was little about today's very bad hair worth protecting.

" 'Bye, Joe," she called, as she walked past the security man on night shift.

He beamed. Joe was her favorite, a vocal old Irishman with strong opinions on everything and a willingness to share them with anyone who'd listen. His all-time favorite was that the Westbourne Grove end of Notting Hill, Annie's stomping ground, was an overpriced hellhole and no amount of money could induce him to live there. Apparently the council had tried to move him there once, about thirty years earlier, but Joe was having none of it. He was right, of course, Notting Hill was a hellhole, just not for the reasons he thought.

Be nice to Joe, Annie had long ago discovered, and you had an ally for life. Consequently, there were many times he'd helped her "borrow" her colleagues' prebooked taxis when she had been running late. She owed him. Big time.

"Ah, 'bye Annie. You'll be back, surely."

"Maybe, who knows?" said Annie, and bundled herself through the revolving door.

Turning left, Annie headed down Old Street, clinging as closely as possible to the walls in the hope of gaining shelter from any overhang. She could have run there in seconds, but Annie wasn't ready to face her workmates yet. Walking slowly from one doorway to the next, Annie watched the windows of The Swan grow closer. It was one of those renovation jobs that fancied itself more wine bar than pub and as a result almost everyone on the paper professed to hate it. But everyone still went there, convenience getting the better of stylistic preferences.

Ken had hired the upstairs bar, a Victorian room that retained traces of the nineteenth-century pub The Swan had once been. Doubtless the brewery would get around to ruining the second floor, too, but they hadn't yet.

From where she stood in the rain, Annie could see enough shadows reflected against the upper windows to make her feel sick. Parties were okay and she liked free alcohol as much as the next person—that was practically a prerequisite for the job. At least it was if you worked for Ken Greenhouse. Birthdays, engagements, promotions, and leaving dos . . . All were fine with Annie as long as one crucial box was ticked: They belonged to someone else.

By now she was standing in the door of a twenty-four-hour newsagent, scarcely ten feet from the pub, rain dripping onto her head and trickling down the side of her face. "Come on," she told herself. "Usual rules: Get in there, get it over with, get out again."

Annie was about to follow her own advice when the pocket of her coat vibrated against her hip. It took a few seconds to untangle the Nokia from the used tissues and taxi receipts that filled her coat pocket. Two words flashed on its screen, JANE, HOME. For all of a second Annie contemplated answering, then she punched the red button to reject Jane's call. Her older sister would already be leaving a message on Annie's voicemail and her voicemail would call and then text Annie to inform her of that fact. It was a system designed to persecute call evaders, and Annie didn't need to play back any message to know exactly how it would go. She'd heard it all before.

"Anderson!" Ken bellowed, and every head in the bar turned toward her. "Call that five minutes! It's a wonder you ever met a fucking deadline!"

There was a ripple of laughter as Annie's colleagues readied themselves for one of Ken's stand-up specials at Annie's expense. But it never came.

Struggling out of her coat, Annie dumped it on top of a precarious pile of about fifty others on a table just inside the door and fixed her air-hostess smile firmly in place as a photographer from the sports desk pushed a glass of lukewarm Sauvignon Blanc into her hand. As she took it, Annie noticed his hand lingered on the stem a second longer than was strictly necessary. She looked at him inquiringly and then remembered. He'd e-mailed her several times a day afterward, seemingly unable to read between the lines of her nonexistent replies. Annie had been bloody glad to be sent to Glasgow after that. By the time she'd returned he'd been in Tokyo for the World Cup and that had been the end of it.

"Come on, Anderson, get over here!" Ken was gesticulating wildly from his position by the bar.

Annie flashed him the grin he was expecting and burrowed through the crowd. She knew what was coming; better let him have his fun.

"Oi, you lot!" he yelled into the racket. "Shut the fuck up! I've got a few words to say."

To Annie's astonishment, everyone did.

"Right, everybody here knows Annie. And if you don't, get out 'cause you're not having another round at my expense."

There was a polite smattering of laughter.

"I won't keep you long, because as you all know I'm not given to flowery words."

More laughter, far less polite.

"I want to pay tribute to one of the best chief investigative reporters I've ever had."

Thrown, Annie caught the smile before it dropped from her face. She'd been expecting ten minutes of Ken's gags about her appalling timekeeping, nonexistent tea-making skills, and weird dress sense; those she could cope with. Plaudits weren't part of the deal.

Christ, she thought, *not the unedited highlights, please.*

"I remember Annie's first day," Ken started. "We thought we'd give her a girlie job, see what she was made of, and sent her out in a skirt that looked more like a belt, told her if she wanted to be an investigative journalist she could investigate a few building sites. A few of you will remember that feature. And Annie, the boys from the sports desk have asked me to give you this."

It was a card, mocked up by one of the designers. A very much younger and slightly plumper Annie stood next to scaffolding, a yellow hard hat crammed onto unruly curls. She wore a child-sized Bob the Builder T-shirt so tight that even her breasts looked large in it and steel-capped boots several sizes too large. Annie was five feet four, not exactly stumpy, but next to the foreman—six feet plus and sixteen stone—she looked tiny.

There were snorts of laughter, and Annie felt her face grow warm. Of course she remembered that bloody feature, how could she forget? It had been pinned on the production editor's wall for years afterward. Annie Anderson in a skirt so short you could practically see her knickers, scowling for the camera.

"Annie soon proved she had real balls and over the years she's made me proud I took a punt on her. Thanks to Annie, cowboy cosmetic surgeons have been struck off, premiership footballers out on the shag before a big match have been caught with their pants down, and a top London hotel that best remain nameless found itself in very deep shit for employing illegal immigrants. And let's not even mention how Glasgow city council feel about us after Annie's investigation into homelessness in their fair city—"

"Yay!"

"Go Annie!"

"Good one!"

The news desk contingent had clearly been drinking a little longer than everyone else. Grateful for the momentary diversion, Annie took the opportunity to tear her eyes away from her feet and glanced around. Almost everyone was looking at her, some staring, others whispering.

Get a move on, Ken, she thought, *for Christ's sake.*

"But that's not all," Ken continued on cue. "Because Annie's last story for the *Post* was her greatest coup yet."

Annie's eyes returned to her feet.

"The rumors had been circulating for months. We had a pretty good idea Eastern European kids were being imported straight into prostitution under our noses, right here in Kings Cross. Could we prove it? Could we fuck. Plenty of far more experienced journalists than Annie tried and failed. Even the Met couldn't get the evidence they needed, until we put Annie on it. Annie and her team blew it wide open and saved a few kids' lives in the process. I think we all know this is where the *Post*'s next British Press Award is coming from."

Ken looked genuinely proud as he stared at her, like Annie's father had looked the day he'd walked up the aisle with his oldest daughter wearing a dress like a meringue. Annie, on the other hand, really did not want to think about those damaged teenagers, not now, not at all.

"So, Annie . . ." Ken was smiling warmly. "Even though you're abandoning us. Sodding off to some bloody poncy magazine to teach them about proper journalism, better known as putting your feet up and pocketing the freebies—"

More uproarious laughter and Annie joined in, confident that the worst was over.

"—we've got a little something for you to remember us by."

Reaching behind him, Ken took a large flat parcel from where it had been lying, facedown on the bar. Annie knew what it was; she'd been to enough leaving dos over the years, and it was always the same. A couple of fake headlines, her face imposed on someone else's body. The usual.

Only it wasn't.

Ripping off the paper, Annie found a framed page from the *Post*. A front page from the previous October dominated by one haunting image. The face of Irina Krodt, barely sixteen but looking far younger, devastatingly pretty with sallow skin and dark hair. It was Irina's eyes that haunted Annie, dark and dead, staring flatly out of the page, making everyone who looked into them culpable.

EXCLUSIVE! screamed the tag. POST SMASHES CHILD PROSTITUTION RING! Underneath, the byline read ANOTHER POST EXCLUSIVE BY ANNIE ANDERSON.

Innocent life lost in process, Annie thought bleakly. Funny how they hadn't mentioned that on the front page.

A Post-it note stuck to the back of the frame read, *I'll be here, call me—* and then Ken's home number scrawled in blue biro.

As if she didn't already know it by heart.

"Speech!"

"Yes, come on, Anderson, speech!"

Clinging to the frame as if it were all that held her up, Annie gazed around, searching for something to focus on. Anything would do. Fifty-odd faces were turned toward her, all willing her to speak. Annie swallowed hard and settled her gaze on an old beer poster above the heads of the people at the back. As she did so, she caught the eye of the *Post's* fashion editor, Lou McCartney, who winked and gave Annie a supportive wave.

Lou, as ever, was immaculately dressed, her Prada coat perfectly offsetting thrift shop boots. Anyone else would have looked like a bag lady but Lou just looked, well, like Lou . . . It was Lou who had helped Annie get an in with *Handbag* magazine.

"Th-thanks," Annie stammered. "I've, uh, had a wonderful time at the *Post*. It's been fantastic. I've loved every minute of it. Well, not *every* minute obviously . . ."

She knew she should be gushing Oscar-style about her talented team, the fantastic paper, those career-making awards, how much she owed Ken Greenhouse. She'd had a speech all planned in her head before she even entered the pub, but now she couldn't think of anything but Irina, couldn't see anything but Irina's haunted eyes. In the absence of any better idea, Annie opted for humor.

"Er, I'll miss you all more than you can possibly realize. Even whatshisname on the sports desk."

"Yeah right!" muttered a girl in the corner and there was a burst of relieved laughter, the tension subsiding as quickly as it had surfaced.

"Sure you will!" yelled another woman.

"You know where to find us when you can't fit any more free gear in your wardrobe!"

Raucous chatter filled the room.

"Attention span of gnats, that lot," Ken said. "Let me put this somewhere safe for you." He eased the frame from her fingers. As he did so he gazed down at the page.

"Good story, that," he said. "And, for the record, Anderson, what happened wasn't your fault. Whatever you think."

Annie wished she could believe that.

For the first time since entering the bar, Annie was no longer the center of attention. She took in the faces around her. The last five years of her life were in this room.

The news desk hard core were propping up the bar, knocking back bottles of Becks with Bells chasers and irritating everyone in the immediate vicinity by reenacting old snatches from *The Office*. Only their choice of sketches had changed in the time Annie had known them: One year it had been *League of Gentlemen*, another *The Fast Show*.

"Annie . . ." A hand settled on her shoulder and she turned to find Al, her partner on the investigations team, standing so close she could feel his breath on her face. Carefully she inched away.

"There's still time to change your mind," Al said. "I mean, why would anyone give up all this . . ." He gestured to the pile of damp coats steaming gently in one corner, the alcohol-slicked floor, steamed-up windows, raised voices, and drunken laughter.

"Why would anyone give up this for posh frocks and champagne parties in the fashion capitals of the world?"

It was disconcerting, she thought, how you could have a passing acquaintance with every single person in a room and still not have anyone to talk to. There was barely a face she didn't recognize, but scarcely one she felt she really knew, except Ken. And Lou.

Lou and Annie had joined the *Post* in the same month and were the same age. Only their star signs and hair colors were different—Annie's dark brown hair had always resisted her halfhearted attempts at DIY bleach, while Lou's came out of a professional's bottle and was topped up every six to eight weeks. They'd hit it off instantly, a rare occurrence for Annie and one that hadn't been repeated since. She could count the people she regarded as real friends on less than one hand. Life was easier that way.

Making a beeline for the spot where she'd last seen Lou, Annie saw the top of her friend's blond head, damp hair piled haphazardly on top, soggy tendrils hanging down her neck. Lou hadn't moved from beneath a real ale poster, where she was locked in conversation with a subeditor Annie couldn't put a name to and one of the senior reporters, Colin Green.

"I mean, it's obvious, isn't it?" Green was saying. "The woman's got a Messiah complex. It's never just a story to her, oh no. She's got to save everybody. I mean what's with that?"

"*Shhhh!* For God's sake, someone will hear you." The voice was Lou's, but Colin Green continued.

"She's bottled it," he said. "One tough story, one job that doesn't go according to plan, and she's out of here."

The subeditor was nodding fervently in agreement.

Annie froze. The noise, the chatter, the laughter, the knackered old jukebox playing "Dancing Queen" all swirling to a halt around her.

"Going into fashion?" Green said. "I ask you. The woman's meant to be an award-winning journalist. What's she going to investigate there? Skirt lengths?"

"Oi!" Lou's familiar voice said. "What's wrong with fashion?"

Standing motionless in the crowd behind them, Annie heard the sub snort derisively and slam what sounded like an empty pint glass down on the windowsill next to him, but Lou persevered.

"You're just jealous," Lou said to Colin. "Because Annie broke that Kings Cross story when you couldn't even get close. You think it was easy befriending those kids, listening night after night to tales of abuse while putting herself in danger at the same time. And then when that girl died . . . well, you can't blame Annie if she needs a break. She deserves one."

Annie wanted to scream, *I'm not cracking up. I fancy a change, that's all. Deal with it!* She knew she shouldn't give a toss what they thought, but it still galled her. Christ, even her best friend on the paper thought she was copping out, and Lou worked in fashion.

Unable to bear another word, Annie glanced around to make sure no one had been watching her watching them and crept away. But by the time she'd fought her way to the pile of damp coats by the door, her resolve had hardened and she kept going, heading downstairs toward the ladies for some long-overdue face repair.

Let no one say Annie Anderson had lost her nerve.

chapter two

"Dumbass!" shouted the man. "You wanna get yourself killed, lady?"

Annie threw herself sideways, narrowly avoiding being kneecapped by a battered yellow taxi, and stepped straight into her umpteenth puddle of slush that evening.

Lexington Avenue was heaving. New Yorkers spilled off the sidewalk into the bumper-to-bumper traffic, filling the February night air with a cacophony of excited babble accompanied by blaring horns and cursing taxi drivers.

"Bloody groupies," Annie muttered as she picked herself up and pushed through the jostling fashion students, paparazzi, and "standing-onlies" forced to queue in the icy temperatures outside. "Anyone would think it was a rock concert, not a fashion show."

She was late, she was cold, and, worst of all, she was spattered with slush from head to toe. When Annie had tried to hail a taxi on the corner of West Broadway and Grand Street, the driver's response had been to accelerate through the nearest sludge-filled pothole, spraying her coat and boots. As she'd stood there, debating whether to go back to her hotel to change and be even later than she already was, a group of guys hanging on the sidewalk had actually laughed. Not just sniggered, roared.

"Welcome to Noo Yoik!" one of them yelled.

She yelled back, but nothing she could have repeated in front of her gran.

That was forty-five minutes earlier, before she started the toe-numbing thirty-eight-block trudge to Lexington and 26th Street. If this was her new life, they could keep it.

Annie wanted to weep. She'd been in her new job barely a fortnight and in Manhattan, to cover next season's autumn/winter shows, less than four hours. Four disastrous hours notable only for the delayed flight, mislaid hotel reservation, no-show taxi, and knee-high sludge that had conspired to make her miss every appointment so far. And now she was late for her most important appointment of all. Thirty-five minutes late to meet up with her new boss, Rebecca Brooks, the one person she really had to impress.

Whipping off a woolen beanie hat that broke every style law in the book, Annie stuffed it into her enormous shoulder bag in the vain hope that no one would notice and scanned the crowd in the Armory's entrance hall, praying not to see anyone she knew. Not that anyone of note knew her. The initial announcement of her appointment as fashion features editor of *Handbag*, at the age of twenty-eight, had been greeted by the fash pack with a derisory chorus of "Who?" and then instantly forgotten. Annie grinned. She couldn't help but be amused that they regarded newspapers with precisely the same contempt the national press held for them.

"ID," demanded an immaculately groomed blonde at the entrance desk, one of an army of black-clad staff murmuring darkly into headsets and wielding clipboards. Annie handed over her passport to be checked against her ticket and her ticket to be checked against the guest list.

So much for my fifteen minutes, she thought grimly, glancing nervously at her watch. *More like fifteen seconds if I carry on like this.*

"You can go in."

The blonde nodded curtly and handed back Annie's passport, giving her a none-too-friendly once-over as she did so. One that said, *They let you work on* Handbag?

Annie suppressed a shudder. Now she knew what Lou had meant by "that fashion feeling." Practically the last piece of advice Lou had given Annie before she left the *Post* was that the plummeting sensation in Annie's stomach would become her constant companion throughout the shows, as comparisons with the glossy women around her found her wanting.

"You'll get used to it," Lou had said. "Just remember, half of us feel precisely the same way. The other half aren't worth bothering about."

Annie tried to see herself as the blond PR saw her. The weather was not what you'd call "fashion-friendly." Subfreezing temperatures, compacted snow, and slow-thawing drifts had been trampled into mushy gray by a constant procession of tires and boots. By the time Annie had completed the obstacle course from terminal one at JFK to downtown Manhattan and then convinced the Donna Karan–clad receptionist at the Soho Grand that she did indeed have a reservation, there'd been no time to transform herself into Annie Anderson, Fashion Editor.

So her new season's wardrobe, the result of a bank-balance-busting trolley dash around Selfridges, had remained crumpled in her trolley dolly suitcase, where it had been for the best part of eighteen hours while Annie did a speed-of-light change. Off came the black rollneck she'd worn to fly, on went a finer, cleaner version. Annie just hoped her favorite Gina boots—spike-heeled, leopard-skin, full-on sex kitten—would carry her jeans through one more night. The very same boots whose eye-catching leopard-skin print was now invisible under a sodden layer of gray goo.

A barrage of noise assailed Annie as she stepped through the main doors. She adjusted her eyes to the darkness that shrouded the outer edges of the enormous room and began maneuvering her way through the crowd, her bag catching people's legs as she went, earning her irritated glances.

Firetrap, Annie thought, instinctively scanning the area for exits, then cursed her mother for her sensible streak and cursed herself for thinking of her mother.

Despite the sheer weight of numbers, it was freezing inside the cavernous space that formed the hub of the old Armory, a huge, echoing chamber with arced ceilings some thirty feet high. Heating in here, had anyone bothered to try, wouldn't have stood a chance. By now, though, Annie's gaze had fallen on the dazzling centerpiece. Running practically the full length of the room, flanked on both sides by a bank of galvanized steel bleachers eight rows deep, stood the point of it all: the runway. With a seventy-foot river of industrial-strength plastic protecting the pristine white catwalk beneath, it almost seemed to ripple under the intense glare of a hundred spotlights set on rails attached to the ceiling high above.

Despite herself, Annie held her breath.

For a moment she stood transfixed, not quite believing she was here. The school swat from Basingstoke was in fashion, and not just in fashion but at the very heart of it, the epicenter of an industry that had held a guilty fascination for Annie ever since she was a tiny girl watching her sister put Sindy through her paces on the floor of a bedroom they shared in her family's semi.

Annie's reverie was shattered by the abrupt realization that she wouldn't be "in fashion" for much longer if she didn't find her new boss and grovel. But where to start? Stunned and not a little intimidated by the studied hipness surrounding her, Annie searched the sea of vaguely familiar faces for anyone who would glance in her direction long enough for Annie to ask about Rebecca Brooks.

The Armory was literally heaving with the great and the good of the industry. Everyone who was anyone in fashion and media—and quite a few who weren't—had turned out for New York Fashion Week's hottest ticket, that hip downtown designer beloved of indie actresses and just about everyone else, Marc Jacobs. They moved around the plastic-shrouded runway, waving and air-kissing, scarcely touching and rarely stopping to do more than exchange pleasantries and price each other's outfits in the space of time it took mere mortals to blink. Magazine executives, fashion editors, buyers and celebrities, models, rock stars, stylists, and photographers, performing an intricate dance of see-and-be-seen to which it seemed everyone knew the steps but her.

"Annie! There you are! Where have you been?"

Having just spotted Liv Tyler chatting to Sofia Coppola a few seats down from A-list but just-indie-enough actress Miranda Lawson and her magazine-magnate boyfriend Robert Dellavecchia, Annie didn't see her editor until it was too late. The voice was piercing, perfectly pitched so anyone tuned to fashion frequency would hear.

And sure enough, at the sound of it, every head in the immediate vicinity turned to see who had dared to keep Rebecca Brooks waiting.

"I've been worried," Rebecca added, as Annie picked her way across the catwalk, taking care not to snag the heavy-duty PVC with her spike heels. But Rebecca's expression said otherwise.

Rebecca's expression said, *Where the bloody hell have you been?*

It said, *You work on* Handbag *now, so start behaving like it.*

What it definitely did not say was, *You poor girl, you must be dying for a hot bath and an early night.*

"Sorry," Annie muttered, "my plane . . ."

Running a perfectly manicured hand through tastefully highlighted, shoulder-length hair, Rebecca dismissed the agonies of Annie's last four hours in an instant. "You should have taken a taxi."

She had a point, thought Annie; if Rebecca had been in Annie's boots none of this would have been permitted to happen. The plane would never have dared to be late, the traffic on the Van Wyck Expressway would have parted like the Red Sea, and the concierge would have had her check-in complete before she'd finished wafting through the hotel's revolving doors. As for the taxi, any taxi driver stupid enough to splash Rebecca Brooks's brand-new Marc Jacobs trench and waiting-list-only shoes would never live to tell the tale.

"Anyway, never mind that," said Rebecca. "I'd better take you backstage after the show now. See if you can pick up some gossip on Mark Mailer. You'll need all the ammunition you can get before your interview with him. He's notoriously secretive."

Excitement roiled in Annie's stomach, reminding her that she hadn't eaten anything that wasn't plastic since yesterday, and according to her body clock it was now tomorrow.

"I'll get what I need," said Annie.

"You'd better," Rebecca replied. "We can't afford to mess this up."

Widely tipped as fashion's next big thing, Mark Mailer was the toast of

Manhattan. He was also Annie's maiden assignment for *Handbag* and the magazine's first foray into semi-serious journalism.

On the surface, Mark Mailer had everything. At thirty-one, he was the hottest up-and-coming designer in American fashion, with a label everyone who was anyone wanted in their wardrobe and a name all the big fashion houses wanted to own. Rumored to be about to sign a massive deal that could set him up for life, Mark Mailer was currently generating as much buzz as Alexander McQueen and Stella McCartney had combined.

By rights, Annie should be in her element. All she had to do was find out what made the man tick, why his girlfriend—the supermodel Patty Lang—spent so much time in rehab, and why, if the rumors were true, Mark Mailer hadn't spoken to his father in almost eight years.

Simplicity itself.

Annie began making mental notes of what she needed to know prior to her meeting with Mark Mailer and how she intended to approach the interview. She wanted to get under the skin of Mailer's relationship with Patty Lang. Industry gossip said they'd met through a mutual friend, heroin, but Annie had also heard from the *Post*'s gossip columnist, not a man known for giving the rich and infamous the benefit of the doubt, that Patty was clean for the first time in five years and this was thanks to Mark, large amounts of cash, and a discreet clinic just outside Aspen.

Anxious to sit down so she could get her thoughts on paper, Annie turned to excuse herself, but Rebecca's attention had already moved on to the well-known boss of an American publishing conglomerate. It was only after Annie had begun picking her way over the bodies of those reckless enough to ignore the bouncers' instructions not to sit in the aisles that Rebecca noticed she had vanished.

"Annie!" she demanded. "Where are you going?" And it seemed to Annie that a sudden hush descended, as if the entire auditorium waited for her answer.

Seat and row allocation are the fashion industry's class system, the front row so fiercely fought over that designers have been known to put their mothers in the second row to avoid taking a seat away from a journalist who might make or break their careers.

The front row is strictly Upper Class: celebrities, editors of the big fashion glossies, and Very Important Fashion Directors. Slightly less significant fashion directors are consigned to Business Class in row two, with Premium Economy behind that in rows three and four. Economy is behind that, with the lowest of the seated low. And then there was standing, which apparently didn't bear thinking about.

According to Lou, the whole fashion pack could be simplified into "Shoes visible," "Shoes just about visible provided you're sitting near the end of a row," and "Shoes? You mean the models were wearing shoes?"

"To my seat," Annie replied confidently. "Third row, two behind you." Top-end Premium Economy, perfectly respectable, also according to Lou.

Rebecca scowled. "Not good enough," she said. "Tell Libby to deal with it when you get back to London." Libby was the bookings editor, whose job it was to fix tickets for fashion shows she would rarely be allowed to attend herself.

Feeling utterly deflated, Annie let her bag fall to the floor with a thud as the people on either side of seat C39 grudgingly shunted sideways to make room. She tugged a crumpled sheet of paper listing the running order of the outfits from its hiding place beneath the woman sitting next to her and perched miserably on a narrow section of bench.

"My," said a familiar voice in her ear, "haven't we scaled the dizzy heights? One row ahead of the fashion editor of the highly prestigious London *Post* and still the mighty Rebecca Brooks doesn't think it's good enough for her new protégée."

Annie burst out laughing, the combination of relief and reality check bouncing everything back into perspective. Lou McCartney had a point. It was, after all, just a seat, and not a bad one at that.

Lou slung her arm across Annie's shoulder and leaned forward conspiratorially. "It could be worse," she whispered. "Only forty-five minutes late so far, and I could swear I still have feeling in my toes. If we were in London we'd have at least another hour to go and probably lose entire limbs to frostbite."

It was a peculiarity of London Fashion Week that, by the end of any given day, all the shows were running up to two hours late and the audience rarely complained, let alone walked out. In New York it was a different story: The über-editors would never stand for it.

"Watch." Lou nudged Annie as a notoriously stroppy British magazine editor bestowed her frostiest glare on a chancer occupying her front-row seat; the young woman feigned ignorance and stared stoically into the middle distance. Annie couldn't help admiring her front; that disengaged indifference essential for quality blagging was a real skill. One it had taken Annie years to acquire.

"What will she do?" asked Annie. "Surely she won't go and sit farther back?"

Lou snorted. "Not a chance. They'll find space somehow."

Annie watched fascinated as a PR foot soldier materialized out of thin air, appeased the editor, and miraculously conjured spare inches before their very eyes.

As soon as the last person was seated, the babble abated and expectation filled the air. This was the show that would dictate the next six months and beyond for the assembled fashion fraternity, and every single person in the room knew, as they sat in rapt acceptance, that their newly acquired spring/summer wardrobes were about to be rendered charity shop fodder.

Slowly the dazzling spotlights dimmed and the backstage crew dashed to the far end of the catwalk, ripping off the heavy duct tape that constrained the edges of the PVC covering and dragging it up and off, to reveal the spotless white runway beneath.

No sooner had they and the plastic vanished than the spotlights swung up again, illuminating a point on the back wall of the stage.

Fifteen hundred fashionistas held their breath.

As the opening chords of the Clash's punk anthem "London Calling" crashed out, bass line reverberating through the bench beneath her, Annie became aware that she was gripping her pencil so tightly her nails had pierced the flesh of her palm. But any discomfort was forgotten as the first model emerged, marching purposefully onto the runway, long silver wig swinging. In the prestigious opening position was the fallen angel of the international modeling circuit, live-in girlfriend of Mark Mailer, Patty

Lang, looking like a cross between Barbarella and Florence from *Magic Roundabout.*

Ice-blue eyes stared from a face that had once been heartbreakingly beautiful. They looked tired and bloodshot and far older than her twenty-four years.

Annie had seen more than her fair share of drug addicts since she began working undercover, and she was pretty certain that the woman stalking down the catwalk toward her, head held high, still counted as one of them.

chapter three

The paparazzi went mad. Poised, cameras ready at the end of the runway, they flared into life, flashes exploding.

"Patty! Patty!"

"This way, darling!"

"Over here!"

They sniffed payday. This could be big, bigger than the first time Patty Lang was papped leaving America's most famous "celebrity retreat" in the well-worn A-list disguise of dark glasses and baseball cap. Bigger even than that shot of her comatose in the corner at Mark Mailer's last after-show party, just weeks out of rehab two seasons ago, hollow-eyed and heroin-haunted.

The world's tabloid press, even the *Post*, Annie thought, would pay through the nose for photographic evidence that Patty Lang had fallen off the wagon, *again*. After all her protestations that this time was different. And the photographer who got the defining shot would be laughing all the way to a Tribeca penthouse.

Patty Lang's career, on the other hand, was now officially over.

Annie glanced over her shoulder and caught Lou's eye. *Trashed,* she mouthed to her friend in the seat behind.

Lou nodded and raised her eyebrows.

Everyone knew that the prestigious Femme model agency had been giving Patty one last chance for the past five years. This had to be it; after this no designer, and certainly not one as reputable as Marc Jacobs, could possibly take a risk on her again.

Annie was gripped. It was a car crash, with each step taking the model closer to the edge of the cliff. And then, just before Patty reached the end of the catwalk and swung her left hip out and down, holding for the customary three-second pose, Annie understood something else. *She knew,* Annie realized. Patty Lang knew that the photographers were already banking the check she was writing for them. And if the price of that check was her career? Annie had the distinct impression that Patty Lang couldn't have cared less. Behind the pinprick pupils was a depth of despair that made Annie shudder.

She grabbed her pencil and, along with the rest of her row, started scribbling furiously. Unlike the others, however, Annie wasn't detailing Patty Lang's futuristic blue-and-orange pinafore (ludicrous, unwearable, will probably own one by August, but only in black) or even making sarcastic notes about the unforgiving white opaque tights, quite the cruelest thing a fashion designer had done to womankind in months. She was adding to her notes for the next day's interview, working out how to tackle Mark Mailer on his girlfriend's renewed acquaintance with hard drugs. If Annie could move quickly enough after the show she might even manage to get backstage in time to catch Patty Lang before she left.

Some hope, she thought, as the subsequent fifty-four outfits crawled by. Impatiently Annie scanned pair after pair of outrageously angular cheekbones in the hope of sighting Patty again, but the model didn't make another appearance.

"Come *on,*" Annie muttered. The autumn/winter trends she was meant to be there to cover were all but forgotten as one skinny leg after another high-stepped down the catwalk in increasingly futuristic-meets-1960s outfits and ever-more-unflattering tights.

The entire production barely lasted fifteen minutes, including a lap of honor, but it still felt like an eternity. The second the final model vanished backstage and the applause began to fade Annie snatched up her bag, gave Lou a perfunctory wave, and, in an effort to beat those shuffling along her row toward the steps, prepared to leap down onto the catwalk. She had a pretty good idea it wasn't etiquette, but right that minute she didn't care.

"Go get her," Lou said, knowing exactly how Annie's mind worked. Everyone else just frowned.

Classy, Annie thought, muddy heels wobbling precariously as she landed as elegantly as a toddler jumping from halfway up the stairs, directly in front of her boss.

"There you are."

The trace of a patronizing smile played at the edges of Rebecca's lips, making Annie feel all of eight years old.

"So," said Rebecca. "What did you think?" Her gimlet eyes were already boring into the scribbled notes on Annie's pad.

Annie thought fast. "Brilliant," she said confidently. *Say it like you believe it and she'll believe it,* she told herself firmly. Ken had told her that and she'd never forgotten it. "Brave . . . a bold statement . . . the 1960s references perfectly capture the spirit of the moment . . . setting the tone for the whole season . . . the high street will be on the phone to its suppliers as we speak."

All of which was true.

Her boss smiled, and Annie tried not to sag visibly with relief.

"Exactly. Right on form," said Rebecca as she steered Annie into the crowd that was moving as one toward the backstage area. "The man's a genius. One of a kind. Come on, we must congratulate him."

Rebecca swept through the crowd bestowing the occasional comment and regal smile as she strode along the catwalk.

"Yes, wasn't it?"

"Absolutely. One of a kind."

"Totally agree."

Almost literally clinging to her boss's coattails, Annie watched fascinated as Rebecca worked the line without stopping. Unlike the preshow schmoozing there was no halting to chat and air-kiss now. Rebecca was a woman on a mission, and that mission did not involve making small talk with lower forms of fashion life; it involved getting backstage fast and installing herself at the designer's side before anyone else.

God, she's good, thought Annie, awestruck despite herself. She was used to getting in through the back door, chatting up receptionists, post boys, and deliverymen. Social engineering, in the terms of the trade. This, however, was something else entirely; this was sailing up the red carpet and watching the crowd part and doors swing open at the merest hint of your presence. In less than a minute they'd cleared the masses and passed through the white curtains separating backstage from front. Now all that lay between Rebecca and her target was a gaggle of models and the handful of journalists, celebrities, and general hangers-on fortunate enough to be sitting a block or two nearer the curtains, and they were no more than a minor irritant to the great Rebecca Brooks.

After ten years climbing the magazine hierarchy in London, Rebecca had crossed the Atlantic to become editor in chief of the American fashion magazine *Trend,* where she'd acquired networking skills and a contacts book that were second to none. Only the opportunity to launch *Handbag* had lured her back to the UK's dreary shores. Something the editor never tired of reminding her minions. Annie had scarcely been in the job five minutes and already she'd heard it a dozen times.

No one in the magazine business equaled Rebecca for clout and sheer chutzpah except U.S. *Vogue's* Anna Wintour. Office rumor had it that Wintour was the only person Rebecca once admitted drunkenly she might never surpass.

Annie knew she should have been watching and learning. There was no question that her new position would be consolidated by being snapped shoulder to shoulder with the designer of the moment and the most significant editor on the other side of the Atlantic, but Annie's instincts were buzzing. Her eagerness to get through the curtain had nothing to do with schmoozing and everything to do with Patty Lang. Annie needed to see for herself if Patty was as far gone as she'd looked out there on the catwalk. If Mark Mailer's girlfriend really had taken another dive off the wagon,

Annie needed to know why, and she needed to know before she met the man tomorrow.

Backstage was bedlam. Voices rising ever louder competed for airtime, their combined volume ricocheting off temporary walls as Rebecca cut a swath toward the center of the throng, dragging Annie in her wake. Annie could barely distinguish a word and could see even less as countless fash pack well-wishers, most of them a good six inches taller than Annie even in her heels, surged into the hastily constructed dressing room.

"Marc, darling, that was inspired." Rebecca broke with self-imposed protocol to actually touch the designer as she leaned in to kiss him on both cheeks. "So refreshing. So creative. I lost count of the looks *Handbag* will be shooting."

Without missing a beat Rebecca segued straight to Annie, who was so absorbed with planning her attack that, once again, her boss caught her completely off guard.

"Meet my new fashion features editor, Annie Anderson, headhunted her from the *Post,* investigative background, just what *Handbag* needs. Annie . . ."

"Pleasure to meet . . ."

Rebecca thrust Annie forward, but the moment had passed, the designer's attention forced in a million different directions. Fashionistas descended, raining congratulations on the designer as Annie watched him vanish beneath a sea of his own designs.

"Good enough," Rebecca said smartly. "We'll visit the studio later in the week, take a closer look at the collection. Then we'll make him your second big conquest."

Annie blanched. She hadn't pulled off her first yet.

As always Marc Jacobs was Monday's last show, and neither Rebecca— silver lighter in one hand, Gitanes in the other—nor the rest of the crowd seemed to be in any hurry to get to the official after-show party. Within minutes the air was thick with cigarette smoke, alcohol fumes, and the conflicting smell of at least thirty different fragrances made pungent by body heat.

Not so different from The Swan, Annie thought, recollecting her ex-colleagues' predictions of champagne parties and silver service. Fag smoke, lukewarm booze, and body odor more like. And that added up to the same, whichever city you happened to be in.

One eye open for an opportunity to escape, Annie surveyed the scene with bemusement. She had always assumed the mythology surrounding the fashion industry was precisely that, urban myth, but quite clearly it wasn't. Only in fashion, she realized, could a roomful of unusually tall, unusually thin women chain-smoking be unremarkable. Even in Manhattan where the last bastion of the nicotine-addicted, the Blue Bar at the Algonquin, was now a cig-free zone and smoke about as welcome as SARS, nobody so much as blinked at the fug collecting above their coiffured heads.

"What the hell." Annie rummaged in her bag until she found what she was after, a duty-free pack of Marlboro Lights, still in its cellophane wrapper. She had given up a million times, but there were some situations where only a cigarette would do.

At the back of the room a few remaining models still stood, sharing a supper of champagne and red-label Marlboros, before a backdrop of garishly lit makeup mirrors, each mirror surrounded by a dozen hundred-watt bulbs. Between drags, a group of three were busy stripping off their final outfits in favor of the regulation model uniform of jeans, T-shirts, and battered leather coats. They were tall, they were thin, and, with the exception of the occasional silicone enhancement, their tits were smaller than Annie's had been at twelve, and she didn't count her 34Bs as large.

Plucking a cigarette from her packet, Annie wandered over.

"Got a light?" she asked the first back she came to. It was naked and hunched over, rifling through a leather bag, each vertebra so clearly visible beneath taut, tanned skin that Annie could have counted them off one by one.

The back straightened and a cream cotton camisole slid over it. Then its owner turned, cigarette burning in one hand, plastic lighter in the other.

"Here." The model flicked the disposable a handful of times before the flame finally sprang to life.

"I was meant to be meeting Patty."

"Patty?"

Annie nodded. "Don't suppose you saw where she went, did you?" She was trying hard not to stare, part envious, part appalled, at the hip bones protruding below the model's tiny vest. Like the majority of the female population of the Western world Annie had always wanted to be thinner than she was, but this?

"I think Patty left," the model said, wriggling into her jeans. "Try Anya. She took Patty's last look, so she was probably the last person to see her."

Waving what was left of her cigarette, the model indicated a statuesque brunette whose dark hair was slicked into a neat bun at the nape of her neck. Anya, over by the exit, was busy shrugging on a leather trench coat and zipping an enormous holdall.

It took every ounce of Annie's willpower not to sprint across the room and fling herself in front of the doorway to prevent Patty's friend from leaving.

"Anya?" Annie called, trying and failing to pull off that trick where you raise your voice but simultaneously keep it low. Needless to say her voice came out loud enough to turn every head in the immediate vicinity. "I don't suppose you've seen Patty, have you?"

The model's dark eyes narrowed. "Not for fifteen, twenty minutes. Why?"

"I . . . um, just wanted a quick word." Thrown by the model's overt hostility, Annie added, "To say hello."

Anya smiled, but it never approached her eyes. In fact, it barely made it to the corners of her full mouth. "I don't think Patty was up for after-show chitchat. But I can give her a message . . . if I see her, of course. Who shall I say was asking?"

Waving her own cigarette dismissively, as if to imply that it could scarcely be of less importance, Annie shrugged. *Annie,* she thought, *what's wrong with you?* The last thing she needed was for Patty to tell Mark Mailer that some Englishwoman had been asking after her. If he made the connection to Annie he might even cancel her interview.

"Don't bother," Annie added. "I'll catch up with Patty another time."

"Whatever." The brunette gave a curt nod, hefted her holdall onto one shoulder, and shoved at the heavy door, an icy draft sweeping in as she stepped into the darkness beyond. The door crashed shut behind her, causing the walls of the dressing room to shake.

Annie had two options. Annie Anderson, Fashion Editor, could leave it, go back to the hotel, and get a decent night's sleep. Annie Anderson, ex-chief-investigative-reporter, could crowbar the lid off another can of worms. And she was congenitally incapable of leaving cans shut—especially other people's cans, as her ex, Nick, had never tired of telling her. Glancing across the room, through the thinning crowd to where Rebecca was deep in conversation with the editor of *Harper's Bazaar*, Annie nodded. Her boss was safely occupied.

Dropping the remaining inch of her Marlboro Light into the dregs of a nearby plastic cup, Annie shook off the encroaching jet lag and followed.

chapter four

The back entrance to the Armory opened not onto a corridor as Annie had been expecting but into a narrow snow-filled alley that led to a cross street. It took Annie a moment to get her bearings as she stood on the corner, struggling into her still soggy coat as a biting wind whipped around her face and nipped at her ears. The streets looked quieter now, the earlier throng having departed for their respective hotels or nearby bars. There was little sign of life and even less sign of Anya.

For a split second Annie reconsidered, longing for her bed. If she jumped into a taxi now she could be back at her hotel in ten minutes, in bed in fifteen, asleep in fifteen and a half.

"Come on," she chided herself, trying not to lose her footing. The slush was rapidly developing that telltale crunch that said the temperature had dropped past freezing and was still falling. "Concentrate. Think yourself into her head."

Annie peered in both directions. There wasn't much to see. Fifty yards away, where 26th Street met Lexington, a taxi pulled up and disgorged passengers who immediately started to quibble about the fare, while a couple walking down Lexington paused at the lights waiting for WALK.

Where would Anya go?

Annie spun on her heels, wondering why she was wasting precious sleeping time playing spot-the-stranger on frozen street corners and increasingly feeling her new job was just the same as all the others, when she spotted what she had been looking for, in the other direction entirely. A tall, slim figure, lugging an enormous bag, who darted out from the shadow of a shop doorway and crossed 26th Street. Once on the other side, the figure vanished around the corner onto Park Avenue South.

"Shit!" Breaking into a run, Annie skidded into the middle of the icy road and narrowly avoided her third conflict with a taxi that evening. Leaning on his horn the driver raised the relevant finger, but Annie was already half sliding, half jogging away toward the corner where she'd last seen Anya.

The sidewalk was all but deserted and most of the shops—nail bars as far as the eye could see—had long since shut. Annie turned a slow circle, squinting into the darkness in case she'd been mistaken or the model had doubled back. Barely a soul was on Park except for a gaggle of teenage boys, padded ski jackets pulled tight as they emerged onto the sidewalk from a brightly lit McDonald's. They looked loaded down with enough take-out carriers to feed a party of fifty.

Annie's stomach growled. And after a brief tug-of-war between her work ethic and her hunger, hunger won. She was on a wild goose chase, her stomach reasoned, Anya was gone, and Annie succumbed to her stomach's suggestion of Filet-O-Fish, fries, and then bed.

Warm air and that peculiarly McDonald's smell hit Annie as she pushed open the glass double doors and stepped inside. There was something about it that, for Annie, always managed to hover between the addictively enticing and the stomach-churningly vile.

The restaurant was close to empty, except for two guys sitting at separate tables near the entrance chewing on quarter-pounders and staring into space. Behind them were two sparse queues, each one only two or three people long. A middle-aged man with hair receding beneath his cardboard hat operated the drinks machine, while a Hispanic boy and girl shoved pastel-colored polystyrene boxes into brown paper bags to the sound of tinny pop music piped through temperamental speakers.

Joining the end of the shortest line, Annie started rummaging in her bag for her purse. She was practically at the counter before she found it at the bottom inside the woolen hat she'd dumped earlier, and it was sheer luck that she looked up in time to recognize the woman who turned toward her, awkwardly juggling a large take-out bag and her even larger holdall.

"H-hi," Annie stammered, cursing her sleep-starved brain.

Without breaking her stride, Anya looked her up and down. "I'm sorry?" Then realization dawned. "Oh, yeah," she said, and stepped around Annie.

Annie could have left it there but she didn't. After all, that would have meant she'd spent the last fifteen minutes behaving like an idiot for nothing. Instead she racked her head for a single good reason why she might waylay Anya. And came up with a bad one instead.

"About Patty . . . ," Annie said, loud enough to reach the model who was now struggling with the door.

Anya turned back, the hostility no longer veiled. "What about Patty?"

"I wondered, is she really okay?"

"God." Anya's eyes narrowed. "What are you?" she said. "*Hard Copy* or something?"

Something like that, Annie thought grimly.

"I heard she was better," insisted Annie. "You know, recovered. But Patty, um, well, she didn't exactly look recovered to me."

The model sighed, a look of genuine sadness crossing a face that, Annie suddenly realized, had been staring at her from almost every billboard she'd seen since arriving at JFK. "You know I can't possibly answer that," Anya said. She turned and headed out onto the sidewalk, holdall now over her shoulder, take-out clutched to her chest, eyes fixed resolutely ahead.

Annie let her go. It might not have been the most professional thing she'd ever done, but that didn't make it wrong.

chapter five

The room was dark, growing colder, silent but for the ever-present sound of a
man breathing. Watching, waiting, biding his time . . .

Annie awoke. That is, she lurched into wakefulness, and for several
long seconds lay completely still, hearing her heart pound in her ears, eyes
wide open, staring at a ceiling it was too dark to see. It wasn't so much
that she wouldn't move as that she couldn't. Every sinew in her body was
tensed to the point that the slightest movement made her feel like something might snap.

Her jaw throbbed, an ache that Annie recognized, a sure sign she'd been
grinding her teeth in her sleep again. And she could feel sweat drying between her breasts where moments earlier it had slid down her skin, soaking into crumpled sheets. But the dream's familiarity didn't make waking
any less terrifying.

It was pitch-black and Annie wasn't yet certain where she was, although
she was pretty sure that someone had woken her. Logic told her that the
someone was the figure who'd been haunting her nightmares since she
was seventeen. A bad dream, nothing more. Trouble was, right now, logic
didn't hold much sway.

It seemed like a cold eternity before, from the corner of one eye, Annie found an unfamiliar green light and finally remembered where she was and why. (And, equally important, where she wasn't.) Taking care not to make the slightest sound, Annie rolled onto her left side to inspect the source of the light: the rectangular screen of a radio alarm clock that didn't belong in her flat at all. It was 3:25 A.M.

Annie watched the numbers change.

3:26 A.M.

New York.

"Come on, Annie," she told herself, saying the words out loud for the reassurance of hearing her own voice. "It's okay. This is the Soho Grand. You're in New York."

It was a well-worn technique, but it usually worked. Cushioned by the carpet and curtains of a hermetically sealed hotel room, her voice held no echo, and when all that remained of her words was silence, Annie could hear only the ever-present background roar of the hotel's heating system and, beyond that, the distant *ping* of a lift.

"Get a grip, will you?" Annie announced, unclenching her fist from the sheets and reaching across, fingers hunting for a light switch. She was ludicrously relieved when the glow of a forty-watt bulb illuminated the room.

Yanking the blankets aside, Annie swung her legs gingerly over the edge of the bed, toes sinking into the kind of beige carpet found only in Manhattan apartments and upscale hotels. She was grubby with sweat, her sodden T-shirt still glued to her back.

"Yeuch," Annie muttered. As she'd suspected, her hair was also wringing. After gazing around, Annie made herself walk toward the door and turn on all the remaining lights, her ears still straining for the slightest noise.

Her room, so far as Annie could see, was exactly as it had been when she'd last looked. A still-damp coat was slung over the back of the fabric-covered chair she'd pulled from underneath the desk, her bag dumped on its side by the chair, notepad and purse spilling out. Mud-splattered boots lay sprawled on the carpet where they'd been discarded, one under the desk, the other next to her jeans, which lay in a heap where she'd stepped out of them. Annie didn't need a mirror to know she'd been too exhausted to remove her makeup or that, judging from the salt taste in her mouth, her mascara was probably halfway down her face by now.

She checked the door instinctively to see if she'd remembered to double-lock it and then checked again, making herself note that it was very definitely locked. That way a third check would not be necessary. Common sense and every other sense Annie possessed told her there was no one but her in the room, but she still couldn't kick her brain's certainty that someone had been watching in the dark, hunting her. It was an old dream, a well-trodden 3 A.M. path in other rooms in other parts of the world, and she knew she wasn't alone; every woman suffered it sometime. But for Annie it was as familiar as family and about as welcome.

The wardrobe was empty, hangers swaying as Annie raked them aside to check the wall behind. Next she checked the windows, beginning to feel faintly ridiculous. Which was good. She knew even before she twitched the first curtain that both windows would be shut, their inner and outer glazing firmly bolted into place.

"Idiot," she muttered.

Annie knew now was the time to call it quits and go back to bed, but she didn't. There was still one place left to check, and until she knew the bathroom was clear, sleep was not an option.

The door was shut. Which was not good. Had she shut it before she went to sleep last night? Twisting the handle, Annie jerked open the bathroom door, not giving herself time to change her mind. Light flowed in as darkness, but nothing else, rushed out. The last of her terrors was gone. From where Annie stood, she could see around the shower curtain into the empty bath and across to a frosted window, via the sink, where a hot tap dripped lazily onto a white hotel flannel that still lay in a soggy ball blocking the plug hole. The room was unquestionably empty.

Opting to leave the bathroom door open, Annie retreated to the far side of her room and sank back on the crumpled bed. She wasn't alone in this small-hour insanity. Plenty of her friends would, in the confessional of a wine bar, admit to the occasional attack of checking their doors and windows half a dozen times before being able to contemplate sleep when home alone, while a few openly admitted to nights spent sitting up in bed, worrying away at a noise outside. But those were flats in Brixton and Camden, not the concierge-protected luxury of a four-star hotel where the bedrooms all had double locks on the doors.

It would be at least half an hour before Annie was able to lie down properly and ten or twenty minutes beyond that before she'd finally bring herself to turn off the light. After that, maybe sleep would come. If Annie still hadn't crashed out by 5 A.M., she'd get up again, order coffee from room service, and collate her notes for the Mark Mailer piece.

"And the nominees for the Best Actress Oscar are . . ."

"What the . . ."

For the second time in five hours Annie went from unconscious to wide awake, blood pounding, in a single beat of her heart. This time she sprang out of bed and lunged for the television, which had burst into life seconds earlier. It was 8:15 A.M. and, although Annie could recall the night's events all too clearly, she had almost no memory of actually going to bed in the first place. That she'd had the presence of mind to set an early-morning call on her room's state-of-the-art television was useful but not unusual. Annie had trained herself well.

"Shut *up*," she muttered, scanning the front of the sleek, silver television for anything resembling a volume control as a self-important voice announced that the Best Actress nominations were now complete and moved on to Best Actor. In the absence of an obvious alternative, Annie stabbed at the STANDBY button with her index finger.

The screen went blissfully blank.

Her bedside light was still on and her pillows sat squashed against the headboard where, until thirty seconds ago, she'd been sleeping upright against them.

"Dozy cow," she muttered before starting to tidy the bed, not-so-subconsciously removing all evidence of last night's dreams.

Snatching up the remote, Annie aimed it at the TV. She needed some real news, a dose of the outside world, but finding it was easier said than done. Flicking through seventy-odd channels, it took her a while to track down CNN and less than a minute to decide that she couldn't cope with wounded children right now. Eventually, almost back where she'd begun, Annie found Manhattan's rolling news channel, NY1.

"Next we go to Bryant Park," the presenter was saying, all toothy grin, "where the fall ready-to-wear shows are in full swing, but first it's the New York weather on the ones . . ."

It didn't take a degree in meteorology to predict that the weather would make unhappy listening for most residents of the tristate area. It wasn't a barrel of laughs for visitors who hadn't come equipped for the Arctic, either.

"It's a case of wrapping up and preparing for the worst," he announced, smile replaced with a look of wide-eyed concern. "Temperatures are expected to reach a low of ten degrees Fahrenheit over the next forty-eight hours, rising over the weekend to bring a strong chance of snow."

Cheers, thought Annie, *either I freeze to death or I get snowed in.* She hadn't made appropriate wardrobe decisions for either. For a second she wondered lazily if it might be cold enough to wear her beanie and get away without washing her hair; then she remembered Rebecca's sleek honey-colored bob and imagined the look on her boss's face if she caught so much as a glimpse of Annie's woolly hat.

Groaning, Annie flicked a switch, and the bathroom was flooded with unforgiving light. She stared hard at her reflection in the mirror, ticking the boxes: bloodshot eyes, matted hair, blotchy skin . . . So much for yesterday's resolution to get groomed. Behind her Annie could hear a young woman extolling the virtues of Betsey Johnson's predictably eccentric show from the previous afternoon before moving on to Marc Jacobs. As Annie had guessed, the collection was described as brilliant, heralding a new era. But there was no mention of the thing that really interested her, Patty Lang.

"Get a move on," she told herself. Her first meeting with Mark Mailer was little more than an hour away, and she needed to turn back into a human before then.

Discarding T-shirt and knickers, rank with dry sweat, Annie stepped under the spray and let water cascade down her skin. It was a cliché, but Annie could literally feel the shower wash away the night's grim memories.

Her body was okay, she supposed, on a good day, at the right time of the month. Better than she deserved at any rate, given she'd been existing for years on coffee, chocolate, and burgers, the traditional diet of investigative journalists. "Only you're not now, are you?" Annie scolded herself. "You're in fashion. You probably need to remember that.

"So," she continued aloud, beginning to lather and undeterred by having to compete with the shower hissing around her. "Mark Mailer. Thirty-one years old. Jewish and Italian parentage. What else do we know? What do we need to know? And how do we find it out?"

She wasn't worried about being able to hit it off with the designer. Annie had done her research and knew that they both came from blue-collar families. That alone guaranteed she'd have enough in common with him to find something to fall back on. As long as he didn't begin the interview already shut down and defensive. And why would he? She was a fashion journalist, for God's sake, nothing to worry about.

The youngest child of a New Jersey plumber, Mark Mailer had come to fashion late. He'd originally trained in the family business but, displaying no flair for welding pipes, went walkabout in his early twenties. Everything Annie had read pointed to a couple of years lost to coke, heroin, and vodka, but he'd been clean for ages now and Lou McCartney swore she'd never once seen alcohol pass his lips in all the time he'd been showing his own collections. Which made his relationship with Patty Lang all the more fascinating.

Although Mailer was said to be close to his mother, several clippings referred to the feud with his father. Which figured, Annie thought. After all, if an only son flunks out of the family business, who gets to keep it going? Not his one sister, a high school teacher whom Mark had publicly credited with encouraging him to go back to college. He had majored in fashion at Parsons, working evenings and weekends for Guido Brasco, an elderly tailor in Little Italy, doing repairs and alterations in return for learning to cut. By the time he left college, Mark Mailer was making made-to-measure suits for half of Manhattan's Italian community.

Washing away the soap, Annie reached for a small bottle of shampoo with the same bright logo.

Just reading the clippings had been enough to make Annie decide she liked Mark Mailer, and she wasn't alone. The fact he'd continued to work part time for Brasco after graduating, while producing his own collection on the side, had earned Mark Mailer his reputation, both for a strong work ethic and for a perverse kind of integrity in an industry that majored in surface flamboyance and flakiness. Mark Mailer was New York's local boy made good, and the press and the fashion world alike loved him for it.

He had it all going for him. So why saddle himself with the junkie?

Hair shampooed, Annie stepped back under the shower, foam gushing down her forehead and across her body to spiral away down the plug hole. Mark didn't need a relationship with Patty Lang to give him a leg up and, apart from maybe right at the start, he never had. Patty wasn't exactly an asset to any power couple, so what was in it for him?

Unless . . .

Annie stopped dead, thinking it through. There was no other explanation, logical or otherwise; it had to be love. For a second, as the last of her own dreams swirled around her feet, Annie felt uncomfortable with what she was about to do.

The message light was flashing on her hotel phone when Annie finally emerged from the bathroom wearing the regulation-issue white toweling robe she'd found hanging on the open door.

"Fuck it," she muttered, flinging herself across the bed, snatching up the receiver, and dialing star three.

Without preamble or introduction, Rebecca's clipped tones cut in. "Annie, you forgot to say goodbye last night and I need to catch up before your Mailer interview, I have a few tips . . . I imagine you're already on your way over there. I'll try your mobile."

The line went dead.

The last thing Annie wanted right now was a pep talk from her new boss. It was ten after nine and she had barely half an hour to get herself dressed, mentally prepared, and into a taxi, which didn't allow for ten minutes on the phone. Not with Rebecca anyway. Worse still, Rebecca might suggest coffee. Taking the hotel-branded pen and a piece of headed paper from the desk drawer, Annie began to lie.

Rebecca, Sorry I missed you last night—you were deep in conversation and I didn't want to interrupt. I'm meeting Mailer at . . . the truth was, her interview with Mark wasn't until 10 A.M., but Annie didn't want Rebecca to know she'd still been in her room when her boss had called . . . *9:30 and expect to be there most of the day. If I don't see you before, I'll fill you in at Narciso Rodriguez. See you at 8. Annie*

She'd leave the note with reception on her way out, ask them to get it delivered to Rebecca at the Mercer where she was staying.

Next Annie called the concierge and booked a cab. After last night's debacle she wasn't going to get caught again taxi-less and knee-deep in slush. Taxi ordered, Dictaphone fully functioning, and a story waiting, Annie was beginning to feel more like her old self than she had for weeks.

By the time reception called to say her cab was waiting, Annie was about as fashion as she was ever likely to get. Unable to spare the time for a clothes crisis, she'd settled on a clean pair of Earl Jeans, an Oriental embroidered shirt that could pass for vintage and always earned her compliments, and her favorite black jacket. It was Helmut Lang and had cost the most money Annie had ever spent on anything. Even now she winced at the thought. The Gina boots were almost destroyed, so Annie opted for a marginally more practical, black leather pointed pair, tucking the Ginas on top of a bag that was now full of her notes, Dictaphone, and mobile. She could drop the boots off at reception on the way out, see if they could work miracles.

Then Annie totally ruined that day's style statement by covering the whole ensemble with her coat, which was still disconcertingly cardboard-like after last night's soaking. After that she swathed her face and neck in a huge knitted scarf and tucked the ends inside the coat.

Shutting the hotel room door behind her, Annie checked the knob from habit, leaning back to test it was locked, then headed for the lift. After yesterday's litany of disaster, today could only be better.

chapter six

Seven fifty-five the next evening and there was still no sign of Patty Lang. And no news of when, if ever, she might actually make it to the venue for her boyfriend's show, a derelict automobile plant beside the Hudson River that was currently doubling as the inside of a freezer. Mark Mailer's girl-friend had been conspicuously absent for the last two days, and frustration was beginning to get the better of Annie.

As the twenty-two models, most of them female, did their final lap of the catwalk, weaving in and out of an elaborate figure-eight seating plan in beautifully tailored Jackie O–style suits, Annie scanned their faces to make sure she hadn't missed the pale blue eyes and cheekbones she'd spent the last forty-eight hours searching for. Not that there was any real likelihood of Patty appearing now. If Patty had intended to make the show, she'd have been backstage earlier; Annie understood that. All the same, she couldn't help hoping.

By now Annie was so cold she could barely concentrate, her ungloved hand unable to feel the pencil balanced precariously between first finger and thumb, her scrawl scarcely legible. The derelict building was the size of an aircraft hangar, large enough for several hundred fashion journalists to get a front-row seat—though some front-row seats were infinitely more front-row than others—and pretty much everyone else to sit in the second. The temperature was several degrees below freezing, and the huge five bar heaters hanging from the ceiling made little impact.

Huddled next to Annie in the front row, even Rebecca had bowed to the elements and wrapped herself in a foil blanket provided to prevent frostbite. Just as well, thought Annie, it wasn't as if her boss carried all that much in the way of natural padding. And Rebecca wasn't the only one reduced to using a space blanket. An entire stretch of front row was swathed in BacoFoil.

And what a front row it was. Impressive by anyone's standards, this was a patchwork of celebrities, friends, and fashion royalty with Mailer's mother and sister sitting between the lead singer of the Strokes and Milla Jovovich. The real star turns, however, could be seen just around the corner, where the models first emerged—Tom Ford, Ugo Baroni, and Mariolina Mantolini. A starrier fashion triumvirate Annie had never seen; Mantolini's severe good looks sat between Ford's film-star presence and Baroni's intense gaze. Annie was surprised. She had seen pictures of Ugo Baroni—everybody had—but she had not expected a man of his age to be so . . . *striking* was the only word for it.

Her brain worked overtime assessing the odds. Ford had snapped up McCartney and McQueen back when he was at Gucci—was he now back in the market and interested in Mailer? If so, Annie hadn't heard that rumor. She had, however, heard the others. The rumors that had both Baroni's label Fava and the House of Mantolini, a recherché family operation currently experiencing a renaissance under only child Mariolina, coveting the Mailer name. Gossip also said that, although both had put together very persuasive packages, Mailer's decision would be based on something else altogether. But Annie was a long, long way from hearing that from Mark himself.

All he had said during the time she'd spent with him in the last two days was that the decision would be announced once the contract had been finalized.

The designer was not what anyone would call an easy interview, but Annie had undertaken far worse. After an awkward first day when Mailer had vacillated between pretending he really didn't have time for this and treating Annie as if she was working undercover for the IRS, he'd suddenly warmed to her, and Annie had a hunch she knew why.

It had taken thirty minutes of discreet button pressing to strike lucky, an intricate sequence of dropping personal information about herself, combined with anecdotes designed to imply that he could trust her, that she was more than just another groupie. And no doubt all that helped. But the defining moment came that morning when they moved back-stage, just after Mark had finished supervising the lighting. They were huddled around a small Calor gas heater, warming their hands like tramps around a street corner brazier. As Annie loosened her scarf and undid her coat, she saw something change in Mark's dark brown eyes. He had de-cided he liked her and would talk to her. And he was going to talk to her because not a single item of Annie's clothing bore the distinctive Mark Mailer label.

From there on in, her fight was, if not exactly won, then well on the way. Mark answered most of Annie's questions, amiably if not entirely willingly, and when the interview had officially finished he agreed to let Annie shadow him for the rest of that day. By the time the first of the models arrived for makeup, two hours before his show was due to start, Mark appeared to have forgotten all about the journalist who sat eaves-dropping in one corner.

She hadn't yet gotten the information she really wanted. In fact, so far Annie hadn't discovered anything she couldn't have unearthed from the clippings, but she'd laid the foundations for a deeper level of questioning. And Annie suspected that when she went back—as they both knew she would—Mark wouldn't refuse to allow her in.

Unless, of course, the questions concerned Patty. The only time he'd balked was when Annie raised the subject of his supermodel girlfriend.

"She's not relevant to my work" was all Mark would say, his voice calm, even friendly. Politely he'd refused even to confirm how long they'd been seeing each other. He was equally unforthcoming on when and where they'd met, the state of Patty's health, and the current condition of their relationship. Well, she'd had to ask. It was what she was paid for.

And now, sitting in the front row, Annie thought she understood his reticence. There had never been a Mark Mailer show that didn't close with Patty Lang, whatever her extremely well-documented problems, but after Monday night's very public career suicide, it seemed that even the ex-über-model's loyal other half wasn't prepared to take a risk on her.

As the final model vanished backstage to rapturous applause, Mark Mailer's head appeared around the white hardboard that separated front stage from back. At first only those closest to the entrance noticed him, but their wild cheering took barely a second to infect the rest of the crowd. The venue erupted. Even Rebecca was on her frozen feet, foil blanket fluttering to the floor. There was no doubt Mark's show had been a success, brilliant even, but standing ovations didn't seem very *fashion* to Annie.

As for Mark, he looked appalled as he braced himself for the adulation and stepped out into the open. Scarcely lifting his eyes from the catwalk, he waved one hand in acknowledgment and was gone, vanishing backstage as quickly as he'd appeared.

"Amazing," said Rebecca. "I always knew he was going to amount to something."

Before the words were even out of her mouth, Rebecca was retrieving her bag from beneath her seat and moving toward backstage. Several dozen other fashionistas had the same idea; Annie was reminded of hounds she'd once seen chasing down a fox in Somerset. *Leave the poor thing alone,* she wanted to yell now, as she'd wanted to yell then. Not an opinion that would endear her to Rebecca, who was busy trampling someone else's discarded foil cape as she motioned Annie to follow.

Taking a deep breath, Annie shook her head. "If it's okay with you," she said, her tone light, "I'll pass. Mark's probably sick of the sight of me after the last two days. If I stay out of his face tonight it'll make it easier to catch up with him again tomorrow, if necessary."

Rebecca raised a single eyebrow and gave Annie a thoughtful look. "Okay," she said. "I'm sure you know what you're doing."

Annie did. She didn't want Mark to see her with Rebecca, or anyone else from the fash pack. That would undo all the good work she'd put in gaining his trust. In his mind she'd already established herself as Annie Anderson, journalist, yes, but okay person, not Annie Anderson from *Handbag* magazine.

And Annie had another reason for cutting loose. One Rebecca would not appreciate. Mark had decided against a big after-show bash, any inclination probably soured by memories of that image of Patty unconscious on a red velvet sofa. He was having a small, select gathering instead, for those who'd helped him with the collection. Family, close friends, cast and crew—and Annie. Quite how she'd pulled that off, she wasn't sure. Mark had certainly looked as if he wanted to take the invitation back as soon as the words were out of his mouth, but there was no way Annie was going to stay away. Nor was she taking Rebecca with her.

"We're here?"

"Yeah, this is it." The driver shrugged to indicate he wasn't responsible for her choice of drinking den. "You want me to take you someplace else?"

"No," said Annie. "This is it."

The Elephant was a typical East Village joint. From the outside, so nondescript as to be almost invisible among walk-ups in various stages of urban regeneration, while the sandblasted interior was so excruciatingly hip Annie's first instinct was to turn around and grab her taxi before it had time to pull away, soft rock from the bar's speakers still echoing in her ears. Cutting Crew unless Annie was very much mistaken. Well, hip and ironic did tend to travel hand in hand.

Annie was used to being an interloper; it went with the territory, and she'd always found other people's parties vastly preferable to her own. All the same, she dreaded those first few minutes standing on the edge, wondering who, if anyone, to talk to.

It reminded her of school, bad discos, and Basingstoke.

To fortify herself, Annie stopped off at the bar before braving the throng.

"Vodka, diet tonic, lime juice, and ice," she ordered.

"Vodka, diet tonic, lime juice, and ice?" The girl behind the bar made it more of a query than a statement. Dressed in a faded Metallica T-shirt, her long dirty-blond hair tied in a rough ponytail, she gave Annie a pointed look that clearly suggested she'd just been asked for some unbearably bridge-and-tunnel cocktail.

"Yes. Double."

Annie was rummaging in her purse for a twenty when she felt a hand on her shoulder.

"Stick it on my tab, Jay," said a familiar voice. "Glad you made it," Mark added, not entirely convincingly, but he leaned in, bestowing a quick peck on Annie's cheek.

Taken aback, Annie smiled.

"You were . . . ," she began. "It was . . . great," she finished, cursing her sudden ineptitude.

She couldn't be certain, but it seemed to Annie that Mark actually shuffled his feet, whether from embarrassment or pleasure she couldn't tell.

"Thanks." He shrugged, shoving a hand self-consciously through ruffled dark hair. "But, you know, it was just . . ."

For a second their eyes met.

He's just a bloke, Annie thought. *Still just an ordinary bloke.* That was true, for now; but tomorrow, instinct told Annie, when the show reports hit the newsstands, Mark Mailer would be reincarnated as the second coming, a kind of fashion god.

"This is Annie," said Mark, when he'd finished steering her toward the sprawling party who'd commandeered a large alcove at the back of the bar. "She's not bad for a journalist." And with that he reclaimed his seat on a battered leather banquette next to a shaven-headed black guy Annie recognized as his lighting engineer. A few people glanced up, vaguely interested, a couple even raised their hands and smiled, but most just carried on their conversations oblivious to Annie's arrival.

Perching on the arm of the nearest sofa, Annie checked the faces around her. Models, plenty of them, both male and female, but no Patty and no Patty's friend, either, although Anya had worn two key outfits in Mark's show. The Latin American model had studiously ignored Annie from the second she arrived and had gone out of her way to be wherever Annie was not.

Assorted technicians added to the numbers, as did hair and makeup artists, Ralf, the sound engineer, and Mark's assistant Rob, whom Annie had met earlier. In the far corner, deep in conversation with a girl Annie was fairly sure was one of the makeup artists, sat a woman who looked to be in her late thirties with dark midlength hair and strangely familiar eyes. A rounder, less cheekbone-blessed version of Mark. Cathie, his sister.

Annie was finishing her third double vodka by the time she glanced at the clock over the bar and realized it had gone midnight. Apart from their own group, which was still running more or less at full strength, the crowd had thinned considerably. A few clusters of twos and threes still loitered at the bar or sat at solitary tables but the place was less than half full, winding down for the night. Some of Mark's crowd were on their cell phones, ringing for cabs, Cathie Mailer among them.

Afterward, Annie would look back and decide that this was the moment her life changed. When she checked the clock over the bar, debating whether to call for her own taxi or risk one last vodka. Rightly or wrongly, alcohol had won.

Disaster arrived with a kick at the door. Although the first thing Annie heard was a voice raw with rage.

"Bastards!" it screamed over the crash of glass splintering against bare boards. "You fucking shits." The bar door crashed into a woman sitting directly behind it, a near-empty bottle of house wine and two glasses tumbling after her onto the beer-soaked floor.

"Everybody else down," screamed the voice. "Now!" The intruder was black, dressed in a ragged coat and wearing a beanie not a million miles away from the one stuffed inside Annie's bag. He glared around the bar.

Nobody at the back took much notice. This was Manhattan—worse than that, this was the East Village, a place habitually full of weirdos, and everyone knew the worst possible thing to do was pay them any attention. Why should this time be any different?

Except it was.

Annie could have told them that the moment she saw his eyes. The eyes of a man with a purpose and a fury unhinged enough to carry it out. She had seen eyes like that before.

"Nobody move," the man said, less aggressive now but far more definite. It could have been Annie's imagination or the alcohol talking, but it seemed to her that he was scouring the bar, looking for someone.

Annie saw Jay reach for the phone at the same time as the black guy did. He shook his head, digging one hand deep into his coat pocket to produce a gun. One wave of his .38 semiautomatic and Jay let the receiver fall, backing away as he approached.

"Stand still," he ordered, "or I'll shoot you." Grabbing Jay, one arm snaking around her neck, the other holding the pistol to her head, the man began dragging her toward the back of the room.

"Get down," he told the suddenly silent room. "I'll kill her if you don't."

Maybe no one believed him or perhaps survival instincts kicked in because four women, somewhat the worse for wear at the end of a girls' night out, stood up very slowly and began to edge to the door of the restroom, then changed their minds, ending up by the jukebox, exposed and terrified. A group ran for the kitchen, sending tables and chairs crashing to the ground, bottles and glasses flying. Someone, somewhere, was screaming. A girl sitting on the sofa behind Annie began the Lord's Prayer.

Our Father . . .

"We need to get out of here," Annie said quietly. "Get the police."

"Someone will have called," said Mark, nodding toward the double doors to the kitchen, still swinging.

"I know, but they'll need to know how many gunmen, how many hostages, layout of the bar . . . the usual."

She realized Mark was staring at her, reappraising.

"Ralf," he said, indicating that the sound guy should stand alongside him to shield Annie from the gunman, giving her space and cover to get to the bathroom and call for help.

"Try the window," Annie heard someone mutter, as if she would do anything else. She stood slowly, unnerving herself by stopping to retrieve her bag. It was nothing special, not exactly Vuitton or Dior, just her life in a battered leather sack.

When she finally reached the unisex restroom there was no window, only two cubicles, a basin, and an extractor fan in an area barely eight feet square.

Shit. How could she, of all people, have missed something that basic? She was still asking herself that question when Mark appeared in the doorway, face frozen.

"It's no good," Annie said. "I'll try the kitchens."

"No you won't," said a voice behind Mark. "You'll shut the fuck up."

After Mark came Ralf the makeup artist and a handful of models, eyes wide with an increasing but unwelcome clarity as alcohol rushed from their brains. Behind them stalked the gunman, his weapon still held to Jay's head.

Casually, almost coincidentally, he raised the gun and slammed it into the side of the girl's head, dropping Jay to the floor. "Now look what you made me do," he said, his eyes on Annie. "Get down," he added, voice flat. "That means all of you."

Annie knelt, tugging Mark's T-shirt as she did so. He turned, glaring, but Annie saw in his eyes the same terror she was feeling. Mark knew as well as Annie that they had no alternative but to do what they were told.

"That's better."

The tiles were cold against the side of her face and Annie could see a lump of chewing gum trodden into the grouting in front of her. She could see Mark's head, but it was turned to the wall, as if he couldn't stand to meet anyone's gaze.

As Annie squinted around the restroom floor at the people with whom she'd spent the last few hours, their faces now gray with fear and intimations of mortality, she made her decision: She wouldn't look at the gunman's eyes again. She should be looking him in the face, memorizing every feature, ready to describe each scowl and facial tic, but she couldn't. More than that, she wouldn't. A gangster in Glasgow had told her never to stare a psychopath in the eye. How was the old man to know he wasn't telling Annie anything she didn't already know?

The gunman was still looking them over. Another gun had appeared from his coat pocket, something small and light, and he was juggling his attention between the two, one covering those already on the floor, the other pointed at the sound engineer, who stood shielding Mark's sister.

"Tell that bitch to lie down," the man ordered. "Then give me their wallets and tie their hands together."

He shoved a handful of plastic cuffs at Ralf. "I mean it," said the gunman.

Ralf did as he was told, starting with Cathie, who handed him her purse without being asked. Annie didn't blame him. God, she didn't doubt for a single second she'd have done the same. But one look at Mark told Annie he disagreed.

Ralf passed Cathie's purse to the gunman, who opened it, emptied out the money, and tossed Cathie's ID on the ground, having given it a quick glance.

"I'm sorry," Annie heard Ralf mutter as he dragged Cathie's arms behind her back and cuffed them firmly. "I'm sorry."

He said it to everyone, one at a time, and it wasn't a quick process. There were eight of them packed into that tiny room, laid out on the tiles like corpses, and Ralf had to clamber over their bodies to get around the room, while the gunman watched from his doorway, following Ralf with his eyes and the barrel of the smaller gun.

Eight hostages, eight purses or wallets, and eight lots of money to be taken, IDs scanned briefly and discarded. It was methodical, Annie noticed, unnervingly out of keeping with the frenzied way he'd entered the bar.

By the time Ralf reached Mark, the last before Annie, Ralf was sobbing, tears running into his small beard. "I-I'm sorry, mate," he whispered.

Mark said nothing. He did nothing, either.

"Please," Ralf implored. "Come on, give me your wallet."

"Do it," Annie hissed, watching the gunman from the corner of her eye. He was moving toward them now, stepping roughly over bodies.

Mark shook his head, his eyes never leaving Ralf's.

"Give him your fucking wallet, asshole," the gunman said, drawing back his foot to boot Mark in the ribs. Annie winced; she could hear the crack from where she lay.

"Moron," said Mark, and the gunman drew back his boot again.

"Don't," said a voice. "I mean, *please* don't . . . And Mark, please don't do anything stupid."

It was the first time Annie had heard Cathie speak, her voice soft but firm, and Mark responded immediately, uncurling from his pain and grudgingly reaching for his wallet, staring hard at Ralf as he did so. Annie was appalled—surely Mark couldn't blame Ralf for any of this? Anyone would have done what he was doing right now.

"Mark Mailer," said the gunman, reading it off a New York driver's license.

"Sorry, boss," said Ralf, wrapping cuffs around Mark's wrist. A look passed between them.

"You do what you have to do," Mark said.

Ralf made a big deal of yanking the cuff tight.

When he reached Annie, she carefully pushed her bag into a stall behind her where she could keep an eye on it once her hands were bound, and let Ralf slip the plastic cuffs around her wrists and pull them tight, so tight the plastic bit into her skin.

The last of them cuffed, Ralf dropped to the floor where he was and sobbed, his wretchedness echoing off the once white mosaic tiles of the small room. The natural thing would have been to wipe his eyes, stuff his hand in his mouth, but Annie noticed Ralf kept both hands behind his back as if they'd already been tied. She watched the gunman count through the money, waiting for him to remember, to reach for one of the remaining cuffs. Instead he just ranted and stormed, stuffing twenties and fifties into his pockets while loading the ills of New York City on their overpriced shoulders, making it clear that every fucker in this fucking city was going to pay. And all the while he darted in and out of the doorway, checking on the now empty bar, never remembering to tie Ralf's hands.

Annie felt a glimmer of hope. She knew Ralf was uncuffed and wondered if Mark knew, too. Desperate to catch his eye, Annie glanced in his direction, but Mark's body was rigid with fury and he had his face to the floor. She was about to risk a whisper when she was interrupted by a voice behind her.

"Let us go. Please God, let us go." Someone had caved in to terror, fear getting the better of prudence as her litany of prayer grew louder. Annie thought it was the makeup artist she'd seen earlier, an Italian woman with cropped hair.

"Shut up!" said the gunman. "Or get your brains blown out."

Annie didn't doubt that he meant it. Nor, to judge from the sudden shocked silence, did the makeup artist.

Whatever you do, Annie warned herself, *don't move.* It was freezing on the tiles, filthy, and the room stank—of fear, disinfectant, and stale loos—but Annie's entire concentration was focused on remaining still and quiet.

"Annie," someone whispered.

She shook her head. The movement slight, almost invisible. *Don't talk,* she wanted to say. *Don't say a word.*

"Annie," came the whisper again. "Kick Ralf."

And then she could hear what Mark had already heard far off in the distance. A familiar wail. First one siren, then another, hardly unusual in this city, but somehow Annie knew these were for them. They all knew, not least the gunman.

"Nobody get clever," he said, and there was something in his voice other than flat anger. To Annie it sounded like fear.

"Got that?" he said. "Move and I'll fucking kill you."

"We understand," said Cathie calmly.

The gunman grunted.

The sirens were so loud now that they rattled glasses on shelves in the bar beyond.

"Nobody moves," insisted the gunman, breaking his own rules by shifting toward the bar to see what was going on outside. Which was the point the makeup artist forced herself to her knees and began to shuffle toward a cubicle. It didn't much matter whether she wanted to pee, vomit, or just find somewhere to hide. It was the wrong move.

"Bitch!" The gunman spun around, raised one of his guns, and pulled the trigger. The sound was deafening, two quick shots reverberating around the tiny restroom. Annie moved as if to clap her hands to her ears, forgetting, until plastic tore into her wrists, that this was impossible.

Ears still ringing, Annie stared at the small woman. A bullet had penetrated her thigh, and blood was welling through her jeans. Frozen with shock, the makeup artist didn't scream or cry, just stared blankly at the stain spreading across the faded denim.

"We heard a shot." A voice that came from beyond the bar door was loud and none too distinct. "Is that right? We heard a shot."

The gunman said nothing, just glanced between the empty bar and the small, dark woman who now lay on her side, half in, half out of one stall.

A second's silence stretched into a minute, and then the voice from outside came again. "What's your name?" yelled the police negotiator. "What do you want us to call you?" He sounded very loud, very close.

Turn it down, Annie wanted to shout back. *If you don't, he's going to hurt someone.*

"I don't have a fucking name," the gunman screamed, kicking out at the nearest body. A woman screamed.

After a moment's silence the police negotiator tried again, his voice fuzzy with feedback. "Okay," he said. "It's okay."

There was a pause that stretched into a silence. Annie could feel her heart pounding in her chest, hear the breath of the other hostages around her.

"Look," the negotiator said. "You've got a bunch of girls in there. Why don't you just let them go? One at a time. We don't want them getting hurt."

The man laughed. "No girls," he said. "Only fucking bitches." His voice was quieter now, almost calm. And the comment that came after was little more than a whisper. "Ain't too sure anyone's getting out of here alive. Especially not . . ."

That must have been the decider, Annie concluded later. One minute she was lying on her front, tiles cold and grimy against her cheek, the next minute someone was scrambling over her, hurtling toward the gunman.

Ralf, Annie thought, but then she saw Ralf push himself to his feet, still on the far side of her. And she realized it was Mark who had thrown himself at their captor.

"Mark!" said Cathie's voice. "No."

"Fuck," said Ralf, mouth gaping in shock.

The first shot was followed by a second, spent cases ringing on the tiled floor.

Someone screamed, Cathie probably, and Annie struggled furiously to get to her knees, wondering what the fuck was going on and all too afraid she knew. As certainty took hold she heard the glass window at the front of the bar shatter and the crump of a stun grenade, just seconds ahead of black-clad shadows opening fire, their .45s blossoming flame.

The gunman jerked backward and went down.

"I should have just cuffed him properly," Ralf was mouthing over and over. "I should have just cuffed him."

But Annie's attention was on the gunman's last victim. Forcing frozen muscles to move, she twisted awkwardly, seeing dark hair, the instantly recognizable T-shirt, and a pool of darkness still spreading across the tiles beneath him. His eyes were open but Mark Mailer was already far beyond being able to return her gaze.

chapter seven

Get through the first twenty-four hours and you can survive anything, Irina had told her. Irina was fifteen at the time, sitting in a Kings Cross café talking about when her parents were murdered and what came next. Annie had just nodded dumbly, fingering her coffee-stained spoon. She couldn't say, *I know,* because she didn't, not on that scale.

Twenty-four hours, Annie told herself. *Survive anything.*

The hospital room had a sour 4 A.M. feeling. Made worse by strip lighting, cheap chairs, and the ancient metal bed on which Annie sat.

"So . . ." Sergeant O'Connell leaned back in his visitor's chair and put his arms behind his head, causing the chair to rock violently. Made from orange plastic, it was clearly not accustomed to the weight of an adult male who was quite so fully grown. O'Connell's shirt gaped over his gut, the gaps between buttons forming a series of elongated O's each exposing white flesh and wiry gray hair.

The sight made Annie's hollow stomach churn.

"You're *sure* you didn't get a decent look at the shooter?"

"No," said Annie. "I didn't."

Her answer elicited an irritated grunt from the NYPD officer. Annie understood his frustration; she'd have expected her to have seen something, too . . .

"I was trying not to draw attention to myself," Annie admitted.

"So you didn't actually see the victim get shot?"

Scowling at O'Connell from where she sat propped against pillows, legs splayed inelegantly in front of her, Annie shook her head then glanced away. There was little to look at in the small room, no pictures on the walls, not even those officious posters found in British hospitals and no window to reveal what was left of the night. In the absence of anything else, Annie stared at her legs, clad in the same jeans she'd been wearing since the previous morning. Same everything, in fact, except her Helmut Lang jacket, which had been taken by the police the moment she arrived in the ER, and her boots, kicked off hours before and not seen since. She'd asked once about her jacket but a nurse had just shrugged and said she thought forensics wanted it.

Annie had been stuck here on this bed, looking at this policeman—or some other authority figure—for hours. Being poked and prodded, literally and psychologically, and not just by the cop sitting in front of her now. A whole procession of interns and nurses had come by, all of them eventually reaching the conclusion that she wasn't hurt.

She was traumatized, they decided. You could tell that by the way she insisted she wasn't. And by her constant demands to be allowed out of this room.

Breakfast had come and gone hours before. It must be 8 A.M. by now, Annie thought. In the real world people would be eating bagels, opening papers, reading the overnight news. Watching NY1, just as she had this time yesterday. Hearing all about the untimely death of Mark Mailer.

The door behind O'Connell swung open.

In came a uniformed officer who'd been sitting with Annie earlier. Easing the door shut with her navy-clad rear, Dana Ramirez slowed its progress with first her thigh, then her knee, then her heel to prevent it from slamming back on its frame. She carried three plastic cups, one in each hand and a third precariously balanced between them, scalding coffee slopping over the edge and down her fingers.

"Damn!" Dana muttered, dumping the mugs on a trolley at the end of

Annie's bed. She shook her fingers. "I wouldn't mind if it didn't taste like shit."

O'Connell fixed Dana with what could only be described as a look. One fierce enough to send her retreating to the uninviting plastic chair by the door. The woman waited until his attention had returned to Annie and then scowled, playground-style, at his back. Annie pretended not to notice. She couldn't help thinking Dana Ramirez looked like an extra from an old episode of *NYPD Blue,* third desk clerk or something: wavy hair resting just above her shoulders, highlighted at some point, but now with an inch of root showing, medium height, built but not too built . . . prototype low-ranking female cop.

"Now. You remembered anything?" the sergeant asked, blundering into her thoughts. "Maybe something you saw?"

Annie shook her head.

"You musta done," he persisted. "You told my colleague, Officer Ramirez, that you're a reporter. You were with the victim all evening. If you were doing a story on this guy how come you weren't taking it all in, making notes . . ."

Shit. Annie held her face immobile and swore inwardly. She should have known better than to volunteer. It was what Annie would have done in Sergeant O'Connell's place, give the poor traumatized witness another woman to confide in.

"Come on," O'Connell said. "What aren't you telling me?"

Annie shook her head hard, trying to dispel the blazing hatred she'd seen in the gunman's eyes and all the other images that came rushing in. The bar girl pistol-whipped into unconsciousness, legs buckling as she crashed toward the floor, blood pumping across the makeup artist's jeans, Mark laughing minutes before the maniac burst in and Mark curled in pain under that man's boot, the dark reddish brown pool that seeped across grubby white tiles toward Annie, blank, dead eyes, Irina Krodt . . .

Aware of Sergeant O'Connell's gaze boring into her, Annie forced her head upward, looking into his face but not quite meeting his eyes.

Come on, she coached herself, *usual rules apply. Get it over with, give the man what he wants, and get yourself out of here.* Annie took a deep breath and began to talk.

"As I've explained to Officer Ramirez several times already—" Annie inclined her head in Dana's direction with a calmness she did not feel. "—I'm a fashion journalist. It was an after-show celebration for his crew . . . Mark is . . . Mark Mailer was a fashion designer—"

"Yeah, yeah, we know all that," said Sergeant O'Connell. "What we want to know is what you saw . . ."

Annie winced. The man shouldn't have done that: Breaking into a witness's flow was a no-no, especially when the interviewee was taking so long to warm up.

"I hardly knew Mark," Annie continued, concentrating on keeping her voice level. "I only met him for the first time the day before yesterday. We spent the first day at his studio, the second out at some derelict car plant on the Hudson while he prepped his show. He felt guilty not having enough time to talk to me. That's why he invited me to his after-show party. It must have been ten by the time I got there. Everyone else was already there. I had a couple of vodkas, a—"

"How many?" O'Connell demanded.

"Three," Annie said, omitting to mention that they were doubles and she'd hardly eaten anything that wasn't a canapé since running into Anya in McDonald's forty-eight hours earlier. Her alcohol consumption was not at issue here.

"Anyway, it was pretty uneventful. We were just talking, about nothing in particular. And then, as it was winding up—people were already calling cabs—the gunman burst in. He was tall, quite thickset, wearing a woolen hat pulled low and a tatty coat that made him look like a down and out . . ." Sergeant O'Connell looked puzzled.

"Homeless," she added.

"He was a bum?"

Annie paused, pulling up her memory of the man who'd stood in the restroom door, that one time she'd seen him clearly. He'd dressed like an itinerant and acted like one, rifling through stolen wallets in search of money and . . . *identity cards.*

"Miss?" Sergeant O'Connell was watching her intently. Obviously feeling he was about to hear something useful at last, the officer leaned forward, elbows resting on his knees. "Miss Anderson? What is it?"

Registering the *miss,* the change in the man's tone, Annie decided to take a risk. To voice a thought that had been growing since the early hours.

"It's just . . ." Annie tried the thought out for size, saying the words in her head before speaking them aloud.

"It didn't seem that random," she said finally. "It seemed like he was looking for something, or someone, from the minute he burst into the bar. Maybe it was Mark."

The second the words were out Annie wished she could take them back. O'Connell looked at her in surprise, his expression changing from interest to sympathy; the kind of sympathy you show a hurt child or a senile, aging aunt.

Annie began to backtrack. "It's probably nothing. I only wondered because, after he grabbed Jay, he seemed to head straight for our group. But, yeah, that could have been coincidence. I went into the toilets looking for an exit and the next thing I knew he'd followed, herding the others in front of him. It just seemed odd, that's all—"

"Why'd you go in the restroom?" Officer Ramirez interrupted. It was a diversion. Annie had done it often enough herself.

"I was looking for a way out and that seemed like the nearest option. I thought there'd be a window, but . . . Anyway, that's where he cornered us. After that I don't really remember much."

Weariness was creeping up on Annie. She had reached capacity. Her head throbbed and her whole body ached, her clothes clung to her with the smell of fear and stale sweat, and something else, the acrid stench of cordite and blood. Sleep was what she needed now, sleep and a long shower. Freshly scrubbed oblivion.

She needed to be somewhere else. Away from here.

"I'm sorry," said Annie, finally looking the middle-aged man in the eyes. "I *really* don't remember all that much. I was having a drink with someone I liked and now he's dead, murdered, whatever you call it. And all I want to do is go home, but I've got to stay here for the next few days and do my job . . ."

She could feel tears in her eyes. *You don't do that stuff,* she reminded herself. *Not these days.*

"I'm not hurt," Annie said, sounding cross. "It was a waste of everyone's time bringing me here in the first place . . . I just want to go home," she repeated.

Visibly softening, O'Connell glanced at his watch and gave Dana another look. One that said they had strayed onto girl turf.

"You were here because of the blood," Dana said gently. "You remember? You were covered in blood. Your jacket was soaked. It could have been yours."

It wasn't.

Annie nodded wearily and shunted sideways to swing her legs off the bed. "I can go then?" she said. "For now at least?"

Another look and Officer Ramirez left the room.

"We'll need to tie up a few loose ends," O'Connell said. "Get you to finish up your witness statement. But if Ramirez can find a doctor to sign you out, then yes, you can go back to your hotel and get some rest. You'll need to stay in Manhattan, though, till the weekend at least."

Annie nodded.

"Ramirez'll be back with your coat and bag," O'Connell added as an afterthought.

Annie didn't have the energy or inclination to ask about the missing Helmut Lang jacket.

chapter eight

It wasn't until Annie stepped out of the hospital doors that she realized why Sergeant O'Connell had given her another of his looks. She'd just rejected his offer to have Officer Ramirez drive her back to her hotel. The look this earned her said she definitely needed treatment.

"Are you sure you're not too tired to walk?" O'Connell said. "It's pretty cold out there." Annie wouldn't have had the officer pegged as a master of understatement, but as the automatic doors of the ER slid shut behind her she discovered otherwise. The frigid air wrapped itself around her exposed face.

"Shit," Annie said, breath and glacial air colliding in her throat. This was beyond cold. Dragging her coat around her, Annie instantly mourned the loss of her Helmut Lang jacket. Not because it had cost a month's wages, but because the jacket would have formed a much-needed layer of insulation between her chiffon shirt and a coat that looked like she'd stolen it from a down and . . .

Not now.

Annie could scarcely recall giving up the jacket, its cloth dried to a stiff black on black, although a nurse had gently prized it from her fingers and handed the garment to a waiting officer, who deposited it straight into a clear ziplock bag and then vanished. That particular film had other scenes, too . . .

If only to distract herself, Annie fumbled in her bag for her mobile. She should call Rebecca, let her know what had happened and arrange to meet her. Not exactly top of Annie's list of fun ways to spend the morning after you've witnessed a murder . . . But hey, the woman was her boss, after all. It was only when she traced the phone to a random inside pocket that Annie remembered it was dead, the battery having died on her the previous evening, just after she entered Mark's party.

Annie glanced back, the noise of East River Hospital assailing her in a short burst as the outer doors hissed open and shut again, allowing Annie one tantalizing moment of warmth, then locking her out.

The story of my life, she thought bitterly. Always the outsider, until she met Tony Panton. An icy wind bit at Annie's face, making her eyes water. Only the wind, Annie told herself, swiping away tears, nothing more.

Only the wind and only memories. Those things she filed away with a promise to herself that she'd examine them later. But she never did. Tony had seen to that, ensuring she had more memories than one girl could stand. Annie was no fool. She knew that in some bizarre way she owed her career to Tony; her career and her anger, because one fed off the other. Not a good feeling.

Tall, fashionable, and popular, Tony Panton had seemed the answer to any teenage girl's prayers and her passport to a life of cool people and cooler parties. A life Annie had only ever eyed longingly from the sidelines. How wrong could she be?

Annie had been seventeen and three days. It was the weekend. His parents were away. Annie and Tony were meant to be going to a party. Their argument began in a pub.

She shouldn't have been there, of course, Annie was still a year underage, but The Plough was full of people she knew, many of them younger. She was proud of Tony, he was in his second year at Cambridge, far hipper, more unattainable than all the boys in the sixth form. And she was proud to be seen with him. She'd seen the way her friends looked at him, the way they looked at her when she was with him, spotted the envy in their eyes and liked it.

"Martini and lemonade . . ."

Annie had asked for it once just to see what it tasted like, and now Tony ordered it every time.

". . . and a Grolsch." He held a twenty-pound note in his fingers, folded with a single crease along the center so it didn't bend. The fact Tony ordered over the heads of those in front of him made one of the boys turn around. Whatever he'd been about to say remained unsaid. Tony was older, dressed in a black suit worn with a white T-shirt, and taller, too. He just looked altogether more grown-up. Annie couldn't believe he was with her any more than her friends could.

It was his *Reservoir Dogs* look, his favorite film, although her parents just saw the suit and the shoes that shone. They didn't know he'd taken their younger daughter to see an 18-rated film on her first real date.

"Drink okay?"

Annie smiled.

"I can change it if it's not . . ."

She shook her head.

Someone had put Bjork on the jukebox, half of Annie's English class were huddled around a table in the corner wondering how she'd pulled it off, and life was close to perfect.

"I wish you wouldn't."

Annie looked up, her fingers frozen in the act of peeling cellophane from a packet of Silk Cuts.

"Smoking's bad for you."

"Everyone does it," said Annie. There probably wasn't a girl in the entire pub without a cigarette in her hand.

"That's not the point." Tony leaned forward and took the packet from Annie's unprotesting fingers. "It's not worth arguing over," he said, slipping the Silk Cuts into his pocket.

"I mean it," he added. "Don't argue with me."

Annie stared at him, hard, but she didn't argue with him.

Somewhere between then and Annie's third drink everything went really sour. She thought about it afterward. God, how she thought about it afterward. Wondering which bit of it had been her fault . . . How she had put that look on his face. Why she'd never before noticed the flatness in his eyes. And, most of all, should she have known? Should she, somehow, have seen it coming?

"You should have told me if you didn't want to go to the party."

"I never said that."

Tony sighed and swung his red Peugeot 205 into a roundabout. "You didn't have to say it," he said. "It's pretty bloody obvious."

This was a Tony she hadn't seen before. A white-knuckle version of the student she'd first met in Our Price six months earlier.

It was possible his pursed lips and frozen face resulted from the speed at which he flung the GTi into corners, not bothering to brake until the final moment. But Annie didn't think so.

"I'm taking you home."

"Home?" It was still only 9:20 P.M. Annie's parents would realize something was wrong and grill her about it, probably for weeks. "Let's go somewhere else."

"You know," said Tony, slamming on the brakes. "Sometimes you can be really fucking boring."

Annie bit her lip, but she didn't cry. Not then. Instead she pushed her nails hard into the palms of her hands and resisted the urge to clutch the door handle as the car screeched to a halt, spraying gravel across the drive of his parents' place.

The house wasn't huge but everything inside looked expensive, in a shabby kind of way. There were Persian rugs on the floor and the pictures were oil paintings, not the John Lewis prints or framed photographs found in Annie's own home. It was the first time they'd been there alone. As it turned out, it was also the last.

"I want to go home," Annie said as he slammed the front door hard behind her and snapped on the sitting room light.

"You just said you didn't." Tony's voice was clipped.

"Well, I do now."

He sighed, looked around the room, and wandered over to a small television, flicking it on with the remote.

"You'll have to wait," he said.

Walking over to the TV, Annie turned it off at the set. "Take me home," she said.

"That's where we *were* going, remember? You changed your mind. So now we're here."

"Well, I've changed it *again*. I want to go home."

"You'll. Have. To. Wait." Tony spoke slowly, as if talking to an idiot or a particularly young child. "We've only just gotten here. I'm not going to get straight back in the car."

"Why not?"

"Because I'm not."

"That's stupid." It was a throwaway comment, nothing more, but the words were enough to bring Tony to his feet.

"Are you saying *I'm* stupid?"

"I don't know," said Annie. "Are you?"

That was when he slapped her. He'd simply stepped forward, raised his hand, and did it. And that was when she locked herself in the bathroom.

"You've got to come out sometime."

Annie shook her head. If she looked hard enough in the bathroom mirror she could just make out the imprint of his hand on her cheek, although that might have been where she'd been rubbing it.

"There's no point crying," he said.

"I'm not."

Annie looked at herself in the glass. All dressed up for the party, black Lycra dress with a scoop neck, her hair newly trimmed and blow-dried so it swung around her shoulders. Winona-esque, she'd hoped when she gave herself a final once-over in the full-length mirror on her wardrobe door three hours earlier. As in Winona Ryder, but there was no sign of that now, just bloodshot eyes and mascara smeared halfway across a teenage face. *Tarty,* he'd called it. *Cheap.*

"Look," said Tony. "You can't stay in there all night."

"Yes, I can."

He'd begged, he'd thumped the door so hard Annie thought it might crack, and now he was trying to be reasonable.

"You'll be late."

Despite herself Annie checked her watch. 10:38 P.M. Her curfew was eleven thirty. She had time yet.

"No, I won't."

Tony sighed. "We shouldn't quarrel," he said. "I'm sorry I lost my temper. Really, I'm not like that . . . It's life. Things have been a bit rough at home."

Annie said nothing.

"Open the door," Tony said, voice soft. "At least let me see that you're okay."

Annie unbolted the lock, backing away slightly as Tony came into the room. His face was serious, and sometime over the last ten minutes he'd taken off his jacket.

"We shouldn't quarrel," Tony repeated. "We're better than that . . ." Reaching out his hand, he waited for Annie to take it. Part of her wanted to make him wait, and part of her now understood that wouldn't be a good idea at all.

"I'm sorry," she said, taking his hand.

What she meant was *I'm sorry I made you angry.*

"Yeah."

Stepping forward, he touched her face, frowning when she flinched.

Annie tried to turn her head. She didn't want to kiss him, she didn't even want to look at him.

It wasn't the first time they'd had sex, it was the fifth, although the original occasion had also been Annie's first. It was, however, the first time he took her in anger, his hands yanking her little black dress above her hips, his knees forcing her legs apart, as one arm wedged across her throat, almost choking her as he held her to the floor.

Annie didn't shout, she didn't even protest. She just lay in shock, waiting for it to be over and feeling hot silent tears seep down her cheeks and fill her ears. He was raping her. She couldn't believe it. Things like that didn't happen to girls like her.

Learn from your mistakes, Annie's dad always said. Well, she'd certainly done that. She should have known a man like Tony wouldn't know the meaning of the word *no*.

Only the wind, Annie told herself, swiping away more tears before heading against the flow of human traffic that flooded through the gates of East River Hospital. By now, news of Mark's death would have spread through the fashion grapevine, his murder becoming a Chinese whisper of tragedy and cliché. She didn't doubt he'd be "cut down in his prime" many times before this thing was over. Imagining the headlines, Annie winced, knowing she was more than capable of having written most of them herself. She could imagine the scene at the *Post* as Ken Greenhouse frantically wrote and rewrote that night's front page himself, reports of Mark Mailer's killing sitting incongruously alongside rave reviews of his show. And all the while, Pete from obits would be hassling Lou for something he could run in his column. The life, death, and career of Mark Mailer, the sum total of his impact on the world, all wrapped up in a headline, a photograph or two, and a thousand words, max. And that was more than most people got.

As memories of the *Post* crashed in around her, Annie's brain finally kicked into gear. It didn't matter where she'd been hiding herself. Or who she was, for that matter, because Annie was back and she, *Annie Anderson,* had Mark Mailer's last-ever interview. It wasn't the best she'd ever pulled off, not exactly hard-hitting and incisive, but it was still an exclusive. The last words Mark Mailer would ever speak on the record.

Cold momentarily forgotten, as she trudged along Annie opened her bag and rifled through the mess. Beneath her dog-eared sheaf of notes, two lipsticks, her mobile, the black beanie hat, and a handful of English coins, she found her Dictaphone and an empty cassette case, its microtape still safely inside the recorder.

"Come on," urged Annie, flicking open the lid to check the reel. Had anything been damaged since she'd clicked the OFF button and dropped the machine into her bag yesterday lunchtime? Not so far as Annie could tell. The tape was just as she'd left it: side two, three-quarters of the way through. About ninety minutes, allowing for pauses and chitchat at the start. Annie felt sick, excited. What had Mark said that she hadn't heard? What questions had he answered that she hadn't expressly asked? She needed to know, and that meant getting back to the hotel.

The icy pavement, frigid wind, and proliferation of pedestrians too bundled up to see more than two steps in front of them made it slow going. She was so preoccupied by the perilous act of putting one foot in front of the other that she would have walked straight past it if an almost-skid into a Second Avenue gutter hadn't pulled her up short.

"Shit."

It was bound to happen sooner or later. *Mark Mailer slain!* And Annie should have known Mark's death would come with a twenty-four-point sans serif headline and a box with a key line around a grainy photograph.

The papers had moved fast, tipped off, most probably, by someone inside the NYPD. That was how it usually worked. A quick call from a dispatcher or an officer on the scene, favors exchanged. They'd used a stock shot, probably the one Mark had mentioned, the one he'd been bullied into by his new PR.

His eyes bothered Annie; eyes did on the whole. It was the knowledge behind them, or lack of it. Annie didn't know what was worse, eyes burdened with secrets or so unsuspecting their innocence made her want to weep. Looking at the dead man's face, Annie decided they were the former. What had Mark known when that picture was taken? What questions had she failed to ask?

Scarcely aware of having crossed the sidewalk, she pulled out a fifty-pence piece and a handful of coins from her pocket. Wrong country, wrong currency. There was no more American loose change in Annie's coat pockets but she found two quarters in her purse, pushing the coins into a slot and tugging at the Plexiglas front of the newspaper dispenser as she did so. One last battered copy of the *New York Post* lay inside.

Snatching it up, Annie let the door go, oblivious to the resulting crash as plastic bounced off metal behind her. *It's just another story,* she told herself. Her eyes raced across the page. She'd been here before. But somehow it didn't feel like it.

New York fashion's hottest news was gunned down last night after a siege in an East Village bar left two others critically injured. Fashion designer Mark Mailer, 31, was killed by two shots while celebrating the success of his new collection shown earlier yesterday evening. The victim, who is as famous for his on–off relationship with shamed supermodel Patty Lang as for his clothes, had been partying with friends and family at The Elephant bar on East 2nd Street before the killer burst in at midnight and took Mailer and some of his party hostage in the restroom.

"He [the gunman] was screaming, telling everyone to get on the floor," said one eyewitness who was drinking in the bar, a favorite of the young and trendy who frequent this neighborhood. "No one took very much notice and that made the guy even more mad. So he pulled out a gun and most of us just ran for it."

Although the motive appeared to be robbery, sources say the killer, Michael Watt, 28, who was slain by a SWAT team as they tried to end the siege, was a known drug addict and small-time dealer from the Lower East Side. "It started out as a robbery," said our source, who asked to remain anonymous. "And ended as a classic case of suicide by cop. If it hadn't been one of our guys, the crack or another dealer would have got him. That guy had a real death wish."

Death wish? Annie stopped suddenly. Drug addict? Where did they get that from? She hadn't heard that. More to the point, she hadn't seen any evidence, either. For all his shouting, the man had been cold and methodical in his search through their wallets.

Frowning, Annie scanned the piece again to make sure she'd read that right. It didn't sound entirely implausible—after all, the gunman *had* taken their wallets, even if he hadn't seemed nearly as interested in the cash inside as in their IDs and driver's licenses.

Careful, she cautioned herself, *don't jump to conclusions.* But there was no avoiding it. She'd felt it then and she felt it now; Michael Watt had been looking for something. And if not for something, then someone. In Annie's mind she was back on that cold hard floor, hands tight behind her back, neck twisted to watch the tall black guy in the too-small overcoat open one last wallet and pull out Mark's driver's license.

"Yeah," she heard the guy say, his voice not that of some Alphabet City junkie on an opportunist's night trip to the East Village, but of a man looking for something he had now found. And whatever he'd been looking for, it wasn't a handful of used bills to pay for his next fix.

There was something else. Annie hadn't been able to put her finger on it at the time, but when Michael Watt had pulled the second gun from his pocket it had jarred. Two guns? It didn't make sense. There had been plenty of junkies in Annie's professional life over the past few years. Not one of them carried *two* fully automatic weapons.

Yellow . . .

Annie flung out her arm and blinked in surprise as the New York taxi screeched to a halt beside her, its wheels spinning on the black run that passed for Second Avenue.

"Where to, lady?" asked the Asian driver.

"Grand and West Broadway." Annie dumped her bag on the backseat and slumped down, planning her next move. Back to the hotel, charge her mobile, put in some calls, first to Rebecca, and then . . . what?

Who should be her first port of call? The police weren't going to tell her anything, Mark's family had issued a statement saying they expected people to respect their privacy, and Annie didn't know where to find Patty Lang. There was always Patty's model agency, of course. Annie could try calling them; not that she expected much in the way of cooperation after Patty's performance on Monday night.

Within seconds the cab was hurtling across St. Mark's Place and into the heart of the East Village. Derelict buildings became restaurants, 9th Street became 8th then 8th became 7th. Scarcely a building sped past that wasn't a place to eat or drink. In the course of four blocks, Annie saw only one shop and that was a local grocer, meager produce freezing on the icy sidewalk out front.

Murderers return to the scene of the crime. Sometimes they even attend the funerals of their victims. Do ghosts? Annie couldn't say. But living victims had been known to return, too. She didn't regard herself as a victim of what had happened last night. How could she? But she still felt more than a witness. The fading horror in Mark's eyes had seen to that.

The cab was at least two blocks distant, maybe three, when Annie first saw the bar. Even if she hadn't been expecting it, bracing herself, The Elephant would have been impossible to miss, thanks to an explosion of yellow police tape advertising its presence. A uniform stood outside the door, stoic expression doing nothing to hide his boredom or undoubted lack of feeling in his feet. Across the avenue, pulled up outside a deli, a white-and-blue crime scene van told Annie there were at least a couple more cops inside. The bar would be dusty with fingerprint powder, restroom tiles still scarred by Mark's dried blood. Would the outline of Mark's body be chalked where he'd fallen?

A small crowd had gathered. They were always there, crime scene tourists whose psychic net curtains twitched at the first wail of a siren, bystanders inexplicably drawn to others' misfortune, appetites insufficiently sated by reality TV. Not so different from journalists, really. And then Annie spotted those, too, chatting blandly to the crowd, waiting for a back to turn so they could make notes or, better still, grab a few words with the weary cop.

Get lost! Annie wanted to scream. *Leave Mark alone!* The hypocrisy wasn't lost on her. After all, in her bag lay a lead to beat all early leads. An early lead that nobody even knew existed, except Annie . . . and Rebecca, obviously. Who else? Well, there was Patty and Mark's new PR and . . .

Then it came to her.

"Excuse me." Annie leaned forward to tap on the Plexiglas window.

An irritated glance in his rearview mirror told her that she had the driver's attention.

"I've changed my mind. Take me to Mulberry Street. Mulberry and Houston."

There *was* someone else who knew. Someone who understood Mark better than anyone, better even than the designer's long-term girlfriend.

Someone who, thanks to Annie's eight-hour plane journey with nothing to do but watch bad films and read a bagful of press clippings, Annie knew precisely where to find.

Guido Brasco. The tailor in Little Italy who'd taught Mark how to cut and probably a whole lot else besides.

chapter nine

It was easy to understand why Guido Brasco had never abandoned Mulberry Street for the more stellar fashion climes of Milan or Paris. As Annie clambered from the cab, shoved a ten-dollar bill through the driver's window (and forgot, as usual, to ask for a receipt), she could see that despite the newcomers who were slowly moving in and taking over, tradition still fought back on the streets of Little Italy.

To the right of Brasco's immaculately glossed black door was a boutique belonging to a young Australian designer whose name Annie vaguely recognized, to the left a self-consciously minimalist sushi bar: not so much Little Italy as Micro Southeast Asia. There were clearly new kids in town, and it didn't take a genius to guess what Little Italy's eponymous inhabitants might have to say on that subject.

As she examined the door and the simple plaque beside it, Annie considered the contradictions of the man who was to have been her first feature for *Handbag*—Mark Mailer, the tailor, versus Mark Mailer, the hot up-and-coming designer. Mark the respecter of Italian tradition versus Mark the hippest new brand in fashion. A man whose clothes every cooler-than-thou fashion magazine wanted on their cover. What was it that had given Mark—on the face of it a dropout with so little regard for tradition that he abandoned his father's business—such respect for an old man and an entirely different craft? A respect so great it kept the young designer working here long after he'd outgrown his mentor, even cutting suits for a few of Guido's elderly Italian clients when he should have been the one opening the shop next door, filling Nolita's streets with a line of Maggie Gyllenhaals and Scarlett Johanssons.

There were no other plaques next to the door, so Annie guessed the old man owned, or at least rented, the whole building. It was a prime piece of Manhattan real estate in mint condition: black glossed windows, sturdy door, and a fire escape as pristine as the scrubbed white brickwork that could have been painted yesterday. The place would be worth a fortune in loft conversions and studio apartments.

Annie bounded up the steps and jabbed at the bell, not giving herself time to change her mind. A harsh, mechanical buzzing came from somewhere deep inside.

"Come on," she muttered, stepping back so far she almost lost her footing on the icy step. It was cold, she was tired, and the stupid thing was she felt more pleased about tracking down Guido Brasco's studio than about anything else she'd done so far at *Handbag*. Her priorities had always been screwed.

"Anyone home?"

Annie considered pushing the buzzer again but decided against it. There was no sign of movement inside, and if anyone was there they clearly had little intention of throwing open the door and welcoming her inside.

I'll come back, she decided, ignoring the practicalities: her day job, Rebecca, the shows . . . *I'll come back tomorrow.*

Sitting on the top step, Annie pulled out her sheaf of notes from the previous morning. Picking the sheet that looked least like it had spent twenty-four hours in the bottom of her bag, she folded the page and tore it in half.

Signor Brasco, she scribbled, cursing the virtually blunt pencil that had been the first thing at hand. *I'm a friend of Mark's. I was with him last night and would very much like to speak to you.*

Annie squinted at the lines, the lead so thick and faint as to be almost invisible in the icy morning sunlight. Keep it brief. Too much explanation reeked of need and bred suspicion. *I can come back anytime. Please call me at . . .* Annie hesitated over whether to add her mobile number, given that the cell phone was currently dead, or give a number from the hotel, when she was quite obviously somewhere else. In the end she wrote both.

Annie had almost cleared the block and was picking up the pace when she tripped over a piece of luck. There was something about the gait of the man who limped dejectedly toward her, the tap of the stick and one shoulder hunched enough to spoil the line of an immaculate camel-hair coat that to Annie's untrained eye looked unmistakably familiar.

"Signor Brasco!"

Guido Brasco looked around slowly. She had the sense he was trying to place her. Perhaps was worrying that his memory wasn't what it was.

"Signor Brasco." Annie was gabbling now. "Sorry to trouble you. I'm a friend of Mark's, was a friend of Mark's, I wondered if I could ask you something?"

"Mark who?" he said.

Annie blinked. "Mark Mailer. That Mark . . ."

At the mention of the name Guido Brasco's face shut down, turning in on itself, mouth tightening so abruptly that Annie was taken aback. It could have been the pain—God knows, less than twelve hours earlier he had lost someone he regarded as a son. But there was something more, something darker in his scowl. Annie glanced at his stick and knew infirmity was all that prevented him from making a break for it, because every muscle in his ailing body tensed, and he was swaying on the spot.

"I cannot talk to you . . . to anyone, right now," he said, his voice measured. "You must understand that."

"Of course I do." Annie had no intention of letting Guido go that easily, not now that she had him. Maneuvering herself until she stood in the old man's path, she added, "I was there. I need to talk to someone. *You* have to understand that."

The old man's expression softened slightly. His eyes were still wary, and his face did not open up. "I'm sorry for you," he said, "but I don't see what I can do."

He was more settled now, leaning heavily on his stick, clutching its handle, resigned to the interruption. From his stance Annie could see that her vain hope of him inviting her back to his studio was precisely that, vain. She toyed with the idea of going in hard and rejected it. If the old man was only going to allow her one question it had to be the right one: Who was Mark Mailer's new backer? That was what Rebecca had told her to find out. And that was what Annie needed to know because soon enough they would come out of the closet, both claiming to have been successful. Annie knew how these things worked, and she knew the leverage that piece of information would give her.

"I was there," she repeated, playing for time. "In the bar when Mark was killed. In the restroom, on the floor, next to him when he was shot."

Guido Brasco looked at her then, his eyes briefly wide and sharp with pain. *Don't fill the silence,* Annie told herself. *If you can hold out long enough he'll do it for you.* They watched each other, discomfort growing, wind chafing their faces, until the old man finally spoke.

"It's a tragedy," he said slowly. "For me personally and for you, for everybody who knew him. Mark was a great talent and a wonderful boy."

Annie nodded and crossed her arms tightly in a feeble effort to keep out the cold.

"It was tragic," the man repeated. "An accident."

"That's the thing," Annie said, keeping her voice level. "I'm not sure it was an accident. I was there, I saw it . . ."

For a second the sadness on the old man's face was overwhelming, and then his expression changed until Annie could read something very different from what she'd seen in the eyes of Sergeant O'Connell. Not doubt or disbelief but anger. An old man's anger that nothing in life was as cruel as the truth.

"It was an accident," he said flatly. "Nothing more. I accept that. I suggest you do the same."

"But I know," said Annie, falling back on an old line. "I know every-thing."

Guido Brasco stared at her.

When he spoke, his voice was cold. "Then you don't need to talk to me, do you?"

chapter ten

It was only after Guido had gone that Annie remembered she was freezing. Although it was now midmorning the temperature had yet to climb above freezing, and without the Helmut Lang her battered overcoat and chiffon shirt were worse than useless against the icy wind.

A couple of doors down from Brasco's was a small, scary-looking boutique. In its window a sheet-metal dummy stood naked but for a neat black jacket, cut from heavy cotton, nipped at the waist and fastened with a single button. It looked roughly Annie's size, assuming there was a bulldog clip at the back of the torso currently wearing it. And Annie was lucky to find anything remotely appropriate for the windchill, since this was February and the shops were resolutely spring-like and pastel.

Perhaps she wasn't meant to die of cold after all, thought Annie. And perhaps, in the circumstances, that thought was in totally bad taste.

Annie was not given to sentiment, but her Helmut Lang had been a David Blaine among jackets, making its wearer appear slimmer, taller, more confident, and more professional. It had been no ordinary jacket; it was alchemical, a worker of magic, a purveyor of miracles. Whether it, too, operated by misdirecting the viewer's attention from reality just didn't seem relevant.

For her mother, Annie had more than halved its price and even then been greeted with cries of, "How much? For another black jacket?"

But Lou had been right. Cost per wear the jacket would have been, if not a bargain, then at least something approaching good value, certainly cheaper in the long run than half the jackets Annie had bought in Topshop for forty quid and worn only twice. Shame she was never going to see it again.

The boutique on Mulberry Street was the least enticing Annie had ever entered. She was in and out in less than five minutes and four of those were spent waiting for an assistant to surface.

Oh, the girl was there, all right—standing at the back of the shop and leaning against a glass box that passed for a counter while doubling as a display cabinet at a Damien Hirst exhibition—she just wasn't *there*.

Having convinced the wraith that, Yes, she really did want the one in the window, and, Yes, she did plan to wear it now, and, Yes, she was planning to wear it under *that* coat, Annie left the boutique with one more layer to protect her from the cold, if not the world.

It wasn't until she was safely back in her room at the Soho Grand half an hour later that Annie looked at the lining and realized the jacket she'd just bought was new-season House of Mantolini, one of the fashion houses bidding to buy Mark Mailer.

She couldn't work out whether that made her feel worse or not.

chapter eleven

"Someone was looking for you."

"Rebecca?" Back at the hotel, Annie smiled, waiting for the young Chinese receptionist to continue. The woman seemed embarrassed, her face conveniently hidden behind a sleek black sheet of hair.

"A police officer," she said. "Ramirez? She was worried when I told her you hadn't been back."

"What else did she say?"

The woman shuffled unseen papers beneath the counter. "That we had to look after you. There was a homicide . . . you might be in shock."

Annie groaned and made for the lift, punching the button and almost falling inside it. Why did everyone think she needed protection? Apart from her mother, obviously. Her mother just thought she was difficult, but that had been a given for ten years and more.

Back in her room, the message light was blinking frantically.

00:55 A.M.: "Annie? It's Rebecca. I'm in the bar of the Mercer with Joel. I just heard about Mark Mailer. Awful, terrible tragedy and after that fabulous collection, too. We need to speak because you didn't get around to filling me in on your interview. What did Mark say? Did you get anything good? I'm won-

*dering if there's still time to get your piece in the April issue. I've already spo-
ken to Claudia . . .*

That would have been six-ish, early morning, London time. Lucky
Claudia.

*She says it's doable, just. It really depends how quickly you can turn this
around. I'm assuming that won't be a problem. Call me as soon as you get in.*

She hadn't told Rebecca she was going to the after-show party, Annie
remembered, heart sinking. Hadn't wanted her to know.

*01:30 A.M.: "Annie? You must be back. Pick up . . . This is not good. The
Post might have been prepared to put up with this sort of thing but I expect
to be told where my staff are at all times. I certainly expect them to return my
calls. I want you to phone me the second you get this. I don't care what time
it is. We need to make a decision on April now."*

*02:10 A.M.: "Annie! Where are you? Did you get my messages? And why
aren't you answering your mobile? I'm not paying the bill if I can't even get
hold of you. Call me."*

That was just the tip of the iceberg. Although perhaps volcano was
more appropriate since Rebecca's voice rose with anger and, Annie
couldn't help suspecting, sheer amazement at having her orders defied, as
predawn turned into early morning with still no return call.

There couldn't have been more than a couple of hours between the first
call and the last, but they grew in ferocity until the final message ended
with Rebecca's own hotel phone being slammed into its cradle with such
force that Annie only just had time to save herself from a perforated
eardrum.

"This is bad," she told herself. "You shouldn't have let this happen. All you
had to do was call her."

The television talked to itself in the corner, Annie having turned it on
the minute she came in to give the illusion of company, a habit carried
over from the West London flat she could no longer really afford now that
Nick—the only man in years who qualified as more than a one- or two-
night stand—had moved out.

She was too old to share with strangers and too skint to stay on her own. She'd have suggested Lou move in, but Lou McCartney had inherited a flat from a great-aunt, whereas Annie had inherited a brooch, a stamp album, and a bald teddy bear.

On NY1 a newsreader continued to talk earnestly, giving an occasional smile that revealed just enough of his perfect teeth. Idly, Annie wondered if he got free dentistry the way Rebecca got free frocks, and then she stopped prevaricating, plugged in her mobile, and woke up an entirely new set of problems.

"Annie? Annie?" Lou's words crashed out of voicemail retrieval. "Annie! Fuck! Are you there? Shit! Where are you? Did you hear about Mark Mailer?" Lou's shriek was so loud it reverberated around Annie's room. "Did you interview him in the end? Didn't see you last night backstage after his show. Where the fuck were you? What are you doing? Call me, okay? At the City Club on . . . Anytime. Jeezus, this is weird. Everyone's freaking out. I've even had Ken on the phone. He wants you to call him."

Sod that, Annie thought, replaying Lou's message and scribbling the number for the City Club on the pad in front of her. Next came a couple of Manhattan-based PRs whose names meant nothing to Annie, calling with seat allocations for shows that had already been and gone. Good seats, too. Second row in both cases.

On the television, the anchor began to wrap up his slot. Annie reached for her mobile, which lay charging on the desk, wondering whether to call Lou or bite the bullet and put her boss out of her misery.

Neither, Annie decided. Instead she lifted the receiver from her hotel phone and replayed Rebecca's last three messages. After the first, she held the receiver away from her ear and watched the ads on NY1. After the third, she let the receiver dangle from her hand, watching as it spun out of the knots into which it had tied. If only life were that easy.

It took Annie several seconds to realize that the jocular banter of a DIY ad on the TV wasn't the only male voice she could hear. Lower and more distant, like a radio heard through a wall, came another voice, one with a broad Yorkshire accent and a way of punching at the important words . . .

". . . You got that? Okay."

"Press one to replay the message . . ."

"Anderson? It's Ken."

Thank God, she hadn't wiped it.

"Lou gave me this number. Said you'd interviewed Mailer. So call me as soon as you can, eh? Doesn't matter what time it is over here, I'll be in the office all bloody night at this rate. Use a pay phone if you think anyone at that magazine will check your calls. You can call me at . . ."

Annie saved the call and carefully replaced her receiver. She didn't write Ken's number down; she didn't need to, she could recite it digit for digit. Her memory was a pain like that. No one had ever told her where to find the DELETE button.

"Think, Annie," she urged, clambering off her bed and walking over to the window. Cars, sky, clouds . . . what did she expect to see?

She had bosses coming out of her ears—old and new—both of them after the same story. The trouble was, Annie didn't have a story, not yet. Not a real one. What she did have was a human interest *I was there* shocker and ninety minutes of nothing much from a disappointingly likable, talented ex-fashion-legend in the making whose stock had just soared thanks to a couple of well-aimed bullets to the chest.

That whole first-person thing wasn't Annie's style, no matter how much the tabloids were willing to pay. It wasn't her style and it wasn't a real story. Annie had barely scratched the surface of Mark's relationship with Patty Lang, and she had no idea who his new backers might be. All she knew was that no article on Mark Mailer would be complete if the journalist didn't speak to Patty Lang, Guido Brasco, and whoever would have been Mark Mailer's backer had he lived.

She should stop putting it off and call Rebecca, Annie decided. *Handbag* were paying her salary, the woman was her new boss, and it was probably time Annie began treating her like it. It was also time to remember that, for the moment at least, she worked in fashion.

Ken could wait. After all, he knew the score.

Secure in the knowledge that her chances of actually getting to speak to Rebecca herself were slim, Annie dialed her boss's hotel and crossed her fingers until, after six unanswered rings, the voicemail cut in informing Annie that "the person you require is not available."

Cheering silently, Annie left a message that told Rebecca exactly what

Annie wanted her to know and no more. She'd been with Mark. The police had wanted to talk to her. The East River Hospital had only just discharged her. Enough to engender sympathy and leave the woman wanting more. And enough to ensure that Rebecca didn't discover those facts from someone else. It was only a matter of time before the NYPD began releasing hostage names from the previous night—the dead, the damaged, and the potential case studies—and then it would be all over. At least, it would if Rebecca found out Annie had been there by hearing it on the news.

Back in the bathroom Annie brushed her teeth twice, rinsing, reloading toothpaste, and repeating as she scrubbed away the night's slime. Gradually the acrid taste of bad memories and fear, too much vodka, and hospital coffee was replaced by a synthetic mint: fresher but equally alien.

She was in a state, again. Although this time at least she had a good excuse. Shower next, Annie decided, blasting the water on full and stepping into its flow, letting it thunder down around her head. She had so many things to do and couldn't bring herself to do any of them—things like listen to the tape, for instance. But the truth was, Annie didn't want to hear Mark's voice again, not yet.

Nick would have laughed, although not without a hint of bitterness. At last, a job too ugly for Annie Anderson to just *do.* Maybe, if she'd been better at dealing with her own cans of worms and leaving other people's alone, Nick wouldn't have left her with rent she could barely afford to pay and space in a bed where he used to fall asleep waiting for her to come home.

Don't start that, Annie chided herself, wrapping a hotel towel around her and tucking it modestly above her breasts. The man was just furniture, a security blanket she'd slept with occasionally, a live-in alarm system. She told herself she hadn't really cared whether he stayed or went.

Until he went.

And then she just bought another lock for all the windows and two for her door and reconciled herself to waking at the slightest noise.

Nick had been her first long-term boyfriend in quite a while. Since Tony, if she had to be specific. There'd been plenty of men, most of them the kind who'd have her mother and sister, Jane, choking on their coffee. A few even made Lou shake her head and that was saying something, since

Lou had a penchant for beach bums and surfers that no woman without a private income could possibly afford.

Although Annie had loved Nick in her way, she was never in love with him. She didn't do that anymore. And though she was pretty sure Nick had been under no illusions about that, he'd stayed. And stayed. For three years in all. While Annie buried herself in work and largely ignored him until, one weekend, about six months earlier, he'd left in a jumble of packed cases and tight goodbyes. That was one of the many reasons why Jane and Mum were furious with her; Nick was something Annie had finally done right and now she'd "messed that up, too."

Peering into the wardrobe, Annie grabbed her last clean pair of jeans. They were her least favorite, her thin jeans, which meant she'd have to spend the rest of the day hoping no one noticed the top button was undone. Stepping into the dark denim, Annie was astonished to find the jeans slid easily over her hips and she could even fasten the metal rivets without breathing in. Bemused, she undid the jeans and checked the label, just to be sure. So that was how you dropped half a stone—severe trauma and four days' starvation.

Basking in the ephemeral glory of her new, skinny self, Annie shrugged on her new Mantolini jacket and debated calling Lou before schlepping the fifty or so blocks to Midtown. There was no point, she had to get out of the hotel and back on top of her schedule. There were important shows later this afternoon and she had to be seen at them, preferably by Rebecca. Plus she'd be needing Lou's help with her homework.

chapter twelve

With a renewed sense of purpose Annie stepped from the Soho Grand and waved her arm assertively at the first cab she saw. Amazingly, it U-turned and screeched to a halt in front of the steps and Annie was soon accelerating up West Broadway, feeling more in control of her life than she had since . . . well, since she'd headed in the same direction to interview Mark Mailer forty-eight hours earlier.

That was what gave Annie the resolve to pick up her mobile and carry on emptying her voicemail; a surge of misplaced confidence and the sense her life might be back on some sort of track. It was the same old same old: several new messages apiece from Rebecca, Ken, and Lou, plus a call from a New York tabloid. Annie didn't even want to think about how *they* got her number. Then, just as Annie was just beginning to zone out, another voice came on the line.

"Annie? It's your mother . . ."

"Christ! That's all I need."

"Annie? Are you there?"

Why bother to ask when you're talking to the voice box on a mobile? Clearly Annie wasn't there.

After leaving a five-second gap, as if waiting for Annie to reply, her mother's voice came again. "I don't like to bother you," she said in a tone that indicated quite the reverse. "And I know you're busy, but Jane's just phoned to say a fashion designer was shot in New York and we're worried. It was on the news at lunchtime. And I called your magazine but they didn't know if you were all right. He was famous, so you probably don't know him anyway, but . . ."

One, two, three, four . . . Leaning forward, forehead propped on the driver's headrest, Annie counted to ten, with the phone wrapped in her fingers as if it was the Nokia she wanted to strangle.

Pressing three to save the message, Annie killed the phone, cutting her mother off midflow. She had to admit the woman had a point. She generally did, that was the infuriating thing. It hadn't occurred to Annie to call home.

"Happy bloody families," muttered Annie. She had been faking Happy Annie while her mum and dad played Happy Families for most of her adult life, but it hadn't always been like this. Not when she was little. Then it had been Sindy dolls (well, knock-offs with hollow legs from the Saturday market), two point four children, and fighting over the top bunk with her sister in their shared bedroom. And if not straight A's at school then at least a decent cross section of B+ and A-. Good enough not to get her pocket money docked, if not quite to earn the Sony Walkman she'd always coveted.

Normal, that's how anyone would have described Annie's upbringing. Normal, even boring. An enviably and overwhelmingly bog-standard working-class/lower-middle-class childhood. A bit brighter but plainer than her older sister. Brownies and guides and netball, but not enough spare cash in the family for ballet or tap or ponies. And, belatedly, boyfriends, though she was slower off the block than Jane and positively retarded compared to most of the girls in her class.

That was when life changed, when Annie was seventeen. That's when the dreams started and Annie was officially relabeled *difficult*.

The first dream Annie remembered as vividly as if it had been last night. And every dream was the same. She always woke from the dreams sitting bolt upright, sweat turning to ice on her skin, mouth open in a parody of a silent scream that never came.

In desperation her mother had dragged her to the GP. "What's the problem?" he had asked. But Annie said nothing, lying rigid while he examined her.

"You can tell me . . ."

Only she couldn't, not then, not ever.

Doctors were meant to know things. They were meant to be able to tell when people were broken. After that Annie had never been able to trust a doctor again.

To begin with, Annie's family had been concerned. Well, Mum had, with Dad it was harder to tell; but then the doctor started using words like *attention seeking* and *difficult phase* and Annie's mother had grasped at them like a woman in need of a life raft. Any life raft, regardless.

"Police now believe Mark Mailer was killed during a daring escape attempt. Eyewitnesses have told officers that he somehow managed to free himself and tried to overpower his killer in an attempt to save the other hostages, among them his sister Cathie, a high school teacher from Short Hills, New Jersey . . ."

The driver had tuned in to WNYC.

"Reports are still unclear but, according to witness statements, the thief shot and critically injured a female hostage, and police now believe Mailer decided to act out of fear that the gunman would fire again."

So that was how they were playing it. Mark Mailer, heroically putting himself between his family and friends and a psycho with a gun. Annie couldn't deny the bare facts. It was just that the official version was missing a few crucial details, like the fact that Michael Watt had grabbed the bartender and headed straight for Mark's group without so much as stopping to empty the till. Without even glancing at it, come to that.

"Where d'you want, lady?" asked the driver, swinging his cab into a stream of people crossing 44th Street and watching the tourists scatter. The hard-core New Yorkers just ignored him, daring his bumper to come a single inch closer.

Annie peered past them. She couldn't see the hotel Lou had named but they were near the Royalton, so it had to be around here somewhere.

"Just here," said Annie. "On the right." She thrust ten dollars into the driver's hand and leapt from the cab, once again forgetting to ask for a receipt. She couldn't imagine Rebecca letting her get away with the usual, random, receiptless kind of expense claim Annie always filed at the *Post,* with a regular promise that documentation would follow later.

As Annie was about to turn back to the taxi, the enormous wooden doors of the Royalton swung open and a small, skinny blonde hurtled through them, nearly taking out the black-clad permatanned doorman and almost snapping a pin-thin, kitten-heeled woman in two, which was two bigger than her dress size.

"Annie!" Lou screeched. "Where the fuck have you been? Come on in, I'm having coffee with Chris and Alex."

Annie had no idea who Chris and Alex might be, and the near-black windows of the Royalton's lobby gave up nothing but Annie's own reflection.

"I'd rather go somewhere quieter."

Lou looked at her.

"Please."

"We'll go there." Lou nodded across the street to the Algonquin. "It's nice and warm and there won't be many fashion people there. Let me just get the others."

That wasn't what Annie'd had in mind at all, but it would have to do.

In the end only Chris joined them, trailing behind as Lou and Annie crossed 44th Street.

"Annie, Chris . . . Chris, Annie," said Lou as they left the frozen sidewalk for the Algonquin's claustrophobic warmth.

Chris put out his hand, so Annie shook it. He had good hands, Annie noticed, surprising herself with the thought. His fingers were long and his grip firm, not the languid shake of so many of Lou's fashion friends nor an uninterested *hiya,* which was all Lou's stable of rent-a-shag surfers could muster.

"I've told you about Chris," said Lou. "He works in Milan. We met during a press trip last year."

Annie nodded vaguely and realized she must be looking slightly put out to find Chris here when she'd come looking for a serious conversation with her best friend.

Chris smiled and shoved his hands in his coat pockets, discomfort writ large with the gesture. He looked nice enough. A well-cut gray wool coat stylishly at odds with his scruffy fair hair and battered jeans. Still, not exactly Lou's type, unless Annie had that wrong. Much more her own, assuming she had the faintest idea what that was anymore.

"Good to meet you," said Annie.

"Yeah." Chris nodded and gave Annie a weak smile that showed he wasn't sure how much she meant it. "I should go," he added.

"Stay." Annie hadn't meant to say that.

Contrary to Lou's prediction the lobby—all wood paneling and huge comfy-looking armchairs—was already filling up, although with a wealthy-looking lunchtime crowd and not the fasherati.

"So," said Lou, when the three of them were ensconced on a low 1920s sofa and Lou and Chris had finished insulting the owners of most of the fur coats in the room, not out of respect for the fur's previous owners, but because the cut was so last season.

"Tell us the truth. Where exactly have you been?"

Coming hot on the heels of her mother's call, Lou's bossy big-sister tone made Annie wince. "Don't nag," she said crossly, conscious of Lou's friend trying not to look at her. "I've got other people to do that."

"Whatever." Lou pinged the bell in the middle of the table, slapping its button hard with the palm of one hand. "Well," she said into the lobby's sudden silence. "That's what it's there for, isn't it?"

Annie watched Chris nod, humoring her.

"I've had Ken on the phone three times already," said Lou. "And then there's your new boss . . . There's not a Brit in Manhattan who doesn't know you've been AWOL since Mark Mailer's show. When you piss off Rebecca Brooks the whole world knows about it, don't they, Chris?"

The guy pulled a face for Annie's benefit. "Our world at least," he said. "Assuming that matters."

Before Lou could say *of course it matters,* they were interrupted.

"What can I get you?" asked a waiter.

"A Bloody Mary," said Lou.

"English breakfast tea," Annie replied.

"Me, too," said Chris.

Lou glanced between them and frowned. "Tea? You two?"

"I'm gasping." Annie's shrug was slight. "Plus I haven't eaten today."

"Like that ever bothered you before." Lou flopped back on her sofa and rested a gorgeous pair of cream boots on the low table in front of Annie. The soft vanilla leather screamed *second mortgage*. And that was before you registered the not-at-all antique leather Marni coat that Lou seemed un-derstandably reluctant to take off.

"Nice boots," Chris said. "Sigerson Morrison, right?"

Lou nodded and Annie did a double take. "How did you know that?"

He shrugged apologetically. "Used to do their PR . . ." He grinned, reading Annie's expression correctly. "Yeah, straight guy in fashion PR shocker."

"How much?" Annie asked Lou, intrigued that Lou's friend had just gone out of his way to tell her he wasn't gay.

This was beginning to look like a setup. And Annie really didn't need that right now.

"Well?"

"Less than in London," said Lou coyly. Which Annie knew was virtu-ally meaningless.

"Their old PR sorted me out a discount," Lou added, nodding at Chris. "I might let you touch them if you're really good."

Annie tried to smile. Lou was okay, she was just worried. Annie seemed to be having that effect on people at the minute. And Lou's boots *were* fabulous, cut from a buttery leather not actually designed to be worn out-doors and certainly not walked in. They'd have been trashed in a New York minute had Lou actually been planning to walk anywhere, which Annie very much doubted. Like most of the fash pack Lou was a firm be-liever in the *when in Rome* philosophy, which meant that when in New York she made like a corporate Manhattanite and firmly refused to allow the weather to influence her dress or behavior in any way. These were chauffeur-driven boots if ever Annie had seen them.

Lou gave Annie thirty seconds' grace and then called time. "Annie," she said shortly. "I know trouble when I see it." Her boots vanished beneath dark wood polished so high Annie could see her own reflection. "Let's for-get my boots. Tell me why you wouldn't come into the Royalton."

Annie raised her head, staring hard at her friend. She couldn't believe Lou would do this to her in front of some bloke Annie had barely met, but Lou stared back, brown eyes unflinching. She knew Annie too well.

"I was there," Annie said at last, steadfastly ignoring the man at the other end of the table.

All the same, it was Chris who registered the significance of what Annie had just said.

"*There?*"

Annie nodded. "Last night. Right next to Mark Mailer on the floor when he was shot." It sounded harsh. But then it was harsh.

Lou's mouth had fallen open, but Annie no longer had the urge to reach out and gently shut it. The gesture, which would have been automatic just a couple of days earlier, now seemed too intimate. Annie felt distant, removed, not just from the woman who passed for her best friend but from the world.

She wanted to get up, pick up her coat and bag, and leave. To leave Lou and Lou's too-attractive friend, their tea, Lou's Bloody Mary, the bill, the lot. Walk away from this city, her life, and the memories she dragged behind her like a line of ghosts. Baggage wasn't in it. Mark's death was one thing too many on top of half a dozen things too many.

"Annie," said Lou.

"*What?*"

"Nothing."

Chris leaned forward and handed Annie a tissue in silence, waiting while she dabbed in irritation at her eyes.

"I'll be back in a minute," Annie said, and disappeared down a spiral staircase to repair her face in private. This was not Annie the journalist, or even Annie the fashion editor, it was just Annie, stripped of armor and staring at her face in the age-damaged mirror. She felt naked.

"You all right?" said Lou when Annie returned.

"Of course I'm not . . . ." Annie caught herself, half shrugged an apology, and settled back into the velvet armchair. She was seated before she noticed they were alone.

"Where's . . . ?"

"He's got a job interview at three so he's gone to change. And he felt, you know, in the circumstances . . ."

The waiter's timing was bang on. If Annie hadn't been facing the room and seen him approach, tray aloft, she'd have suspected the man of lurking. Dealing a handful of paper coasters onto the table between them, he gave Annie not a cup of tea but a pot, tea bags, milk, extra hot water, a saucer of lemon slices, the works, and took away the now spare cup and saucer with a shrug.

Grateful for something to occupy her, Annie pretended not to notice as Lou fell gratefully on the largest Bloody Mary either of them had ever seen, only to choke on its potent spicing and generous lacing of vodka.

"Look," said Lou, "perhaps you could take it from the top?"

"The shooting?"

"What else?"

Annie shook her head.

"Then how about starting before that? With how you—a fantastic journalist but, let's face it, a fashion virgin on her first job—came to land an after-show invite that would have been this week's hottest ticket, had anyone actually known Mark Mailer was having a party."

Lou paused, thought about how to word what she wanted to say next. "I mean, I know Rebecca's got clout, that's how you got the interview. But Mailer's not the kind of guy who invites someone he's only just met, let alone a journalist, to a bash that only his crew knew was happening."

"I didn't blag a job behind the bar, if that's what you mean," said Annie.

"It wouldn't be the first time." The words were throwaway, but Lou's face was serious. She wanted to get back to the important stuff, like what had really happened and was Annie all right in there.

"Mark invited me . . ." Annie caught sight of Lou's skeptical expression. "He invited me because he trusted me and Mark trusted me because that's what I do. Build trust. Like you said, I'm a good journalist. Plus he didn't really have much choice. I was under his feet for two days and when the makeup artist asked Mark which bar it was at again, Mark had to invite me because I was there. The man was just too polite for his own good. And he's not *that* kind of guy, either."

"What kind?"

Annie looked at Lou.

"I thought you were implying, well, you know . . ."

There was an uncomfortable silence.

"What you do is your own business," said Lou eventually. They both knew she didn't believe that. But Annie couldn't even begin to explain that she'd never have slept with Mark, because she only had sex with men who didn't matter. (And then only if lust and alcohol got the better of her.) What's more, Annie would never, ever fuck someone to get a story.

"I didn't take Rebecca with me," said Annie, steering the conversation to safer ground, "because her very existence would have reminded Mark that I worked on *Handbag* and wrecked the trust I was trying to build. And then . . . And then it all happened, and I've been with the police and in hospital and giving statements . . ."

"Hospital?"

"They said I was in shock."

Lou looked appalled. "When did you last sleep?"

Annie shrugged.

"You've been awake since yesterday?"

"Stuff to do."

"Old habits die hard, huh?" said Lou, having stirred her Bloody Mary clockwise, then counterclockwise, then in an interesting figure-eight, and, finally, when all other possibilities were exhausted, actually taking a sip. "Why don't you tell me what you can?"

"Take it from the top?" said Annie bitterly.

"Yeah," Lou replied. "It's worth a try."

Reluctantly Annie recounted the edited lowlights, partly because Lou deserved it but mostly because doing so let Annie get things straight in her head. As she talked she clutched the holdall tucked on the sofa beside her, feeling for a small hard bundle, reassurance that the Mailer tape hadn't moved since she last checked.

chapter thirteen

"Christ it's cold," Annie blurted as the Algonquin's concierge heaved open an outer door and they hit a wall of frozen air. Slush still lined the lip between sidewalk and road, turned to a froth of dirt and ice by the plummeting temperature.

"My hotel's only a couple of doors down," Lou assured her, speeding ahead, coat flapping open in the wind that roared along the cross street. "If it was any farther I'd get a cab. These boots weren't made for walking."

They were on their way to Lou's room at the City Club where she'd left her precious show schedule, the list of the shows Annie had already missed that day, and her own notes so Annie could do a crash course before she met Rebecca.

"Hey," said Lou as Annie's spiked heel caught in one of the many metal air vents that peppered Manhattan's sidewalks, doubling as impromptu ashtrays for the city's exiled nicotine addicts. "Mind that grid."

"Shit."

Lou's warning came too late.

Annie extracted her heel from the grid and took a step, going down on one ankle. "Fuck, that hurt."

"Annie," said Lou. "Your foot."

"I know . . . I know." Annie followed Lou's gaze and wished she hadn't. Her left heel protruded at a right angle. The spike hadn't gone through a hole in the grating at all; it had snapped, a clean break about half an inch from where heel met sole. Lifting her foot, Annie balanced precariously and watched two inches of leather-coated plastic swing from a narrow thread of black leather, all that kept her heel from plummeting through the grid and into the heating system under Manhattan's sidewalks.

"Not your day, is it?" Lou said, then looked abashed. It wasn't the most tactful thing she could have said.

Stepping closer, Lou crouched in front of Annie and took the heel in her hand. "The pin's slightly too short," she said, pointing to where the plastic had snapped. "It's meant to run the whole depth of the heel . . . design fault," she added knowledgeably.

"Bugger that," said Annie. "What am I meant to do now?"

"There used to be a cobbler down here," Lou said, taking Annie's elbow and steering her toward Fifth Avenue.

Emblazoned in flaking gold leaf over the first stall in the atrium were the words SHOE STUDIO. *Studio* clearly being real estate agent speak for *cupboard on wheels*. Inside, the place was barely six feet by eight, lined with shelf after shelf of shoes in various states of malaise. Behind the counter, a balding New Yorker was hammering a small steel cap onto the kind of stratospheric stiletto heel that gave even supermodels vertigo.

Grabbing his counter for support, Annie unzipped her boot and tugged it free, taking care not to detach what was left of her heel. The man regarded Annie's offering, and then Annie, with interest.

"I, uh, snapped my heel." Annie stated the glaringly obvious. "It caught in a grid. I was wondering if there's anything you can do?"

Turning the boot over in his hand, the man waggled the heel and looked at the steel pin, curiosity mixed with amusement in his eyes.

"No ma'am," he said at last.

Annie waited for some explanation but none came.

"Can't you glue it back?"

The man smiled, not kindly. "Howdaya expect me to do that?"

"Okay," said Annie. "Just nail it then."

The man shook his head. "Whaddaya think I am, a magician? Lady, it's broke."

"I *know* it's broke." Annie struggled to keep her voice even. "That's why I'm here. I just want it fixed so I can get where I'm going."

"Like I said." The man shrugged. "It's broke. Ain't nothing anyone can do about that. They're cheap, Chinese probably . . . That's what happens if you buy cheap boots. Hell, that's why they're cheap."

Annie stepped forward on one stockinged foot and felt Lou's hand on her elbow.

"What d'you mean *cheap?*" She snatched the boot back and began examining it. Admittedly her boots bore little resemblance to the gorgeous pair she'd spent two hundred pounds on a couple of months earlier; both heels were trashed from where she'd let them get too low before reheeling and the New York slush had liberally decorated their black leather with a white tide mark.

All the same . . . All the same, they looked terrible.

"They're not exactly Manolos," Annie admitted, the fight draining from her, "but they're Franco Borgias. They weren't cheap."

"I don't care how much they cost," said the cobbler, returning to his hammer by way of terminating their conversation. "They're still cheap shoes."

Annie and Lou had barely completed the bizarre two-hundred-yard three-legged race back to Lou's hotel when Annie's mobile buzzed against her hip. She would have ignored it, but instinct told her to check the screen: REBECCA, MOBILE.

"Hi, Rebecca, I tried to . . ." This was as far as Annie got. Moments later, the phone was back in Annie's pocket and she was under strict instructions to be in the Royalton lobby in thirty minutes sharp. Or else.

Ten words, ten seconds. Round one to Rebecca Brooks. Annie didn't like the way this relationship was shaping up at all.

"Be humble," Lou advised once Annie's feet were safely tucked into a borrowed pair of too-big tan boots with three-inch heels. "Grovel, if necessary. Milk what passes for her human kindness."

Annie was skeptical. She didn't do groveling on principle and she certainly wasn't about to let it become her default tactic where her new boss was concerned, über-editor or no.

"What are the chances she'll be traumatized by Mark's death?" Annie asked. "I mean, she did claim to be a friend of his."

"Yeah right." Lou grinned. "You mean she met the man once for five minutes two years ago and didn't think him worth any more of her time."

And then Lou's grin faded. She'd just taken a look at the bleakness on Annie's face. For someone who didn't do crying, Annie looked awfully close to breaking her own rules.

"It shouldn't bother me this much," said Annie, grimacing at her reflection in the mirror on Lou's hotel wardrobe.

"Mark?" said Lou. "Of course it should. You saw someone murdered. It's bothering me and I wasn't even there. What kind of person would you be if it didn't?"

"No." Annie shook her head. "Not that. Well, yes, that, too, of course. I meant my boots."

"Annie!"

"Listen to me for a moment, will you?" Annie took a deep breath and tried to put her thoughts in order. "Those boots were Franco Borgias."

"Yeah, you said that already."

"I've bought Borgias before," Annie persisted, "and they're pretty hard wearing for designer boots. I still have an old pair at home. I might have bought this pair from a boutique in Portobello, but *they were not cheap . . .*"

"That's what's riling you?" said Lou, sounding surprised. "Some Manhattan cobbler thinks you're tight?"

"You're intentionally missing the point." Annie rescued her dead boot from its resting place in Lou's bin and thrust it at her friend. "I bought a pair of Borgias boots and paid a Borgias price. Did I get the real thing?" She glared at Lou, as if daring her to say it didn't really matter. "Either Borgias aren't bothering with quality control anymore or this is a fake."

Lou took the boot, turning the battered object over to examine it carefully.

"Does that look real to you?"

"Well," said Lou. "This heel doesn't look like it would pass any decent quality control and the leather's not that good. The stitching is a little crude, too . . ." She paused. "I don't get it. Mark's dead, Rebecca's furious, and you're worried about this."

"I'm not in shock," said Annie. "If that's what you're worried about. And it does matter." Annie couldn't really say why, only that it did. She hated fakes of every kind. "You agree they're knock-offs?"

Lou nodded. "They're certainly not a six-points-of-difference imitation. Not with that logo."

"A what?"

"Six points," said Lou. "Otherwise known as the high street version. When a high street chain produces an item "inspired by" a designer piece there are supposed to be six points of difference. The heel may be slightly different—a little higher or a little thicker—stitching another color or thickness, the fabric cheaper. Nine times out of ten, the differences are so subtle you won't spot them unless you have both items side by side—"

"But the point is," Annie interrupted, "when you buy high street you know you're not buying Prada. It's got a high street label inside and you pay a high street price. The difference is, I didn't pay a high street price. I thought I was buying the real thing. That isn't an imitation, homage, inspired by, or any other euphemism. They're knock-off and not from a market stall on Canal Street or Brick Lane. These boots aren't the kind of fakes you know are fake and decide you don't care. These are fakes you think are real and discover later that they're not." She'd known several men like that, and one who stood out above all.

The Royalton lobby was like being inside a fantastically expensive filing cabinet where, Annie couldn't help feeling, she had been incorrectly filed with the beautiful people.

Ahead, at the far end of the room, was the restaurant. To Annie's left, down a handful of steps, was the lobby bar, sunk into the ground like an empty swimming pool. Ken Greenhouse would have had words for this place and the kind of people who frequented it. It wouldn't have been Annie's venue of choice, either, but the sheer scale of the room was undeniably impressive. Even the noise of the after-lunch brigade, which anywhere else would have been reminiscent of a football match, was hushed, rendered reverential by the cavernous gray interior and double-height ceilings.

This, decided Annie, must be what hell was like, full of people who were infinitely thinner, richer, and more attractive than you. People who looked like they slept, went to the gym, and had lives that were under control. And you, as usual, were the only one without a table.

Suppressing the urge to make a break for it, Annie tried to find a seat without appearing to look for one. As far from everybody else as possible. She could do without the whole bar eavesdropping on her imminent conversation with her boss.

Annie walked the length of the aisle overlooking the bar, self-esteem shrinking with every step as she looked down on table after table of the self-consciously gorgeous and/or fashionable. By the time Annie reached the end she felt about three feet tall and twice as wide. There was no sign of Rebecca and, almost as worrying, no empty tables. Annie had two choices: hang around inside looking conspicuous or drag what remained of her confidence outside. In the battle between death by condescension and hypothermia, hypothermia won.

She was almost at the door when it swung open and Rebecca was ushered in, coatless, glamorous, utterly, effortlessly intimidating. With no opportunity to smooth her hair or belt her coat, Annie was instantly rendered a mess by Rebecca's slim-line black Gucci trouser suit and swingy shampoo-ad hair.

"Darling!" Rebecca declaimed, as always managing to pitch her voice just loud enough to announce her presence to everyone in the vicinity but without apparently raising it. "I'm sorry if you've been waiting."

Was Annie going soft in the head? Her boss sounded as if she genuinely meant it.

"A few seconds," Annie lied, air-hostess smile sliding into place. "A couple of minutes at the most. There are no tables, though."

"Of course there are." Rebecca glided toward the back of the room. "This one will do."

Doing a quick 360-degree turn, Annie scanned the bar for the group who'd been sitting on the corner banquette just seconds earlier. Nothing. The women—their bags, coats, cell phones, and all—had vanished. A waiter was busy wiping the table. Despite herself, Annie was impressed.

"Sit down," said Rebecca as she told the waiter to bring two black coffees without first asking Annie what she wanted. Sending the man on his way, Rebecca tucked her Manolo-shod feet under the sofa and crossed them at the ankle so she neither collapsed back into the cushions nor perched uncomfortably on the edge. Her eyes were on Annie and she looked troubled, almost as if she was searching for the right words. Except Rebecca never searched for the right words. What would be the point? Anything she said became gospel by the mere fact she'd said it.

Annie waited for the first blow to fall. And waited. The frenzy of rubbernecking that had blown up around Rebecca's entrance had abated and Rebecca, her face a mask of concern, kept staring at Annie with something that looked disturbingly like pity in her eyes.

"Look," said Annie. "I'm sorry."

Before she could say anything else, Rebecca stopped her.

"You mustn't be. I've been so worried . . ." Rebecca smiled. It was an unnerving sensation. "I'm not accustomed to my staff going AWOL. As you can imagine . . ."

Annie could.

"So I knew something dreadful must have happened. Nothing else could explain your not answering my calls. And, well, it had, obviously, something horrible, but that wasn't what I had in mind. I never dreamed anything so terrible could happen. Poor, poor Mark. And how absolutely awful for you."

There was a pause that Annie was obviously meant to fill. "I'm okay," she said obligingly.

"So brave," said Rebecca. "How much did you see?"

Once more, Annie was impressed. The woman was such a pro, she could teach Ken Greenhouse a thing or two about manipulating and motivating staff. It had taken less than a minute for Rebecca to bring the conversation around to where she wanted it. The interview as therapy: Play on the interviewee's need to get something off her chest, turn on the tape recorder, and watch the subject spill. Annie had used it herself a million times and watched it work every time. It would work now if she wasn't careful, and Annie couldn't afford that luxury. Then again, she couldn't afford to piss Rebecca off, either, not when her boss was being so . . . considerate.

The coffee's arrival bought Annie a few seconds. She decided to take the same route she'd used with Lou, give just enough information to satisfy Rebecca, only this time play up the trauma.

"How much did I see?" Annie repeated as the waiter turned his back. "Too much." She proceeded to run through last night again.

"God," said Rebecca when Annie had finished. "Horrible . . .

"And the interview," she added. "How did that go? At Mark's show you said you had a lot of background. Do you think we can use that?"

Annie had seen this coming, tried to legislate for it, but she still found herself facing a blind alley: claim she didn't have enough background for her feature to work or pretend she did and then try to get out of writing it.

"The thing is," Annie said, more confidently than she felt, "I've nowhere near finished my research for the piece. Hardly started in fact."

"But this changes everything," said Rebecca. "It's an entirely different feature now. You interview America's greatest up-and-coming designer— the future of American fashion—and a few hours later you see him die. You're in a unique position. Whatever Mark did or didn't tell you is just background. *You're* our story now."

Aaaaaaaaaaaaaaaagh! This was what Annie had been dreading. *Mark Mailer was murdered right in front of me!* Handbag *exclusive!*

Annie didn't *do* being the subject. Her life worked precisely because she was invisible . . .

"There's just time to make the April issue," Rebecca was saying. "The printers will push our print slot a couple of days so we still hit the newsstand on time. No one else will be able to touch us. We'll get masses of pickup. How much space do you need . . . ? Claire's pulling together pictures now, we'll need a new shot of you obviously. I was thinking we could hold over the Clements Ribeiro story but I'm not sure four pages will do Mark justice. Still, I can probably drop a couple of still-life pages and get you six, what do you think?"

Annie knew exactly what she thought, but Rebecca wouldn't want to hear that. Her best option was to continue playing it traumatized and try to win herself some time that way. Ignoring, of course, the fact that she probably was traumatized, whatever that was supposed to mean.

"I . . . I, uh, don't know, Rebecca," said Annie, so weakly she made herself want to cringe. "I mean . . . I don't know if I'm up to writing it right now. It's too soon."

"Oh you poor thing." Reaching forward, Rebecca stroked Annie's arm, and Annie tried not to flinch. She figured it was all part of the "considerate Rebecca" act but still the whole touchy-feely thing unnerved her.

"I do understand," Rebecca continued, steely gray eyes boring into Annie's. "So here's Plan B. How about I take your tape back to London with me tomorrow, get it transcribed over the weekend, then, if you're still not back by Monday, I'll get Ginny to talk to you over the phone to get your perspective and write it up for you. We'll e-mail a draft to you to read through, obviously, but spare you the agony." Rebecca nodded, pleased with herself. "By the time you get back to London it will practically be printed."

Could this get any worse? Annie didn't even have the beginnings of the real story yet, but the last thing she needed was for Rebecca to know that.

"I . . . I'd really rather not." Annie stalled frantically. "I mean, the tape was recorded backstage and it was really noisy so it probably isn't very clear. Anyone else will just hear great swaths of Mark mumbling but I'll be able to remember the bits that are indecipherable. Why don't I transcribe it this weekend, when I've had tomorrow to collect myself, see what I come up with?"

Rebecca considered the suggestion. She wasn't buying it, Annie could tell, although she was doing a good impression of giving it some thought.

"And you know," said Annie, clinging to the air space now that it was hers. "It would be great to get this out at the beginning of March but I could write a much better feature if I had longer." This was anathema to a newspaper journalist but Annie was getting desperate. "As well as calling in pictures of Mark's last show," she continued. "Claire could hunt down images of the bar and the models and crew who were held hostage. What's more, I could interview them, too. They'd trust me because I was there and, given time, I'll be able to get to Patty Lang . . ."

She'd said it. Used her Get Out of Jail Free card and probably used it far too soon.

"Okay," Rebecca said briskly and, grim as Annie felt, it was all she could do not to smile. After all, what self-respecting editor would turn down the chance of an exclusive with the newly bereaved fallen super-model? Not one with the rottweiler reputation of Rebecca Brooks, that was for sure.

"But if we're going to give away our time advantage," said Rebecca, "I'll need serialization potential, probably with a good Sunday, so I want lots of emotive description, first-person observation, what it was like to be there. The kind of thing people won't be able to get anywhere else."

Everything about Rebecca's attitude told Annie they were back to business as usual. A waiter materialized, the bill was paid, and Rebecca was on her feet, Balenciaga Lariat bag in the crook of one arm.

"Balenciaga starts at three," Rebecca said. "Come along, my driver's waiting."

chapter fourteen

The A-list actress sitting in the front row opposite was wearing flip-flops, in Manhattan, in February. And not particularly covetable flip-flops at that. No diamante thongs or Perspex kitten heels, just the bog-standard plastic kind. The ones you used to be able to buy in Woolworth for ninety-nine pence when that was Annie's preferred pocket-money destination.

Mundane the actress's shoes might be, but these had doubtless been produced by a Brazilian street kid and cost her far more—assuming, of course, Miranda Lawson had paid for them at all. And the paparazzi were loving it. At least five photographers clustered the catwalk in front of her, taking shots of the actress's purple toenails.

Miranda Lawson had a rep for quirky—quirky hair, quirky temperament, and quirky love life, but not, a cynic would note, quirky movies that might mess with her box-office receipts or *Variety* Top Twenty Most Influential Women in Hollywood status. *Quirky* spelled with a capital *I* for *Image*. And *F* for *Freezing*, thought Annie. Although the woman had not a goose bump in sight, unlike the rest of the room.

Annie scanned the brightly lit meatpacking loft where the international fasherati were simultaneously trying to appear effortlessly chic while hunkered down under numerous layers. Even Anna Wintour hadn't removed her hip-length fox-fur jacket. Or her Chanel sunglasses.

It was Friday, early evening, and nobody waiting expectantly for the final show of the week was wearing as many layers, or shivering quite so conspicuously, as the British contingent. Most of whom were already far more concerned with their next seat allocation, the one waiting for them on the flight home. Except, of course, for Rebecca Brooks. Clad only in an ocher Daniel Niven suit and with a fine cashmere trench slung over one arm (fresh from his spring/summer collection and couriered over to the Mercer that very morning), Rebecca had squeezed in next to Miranda Lawson and was chatting animatedly, professionally oblivious to the Oscar winner's unflattering A-line denim skirt and skinny white vest, which looked as if it had come from a Wal-Mart three-pack.

Full marks, thought Annie. It took style to leave the house looking that cheap. Although Miranda's outfit was more nipping to the corner shop for a pint of soya milk on a Californian morning than front row at New York Fashion Week, even if you ignored the fact that it was the middle of February and the temperature, both outside and inside, was what Annie had come to think of as So-Zo, south of zero.

"If I was Daniel I'd bin her," said Lou from a seat behind Annie. "He pays her a fortune to stuff her wardrobe with those boring bias-cut gowns he keeps churning out and then she leaves the house dressed in Kmart the minute her stylist turns her back."

"She didn't," insisted a young besuited guy whom Annie recognized as fashion editor of the *Sunday Herald.* He was one of a small but influential phalanx of man-boys whom Annie had noticed scattered along Manhattan's front rows. Neither overtly gay nor obviously straight, their ambiguity was part of their currency.

"Didn't what?" Lou sounded puzzled.

"Turn her back, I mean," he said. "The stylist . . . Christy always does Miranda."

Christy who? Annie wanted to ask but held her tongue, knowing it would be tantamount to asking *Rupert who?* on *The Times.*

"Oh." Lou's voice was scathing. "I believe you. But it just makes it all the more bizarre for Miranda to be one of Daniel's rent-a-celebs. And I wouldn't have thought it was Christy's style either, way too much like clothes people might actually wear."

"Juxtaposition," said the man-boy. "It's about defying expectations, creating conflict. Always surprise, that's Christy's motto. Where would be the originality in turning up for a Daniel Niven show *wearing Daniel Niven?*"

With the exception of Miranda Lawson, almost the entire front row on both sides of the catwalk had done precisely that, including him. Although his had been paired with old-school plimsolls and a battered band T-shirt in what Annie suspected was a none-too-subtle attempt to subvert the designer's intentions, create conflict, even.

"Christy's entirely responsible for Miranda's look," he said, warming to his subject. "She creates the entire image, on set and off. What Christy says, Miranda does, and what Miranda wants Miranda gets. In my view, it's Christy, not Miranda, who's the most powerful woman in Hollywood right now."

Annie tried, and failed, to conceal a smirk. The man flicked her a look that began as disdain, merged with uninterested contempt, and slid into reluctant recognition, the merest trace of acknowledgment lifting the corner of his mouth as he turned to Lou. Annie knew why. Since her previous afternoon's conversation with Rebecca at the Royalton, word of Annie's presence at Mark Mailer's death had spread through the British fasherati like news of a sample sale at Chanel. Now people who'd effortlessly ignored her since Monday still shunned her; it just took them a little more willpower.

You had to hand it to Rebecca. Apart from the six hours when Annie had been allowed to return to her hotel to sleep, the woman hadn't let Annie out of her sight. *Keeping your mind off it,* she called it, but Annie was more inclined to think it was Rebecca keeping an eye *on* her little publicity gold mine.

The past day and a half had been a crash course in fashion etiquette. Annie hadn't been allowed to leave her boss's side, forced to listen in on every bit of small talk Rebecca talked and watch every spectacle that her boss had seen through newly fashion-conscious eyes.

She had gasped as Nicholas Ghesquiere's new collection for Balenciaga rushed straight to the top of every fashionista's want list. She had been intrigued by the celeb-packed front row and 1920s-style Oscar frocks at Zac Posen and choked on Scandinavian-Thai fusion canapés—lemongrass meatballs anyone?—at a succession of after-parties. She had been impressed, almost to the point of purchase, by the grown-up models in body-hugging black wool dresses who stalked the catwalk at Donna Karan.

Most of all she'd longed for big, fat chip-shop chips with ketchup as she watched Rebecca push a Caesar salad . . . "Hold the croutons, hold the Parmesan, and I'll take the dressing on the side" . . . around and around a plate during lunch with a Manhattan power PR at the Mercer Kitchen.

Having been instructed to watch and learn, Annie wasn't sure whether she was meant to be learning how to talk the talk or how to make a plate of lettuce last more than an hour.

It had been an education all right, and the muscles in Annie's cheeks ached from smiling politely through the whole charade. But her air-hostess smile was still in place and had to hold out only for one last show. Then, thanks to Sergeant O'Connell who insisted she could not yet leave Manhattan, Annie could get on with her job while Rebecca and the rest of the British fashion pack boarded the 747 that would double as their fashion bus home.

Praise the Lord and the NYPD, thought Annie. Who knew that a balding Irish American detective with middle-aged spread could inspire such gratitude?

"Shame you didn't make it to Tom Li this afternoon," said Lou, leaning forward.

The 747 in Annie's head screeched to a halt as Lou named what Annie felt must be the only damn show she hadn't attended in the last twenty-four hours.

"Tom . . . ?"

Reading her blank expression, Lou smiled. "Chinese American, LA-based, but he's been all over, Milan, Paris . . . worked for some really big names."

"He's not that big in Britain yet," added the man from the *Herald*. He seemed to regard talking to Annie as contagious. If Lou was doing it, then maybe he should, too. "You can get Tom Li in Browns and Harvey Nicks, but that's about it. It's pretty but not too pretty, wearable but with a quirky edge."

"Amazing to think he started out as a copyist," Lou said.

Annie frowned.

"You know," said Lou. "A counterfeiter. Your favorite subject. Urban myth is he was churning out Fava knock-offs when Ugo Baroni tracked him down to Hong Kong, not to mention knock-offs of Armani, Gucci, Mantolini, and Vuitton."

"I don't get it." Annie was shocked. "How come that doesn't make him a crook, rather than an international design sensation?"

The man from the *Herald* laughed, and Annie felt like she'd just asked if you could get pregnant from sitting on a loo seat.

"He was just a kid," said Lou. "You know, ripping off famous designs to earn a buck, that's what I heard. It's not like he was the brains behind the whole operation. Tom Li was way down the food chain, he just happened to be good at what he did."

"Very good," said the guy from the *Herald*. "Think about it. Here's a guy who's learned his skills the hard way. I mean, imagine a tougher apprenticeship. You have to be pretty talented to do other people's stuff as well as they do and, since he already knows how to do your stuff, and do it well, you bring him in-house and there's one less knock-off merchant to worry about. I'd have done it, too, if I was Ugo . . ."

It made a strange sort of sense, Annie had to admit.

"But don't the other designers mind?" she said. "The ones he was ripping off?"

Lou laughed. "Well, they didn't while Ugo Baroni was employing him. Now Tom Li's gone it alone he's more of a threat. So it's only a matter of time before one of the big houses tries to buy him."

Returning to her rightful place a split second before the lights dimmed, Rebecca nodded politely at Suzy Menkes on her left, then twisted on the bench and beckoned to Annie.

"Cover," she hissed when Annie obediently leaned forward. "The June issue coincides perfectly with Miranda's new movie. Everyone's after her, of course, but she's definitely interested in *Handbag*. We're in a whole different league, edgier, more thought provoking, perfect for Miranda's image. We'll put together a dream team. You can do the interview. I've explained that you'll be huge once the Mark Mailer piece hits the newsstands."

Annie thought she was already a name. Not in fashion, obviously.

"Any ideas on who should style?" asked Rebecca, staring at Annie expectantly. A minute earlier Annie would have been completely thrown, no more able to tell one stylist from another than she could tell a chassis from a carburetor. Now she knew the answer instantly.

"Christy," Annie said firmly, crossing every limb in the hope that Rebecca wouldn't ask which Christy. "She'd bring that cutting-edge accessibility both Miranda and *Handbag* are famous for. You know, defying expectation, creating conflict. Plus, she's a favorite with Miranda already."

Something in Rebecca's expression shifted slightly. "You're absolutely right," she said. "Absolutely . . . Miranda, *Handbag*, Christy, and TJ Nickson." Naming a photographer who'd made his reputation by making beautiful people look ugly, but lately softened his look so it was altogether more cover-shoot-friendly, she smiled. "It's perfect. She's ours. I'll call her publicist on my way to JFK, then we can put the entire proposal to her personally at Mariolina's party."

Mariolina's?

"In Milan. You know, Mariolina's throwing a party at Lake Como in Miranda's honor. Very exclusive, only close personal friends obviously, so we'll have plenty of time to get Miranda on board then."

Opening her mouth to point out that if the guest list was so exclusive, she wouldn't be on it, Annie shut it again. She should have learned by now. Mark Mailer, Miranda Lawson, TJ Nickson . . . What Rebecca Brooks wanted, she got. So a plus-one on her invitation would be unlikely to lose Rebecca any sleep.

For the next fifteen minutes models unfailingly clad in more shades of tan than Annie knew existed blurred before her eyes. Trends clearly cut no ice with Daniel Niven. Until now, autumn/winter had been relentlessly 1960s with a '40s twist and a hint of '20s. No one, it seemed, had informed Daniel. Scanning her running order in bemusement, Annie frowned. The descriptions bore little resemblance to the outfits parading along the catwalk. The words in front of her described a rich array of chocolates and coffees and honeys and ambers. All Annie could see was brown and cream.

Handclaps had barely begun to falter before Annie was on her feet, coat and bag in hand, ready for the ritual backstage rush. She was a quick study, and the past day's experience had taught her that if she didn't move fast enough her boss would leave her trailing in her wake.

The rush never arrived. Instead Rebecca got languidly to her feet, slipped one arm then the other through the sleeves of her trench, and, with the slightest inclination of her head, indicated a small back staircase away from the crowds surging toward the cargo lift.

"Come on," said Rebecca. "I've got a flight to catch. And you've got that feature to write."

Annie wasn't the only one to be taken aback. Her surprise was echoed in meaningful stares from those around them. Rebecca omitting to schmooze a designer was serious, forgoing the backstage ritual unheard of . . . What was the story? Because there had to be one. If Rebecca Brooks was passing up an opportunity to consolidate next season's advertising, then either something was seriously wrong or *Handbag*'s editor had bigger fish to fry. Annie had a horrible feeling she was about to be battered.

A tug at her belt caused Annie to file the thought away for further consideration.

"What's that about?" Lou hissed, nodding to where Rebecca was knotting her belt. "And while we're at it, what should I tell Ken?"

"Why do you have to tell him anything?"

Lou glared at her. "Come off it, you know Ken. As if I'd be able to get away with that. Give me a break. What shall I tell him?"

"Tell him . . . tell Ken I'll call. As soon as I get back to London, that's a promise," Annie added, when Lou's glare turned to a scowl. "Tell him I'll talk then."

chapter fifteen

It was strange the things you remembered. All the things it was impossible to forget. When Mark had finally detached the microphone from his
top it had pulled a little looping thread, creating a tiny hole in the fabric.

Annie's interview had begun with the usual inane chat of the above-
board interview: the weather, traffic, polite inquiries about children or
pets. Interviews done wired up on the sly used different rules, obviously
enough. This time around her chatter was even more humiliating. Winc-
ing, Annie heard herself spout platitudes. Was New York always this cold?
Wasn't he freezing in that jacket? Was the traffic on Eighth Avenue always
that bad . . . ?

Fast-forwarding, Annie heard other questions squeal past. She'd had
enough of the niceties and so, if his tone was anything to go by, had Mark
Mailer. This part always made for interesting observation, though. You
could tell a lot from how an interviewee responded to polite chatter, and
Mark Mailer's response had been borderline rude.

Rebecca had mentioned, very much in passing, that this interview was
the idea of Mark's new PR company. Translated, that meant Mark was answering questions under protest and through gritted teeth.

So, Annie heard herself say. *From plumbing to fashion design—how did that happen?* Mark clearly thought the question banal, because his answer reeked of crib sheet, but it was meant to. Start the way you have no intention of going on, that was Annie's motto; lull them into a false sense of security. *I just wasn't a natural,* he said politely. *Plumbing is a skill the same as tailoring, just not one I was blessed with. Unfortunately it took me a while to work that out.*

What had the man really wanted to say? Annie wondered, as she always did when off-pat answers were trotted out in response to formulaic questions.

Recalling the circuitous route she'd had to take to get Mark talking, Annie began whizzing through the tape, stopping and starting only to note down terse one-liners about Mark's childhood, school, family business, whatever. Gradually Mark's one-liners became two as Annie carefully followed up each of his comments with a snippet of information of her own.

That's the good thing about not being the oldest, she heard herself say, *sometimes you can get ignored.*

Yeah, he said. *There were times when that would have been good.*

Or, *At least you didn't have to share a bedroom with your sister! I never got a moment's peace.*

Or, *I know what you mean, I never saw much of my dad, either. He was always at work.*

If Annie wasn't mistaken, that was the first time she heard a shift in Mark's tone. *Hey,* he said a few minutes later, *how long have your fingers been blue? Let's go out back and see if we can find some heat.*

It had taken more than a day, but Annie had finally made it to second base. Doddle.

The sound clunked as Mark picked up Annie's recorder, diode still glowing and clip mike banging gently against his chest, and carried it toward the temporary walls erected to separate front stage from back.

Let's try here. He was talking to Annie again. *Can I get you a coffee?*

Annie heard herself accept. She stood a little farther from Mark now, she remembered, tape recorder between them on top of a portable heater. It had been easier to see Mark's face from that position, to watch him avoid eye contact, but the microphone was less able to pick up Annie's words and her questions became muffled.

Better? asked Mark, returning with two polystyrene cups of scalding black water from an urn in the corner. It was vile, but it was hot.

There was more rustling. The sound of Annie's own coat being unbuttoned and scarf discarded.

Much, Annie said, *thanks. I almost have motor functions.*

Mark laughed then, short and sharp. *So*, he said, *where were we?*

Would the change in his approach have been perceptible to her now if she hadn't known it was coming? Annie found it hard to say. But the next time she picked up her own voice it had relaxed, reflecting Mark's warmer tone.

Tell me again about your transition from plumbing to fashion college . . .

It wasn't that straightforward, unfortunately. It took me a couple of years to pluck up the courage to tell Dad things weren't working out. He never really got it. I mean, he never really got why I thought I was entitled to a job I loved, when he was offering me the family business. And, you know, family's important. Dad's lot are Jewish—not strict, obviously—my mom's Italian. You don't get much more family than that.

Annie laughed.

The way Dad saw it, the business wasn't good enough for me. He just took it personally, I guess.

Sounds rough.

Yeah, said Mark's voice abruptly. *It wasn't great.* He'd taken her comment as sarcasm.

And it was a couple of years before you went to fashion college?

Uh-huh.

Was that because it took you a while to decide what you really wanted to do? Annie knew it wasn't but she'd made herself ask.

No. Mark's tone was slightly lighter, Annie thought. Maybe she was just being optimistic. *It was because I fucked up! You wanna know what I did with those missing years?*

There was a moment's silence, while Mark waited for Annie to say *yes* and Annie waited for Mark to back down.

I wasted them, he said more quietly.

Yeah. Annie's own voice was barely a whisper, but it didn't matter. *I know the feeling.* She remembered that moment as clearly as if she were standing opposite Mark right now.

Two, maybe three seconds, then Mark's laughter exploded from the tape. Annie, who'd forgotten it was coming, noted again the surge of relief she'd felt at the time.

Cathie got you through rehab? That might be common knowledge, but better she got it from him than from the clippings.

Yes and no. Mark hesitated. *At the risk of sounding like some twelve-step evangelist, I had to take responsibility for myself, my sister made me see that. Cathie helped, definitely, but she made me realize I couldn't blame other people for my fuckups. Okay, so Dad was angry but the only person wasting himself was me. I'm not going to let that happen again.*

Mark took a deep breath, and Annie could still see him sweeping his hand through his messy dark hair. *There comes a point, you know, when you have to stop looking for someone to blame. You just have to say, Shit happens, and put it behind you and face up to life. You can't go on drowning forever— in guilt or fear, whatever it is—because the only person who drowns is you.* He'd paused. *And sometimes you have to do what's right, whatever it costs.*

Annie paused, staring at the white words on the blue screen of her laptop. Her head ached and she needed a drink. Stopping the tape, she rewound and played Mark's words over again.

You can't go on drowning forever—in guilt or fear, whatever it is—because the only person who drowns is you.

He might as well have been talking about her, except Annie knew from Mark's voice that he was talking about himself.

Was that all it took? Annie wondered. Just call time and move on? Were her own problems really that basic? For a moment she longed for a Cathie to kick her butt, rather than her own sister whose specialty had always been to sit in judgment without bothering to get the facts first.

Anyway, Mark was saying, *when I got out of rehab I applied to do fashion design, got accepted, and everything fell into place. It was what I'd always wanted, I just hadn't realized it was an option when I was in high school. Of course, for my dad it still wasn't. He thinks the fashion industry is full of fags, I guess. And he's wrong, it's full of fakes. Ask Tom Li . . .*

Ask Tom . . . ? Annie hunted down the reference and came up with the ex-counterfeiter-turned-independent-label, the one Lou had been talking about a couple of hours earlier. How come she hadn't noticed that on Wednesday?

A pause in the tape indicated that Mark was waiting for Annie to respond. When she didn't he said, *I worked my butt off studying at college, paid my way through and kept away from the scene. The rest, as they say, is history . . .*

Annie could almost hear her own brain whirring as she considered her next question. Was Mark Patty's Cathie? Dare she go there? Now would have been the logical time to ease his famous girlfriend into the conversation.

Annie listened hard, following her own taped thought process. It took a second, but the decision she made defined the whole interview.

Talking of history . . .

She could almost hear him wait for the wrong question, the one that would have blown it.

You go back a long way with Guido Brasco. I've seen you quoted as saying he taught you all you know. How did you meet?

I did my internship with him.

What made you go to Brasco? I mean, why not Ralph Lauren, Calvin Klein, Marc Jacobs even?

Mark's gaze had flicked over her, causing Annie to wonder what she'd said wrong. This was meant to be an easy question. For both of them.

Why Guido? Lots of reasons. For a start, everyone was applying to those guys. Not Marc Jacobs, though, he wasn't as big as he is now. Still finding his way back then.

Damn it, Annie should have known that, but her homework hadn't included a potted history for every designer whose name might possibly crop up.

I know, said Mark. *Hard to believe, isn't it? The guy can't put a foot wrong. It's kinda reassuring in a way.*

And Ralph Lauren? Calvin Klein? Annie prompted, dragging him away from her woeful grasp of fashion history.

Yeah, right. Well, I guess I just didn't have that kind of front. I didn't think they'd even let me through the door. You know, that thing where you think everyone's going to find you out. And there was more to it than that: I wanted to learn to cut and I wanted to learn the trade from the bottom up, so I knew everything there was to know.

But surely . . .

College? Sure, they taught us the basics, but I wanted to learn from scratch from a master, someone hands-on who was doing it day in, day out. It's not just about talent and creativity, there's skill and learning and I respect that, still do. I guess I'm more my father's son than he realizes.

There was a silence, as if Mark, rather than Annie, was digesting that particular piece of information.

And . . . ? she said eventually.

He's the very best, right up there with Brioni.

It took Annie a second to connect the name to an old-school Italian tailor, a firm that made their name dressing the film icons of the 1950s; Frank Sinatra, Clark Gable, and Gregory Peck all had worn Brioni's flamboyant but classic suits. There'd been a name-check for the firm somewhere in Annie's clippings.

Menswear wouldn't be what it is today if it wasn't for Guido. Just because he's never shown in Milan or Paris doesn't mean his work has been without impact. You didn't have to play the international game in the same way back then because fashion wasn't so corporate, so ruthless . . . at least not on the same scale as it is now. Now, of course, it's a case of play the game their way or die.

Just as quickly as he'd warmed to his subject, Mark had stopped. Annie had waited for him to continue and then waited some more. Rewinding the tape, she listened to the designer's last answer. Wondering if it said what she thought it said . . .

Brasco taught you to cut? she heard herself ask above the heater's din.

Uh-huh.

And you stayed on? I mean, after the internship finished.

Yes. I owed Guido, still do. Life is about debts owed and debts paid. Some people, they say they're your friends and they want to help you get rich or famous, they're the ones who are the most dangerous of all: They want your soul.

Guido entrusted me with everything he knew and, it's kinda cheesy, treated me like a son at a point when I guess I needed that. So, if he thought Mark Mailer was good enough to be some use to him, who was I to argue?

He taught me the rules I've been trying to live by ever since.

I went in one or two days a week and every day during vacations. But, you know, this was Guido Brasco, I'm not stupid, I know a good thing when I see one. Guido was paying me a decent wage to help me work my way through college. And he gave me my own customers, let me try my own thing, experiment with cut and shape. The older ones didn't like it, of course, they preferred the classic Brasco, but some brought their sons or nephews, sons-in-law, new members of their family. So it worked both ways, younger clients came to Guido's business because of me.

Skimming through the rest of Mark's time with Brasco, Annie moved on to his own business, how he'd taken the tailoring skills he'd learned and started making his own designs in the evening, working from his apartment and selling them to his—read, Patty's—friends. Word had gotten out, and he found himself taking calls from *Vogue* for samples he didn't even have.

His first ready-to-wear collection, of less than twenty pieces, eventually showed in a friend's loft four seasons ago and was immediately snapped up by Bergdorf, Barneys, and Saks. Mad as it seemed, he'd only moved out of his bedroom and into a studio six months before the show Annie had seen and his staff still totaled only three: a sourcer, a salesperson, and an intern. Everyone else involved in the show was hired in, working for peanuts, samples, or on a promise of future greatness, including the PR who'd lumbered him with Annie.

Mark Mailer had gone from fashion student and tailor's apprentice to U.S. Top Ten—Top Five, even—in barely two years, a dead cert to scoop the Council of Fashion Designers of America award for best newcomer. It was remarkable, to say the least. Remarkable, and unlikely.

It wasn't hard to see why even the world beyond fashion was fascinated by the Mark Mailer story.

Whichever way she looked at it, it didn't quite stack up. You could no more launch a label on pocket money than you could a newspaper. Okay, so Mailer's label had been low-key and he'd had no shops to fund, but everyone knew setting up a label could cost well over a million dollars, even on a tight budget.

Frustrated now, Annie kept listening. How had he met Mariolina Mantolini, for instance? And Ugo Baroni? Why sudden bids from two major houses? Had the word gone out that Mark Mailer was for sale? Annie was there, inside the interview, reliving it, unasked questions on the tip of her tongue. Questions probably no more welcome than the one she'd thrown in once Mark began to trust her.

I can't work out where Patty fits in to all this, Annie heard herself saying. She'd tried to make it more of a statement than a query.

Mark was silent for a moment. *She doesn't,* he said flatly.

I mean . . . where she came into your story. When did you and Patty meet?

Patty is not relevant to this interview. Polite, but very, very firm.

Try telling Rebecca that, Annie thought.

She heard herself appeal to the generosity she'd worked so hard over the previous day to uncover. The Mark Mailer who'd defrosted her hands, brought her coffee, confided to her about rehab.

I just need a bit of background, she said. *My editor . . .*

He'd smiled, Annie remembered, although she couldn't hear any trace of it in his voice now. *You can get that from clippings,* he said. *They're pretty extensive on that subject.*

Maybe, said Annie, trying to bring herself back on his side. *But not ac-*curate. *Every clipping tells a different story. How long have you and Patty been together? Three years? Five? Seven? I can find you printed evidence for all of those.*

That's journalists for you!

Now at least Mark's humor came through, although Annie didn't doubt that he meant every word of it. Buoyed up, she'd given it one final shot.

Look, she said. *Maybe now would be a good time to set the record straight. Get a few definitive and accurate facts out there?*

Mark sighed. *I've told you,* he said. *I'm not prepared to talk about this. It has nothing whatsoever to do with Patty.*

And that was pretty much it. Subject closed.

Now Annie wished she'd gone the whole hog there and then: *So Mark, was your girlfriend a junkie when you met her? Were you the junkie, is that it? Is yours a rehab romance? How many times have you cleaned her up? How many more times before you dump her? Have you any idea why she threw her career down the toilet Monday night, and have you seen her since?*

But that would have been the biggest mistake of all and Annie would never have made it, not even to get a reaction. If she had, she wouldn't have been allowed to spend the rest of the afternoon backstage watching Mark prepare for the show of his life, and the night watching him die.

chapter sixteen

Swinging her legs out from under the sheets, Annie hit STANDBY on the remote and automatically punched zero three. NY1 flooded into her hotel room.

"So we'll let you have that again," the voice came from the TV. "That's Kennedy airport closed, Newark closed, La Guardia closed. All flights in and out of New York, Washington, and Boston are canceled because of snow until further notice. Please call your airline before attempting to travel."

Snow?

A reporter who looked like the Michelin man but was probably just wearing a lot of layers stood hip-deep in a drift, red woolen fingers fumbling with the microphone. Behind the portion of his body still visible, roofs were shrouded a Christmas card white; to his left, at least as tall and three times as wide, was a lump that only the night before had undoubtedly been an SUV.

"Out here in Jersey the blizzard has finally slowed," he was saying, "but as you can see this is one Saturday morning we'll all be going nowhere fast.

The snowplows have been out in force since midnight clearing main roads, but the heaviness and speed of the snowfalls have caught us all by surprise. The going is treacherous, and the highway department has requested that no one leave home unless absolutely essential."

As if expecting some sort of spectacularly elaborate practical joke, Annie crossed over to her window and pulled back the curtains.

The world was white. Fat flakes swirled so thickly beyond the glass that it was no longer possible to tell what was snow and what was not. Far from the storm's having passed over Manhattan, the sky above Annie's head was fat with snow as yet unspilled and the hotel's main air-conditioning unit on a roof far below was hidden beneath an unsullied white cloak.

"Shit," said Annie, then shrugged. It wasn't like she was allowed to leave the country.

On the screen behind her, five red-clad reporters rotated time and again, perched like crimson gnomes on giant icy molehills, endlessly recounting the snowfall and road situation in their boroughs. All saying pretty much the same thing: No one is going anywhere—and especially not you, Annie Anderson.

"O'Connell."

The phone was picked up on the first ring. The Irishman's voice buzzing with irritation and, beneath that, the slur of insomnia. He sounded like a man who'd done the night shift and at—Annie glanced at the alarm clock—10 A.M. was still waiting to be relieved.

"This is Annie Anderson."

Only at the last second did she remember that, so far as the NYPD was concerned, she was Annie Anderson murder witness and not journalist. She'd need to keep her questions as innocent as possible. "I'm sorry to bother you," she added, hoping it didn't sound too much of an afterthought.

The cop was taken aback. Whoever he'd been expecting, it clearly wasn't Annie; probably his replacement calling in snowbound. "Yes, I remember. What can I help you with, miss?"

"We-ell," Annie said, reaching for her notepad. "I was just wondering . . . A couple of things really." At the other end of the line a wooden chair scraped scuffed lino, and Annie heard its frame groan as the man sat.

"First," Annie ventured. "I was wondering when you were going to finish taking my statement?"

O'Connell sighed, making it sound like he was fighting a yawn. "When we have time, miss. I realize it's inconveniencing you having to stay in the city but we're shorthanded and the snow's going to make it worse. If it wasn't for all the press this case wouldn't be a priority at all."

Conscious that the officer was still unaware she was partly responsible for the press interest, Annie chose her next words carefully. "Surely all murders are a priority?"

His sigh this time was for her benefit alone. Annie didn't need a videophone to know O'Connell had treated her to another of his looks. "That, ma'am, is for us to decide."

"How do you mean?" said Annie, ignoring his change of her title.

"Look, Ms. Anderson. We know Mr. Mailer's death was a homicide. A 125.27. That's an A1 felony, if you're interested . . ."

Annie was.

"But the shooter's dead and if you wanna know what I think, that's the best place for him. What do you expect the NYPD to do? This case is pretty much a closed book."

"But I was there," said Annie. "I told you . . . The guy seemed . . . I don't know, to be targeting Mark."

"So you said, but we've talked to everyone else and that isn't the picture we got. What we have is a crack addict and small-time dealer—word on the street is he used to drive for one of Donnie Cassano's lieutenants before they fell out. Michael Watt was down on his luck, out of a job, and robbing for his next fix, that's all. It was a heist that went wrong 'cause the guy was an amateur, pure and simple."

On the pad in front of her she'd doodled two guns—a child's take on the weapon, admittedly, all right angles and bang-bang, but dangerous all the same.

"But he had two . . . ," she began halfheartedly.

"I'm truly sorry for your loss, Ms. Anderson. It's not unusual for people in your position to want a friend's death to have some significance. Not be just . . . But it was random. Just a waste. Look—" His tone softened. "—I think we got pretty much all we need on that statement. I just need you to clear up a couple of points here and there. Then we can let you go home. So as soon as I got someone to send, I'll send him. Not gonna happen today, though, this snow's kind of a problem."

Annie tossed the phone onto its cradle and returned to the window, peering into a haze of white. Looked like she couldn't believe everything she heard on the news: The clouds seemed to have some left for Manhattan yet.

After a while Annie turned her back on the outside and logged on to the Internet, Googling for articles on Brasco, Fava, and the House of Mantolini. It was all more of the same, nothing that hadn't been there last time she looked. Apart from the inevitable platitudes about fashion's loss.

Random.

Tragic.

Unexpected.

A waste.

She went over the same sites again, looking for anything she might have missed, but there was nothing. The tapes, too, hadn't changed overnight, the chipmunk chatter of Mark's voice filling the room as she fast-forwarded from one answer to the next.

This has nothing to do with Patty.

Oh, but it did. The more Annie listened to that, the more she knew she just had to find the supermodel. Pulling an old-fashioned spiral-bound reporter's pad from her bag, Annie checked the model agency's number and turned on her mobile.

Predictably enough, the Nokia throbbed with a whole new list of missed calls: Mum; Rebecca, mobile; Jane; the *Post;* a number withheld . . . Curiosity made Annie dial voicemail retrieval.

"Um, Annie?" It was a quiet voice, unfamiliar, but still its tone sent Annie scrambling for a pen. "It's Cathie Olsen. We met the, uh, other night, I'm sure you remember."

Cathie Olsen?

"Patty asked me to call you. She wants to talk to you about what you're going to put in your article." The caller's voice was layered with doubt, as if, in her opinion, talking to Annie was the last thing Patty should do. "I don't know when you're planning on writing it. I guess you might have done so by now. Anyway, I'll be at the Red Flame Diner at noon tomorrow. It's on Forty-fourth Street. Head east from Sixth, you can't miss it. I'll wait till twelve-thirty. If you don't show I guess we're all done."

The line went dead.

"Shit!" How could Annie be so stupid? Cathie Olsen had to be Cathie Mailer. Somewhere in the depths of her memory, Annie remembered reading that her husband worked for the Mailer family firm. Mark's sister must have taken her husband's name.

It was now 11:40 A.M. and Annie had fifty minutes to get uptown. And if Cathie Olsen née Mailer didn't show? So what . . . She might. Annie couldn't take that risk.

The young black guy who spun his battered yellow cab into a three-point turn at the sight of Annie's arm either had a death wish or needed the fare. Possibly the latter. Manhattan had shut down, streets silent, shops shuttered. A handful of brownstones in Greenwich Village had begun to dig themselves out and then given up, shovels abandoned. Annie wasn't even sure it was possible to get where she wanted to go.

"Sixth Avenue and Forty-fourth," said Annie, collapsing onto ripped leather.

The blocks didn't exactly fly past, but as 8th Street became 9th Street and 9th Street became 10th, it was definitely faster than walking, if a little more scary.

"Hey, lady," the cabdriver said, brown eyes watching her earnestly in his rearview mirror. "You like poetry?"

Damn it. She should have realized only a nutter would be willing to drive in this weather. Annie considered the wisdom of ignoring him and rejected the idea. On balance, given she was sliding precariously up Sixth Avenue on several inches of packed ice and he was behind the wheel, she didn't much fancy pissing him off.

"Well," said Annie, reluctant to commit herself. "Some. Sylvia Plath,

Margaret Atwood, Alison Fell, that kind of thing . . ." In truth she couldn't remember the last time she'd read anything resembling poetry.

It was all he needed. "Take a look at this." The guy leaned back and, in one deft move, passed a white perfect-bound A5 booklet that screamed, *All my own work.*

Politely, Annie leafed through, catching a line here and there about blossom and hearts bursting. She groaned inwardly.

"Whaddaya think?" he asked with Macy's hoving into view like a retail ocean liner.

I think I've still got ten blocks to go.

"It's . . . lovely."

"Wrote them myself," he said unnecessarily. "And made the books. Ten at a time in my bedroom. I've sold forty-seven so far, nine ninety-five. Passenger yesterday said they were so good they made her want to cry."

Annie sympathized with the last part of that statement.

Bryant Park loomed to Annie's right, like a deserted fairground. Just yesterday the park had been a hive of activity, tents pitched to house New York's biannual ready-to-wear shows. Now the big top was abandoned in the midst of being dismantled; canvas awning removed; café, press office, and catwalks all gone, as if they'd never been. If not for the tent's steel skeleton, shivering dinosaur-like under a layer of snow, no one would have known that hours earlier it had been September in Bryant Park. That surreal twisting of the seasons where outside it's February, the shops are selling summer, and in the tents it's autumn.

"So lady, you gonna buy?" The driver's teeth flashed yellow in the rearview mirror. "See that one, the one on page twenty-eight, 'Tush'? I wrote that for my lady. She keeps her body really tight."

Christ, thought Annie, *too much information!*

Still, unhinged or not, she wouldn't have made it any farther uptown than 10th Street without him. As the yellow cab lurched, wheels squealing into a snowdrift on the corner of 44th, Annie shoved a twenty through the plastic partition and flung open the door, removing herself, bag, book, and all, before he had time to give her the rundown on "Wet1" and its companion poem, "Wet2."

chapter seventeen

The Red Flame Diner was remarkable if only for the fact that it was actually open. Open and apparently heaving with tourists, its windows half obscured by steam. As she raced through the inner door, Annie was hit by a familiar wall of heat, cloying and claustrophobic, that made her instantly want to start stripping off her coat.

"How many?" asked a teenage girl perched at the till on a small island inside the door.

Good question.

"You waiting for someone, you gotta wait to be seated till the other members of your party arrive," recited the girl. It was probably written on a card on her side of the till.

"Just one. I was meant to be meeting someone . . ." Annie glanced at her watch. "But that was forty minutes ago."

"What she look like?"

"Small, dark hair. Thirty-something."

"I sat her at the counter," the girl said. "Over there . . . I think she already ate."

Adrift in a sea of ample middle-aged couples and Gap families, Annie spotted her.

"Cathie?"

The dark-haired woman took a while to focus, and then smiled wanly. She looked smaller than Annie remembered, her eyes watery. She looked older, too.

"I'm sorry," said Annie. "I'm so late. The snow . . . I had no idea it would take so long and I wasn't sure you'd even make it."

"That's why I'm still here," said Cathie, polite but short. She waved Annie's apologies away. "I figured I'd give you till one."

Suddenly Annie realized that for the best part of two days she'd been desperate for this encounter—and not just for Cathie's intimate connection to Mark and Patty, although she'd be a liar to pretend that wasn't an added bonus. She'd been longing to see someone, anyone, who'd shared the smallest piece of that waking nightmare. But now that she had Cathie's attention, Annie was at a loss, painfully aware that the other woman's experience of this particular bad dream was so much more personal, more . . . permanent, than her own.

One look at Cathie's face told Annie all she needed to know and much more.

The waiter's appearance with a stainless-steel jug of coffee provided a second's reprieve from the uneasy silence, both women watching the steaming liquid as it sloshed over the edge of Cathie's beige cup and into her saucer. Anyone watching would have thought it was the most fascinating thing either woman had ever seen.

"You've lost weight." Cathie's tone was suspiciously maternal. Annie shuddered. *You haven't been looking after yourself,* came the translation in her head. Thin was good in Annie's book, although there was thin and there was skeletal, she knew that now. *You're looking well,* on the other hand, translated as *Haven't you put on weight . . .*

"Yeah, you, too," said Annie, surprising herself. It seemed a very adult thing to say. She meant smaller, more tired. Cathie nodded distractedly, and Annie noticed that the dark hair that framed the woman's face hung in damp tendrils, hard evidence of an hour or more spent nervously twiddling while Cathie waited for a brunch companion she had no inclination to meet.

"Patty wants to see you," Cathie said, swirling what remained of her coffee around the bottom of her cup.

Casually sipping her own coffee, Annie tried to concentrate on the surge of caffeine hitting her brain. She could have done with that three hours ago.

"Guido doesn't think she should," said Cathie. "Talk to you, I mean. Neither do I, but once Patty found out Guido had your number she wouldn't back off. That's why I'm here, I wanted to see you first."

Well, you couldn't say it straighter than that.

Unsure how to respond, Annie said nothing.

"Patty's in a state," Cathie continued. "Obviously enough. We all are. Guido especially. And Mom and Dad . . . Well, Dad hasn't said a word since he heard or even been home. He's sleeping at the factory. But Patty . . ."

Annie waited.

"You don't need me to tell you how fragile Patty is, and this is more than she can bear. She thinks Mark was murdered. She's hysterical. Maybe you can make her see sense."

And maybe I'm the wrong person to ask, thought Annie, *since I agree with her.*

The waiter waved a coffee jug at Annie and she held out her cup for a refill, her gaze still on Cathie. The older woman was holding it together, but there was something other than grief behind her eyes. Annie had been meant to say, *Yes, of course I'll help you make Patty see sense.* But she hadn't. Along with the guilt and pain, Cathie's eyes revealed suspicion.

"What was it you really wanted from Mark?" Cathie asked suddenly. Her voice was sharp, motored by a rage that had little, if anything, to do with Annie and everything to do with the days of pain she'd just lived through. It was just Annie's tough luck she was within shooting distance. "I'm only asking," said Cathie, "because it wasn't two thousand words on how to cut a nice pantsuit, that's for sure."

It took Annie a second too long to conceal her surprise.

"Did you think he wouldn't notice?" the woman continued. "No questions about form, inspiration, or influence, just family and background and his private life. But it was only when Anya recognized you backstage that it sunk in. She'd already told Mark someone had been asking after Patty on Monday night, so when she spotted you at Mark's show she told him you were a fake. You people, you don't give a damn, do you? You'd do anything for a story."

How right and how wrong could one person be. Annie knew that wasn't Mark's opinion; she'd felt his hand on her shoulder, turned to see the amusement in his eyes at The Elephant. Mark had not been angry with her, she knew that for a fact. She knew what anger looked like.

"He was going to talk to you when you got to the bar that night, tell you to get out of his life, at least that's what Anya says. But it seems he didn't. Maybe Anya got it wrong. Or maybe you did something to make him change his mind. You wouldn't have been there otherwise." She looked puzzled. "And now Patty wants to trust you, too."

Annie stayed silent, waiting for the storm of Cathie's fury to blow over as she knew it must. The woman was too tired to maintain that level of bitterness for long. And, while she waited, Annie retrawled her subconscious for any memory of suppressed anger in the way Mark had greeted her that night. He'd been cool, but laid-back cool, not standoffish, and no more so than earlier in the day. And when he'd met her at the bar and told Jay to put her drink on his tab he'd been friendly, even kissing her hello. If he'd wanted to tell her to go, that would have been the time, in among the crowd and the noise, before anyone even knew she'd been there. Except her. And him.

But he hadn't.

Why not? Annie couldn't help feeling he still had things that needed to be said. As if he'd wanted her there for some reason.

Tears were welling behind Annie's eyes and she was ashamed to realize they weren't for Mark, still lying cold in the city mortuary, but for herself. The idea that she might have read things wrong, that Mark had died mistrusting her, despising her even, as she lay oblivious on the cold tiles of a restroom floor bothered Annie more than she cared to analyze.

"Patty is the most important thing now, you know that, don't you?" Cathie said. "That's what Mark wanted, that's how it is."

Yes, Annie thought. *I knew that all along, I just didn't know why. Still don't.*

The gaze watching Annie was brittle, but Annie couldn't be sure whether Cathie was about to throw her cup at her, storm out, or deflate as rapidly as she had ignited.

Out of the corner of her eye Annie saw the waiter hovering. He caught her glance and wandered over, jug in hand. "More cawfee?"

"Yes."

"No."

The two women spoke simultaneously. Aware that the upper hand was not hers, Annie deferred. If the interview was over, it was over, and she didn't have the spirit to fight someone who held so much higher moral ground. Someone who only days earlier had watched her only brother's blood seep across a restroom floor.

"Just the bill," said Cathie firmly, and then added, taking Annie entirely by surprise, "we should be going. Patty's waiting."

chapter eighteen

Home for American fashion's late First Couple was not what Annie had been expecting. No two-thousand-square-foot warehouse in the meatpacking district or impossibly hip and minimalist loft in Tribeca, not even an ex-flophouse on the Lower East Side in the midst of elaborate and expensive restoration. Mark and Patty had shared an unprepossessing top-floor flat in a Murray Hill walk-up. Over the past six days Annie had walked past Mark Mailer's front door more than once without even realizing it. Had she turned right when she'd left McDonald's instead of left on the night of Marc Jacobs's show, she'd have been a mere two blocks from Patty Lang. For all Annie knew, that was where Anya had been heading . . .

Sensibly shod for the weather in fur-lined hiking boots, Cathie had marched sturdily down the snow-covered sidewalks of a ghostly Midtown, making Annie feel shallow and useless, more schoolkid than journalist. Exactly like the kind of idiot who wore three-inch killer heels to trek through two feet of snow, in fact.

Other than issuing occasional directions Cathie spoke only once during their thirty-minute trudge along the cold canyon of Fifth Avenue.

"You might as well know," Cathie had announced irritably, before taking a sharp left off Fifth Avenue and onto East 30th Street. "I told Patty we shouldn't let you come here and Anya agreed."

Fuck Anya, thought Annie. *What was her problem?*

"We both said she should call you at your hotel, if she had to speak to you at all, but she wasn't having it. Said you'd need to see where he lived." The woman had shaken her head then, whether in despair at Patty's naïveté or to dislodge the memory of her brother, Annie couldn't say.

They covered the final two blocks in silence, passing rug traders with their security grates locked tight over shop windows and Italian restaurants that had seen no point in opening for nonexistent customers. The Paradise Hair Salon and Esther's Cozy Nails were also customerless, and even the first-floor windows of Dina Guardian Angel, Spiritual Reader, Healer, and Adviser (who'd presumably seen this coming), were dark.

As they crossed Park Avenue the area turned abruptly residential, the trees plastered with homemade posters begging anyone who knew the identity of an old man who got up at 5 A.M. to feed the pigeons to please grass him up. It was a very New York kind of Neighborhood Watch.

Cathie didn't bother to buzz, just let herself in with her own key and told Annie to follow. They climbed the six flights of stairs in silence, a silence that was disturbed as they climbed higher by a blur of competing sounds that became a roar as they reached the final flight.

Radio, television, CD player, a washing machine . . . Annie wondered if there was any appliance that wasn't switched on.

The noise was matched by a scene of chaos. The living area looked as if, in rage or grief, someone had thrown its entire contents, rugs, sofas, and all, into the air and left them where they fell. As a teenager Annie had read an article in *Just Seventeen* that said your room was a reflection of the inside of your head. It was no big leap to see that the contents of Patty's subconscious—along with her conscious—were scattered across the apartment's floor. Dark-stained boards and well-trodden Indian rugs were barely visible beneath a snowfall of newspapers and weekly magazines, their pages spread, most of them revealing stories about Mark.

"Patty?" Cathie's voice was immediately drowned in the din.

Floor-length wine-colored curtains were flung, neither open nor shut, across the room's windows so a dying afternoon sun barely made an impression on the gloom. In one corner a rerun of *Sex and the City* fought for air space with Nick Drake, who was still contemplating the meaning of life and death from an unseen CD player.

And if it hadn't been so surreal, Annie would have sworn that someone was vacuuming.

"Patty?" Cathie repeated.

Someone banged in a room next door.

Gesturing vaguely in the direction of the sofa, Cathie stomped across the room, newspapers crumpling beneath her boots. A second later Nick Drake and the vacuuming ceased.

Annie had never really known the meaning of the expression *hollow-eyed* until she came face-to-face with Patty Lang that afternoon. She'd used it often enough over the years; immigrants working eighteen-hour back-to-back shifts had been hollow-eyed, as had homeless adolescents on the streets of Scotland's second city. Even Irina Krodt, damaged as she was, had not been so transparent or so deeply cut. Whatever Annie thought she'd been through, the waking agonies, the nighttime terrors, she'd never been close to what she saw etched in Patty Lang's face now.

"Sorry about the cold," said Patty, her accent carrying a hint of the South. Calm and deep, her voice belied the trauma in her eyes. In her arms she carried a small black cat, which she put on the sofa.

Still wrapped against the snow, Annie had been too busy memorizing the scene to notice the temperature, but now that Patty mentioned it the place was quite obviously freezing.

"The heater broke," Patty added, draping an immense floor-length cardigan so far around her body it was almost doubled. Beneath it men's jeans hung from bony hips. "It breaks all the time but Mark always . . ." Patty paused before correcting herself. "He used to mend it so I never bothered to find out how. Lame, huh?"

Annie shook her head, at a loss for something to say that wasn't patronizing or presumptuous.

"I'll sort it out," said Cathie. She vanished around the corner, a light switch clicked, and the back of the room was illuminated. It was even more chaotic than it had looked in twilight.

There was a rattle as Cathie unscrewed a fuse box and then a second click. "All done," she shouted, then, "I thought you said you were going to clear up in here."

Patty ignored her. "Weird the things you notice," she said. Annie did a double take as she swept her hand across the sofa, shifting everything onto her filing system on the floor. Slumping back against the cushions, she pulled the cat onto her knee to make room for Annie beside her.

"Thanks for coming," said Patty. "Mark would have appreciated it . . . I appreciate it."

Annie couldn't help feeling she was the last person Mark might want sitting on his sofa, but she refrained from saying so. After all, no one would ever know now what Mark might have wanted.

A week ago this was exactly how Annie had pictured herself: sitting here in Mark Mailer's own living room, coffee in hand, as he told her more than he meant her to know. There was one crucial difference. No Mark. Also, no coffee and a different story altogether.

"It's okay." Annie shrugged. "It's the least I can do. How are you?" she added. It sounded ridiculous, but what else was she supposed to say?

It was Patty's turn to shrug. "I've watched four seasons of *Sex and the City* back to back. I'll start on *Will and Grace* next. At least they're safe."

Annie wondered why a woman who didn't trust herself to watch television would have a living room full of discarded newspapers.

"I'm avoiding the soaps," Patty continued. "Current affairs are almost as bad and anything about fashion is out of bounds, obviously. I tried watching movies but the ones that aren't about love are about death. They get you one way or another."

"*Sex and the City* is better?" Right now Annie wouldn't have been able to face back-to-back episodes of anything in which the main themes were love, sex, inability to keep a man, oh, and rampant mortality. And she wasn't the one whose boyfriend was filed in a drawer at the morgue.

Her question was greeted by a weak smile. "My alternative is silence," said Patty, folding long legs under her. "In the circumstances, which would you choose?"

She looked about twelve years old, a bag of bones and anxiety.

"I got a question," Patty said. "You gonna tell me Mark was just unlucky, too?" Her eyes locked on to Annie, right hand repetitively stroking the watchful cat.

"No," said Annie, suddenly aware that the clattering of china and running water from the kitchen had stopped, a sure sign that her talk with Patty had reached a point Cathie felt was no longer safe. "I'm not sure you can call what happened to Mark bad luck."

"Suicide by cop, that's what they're saying. Apparently the asshole was in deep shit with his supplier. Creamed off some smack and used it himself. You know what happens around here if you do that? They feed you through a wood chipper feetfirst. The NYPD reckon he didn't have the guts to off himself and this was the only way out. Mark and Isabelle just got killed in the crossfire."

Isabelle?

Annie said nothing. The slightest reaction would be like alarm bells going off above her head, alerting Patty to the fact she hadn't known the makeup artist was dead, too.

Call yourself a journalist . . .

Why hadn't Sergeant O'Connell told her when she spoke to him that morning?

Because you're not a journalist. Annie answered the question herself. *At least not to O'Connell. To him you're just a witness, and an annoying one at that.*

There was a moment's silence. The sound of water filling a bowl resumed.

"Tell me what you saw," Patty ordered, wrapping her fingers around and around the cat's ear.

"I'll try," said Annie, then hesitated, needing time to put her thoughts in order. "He—the guy, the gunman—didn't seem to me like a man who wanted to die. If anything, when we heard the sirens I'd have said—from where I was lying, so you have to remember that I couldn't really see much—he seemed scared and almost like this wasn't how it was meant to be. If anything, it was the sirens that made him lose his nerve. But Cathie can tell you all this, she was there."

"Yeah." Bitterness soured Patty's laugh. "Only she says she can't remember or doesn't want to and thinks I should leave this alone. Guido, too. He just keeps saying Mark didn't understand the rules. I don't know what you said to Guido, but he's totally pissed with you. They're both on at me to leave well—"

There was a screech and the cat, all out of patience at being fondled, flung herself off Patty's lap and stalked from the room just as Cathie re-entered, attention pointedly obviously focused on the steaming mugs in her hands.

"Poor Winona," said Patty sadly. "Another stray. Mark found her, too . . . You know how Mark and I met, don't you?" Patty suddenly brightened. For the first time the flip in Patty's mood didn't catch Annie unawares. She was adjusting to the model's mania. She recognized it. Part grief, part constant battle not to score. Irina had been the same.

"You know she doesn't know how you met," Cathie interrupted, banging the mugs down on a side table. "You know Mark never talked about you. Why can't you give him the same respect?"

"She needs to know," said Patty. It was obvious that she wanted her voice to sound determined, and equally obvious that it quavered.

"Does she?"

"Yes. She has to know every last thing if she's going to write Mark's story."

"She's not, though, is she? She's a journalist, she'll write her own story. Whatever that is."

Patty's face set, stubbornness etched into every line. "Mark trusted her," she said. "So I trust her." Her tone said she would tolerate no argument.

"Tell her if you must." The words came after a long silence while Cathie waited for Annie to do the decent thing and Annie didn't. She stayed where she was, and waited. "But it's your decision. And for the record, I think it's a big mistake."

"I understand that," said Patty quietly. "But *I* think it's what Mark would have wanted."

"All Mark ever wanted was to protect you." Cathie's voice trailed away. In the silence that followed Annie heard the layers of resentment, years of blame, and unspoken accusations fighting to be heard.

Cathie let herself out of the flat without another word.

chapter nineteen

"We met, as you may know, depending which bit of gossip you believe, in rehab," Patty began, as the door slammed behind Cathie and an old sash window rattled in its frame.

"Don't mind her," Patty said, waving the first of many Camels in Annie's direction. "She's old school. Mark loved her, but they never saw eye to eye on that stuff. Now where was I?"

"In rehab."

"Oh yeah, right. Mark hated the fact we met there. He'd have given anything to change history if he could. But, the way I figure it, history is exactly what it is. That was then, this is now, and it's nobody's business but ours.

"It wasn't my first time there and it wasn't my last, I guess you know that, too?" Patty looked at Annie, trying to gauge her reaction from her stolidly neutral expression. How much did the journalist know already? What had Mark told her? Patty had no idea, she hadn't seen Mark before his show and now . . . now Mark was dead. She swallowed hard, tasting the tears that had taken up permanent residence at the back of her throat.

Trust the journalist, Mark had written. *If anything happens, no matter what anyone else says, talk to Annie Anderson.* It hadn't made sense when she'd found the note, and now that something had happened . . . You know what? It didn't seem any less odd.

Flying in the face of public opinion and pretending she didn't care: Both were second nature to Patty Lang, but she wasn't used to doing them without Mark to back her up. Alone it was a different story. But she wasn't alone really, there was a journalist sitting beside her on the sofa, notepad balanced on her lap, blue pen poised, waiting.

"But it was Mark's first and last time in rehab," resumed Patty. "It's real important you understand that. I've been in and out of clinics all my life—big, small, expensive, bargain basement . . . Aspen, Brooklyn, you name it, although nothing like as often as you'd think if you believe the tabloids. And nothing like as many times as I might have been if I hadn't met Mark."

Annie made a couple of notes on her pad and Patty wondered idly what she'd just said that merited the attention.

"I'd like to say it was love at first sight, readers like that, don't they? Some sort of rehab fairy-tale romance. Junkie model finds her cleaned-up Prince Charming, their eyes meet across group therapy. But it wasn't like that, not for me and not for Mark . . . How could it be? We were in rehab for fuck's sake, scrubbing floors and examining our messy childhoods. Me, I just wanted to get out of that place and get a hit or a drink. Mark, he just wanted to get out of that place—period—and never go back."

Pausing, Patty took a long, deep drag before continuing. "Those first few weeks and plenty more besides I couldn't see farther than my own needs, my own problems. I'd sit in that circle of deadbeats and once I started talking I couldn't stop. It was me, me, me, me. And me. But Mark, you know . . . All he wanted was to start his life over. He could see more clearly than the rest of us. Mark was never a real junkie. And I don't mean like it was some exclusive club that wouldn't have him in. He just fucked up one time and let his life spiral out of control. He was in that clinic clawing it back. God, was he hell-bent on getting it back. If Mark was ever really addicted to anything, it was proving himself and showing the world, showing his dad, he could be something."

A trace of a smile flitted across Patty's face as Annie started scribbling intently. That was one of the many things she'd loved about Mark, his determination and his pride, and the fact that he'd been as obsessed with her as she was with him. For her, Mark had been better than any drug, although at times he could have been forgiven for not noticing.

"That was what attracted me," Patty said, after she'd given Annie a chance to stop scribbling. "You know, when I got smart enough to look, I saw how important his life was to him. How much he needed it back when all I cared about was throwing mine away. And, you know . . ." Patty hesitated. "He didn't just want to screw me and toss me away. About the first guy my whole life who didn't. And when we did, months after we first met . . . Well, you know, I figured I'd never been to bed with anyone I was in love with before."

Tears, which had been leaking slowly, now splashed down Patty's cheeks until she wiped the back of one hand across her face. "Mark made me feel like life was worth living, any life, even mine. I'd never met anyone so . . . I dunno, decent I guess. Not before or since. I never believed in anyone like I believe in Mark, believed . . . He could always talk me down off the ledge, you know, and he did it time and again. Wherever I was in the world, whatever hour it was, I could pick up the phone and he'd be there. Fuck, he was the first guy I ever met who never fed me bullshit like I was just some stupid, skinny blonde.

"Until I met Mark it was all, Patty you're so beautiful, Patty you've got such a great body, Patty you're gonna be a star, Patty you're gonna be on *Vogue* . . . All that time and I never was on *Vogue,* you know. With Mark there was none of that. He's the only person my whole life who always told me the truth."

Shit, this was tough, Patty thought, tougher than she'd expected. Thinking about Mark, talking about Mark, about how much she'd loved him. But he'd told her to trust the journalist, so trust her she would.

She took a sip of her now cold coffee and said, "It was Mark who got me back on the catwalk, you know, that very first time, when he was starting college. Even then, right at the beginning, he didn't want anyone to know about us, preferred to keep it private. I'd been on the runway, done a lot of editorial work. He was nobody. Mark didn't want people thinking he was using me to help his career. At that point maybe I could have been some use! And I, well, I just didn't want yet another thing in my life trashed, so I agreed we keep it quiet . . ."

"How old were you?"

Considering Annie's question, Patty counted back on her fingers, like a small child. "Eighteen," she said finally. "I was eighteen, but by then I'd lived two years in front of the tabloids." The model grimaced. "And, if I've learned one thing, it's that thanks to the Internet the rumors are no longer tomorrow's trash, they're there forever. Ask anyone, go on, pick a stranger, go up to them and ask them what they think of Patty Lang and they'll tell you. She's a junkie, a has-been, a liability. Probably even a ho."

Aware that her voice had risen, Patty paused, listened to her own echo around the darkening room.

"Anyhow," she said, "we got ourselves a place about halfway through Mark's college course. It seemed pretty stupid by then, paying two rents, especially when only one of us had a real paycheck and, even then, only when I was clean. Just after Mark started working for Signor Brasco he called me one morning and said he'd heard about this place. We've been here ever since, not because it's rent-controlled, we just don't wanna leave . . ."

Catching herself, Patty paused, picked idly at her cigarette pack's cellophane wrapper. "I guess I'll stay," she said. "It's got its own little bit of Manhattan skyline. If you climb out the bathroom window and up the fire escape, the roof's all ours. Not a real roof terrace or anything like that, but Mark loved it and spent hours up there—all weather—thinking, working, and just looking at the sky. It was his space. He used to say, you know, how weird it was after the Towers came down, how it seemed like the sky was bigger. More . . . I dunno . . . empty, I guess."

For a second Patty's eyes clouded. Her mind full of an overcast night sky, empty as ever of stars thanks to the overpowering afterburn of Manhattan's sodium glow, full of Mark standing up there in the dark, cell phone clamped to his ear, talking to someone, arguing . . .

Conscious that Annie was watching her, Patty collected her thoughts. She wanted to tell Annie what she knew, what she thought, she just wasn't sure how.

"There was so much going on with Mark's collection and the buyout and still he went up there most nights," she said. "The night before . . . Sunday night I guess, he didn't even get back from his fittings until three A.M. and still . . . Anyway, I heard him talking but he always said he was just thinking out loud." She stopped, stared at a nondescript gold band on the little finger of her left hand. "We'd been together five years before we got married. February. A year next week. We didn't even make it a year."

The shock on Annie's face made Patty smile with relief. No, Mark hadn't told her. He hadn't told the journalist anything at all, he'd left that up to Patty, should the need arise. There was no point wishing it hadn't.

"You look surprised," she said. "You wouldn't have known that, no one does. Well, only Cathie and Anya, and Signor Brasco. Guido knows everything. There was nothing Mark kept from Guido so far as I can tell. You could ask Guido anything about Mark's business . . . Not that he'd tell you, of course, but he knows.

"Anyway, we married last February at city hall, Anya and Cathie were witnesses. We figured we'd just drag a coupla strangers off the street, tourists or something, but it was too risky, in the end we asked the only people we could trust. Looking back it was too much, we didn't think what we were asking, what a big deal it was, especially for Cathie. She couldn't even tell her husband because he'd probably have told Judd. That's Mark's dad," Patty added, by way of explanation. "It took five minutes. Five years to decide, five minutes to say "I do" and sign some forms. Even now I can't believe no one spotted us, sold us to *Us Weekly* to make a few thousand bucks. It was the best day of my life, the best thing I ever did, and I really thought it would be forever. We both did. In a weird way, I guess, for Mark it was."

Annie nodded. Patty was reliving memories, the tears that scoured her throat and rolled down her cheeks a kind of comfort.

"For a while things were perfect," said Patty. "I hadn't been anywhere near a clinic in over a year. Ever since I cleaned up after that picture hit the tabloids. You know the one, me unconscious on a sofa, one tit hanging out."

Annie started to deny it but Patty held up her hand. "Don't bother to lie," she said, "I know what it made everyone think of me. Believe me, I felt the same way. So did Mark." Patty paused, gathered her thoughts. "He was so pissed," she said. "I really thought I'd lost him that time. For a week I didn't see or hear from him and no one knew where he was, except maybe Guido. And then he came back, just walked through that door one night and I promised, I really promised, this time I'd get clean and stay that way. And I did, you know, I really did.

"I'd started working again, editorial mainly, a bit of runway. Only New York, though, where I could do the job and come straight home to Mark. I knew from experience to stay away from Paris and Milan if I was feeling frail. Milan . . ." The model took a breath. "Even worse than Tokyo. You have no idea what a terrible idea that place is for a young model, away from home and vulnerable. I'm getting sidetracked," she added, pulling herself back. "The point is, I was beginning to make my name again, to believe in myself, I'd even done a job for *Jane,* been offered a cover, the first in a long while.

"Aside from that, I can't tell you a whole lot about Guido. He seems like a nice enough old guy and Mark adored him but he never talked about him a whole lot. I guess that strikes you as weird, because, like I said, Mark told me pretty much everything. But Guido . . . nothing, no personal stuff and certainly not about his business, I couldn't even tell you who his clients are. Guido never married and there are no kids, I know that much. I always figured that's why he got so attached to Mark. That Italian thing, family being important, all the more when you don't have any.

"You need a coffee?" Patty asked suddenly, unfurling long legs from underneath her. "Warm you up."

Annie shook her head. "Guido," she said. "You were talking about Guido."

Patty knew when she was being prompted, but she let it go. The journalist could clearly spot the stuff that mattered, and that reassured her.

"I used to meet Mark at the studio sometimes, and Guido was always pleased to see me. Like, 'Ah Patty, Patty, bella, bella.' The whole bit. As far as Mark was concerned, Guido could do no wrong. He was the father he'd always wanted and he felt he owed the old man. I bet Mark told you that, didn't he, when you interviewed him?"

Annie nodded and Patty managed a wry smile.

"I bet. How great Guido is, how Mark Mailer would never have been Mark Mailer if it wasn't for Guido Brasco, yada yada yada. It used to make me so mad. I'm not denying Mark learned pretty much everything he knew about tailoring from Guido but he could have made it without that old man, Mark had the eye for it. Not that Mark would ever let me say that.

"When Mark started his own label for real and finally got his own studio, I thought—okay, I confess I hoped—maybe he'd quit working for Brasco, but he didn't. I asked, you know, when was he going to stop? And Mark just said he owed Guido." Patty sighed. "I guess it's all to do with Mark's dad," she said. "The way Mark saw it he'd let down one father by leaving the family business, he couldn't do it again. That's just my opinion, though, I never heard him say that. Mark met a lot of important people through Guido." Patty stared pointedly at Annie to make sure she was listening. "And Guido's connections in Europe are pretty extensive, even though he was born here and has lived locally his whole life.

"So far as anyone knows, Guido's never even been outside Manhattan, not once, but he doesn't have to, customers and contacts come to him. That's how Mark established his contacts with the House of Mantolini— Guido and Mariolina's father went way back. That's when Mark began to change," she stressed. "After he first met Mariolina Mantolini."

"Change?" demanded Annie.

"He wasn't happy. I'm not entirely sure what happened but he wasn't happy and after that things changed."

"You mean Mark was in trouble?" Annie was staring intently at her, and in that moment Patty decided to do it. She had to trust someone and, now that Mark was gone, there was no one else. This was the person he'd chosen and now Patty understood why. Everyone else, even her closest friends, had looked at Patty with the thinly veiled pity reserved for the recently bereaved when she suggested Mark's death might be more than a tragic accident; everyone except for the English journalist who sat beside her now.

"I want to show you something," said Patty, leaping up from the sofa before she could change her mind and vanishing through the bedroom door.

Seconds later Patty was back with a brick-like PC, which looked archaic even to Annie, who still used an original gray Mac laptop. This one weighed far more even than her ancient PowerBook, Annie discovered when Patty dumped it on her lap.

Whether it was geriatric or just cold, the computer took several long minutes to chug to life, its screen turning from black to gray as it warmed up.

"This is Mark's old PC," Patty explained, clicking on a series of icons. "His main machine's at work, along with all his sketches, and I haven't been able to get into the studio yet. It's padlocked and sealed off with police tape."

Nodding, Annie tried to suppress her excitement, hiding it not just from Patty but from herself. There was every chance this was just another dead end, and she couldn't afford to let Patty see her disappointment if it was.

"Look!" Patty yelped triumphantly.

Dear Mariolina

Annie gazed at the words that appeared. A block of four lines of black type inside a white box.

Thank you for the meeting yesterday . . .

Annie read and reread the lines in front of her, until Patty, irritated at being ignored, actually shook her shoulder. "It is," said Patty. "Isn't it?"

"I . . . I think so." Annie's heart raced.

There are still some questions that need to be addressed regarding how the funding operations would work and the strength of your guarantee that the labels would retain their separate identities. As you know, creative control . . .

It was, at the very least, a rough draft of a letter of intent to Mariolina Mantolini. Annie checked for a date but it was absent, as was any address, so she made a note of the file name and its location, shut down the letter and found the file, right-clicking to throw up its properties. It had been created on January 25.

In the last week of January, just a fortnight earlier, Mark Mailer had been intending to accept an offer from Mariolina Mantolini to fund his label. In return he would design two ready-to-wear women's wear collections a year for the House of Mantolini.

It had been dark and cold in the apartment when Patty started her story and darker and colder still when she finished, the heating having failed again the moment Cathie slammed the door behind her. And the dregs in the bottom of Annie's original coffee cup were so cold they could have come straight from a fridge.

Annie's hair—short as it was—stank of the hard-core Camels that Patty had chained all the time she'd been talking, smoking each one down to its nonexistent filter before lighting the next from its remains. A pile of twisted stubs overflowed from a tiny blue-and-white Chinese bowl that balanced precariously on the battered arm of the sofa. If ever there was a woman exchanging one addiction for another . . .

Come to think of it, Annie realized as she trudged across Washington Square, leaving deep footprints in the newly fallen snow that crunched crisp and icy beneath Lou's ruined boots, the thick fug of smoke and nicotine could have accounted, in part at least, for Annie's growing sense of unease. Her feeling that the apartment, not large to begin with, had begun closing in on her.

Exhaustion had seeped into every bone of her body. She was wiped, so exhausted that every bone, muscle, and part of her body, including her brain—especially her brain—ached with tiredness. She knew so much more now than she'd known three hours ago. Now it was the sheer scale of what she didn't know that troubled her.

Part Two

chapter twenty

"And get it *right* this time! Do I look like a woman who eats butter?" The voice was unmistakable and there was no avoiding it, even before the lift doors slid open to reveal *Handbag's* reception.

"You don't look like a woman who eats anything," muttered the young peroxide blonde, entering the lift as Annie exited. The girl was holding aloft a white paper bag blotched with grease stains.

Annie couldn't help it: She smirked.

"Bagel," said the blonde, waving the parcel in front of Annie's face by way of explanation. *"Marmite no butter."* She aped Rebecca's imperious tone. *"How many times do I have to tell you?"* The girl scowled. "Don't tell *me,* try telling the morons in the café downstairs. Still, at least they got the coffee right today. *Black! How many times do I have to tell you, do I look like a woman who drinks milk . . . ?* No." The scowl grew fiercer. "She looks like a woman with a first-class ticket on the osteoporosis express."

And the lift doors slid shut between them.

The *Handbag* offices—or should that be *space*—were a tasteful ensemble of neutrals, if such a thing was possible. Annie had never seen so many variations on beige. Taupe, mushroom, champagne, almond, latte, blush . . . Even the receptionist busy doing nothing behind her Philippe Starck blond wood desk was resolutely neutral, from her sleek caramel lowlights to her gravelly "Hello, *Handbag*."

The inevitable comparison with the gruff security men who guarded the *Post*'s tatty gray reception made Annie groan inwardly. Christ, could Rebecca be any more of a cliché? Although obviously the woman had to have hidden depths, since she was an internationally renowned magazine editor at the helm of a multimillion-pound business. And Annie had it on good authority—i.e., Lou—that the move back to London to launch *Handbag* had cost Rebecca her marriage, something that had devastated the woman. But still Annie knew she'd be struggling to defend the editor's corner if the boys on the news desk knew even a quarter of it.

Pushing through an opaque glass door into the corridor beyond (walls just a shade south of almond), Annie found herself faced with a row of opaque glass doors, each a mirror image of the one through which Annie had just passed. And each door leading to the lair of a different executive: commercial director, publishing director, advertising director, marketing director, and finally editor in chief.

At strategically erratic intervals between each door was a gigantic blow-up of a different *Handbag* cover. Gisele, Nicole Kidman, Scarlett Johansson, Kate Moss . . . Each cover more impossibly glamorous than the last. It was like running the gauntlet of a fun-fair hall of mirrors, although in her case, Annie couldn't help thinking, she was the odd-looking one as tall, skinny, groomed visions morphed around her.

Fun? Hardly.

Annie had cleared the corridor and was halfway across the huge open-plan editorial office, features desk—and sanctuary of sorts—in her sights, when the first grenade of the day was lobbed.

"Annie! At last!"

Every head swiveled in Annie's direction, faces suffused with ill-disguised relief that their editor's first missile had been launched and hadn't landed on them. Not that there were many people at desks by 9:15 A.M. The entire fashion department were at the first London Fashion Week show of the day, or would be prepared to swear on the life of an elderly relative if ever called on it. Most of the art department were still in transit, from bed to bathroom probably. Only the subs' desk was fully staffed, each one throwing pointed looks at the clock and glowering.

"Annie! I need an update. No, don't bother to stop off at your desk, I'm sure you have everything you need in that bag." There was no hint of a request in Rebecca's voice as she stood in the doorway of her corner office. Editors always got corner offices, or they did if they carried any clout. Bright winter sunlight radiated around Rebecca, bouncing off creamy highlights and silhouetting her wiry black-clad frame against the wrap-around windows.

As ever, Rebecca dressed as if she might be required to attend a five-star function at a moment's notice: nipped-in black jacket with a matching pencil skirt that stopped just below the knee. YSL, Annie found herself guessing, although given that it was London Fashion Week surely her boss should have been wearing Paul Smith or Julien Macdonald? Not that real women, even magazine editors, wore Julien Macdonald. That was Annie's opinion, anyway. Rebecca's outfit was completed by vertiginous black patent heels that clipped on the ash floorboards. Annie's head swam just looking at them.

"Why didn't you call me?"

Searching for the edge in Rebecca's tone, Annie found none. If she'd been expecting fireworks, and she had—rockets—there was no sign of them now, and that made Annie nervous. She'd been on the receiving end of "Rebecca cares" before and nearly found herself the subject of a first-person story ghostwritten by one of *Handbag*'s pet writers.

Deftly smoothing her skirt, Rebecca sat herself behind her enormous, if unnaturally tidy, brushed aluminium desk. It was no surprise that Rebecca Brooks was one of those scary people who quite literally cleared her desk by the end of every working day. A state-of-the-art aluminium PowerBook, a small neat pile of papers, and a brushed steel Lamy cartridge pen were the only indication that someone actually used the desk to work. Someone who was hedging her bets wildly on the technology front.

The editor gestured toward one of several camel leather chairs set around a glass-and-metal trestle table that fit perfectly into an impressive floor-to-ceiling bay. On the table were production notes, remnants of last night's knife-edge meeting where Annie's name had been mud, no doubt. Annie still couldn't get her head around the whole monthly deadline thing.

On the *Post,* even if an investigation had taken several months to complete, once it was finished it was finished. Through subs and, inevitably, lawyers one day; on the front page the next. At *Handbag* the April issue printed mid-February. Annie knew the April issue hit the newsstands on the first Thursday of March and she was well aware that while the editorial team were working on May now, the fashion and beauty departments had already finished shooting July. The logic defeated her.

Rebecca leaned back and swung one slim leg across the other, the toe of her elegant stiletto angled in Annie's direction. Too late, Annie became conscious she was still wearing the weather-beaten black coat that had scarcely left her back for over a week and was now nothing short of a health hazard. Why hadn't she taken a detour via her desk to dump it?

"I left messages for you," Rebecca continued, voice still suspiciously mild. "On your mobile and at the hotel. I even left one at your flat."

Annie knew. Well, she didn't, because she hadn't listened to any of the messages, but she knew they were there, flashing and vibrating. Mothers, bosses, friends . . . She'd always been one of the telephone's greatest junkies, regarding it as a lifeline to sanity, success, and, quite possibly, salvation. Now, however, it was a curse, stalking her every move and haunting her waking hours. Frankly, the flight home had been a relief, a ringing-, vibrating-, beeping-, and flashing-free oasis of calm. Better Rebecca didn't know that, though, better her boss thought her messages had been received and ignored. Apart from anything else, it would help perpetuate the myth that Annie was in control of the situation.

As if on cue, Annie felt the phone buzz silently in her bag, taunting her.

"I could have done with an update Monday," said Rebecca. "Or even yesterday. Yesterday would have been better than nothing. We had to give the printers the go-ahead on April by six."

"I had no idea that the subs were still holding the issue." Annie met her boss's steely gray gaze without flinching. "I thought we'd agreed to put it in May."

Rebecca nodded. "True. But *I* decided it was worth holding on in case you got something worth rushing through. And, if memory serves, we agreed you'd give me daily updates."

You agreed, Annie thought. *I said nothing.* Saying nothing and then doing exactly as she pleased. It was a habit that had gotten her into trouble more than once.

"I was tied up," said Annie. "What with all the research, interviewing, not to mention the blizzard, getting the NYPD to finish up, and then prizing a new flight allocation out of Virgin when the snow thawed, I was up to my eyes."

Every word was true. It's just that there were a couple of words missing, ones that would really interest Rebecca. Words like *Patty* and *Lang*.

Leaving New York had been more of a wrench than Annie anticipated. Although nothing like as tough as leaving her source behind. When Officer Ramirez had appeared at Annie's hotel on Monday and, after handing Annie a copy of a witness statement to sign, told her she was free to leave, Annie found herself praying for more snow. Not because she needed any extra time to grill Patty but because, in some weird way, leaving Patty to the demons Annie had watched dance behind the model's eyes felt like letting her down.

And not just Patty, her dead husband, too.

As she was packing to leave, the phone in Annie's hotel room had rung three times and then gone silent. So Annie counted down from sixty and picked up the next call on the first ring. It was an old code, much used by the tabloids. A way of getting through to people who weren't answering their phone. You fixed how many times you'd ring before hanging up, how long you'd wait before calling back.

Moscow Rules, Ken Greenhouse called it. Whatever that was meant to mean. Annie and Patty had agreed to use the system when they'd met again the day before. Annie hadn't been remotely surprised that Patty already knew the system. You didn't have her relationship with the press without learning their tricks.

"Annie, you've got to listen to me . . ."

The first words were practically inaudible beneath Patty's jagged, almost hysterical gasps, and several seconds passed before her sobs abated sufficiently for Annie to make any sense of what she was saying.

"We . . . need . . . to talk."

"When?"

"Now. There's so much you don't know. You're my only friend." Patty gulped air between the sobs. "No one else will listen."

Annie put down the coffee she'd ordered from room service. It had gone cold anyway and now it tasted bitter. *I'm not your friend,* she wanted to say. *I'm a journalist.*

"They won't listen," Patty repeated. "They just keep saying Mark's case is closed."

"I know." Annie wasn't surprised, since that was what Officer Ramirez had just told her.

"How can it be closed? Mark was shot, killed . . ."

"I don't think they're questioning that," Annie said, sounding calmer than she felt.

"Homicide, the cop said. It was that O'Connell guy. Murder in the first degree. Mark was shot in the pursuit of a robbery, that makes it first, but since that creep is dead there's no case to pursue. So, it's closed . . . over."

"It's okay," Annie promised, knowing it wasn't and never would be. "Look, I'll come around. Give me twenty minutes. Do you need me to get you anything on the way?"

Patty's only request was for three packs of Camels unfiltered.

By the time Annie had put in a call to O'Connell and managed to enrage the cop one final time, it was more like an hour before she made it to Patty's Murray Hill apartment.

"Are you calling as a witness or a journalist, ma'am?" Sergeant O'Connell had asked, the last word heavy with sarcasm, as if the statuses of *journalist* and *human* were mutually exclusive.

"What?"

"Apparently you don't just write about clothes," he said. "In fact, according to Ms. Lang you're a *serious* journalist. What's more, she says you're going to dig out the truth about Mark Mailer . . ."

"I am?" *Damn,* thought Annie. But she'd expected O'Connell to figure it out eventually, with or without Patty's help. What kind of cop would he be if he couldn't unearth a little fact like that?

"Because, if this is a press call," the cop continued, "I'll put you through to our liaison officer. I'm sure you'll find her most helpful."

O'Connell didn't follow through on his threat. Instead he gave Annie what he insisted was the very last word on the subject—the coroner's. Mark Mailer had died as a result of being shot twice in the chest with a .38 hollow-point. The cause of death was a gunshot to the heart, the mechanism was a massive rupture wound, causing internal bleeding and asphyxia, and the manner was homicide, nobody was arguing about that. Both guns recovered from the crime scene had been test-fired, the bullets from the Colt matching the slugs recovered from the restroom. There was a lot more involving stippling, powder patterns, and distance, but it was largely irrelevant, since the man who committed the homicide was also dead (and those details were on a different report and, with all due respect, none of her damn business). Budgets were tight, the DA's office was overworked, and the case and the subject were closed. *Ma'am.*

All of which cut no ice with Annie and even less with Patty when Annie related O'Connell's views to her forty-five minutes later. If Patty was distressed when Annie arrived bearing three packs of Camels, she became desperate when Annie told her she was leaving town that night.

"I'll call as soon as I get back to London," Annie promised, mentally crossing her fingers behind her back. "And you can phone me—anytime—on my mobile. Then it's only a few days until Milan."

Patty smiled weakly. "A lot could happen in five days."

Annie nodded, and prayed it wouldn't.

Never allow yourself to get attached to a case study. That was one of the many rules Ken Greenhouse had taught her. Rules Annie invariably broke. As he'd said when she'd insisted on going to Irina's funeral, "Trouble with you, Annie, you think you're their friend. You're not. You're not there to save anyone. You're there to get the story."

It was ironic, really, that Annie had no trouble lying through her teeth or pretending to be someone she wasn't, but still needed to carry her conscience with her. It made for a tough call when the time came to shaft her subjects—as it always, inevitably, did.

"You see," Annie told Rebecca, "I got Patty."

Rebecca stopped, polystyrene cup poised a hairbreadth from her mouth, waiting for Annie to elaborate. Annie didn't. Instead she watched the tiny black beads of coffee seep through the polystyrene and hang there, like the intricate beginnings of a henna tattoo, until gravity won and the beads trickled down to pool beneath Rebecca's fingers.

"Patty Lang? You tracked down Patty Lang? Why didn't you tell me? Why didn't you call?"

She found *me,* Annie thought, but she didn't volunteer that information. "It was delicate," she said. "This kind of work always is."

Easy does it, she reminded herself. Rebecca was more than capable of running away with the story, Annie knew that from recent experience. Last time her mishandling of the situation at the Royalton had cost Annie thirty-six valuable hours schlepping from show to show in Rebecca's wake when she could have been investigating Mark's death. The trick was to give Rebecca just enough information to get her off her back, but not so much she'd start publicizing her scoop.

Working for Ken had been easier, because Ken understood the rules. Hell, he'd been around so long the man had probably written half of them. Rebecca was different. She'd written rules, too. Her own.

The last thing Annie needed right now was for Mark and Patty's marriage to be all over the papers. If that happened she wouldn't see or hear from Patty again, and Patty would never substantiate the facts—the truth about what happened to Mark—and then Annie would have no story.

No tape, no story. That was a golden rule, and Annie had risked everything on building Patty's trust by not recording a single word of her face-to-face conversations with the model over the last three days. Ken would have killed her.

"I'll clear the May cover," Rebecca was saying. "It was no one who mattered anyway."

Annie, who had definite memories of a much-vaunted cover shoot with Brit packer and rock-star daughter Megan Stroak, did a double take; that was Megan's fifteen minutes gone, then, front cover of *Handbag* one minute, consigned to the back of the filing cabinet in a file marked PENDING the next.

Rebecca smiled, took a sip from her cup, and managed to keep the smile in place. "This is a real coup," she said. "Miranda Lawson on June, Patty Lang on May. Well done, Annie, two exclusives in a row. I'm assuming this *is* an exclusive. Nice work. Of course, no one has touched Lang for years, but now . . . This is different, she's hot. Patty Lang's first— only—interview since Mark Mailer's tragic death, plus cover. We'll be a major news story."

Noting the *we,* Annie decided to ignore it. That was the least of her worries. There was no way Patty would do a cover shoot for *Handbag* or anyone else. As far as Patty was concerned this was all about Mark, he was Annie's story, no question. Rebecca, however, was on a roll. She had the front covers the competition would kill for and she knew it.

"Why did you come back?" asked Rebecca suddenly.

Annie smiled through clenched teeth. "Because," she said patiently, "you told me to get on the first plane out of New York." And for once Annie had decided the smart move would be to do what she was told. Rebecca was the key that would open all Milanese doors, and Milan was where Patty would be. If Annie was to benefit from the unrestricted access *Handbag's* editor could provide, it was in her interest to keep Rebecca sweet.

"Yes," said Rebecca. "But that was then. Wouldn't it have been better to stay there and do the interview? You're not planning a phone interview, surely?"

"Of course not." Annie was a journalist, not a clippings merchant. "Phoners are worse than useless with a subject this sensitive. I'll need to connect with the interviewee, make her trust me. Patty's decided to go to Milan; Enzo Cotta wants her for his show."

Rebecca's face was blank, not because she'd never heard of the small avant-garde designer, but because she was unimpressed. Enzo Cotta was two or three years away from mattering, if he ever came to matter at all. At least as far as Rebecca was concerned.

"He's got backing," said Annie.

"Who?" Rebecca was now looking interested.

"Good question. Mantolini's been mentioned again. Anyway, Patty's going to Italy over the weekend and I've agreed to meet her there. You'll see her, too, at Mariolina Mantolini's party."

chapter twenty-one

If pastel yellow was this season's black (and according to the March issue of *Handbag*, it was), then Annie's desk was utterly of the moment. It was awash with Post-it notes as far as the eye could see. And in the middle, afloat on a sea of yellow, stood a huge bunch of daffodils.

"Flowers," a tall slim girl sitting opposite said unnecessarily. "They came yesterday."

"Who from?"

The girl shrugged. "Some PR probably. Didn't think you'd want me to open the card. Anyway, I was too busy taking bloody messages. Full-time job where you're concerned," she added, watching Annie dump her bag on the floor and tear open a small white envelope.

Hope life looks better now that you're back in London. Maybe see you in Milan? Chris x

Annie read the message twice. She didn't know any Chris, except that friend of Lou's from New York. An image of messy fair hair and a lanky shrug came to mind. Surely he wasn't the flower-sending type?

God, Annie really hoped her radar wasn't off by that much.

Never trust a man who sends flowers, Annie had learned that the hard way. Tony had been big on flowers, sent them every time he did something he shouldn't, like screw her older sister's best friend and then lie about it. Still, it could be worse, they might have been roses. In Annie's experience people who sent roses were the worst.

"Anyone I know?" Viv asked.

Annie shook her head and shoved the card in her coat pocket.

"There were so many calls," said Viv, "that in the end I started you a message book. I've never known anyone to get so many. I began transferring the Post-its but that was so dull I gave up." Viv handed Annie a spiral-bound notebook bearing the legend YOUR MESSAGES.

Kicking her bag under a desk Annie was still struggling to think of as her own, she pulled out a black-padded typist's chair and sat. The desk was a bomb site. Had she been able to see her computer for all the junk, she might have turned it on and downloaded that day's headlines, but that also meant facing an inevitable deluge of e-mail, so Annie decided to tackle the message pad first.

If she'd been hoping for a groundbreaking lead or a call from a vital contact, she was out of luck. The first page went like this:

Your mum called x 3. Can you call her back "when you get time."

Your sister called, no message.

Lou McCartney called, something about a guy called Chris wanting your mobile number. She knows what you're like about anyone giving your number out.

Annie glanced at the daffodils blocking her computer screen. So it *was* that Chris. Okay, maybe she'd call Lou, maybe even allow herself to call Chris, if only to thank him for the flowers.

The next page was more of the same, plus a few names she didn't recognize, presumably PRs.

God, thought Annie, *is this it? The sum total of my life. A nagging family, my one good friend, and PRs who want something.*

After the message pad and a cursory glance at the Post-it notes came her mobile. At first the Nokia's inbox contained few surprises, Mother, Lou, mother, Jane, Lou, mother, Jane, even a couple of messages from Ken, both impatient.

Damn it, thought Annie, she was going to have to face down the *Post's* news editor sooner or later. Hiding only made things worse. Viv having vanished to the coffee machine, Annie picked up the phone on her desk and dialed Ken's number from memory.

A woman answered, another new secretary probably.

"Ken Greenhouse please."

"He's in a meeting."

Yeah, yeah. She'd been in those meetings, they involved a lot of feet on desks, a lot of polystyrene cups of sludge, and not a lot else.

"Who shall I say called?"

"Annie Anderson." Annie didn't bother to expand. She knew that the second Ken Greenhouse heard her name he'd be on the line in a . . .

"Annie, where the fuck have you been? You could have fucking returned my calls. Have you seen today's papers?"

It pained Annie to admit it was gone 10 A.M. and she hadn't.

"Business pages. I'll give you ten seconds to find one and then tell me what you've been doing for the past week. Painting your fucking nails— different color for every day of the week by the fucking look of it."

Stretching her phone's cord around the partition dividing Viv's desk from her own, Annie grabbed the pink pages of the *Financial Times* from the bottom of a pile, where she suspected it would have stayed all day.

"Okay," she said. *"FT."*

"Page three."

The headline smacked her in the eye. MAILER DEAL SPARKS WAR OF WORDS.

"Well?"

"Give me a chance to read it," Annie muttered. There was no bullshitting Ken in this mood.

There was nothing in the three half columns of print not covered in the headline. Mantolini and Fava were engaged in a war of words over the dead designer's name, both claiming they had finalized deals with him in the week before his death, both adamant they'd been his new backers.

As both were private companies all this had no impact on the Borsa, but the spat could only help the perceived value of both fashion houses, which couldn't hurt either of them given it was only six months since the

House of Mantolini's future had been in doubt and rumor had it Fava was considering flotation. Both Mariolina Mantolini and Fava's finance director, Silvio Vianni, were pictured and quoted, fiercely claiming the moral high ground.

"Bastards!" exclaimed Annie. "The poor guy's only been dead a week and he wouldn't have double-crossed them. That wasn't his style. If anything, I had the distinct impression he'd have preferred not to sell at all."

"Really?" Ken sounded calmer now. "So who's telling the truth?"

"I don't know," Annie admitted. "But it should be possible to find out."

"How? After all, he can't tell you now, can he? He can't tell anyone."

Annie said nothing.

"What aren't you telling me?" he said finally. "I don't like my journalists holding out on me."

"I'm not," Annie said, conscious that Viv was back and making slow work of depositing a plastic cup two-thirds full of cappuccino on Annie's desk. "I'm working for *Handbag* right now, remember?"

"Point taken. There's someone listening at your end, right?"

"Uh-huh. Pretty much."

"Okay, I'll leave you to get on with it, but keep me in the loop."

Annie hung up. The art department was filling, the office buzzed with noise, but no one paid the slightest attention to Annie as she spun back to face her desk. As ever, when trying to stand up a story, Annie sorted her thoughts into two distinct piles. What she knew and what she suspected. The trouble was her "know" pile was almost nonexistent. Too exhausted to sleep on the flight home, Annie had listened to the Mark tape again. And though she found herself drawn to the same points over and over—her talks with Patty adding meaning where previously there had been none—Annie suspected herself of hearing things that weren't really there.

Why would Mark, a man whose mistrust of journalists was notorious, be trying to tell her anything? Questions jostled for space in her brain. What if Mark really *hadn't* made up his mind or, worse still, had changed it at the last minute, leaving Fava and Mantolini both believing a deal could be theirs?

There was only one person who could answer that question right now: Guido Brasco. Trouble was, he'd already made it clear he had no interest in speaking to Annie. Pushing the daffodils aside, she flicked on her computer, logged on to the Internet, and typed GUIDO BRASCO, MULBERRY STREET into Switchboard.com. Success! She keyed the row of numbers that appeared into her mobile phone's address book and then glanced at her watch. It was ten fifteen in London, way too early to call New York.

Why did people keep saying the same thing over and over? Annie wondered, sipping at her cappuccino's watery froth while she held her mobile to her ear. *Annie . . . it's your mother. Annie . . . it's Jane.* Lou, her mother, Lou, her sister, Ken.

Annie. The *Annie Anderson!* At Handbag. *Well, well, long time no hear . . .*

Annie's stomach fell away as bile and a last gulp of cappuccino rose in her throat. For a second she thought she was going to gag. The fine downy hairs on her arms and the back of her neck bristled.

Tony Panton, what the fuck did he want?

Without thinking Annie thrust the mobile away and watched it crash onto her desk.

"You okay?" Viv had glanced up to see what the noise was about.

"Sure." Managing a smile, Annie nodded. "Lost my grip."

Annie had to find somewhere to listen to the message properly, in private and away from Viv's not-remotely-subtle stare. There were any number of conference rooms and offices set aside for meetings, but there was no way of knowing if they were occupied without going in.

She could see no alternative. It would have to be the ladies.

For the first time in living memory the room was empty. No fan, which Annie suspected was in direct contravention of some kind of health and safety regulation, no locks where there shouldn't be locks, no light switches where there shouldn't be light switches. Instinctively Annie gave each of the four cubicles a gentle nudge and waited for its door to swing open, just to check that she really was alone. Annie slipped inside the last one, locked the door behind her, closed the lid, and slumped onto it.

Oh God.

Tony Panton. Why now? wondered Annie, leaning back against the cistern. The steel was cold and hard against her back. She shuddered, more from memory than chill.

Her body remembered, even if her mind refused.

Why, after all this time, had Tony decided to track her down? It gave her the creeps just framing that question. She could smell the fear on herself, feel sweat pool under her arms. Her eyes pricked with tears she'd never allowed herself to cry.

It wasn't as if she'd have been hard to find. Bylines and photographs were an occupational hazard of working on a national newspaper. Yet in all that time, ten years—almost eleven—Tony had never bothered to call. Until now. Talk about impeccable timing. And how the hell had he gotten hold of her mobile number? Her work number Annie could handle, but her mobile . . . Annie's mobile was her lifeline, her professional and personal life rolled into one handy package. If she had to change that number, she'd lose everything.

Annie. The *Annie Anderson! At* Handbag. *Well, well, long time no see . . .*

"Not long enough," muttered Annie.

Saw your name in the papers. Nasty business with that designer, can't have been very much fun for you. Thought I'd give you a bell. Didn't know you'd left that paper and gone to work for a magazine. Doesn't sound like you, always took yourself a bit more seriously than that. Spoke to your mother, lovely woman, always liked her. Seemed very concerned not to have heard from you. Anyway no time to chat now, up to my eyes in meetings, you know how it is. I'll catch up with you soon, maybe tomorrow . . .

There was a silence. Annie knew he was still there, waiting, and he knew she knew. And then, nerve of nerves, he left his number, signing off with a smug *If you don't fancy calling me first,* like he'd just given her the birthday present to end all birthday presents.

Fear gave way to fury. *Call him first?* When hell froze over and not a second sooner.

The bastard hadn't even bothered to announce himself. No *It's Tony,* nothing. He'd known she would recognize his voice. By the sound of it, the self-centered tosser even thought she'd be glad to hear from him. But that wasn't what was really making Annie furious.

Her mother, thought Annie, tears biting the backs of her eyes. That was where he'd gotten the number. Her bloody, bloody mother.

The number was dialed before Annie had time to think and answered before she had time to prepare.

"Basingstoke—" Her mother started to give the number in a singsong voice.

"How could you?" Annie cut in. "How could you be that stupid?"

There was a moment's silence.

"So you're back then, I take it. It might have been nice if you'd—"

"You gave Tony my number." The space Annie left between each word was filled with fury and impotence. "Don't you understand anything?"

"Clearly not." Her mother's tone was icy. "He was a nice boy and you treated him badly."

"What?"

"He wanted to get engaged, you know. Mrs. Phillips told me, she met his mother in John Lewis just after you broke up."

For a second Annie was speechless. She'd always suspected her parents were blind where Tony was concerned.

"What do you think happened?" she demanded, concentrating on keeping her voice low and conscious that at any moment Viv might return to her desk and end the conversation before Annie had finished.

"Why did you think I failed my A's?" added Annie, her voice almost a hiss now. "Why did you think I left home? Where do you think the dreams came from? Didn't you ever wonder?"

Her mother sighed, almost sadly, and Annie could picture her plumping cushions on the seat next to the telephone table before she sat. "You can't blame the A levels on us. Your dad warned you about boyfriends and homework. And we thought you were just upset, I mean . . ." Annie's mother hesitated. "He was your first serious boyfriend."

Annie knew exactly what her mother was trying to say.

"And Dr. Francis insisted you'd get over it. I mean, it's not like you were starving yourself or taking drugs. We were all upset when you broke up; Tony's a lovely boy and your dad and me had hoped . . ."

"You gave him my number," Annie said flatly.

"Of course I did." Her mother sounded exasperated. "I was pleased to hear from him. He asked after your dad and Jane . . . I told him all about the grandchildren."

"The grandchildren?"

"I thought you'd be pleased. I knew you'd quarreled—everyone knew you'd quarreled—but it was a long time ago. You're not very good at letting bygones be bygones, are you?"

Bygones!

You don't get it, do you? He raped me . . .

And what would her mother say to that?

Don't be ridiculous, Tony wouldn't do a thing like that. Or, *Boys can be a bit rough sometimes. They don't mean it.*

Oh, but he did. I saw the look in his eyes as he held me down.

Annie stared at the stainless-steel door, seeing it through a blur of tears as her mother continued to talk, mostly about Tony's new job and his BMW. Why had Annie allowed him to do this to her? Again. After all these years. Why was she even having this conversation with her mother . . . ? Why didn't she just tell her the truth?

Because Mum might not believe her, and that would be worse. That was why most people didn't say, wasn't it? Shame, and the fear of not being believed.

"Look, Mum," she said. "I'm at work, and I've got to go. Just do me a favor. Don't give any more of my old school friends this number."

chapter twenty-two

"So, can I give Chris your number or not?" It wasn't the first time Lou had asked that question in the past two hours.

"Yes . . . no . . . ," said Annie. "I don't know, okay? Ask me later."

"This is later," Lou said crossly. "The poor guy just wants to take you for a drink, for God's sake."

Annie shook her head. She knew that, and she wanted to go for the drink. That was the problem.

"You're my friend. Chris is my friend. You're both single. It just occurred to me you might get on."

Annie didn't even bother to answer that time. She had been on the receiving end of Lou's matchmaking before, although this time it looked as if her aim was improving.

"Look," said Lou. "What's wrong?"

"Nothing."

"I don't believe you."

Annie shrugged. It was a childish shrug, sulky. The kind she used to specialize in. "I need some air and a cigarette."

Lou sighed. Digging into her bag, she pulled out a pack of duty-free Silk Cuts and handed it over. "Keep them."

"Thanks." Annie took the familiar white-and-purple packet and elbowed her way through the crowds. She didn't want a fag, not really. She wanted to make a phone call.

The street outside was quiet, just the occasional latecomer rushing toward Smithfield meat market, an hour and a half late for a show that still gave no sign of starting.

For what had to be the tenth time that day, Annie listened as, on the other side of the Atlantic, a phone began to ring. She didn't expect Guido to pick up; after all, he hadn't so far.

"Hello?"

The voice was unmistakably that of Guido Brasco. Tired, more exhausted even than on the day he'd learned of Mark's murder, but definitely his.

For a second Annie didn't reply, waited to see how he would respond to the silence.

"Who is this please?" The old man sounded nervous, as if he was expecting something and Annie would have bet a month's wages that it wasn't her.

"Signor Brasco," she said firmly. "It's Annie Anderson. You might not remember me—"

"Oh yes, signorina," he said wearily. "I remember you. I was under the impression you had no need of me. It is you, is it not, who knows everything?"

Touché, Annie thought. "I have a question for you," she said. There was no benefit in hedging her bets this time. "I need to know who Mark's new backer was going to be."

Guido Brasco didn't even sound surprised. "That I cannot tell you." From his voice, Annie was unsure whether he couldn't because he didn't know or because he wasn't prepared to share it.

She opted for the latter. "I'm sorry, Signor Brasco," she said. "I just don't believe you."

"Signorina Anderson," he said, "and I assure you these are my very last words on the subject . . . Mark was a wonderful boy and a talented designer but he did not understand the rules. Or, if he did, he chose to ignore them. Which is it with you, signorina? Don't understand or won't?"

Annie began to interrupt, but Signor Brasco stopped her. "I will tell you this once and then I do not wish to speak with you again. You do not know how serious this business is. Mark did not know, Patty does not know, but you . . . You should know better. Put yourself in danger if you must. You have no right to endanger Patty."

"But—" Annie started. "What do you mean *endanger Patty?*"

The old man's sigh spoke volumes. It was the sigh of a man who'd seen the passage of years, watched the change, and wasn't entirely sure he liked the way things were going. It was the sigh of someone who had quite simply had enough.

"Must I spell it out?" he said. "Stop now, Signora Anderson, or I assure you it will be too late."

Three minutes later Annie had noted down every word she could remember of the conversation and was back inside Smithfield, heading for the vacant seat next to Lou. With Guido Brasco's warning still ringing in her ears, a fashion show was the last place Annie wanted to be, but she knew how it would look if she vanished. Annie was beginning to see just how much appearances mattered.

Male or female, gay or straight, the fash pack who filled the Smithfield meat market fell into one of three distinct tribes . . .

The fashion forward: haircut, as perverse and unflattering as possible; clothes, either shapeless or brutally unforgiving; makeup, none or harsh in the extreme; overall effect, as ugly as possible.

The fashion victim: haircut, curls/cropped/poker-straight, whatever the hairdresser du jour says it should be; clothes, 1960s mod/librarian chic/supervixen/whatever Tom/Marc/Miuccia say it should be; makeup, ditto; overall effect, totally over by Friday.

The fashion guru: haircut, whatever suits, with subtle seasonal changes; clothes, ditto (would rather be dead than caught wearing the signature piece of the season); makeup, also ditto; overall effect, enviably on the button.

There was no doubt Lou fell into the last camp, great at telling other women what they should be wearing but rarely deigning to touch it herself.

"What?" said Lou. "Why are you staring at me?"

Annie looked away. "What are the chances of this starting in the next week?" she asked.

Lou shrugged. "Probably get going by eleven P.M. If we're lucky." Huddled inside her enormous vintage fur (courtesy of that well-known retro clothes shop, Granny's Attic), Lou was unable to stop herself adding, "Anyway, I told you we didn't need to get here till ten at the earliest."

Annie had to concede Lou'd been right to plead for another hour and another glass of red in the Eagle. Why hadn't she agreed? Probably because she was still furious about Ken.

"It's running tomorrow," Lou had announced.

"What is?"

"That stuff about Mark not having signed for either fashion house."

Annie stared at her.

"That's what you told Ken, isn't it?" Lou said. "What did you think he was going to do with it? Usual stuff, inside source, reliably informed, yada yada . . ."

"But they'll know it was me."

"Who will?"

"Rebecca, for a start."

"Oh come off it," Lou said, her voice cross. "Ken's been good to you."

"Yeah, but that wasn't the deal." Annie knew she'd made a mistake as soon as she said it.

"What deal?" said Lou, putting down her glass with a bang. Friends confided in each other, Annie knew that, she just wasn't very good at remembering how to do it.

"I'm writing a piece," Annie said.

"For Ken?"

"Yeah."

"What, freelance?"

"Not exactly."

Lou scowled. "You mean you're still working for the *Post*?"

Annie had no choice but to admit the truth. She was working for the *Post* and *Handbag,* only *Handbag* didn't know that.

"Nor did I," said Lou, voice tight. "So what's the great exposé?"

"There isn't one," said Annie. "It's just a piece about life inside the fashion industry, that's all."

She hadn't expected Lou to approve.

"I don't blame Rebecca for giving this a miss," said Annie, after another half hour had passed and still no action. Casting around, she realized that her boss wasn't the only fashion grandee who'd elected to miss this show. No *Vogue* or *Elle* and just a smattering of big names from the nationals. No Suzy Menkes, either, and the American press were conspicuous by their absence. Mind you, most of them hadn't even bothered to turn up for London Fashion Week. Again.

At least it explained how Lou and Annie happened to be sitting in the front row. No one more important had turned up.

"I thought you said Mons was meant to be London Fashion Week's hottest ticket?" Annie said.

"It will be," Lou assured her. "In retrospect." She nodded to a small huddle of photographers. "Those guys don't turn out for nothing . . . *Voices* will be *the* fashion event of this season, believe me. Some things I know."

It was 11:10 P.M. before the stagehands finally emerged and began peeling back the catwalk's PVC coating to reveal a matte black space beneath. It took Annie less than a second to realize that was a bad sign. And not the first that evening.

Lights dimmed to a deep, impenetrable black and white noise filled the meat market, cutting suddenly to a lone plaintive wail. Slowly the voice gained in volume until it became a banshee shriek, then two, then three. A cacophony of wails added their agony to a sound track of pain echoing around the old abattoir.

Subtle, it wasn't.

"At what point would it not be a hideous faux pas to leave?" Annie hissed.

Her friend scowled into the blackness, and Annie could have sworn she heard Lou mutter, "Philistine."

The lights stayed down, the screeching fell away, and in the darkness Annie felt, rather than saw, something move. Not at head height, so not a walking model, but low down and sprawled on the ground like a sleeping dog or, dear God, please not an animal carcass.

Meat market.

Abattoir.

Carcass.

Annie allowed her head to slump into her hands. She really, really could have done without this, especially today. That's when the shaking began. Involuntarily at first, but increasingly violent.

It's the cold. Annie listened to the voice in her head. *Just the cold, it must be minus ten in here.* But this wasn't New York, nowhere near. And it wasn't the cold because that Annie could cope with. It was the darkness. And sudden silence.

Why this hushed . . . reverence, almost? Why had no one so much as sniffed? Annie swayed slightly to her right, reassured to get an elbow from Lou in her ribs. But still nobody spoke, not a whisper or a snigger, and Annie couldn't bring herself to look up.

It was only when she became aware of the darkness breaking like a bleak dawn over the hushed crowd that Annie slowly began to raise her head.

Fuck. She badly wanted to laugh, not a mocking *you pretentious bastards* kind of laugh, more the nervous, panic-stricken front-row-at-a-funeral kind. But none came.

"Shit," said Annie, aware she was swearing too much.

"Yeah," whispered Lou. "Impressive."

There were corpses all right. Not cattle, skinned and flayed, although that would have been bad enough. And not entirely corpses. Naked female bodies, some sparsely clad, others entirely nude, their hair flattened under latex skullcaps above blue-lipped, white faces.

Naked or not their bodies were covered with the livid purple and black of bruises, some fading to yellow, bodies that were literally skin and bone. Victims.

Annie vomited.

And an entire front row pretended not to notice.

"Now I know why there was no running order on our seats," Annie ventured in a shaky attempt at humor as the crowd filed out, noiseless but for the sound of fingers ripping cellophane from fag packets and the frenzied flick of lighters. "No clothes to list."

Lou didn't even glance in her direction. A Silk Cut already hanging unlit from her own lip, lighter poised and ready, she picked up her bag and joined the throng moving toward the exit.

"I'm never going to a show with you again," Lou spat when they finally got outside.

"I'm sorry," said Annie, and she meant it.

"What you need to understand," said Lou, "is there are two types of fashion." Waving her now lit Silk Cut, she marched ahead of Annie to start the long and probably fruitless search for a cab. "First, there are clothes. That's what New York's all about. New York and Milan. Clothes designed primarily for women to buy and wear."

Annie nodded obediently.

"Then there's what happened in there, which has little or nothing to do with clothes, but can be far more interesting. At its best it's bold, exciting, and thought provoking. That's where London excels—or did before everyone started moving to Paris. Think McQueen, Galliano, Hussein Chalayan . . ."

Annie threw out her arm and a black cab sailed past, barely pausing to turn off its light.

"What's their work about?" demanded Lou. "It's not just frocks, that's for sure. It's about the role of women in society. I'm not saying it's art—actually scrap that, sometimes it is—but it makes a statement. That's what Mons were doing. Surely you of all people could see that? Okay, so it wasn't the most original statement they could have made. I mean, McQueen did it years ago with his Highland Rape collection. But the point is, it's a statement that still needs making. That's the shocking thing. That in the twenty-first century, the statement still has to be made and it's left to people like Mons to do it."

Lou stopped and looked at Annie. "What are you crying about?" she said.

chapter twenty-three

If Annie had been hoping for blue skies and bright sunshine, her plane was touching down in the wrong part of Italy. Milan, home of industry and commerce, football and fashion, was so far removed from the sun-drenched climate of the Neapolitan coast it might as well have been on the Swiss side of the Alps. A fine, misty drizzle filled the air as Flight AZ237 from Heathrow (also known as the fashion bus) taxied into Malpensa airport.

It was past midday but the sun, assuming there was one behind the low blanket of clouds, was too weak to break through a leaden gray sky. And the combination of drizzle and cloud meant Annie's plane seemed to glide in to land in its own shroud of fog, the terminal building and even the single-deck courtesy coach waiting to transport her there rendered almost totally invisible.

Anyone would think the first ten off the plane got front row at Gucci, thought Annie as she watched the jostling of her colleagues with bemusement. It was all one big competition, she realized. The tickets you were sent and the seats you were allocated, the press gifts you received, the flesh you pressed, were all a reflection of your status, and that status was a reflection of the esteem in which your publication was held.

Handbag deserved the best. Apparently it was part of Annie's job to make sure that it got the best, which translated as her getting the best or, at least, better than anyone else in an equivalent job.

"Never say that's okay and let it go at that," Libby had explained when Annie told her about the Marc Jacobs seating debacle in New York. It seemed like a storm in an espresso cup to Annie. "If you don't get a good enough seat, that's not okay. It is *never* okay. There are three rules . . ."

The bookings editor had blinked when Annie pulled out her notebook. "Okay," she said. "Fire away." Viv was also staring but Annie didn't mind about that. Annie's reaction to the Mons show had been greeted by Viv as the ultimate in instant reviews.

"Never be grateful," said Libby. "Never be understanding, and never, ever show up if your seat allocation is shit. You have to make a fuss. If you don't the PR may be grateful, he may smile sweetly and promise to love you forever, but he'll also know he can get away with it next time. Giving *Handbag* crap seats will become a habit. And Rebecca will undoubtedly fire you!" Libby grinned. "Seriously," she said. "If Rebecca didn't get front row every time, I wouldn't let her attend the shows at all. It would be an affront to Rebecca personally and us in general. *Handbag* is a front-row kind of magazine."

While Annie secretly suspected she might be a third-row kind of girl, she was beginning to get the point. What looked ridiculous from the outside became less so when you understood the mechanics. This was not just about ego—it was about business, an international business with billions of dollars riding on it. Competition it might be, but a game it certainly wasn't.

Slumping back in her airplane seat, Annie resolved to move only when everyone else had finished squabbling. She felt utterly drained.

Right now she couldn't tell a red-hot lead from a red herring and if she listened to that damn Mailer tape one more time she was going to combust. On the plus side, there'd been no more calls from Tony, but it might make her feel better if there were; at least she could give him a piece of her mind.

The queue still wasn't moving, and Annie stifled a yawn. It had been a long night and an insultingly early start. In place of Patty's smack support system, Mark had become that prop. Now that Mark was gone, Annie had somehow taken his place. It was exhausting but, for reasons Annie chose not to examine too closely, she felt she owed it to Mark. And anyway, Annie needed Patty as much as Patty needed her, for the information she was slowly extracting.

Patty, who'd arrived in Milan a day earlier with her body clock still set to Eastern Standard Time, had been on the phone most of the night, lonely in the model flat she'd been assigned, and full of theories about things Mark had said—or not said—before his death.

It had been the same every night that week, each call bringing a new theory. At least last night's had been significant.

"I went to Mark's studio," Patty told her, without even waiting for Annie to say hello.

About time, Annie thought, though she didn't say so. She'd been angling for Patty to visit the Hell's Kitchen warehouse for days, but it had taken this long for Patty to find her courage and the keys.

"What did you find?" Annie asked.

Patty began to sob quietly.

Half dressed, mouth full of toothpaste, and case only half packed for a 7 A.M. check-in, frustration welled up in Annie. It was nearly midnight. "Patty . . . Patty . . . calm down," she said. "Talk to me. Didn't you look on Mark's computer?"

Patty took a gulp—whether it was air or nicotine Annie wasn't sure, but when she spoke again her voice was more measured. "It wasn't there."

"Whoa! What d'you mean it wasn't there?"

"It wasn't there, nothing was. It's all gone. Everything, pretty much. There were his old box files, that kind of stuff, but no computer, no sketches, no drawings for his collection, nothing in his desk . . . It's all gone."

Annie sat heavily on her bed and wiped the last of the toothpaste from her mouth with the sleeve of her dressing gown. "Have you called the police? Did you try speaking to O'Connell?"

There was a hollow laugh and Annie heard a Zippo firing into life at the other end of the phone. "Oh yeah, I called Sergeant O'Connell, but it's pointless. I know what that cop thinks. I don't know why he didn't just come out and say it. He thinks Cathie, or Mark's father, got in there and cleared the place out before I could get my dirty junkie hands on Mark's possessions."

Annie chose her next words carefully. "Is there any possibility of that?" she asked, bracing herself for a stream of tears. "I mean, could Mark's parents or Cathie have been there?"

"No." Patty's hooped earrings clanged against the receiver, she shook her head so violently. "They didn't have keys. I know Mark didn't give them keys. And anyway, I called Cathie and she said she can't bear to come anywhere near Manhattan."

"How about Rob?" Annie named Mark's intern.

"I don't know. I guess he had keys. Maybe Guido did, too."

"Did you get hold of Guido?" Annie asked, half dreading the answer. What would Guido—not exactly Annie's number one fan—have said to Patty if he'd spoken to her?

"Uh-uh. I tried but he wasn't around and he hasn't called back."

Realizing she was in for a long night, Annie slid a fresh tape into her Dictaphone, dropped the machine into the pocket of her dressing gown, and set about finding her ear mike.

It was a habit she'd started several nights before, the first time she received a midnight call from Patty. Face-to-face, tape recorders were out of bounds where Patty was concerned—they made her jumpy and reminded her that Annie was not a friend—but on the other end of a phone Patty would be none the wiser. The mike slotted into Annie's ear, amplifying Patty's voice as it recorded it.

As the time for Annie to leave for Heathrow drew closer, Patty audibly chain-smoked her way through a four-hour conversation while Annie, fueled by an endless stream of black coffee, stalked the four rooms of her first-floor flat. At best the conversation, one-sided as it was, was random and inchoate. Annie had become used to this over the previous nights. Their first meeting and Patty's subsequent calls from New York had filled Annie with the familiar exhilaration of a story taking shape.

Patty's theories about Mark's murder stemmed from a long rooftop conversation she'd overheard when he was up there, supposedly alone and supposedly thinking.

"Just talking to myself," Mark had said, when questioned. "You know, thinking things through."

"I'm not stupid," Patty told Annie. "I might be an ex-junkie, but I'm not stupid."

And that was the whole problem with this investigation: Her main source was an addict. And nobody, least of all award-winning journalists, believed addicts. Especially not addicts who'd leapt off the wagon in very recent public memory.

Mark might have been alone up on the roof, probably was. Patty accepted that, but he hadn't been talking to himself and she didn't call him on the shape in the pocket of his jeans: a cell phone, Patty insisted, and not the one she'd bought him, which had been lying on the bedside table.

He'd never lied to her before, Patty was sure of it. "If anyone was sparing with the truth," she'd told Annie, "it was me. Mark never lied, never made a promise he didn't keep. If anything he was too honest."

Annie didn't doubt it. Of course, he hadn't been entirely honest with *her*, but then journalists probably didn't count. Privately Annie's theory was that Mark's numerous rooftop appointments in the days before his death were with Guido, on that cell phone Patty had mentioned. But Patty had other ideas.

Adamant in her conviction that his final and most vocal rooftop conversation had been with one of his potential Italian backers, Patty would not be budged. It had come soon after Mark told Patty he'd finally reached a decision, two days before his show, the night before Patty's very public dive from the wagon. And it turned out that one explained the other.

"I've never seen Mark so mad," recounted Patty, for the *n*th time. "Not even Mark's dad could make him that mad. I was lying in bed. It must have been after three in the morning, really cold, and I could hear him up there talking to someone. A proper conversation, you know. Pauses and stuff. His voice getting louder. Even then, it was firm, not angry, the kind of tone I'd only heard in his voice once before. That last time I did smack before we got married. A scary, serious kind of calm that said he couldn't bear even to look at me. That's how he was when he came back through the window."

Annie wasn't sure Patty had told her about that before.

"I was pretending to be asleep, but I was so shaken when I saw his face I couldn't keep quiet. Mark looked, well, he looked frightening. Frightening and frightened, like he'd scared himself maybe . . . I don't know . . ."

"Worrying," Annie said, to fill the gap.

"Anyway," Patty said. "I asked him what was the matter and he said nothing. I should have let it lie, but I didn't. I asked him who he'd been talking to and Mark said no one, he'd been thinking out loud, and I said, 'Yeah right.' How dumb was that?"

Pretty dumb, Annie had to admit. She also had to admit she'd done it herself, many times, and mostly regretted it.

"That's when we had the fight," said Patty. The fight had also been news to Annie. The kind of news that made her want to shake the woman for not telling her sooner, the kind that found her sitting up all night, fast-forwarding and rewinding her interview with Mark, an interview she now knew had taken place forty-eight hours after a bust-up with Patty.

Addict or not, Patty was smart enough to have her own theories about her husband's business. Only not smart enough to pick the right moment to share them. When she'd told Mark what she thought—that he was arguing with his new backer, having second thoughts, and she wanted to know who and why because it was her life and future, too—Mark had erupted.

The result? A four-dollar cab ride to a grim part of the Alphabet, a wrap of heroin, and, hey presto, thanks to a showstopping turn on the catwalk the following night and Mark's subsequent murder, Patty had a starring role in her own personal *Valley of the Dolls.*

"Shit," said Annie. "That's rough." It was hard to imagine, being newly bereaved and carrying around baggage like that. No wonder guilt was eating Patty up inside.

"And you really don't know who Mark could have been talking to?" Annie could almost hear Patty shaking her head down the phone.

"Not at that time of night."

"No one had been trying to get hold of him? You didn't take any messages?"

Patty thought about it. "Well, Tom Li called."

"He did?"

"Yeah, that was the day before. I left Mark a note. And there's something else you gotta see, I'm not sure what it means, but I know it's important."

"What?"

"I can't tell you now, my phone might be bugged."

"Patty . . ."

"It could be . . . ," said the voice on the other end.

Exhausted, Annie let out a long, silent howl. Four hours! Four hours it had taken Patty to get to the real point and now she was stalling.

Then a sick feeling hit her. What if Patty wasn't paranoid. What if Patty was right?

chapter twenty-four

Her colleagues were systematically stripping the baggage carousel when Annie caught up with them. Annabel, the fashion editor, a tall, slim girl in drainpipe jeans and ballet pumps, heaved matching Louis Vuitton luggage onto one of two already laden trolleys, while another woman, slightly older, with a fake-bake tan and artfully tousled honey highlights, prowled the conveyor belt, pointing at cases. You could tell Iona, the fashion director, was more senior because she regarded her role as supervisory.

"Rebecca was looking for you," Iona said as Annie approached.

"I was late."

"Yes," said Iona. "We noticed."

Counting the Vuitton off the carousel and onto the trolley, Annie just knew the cases had to belong to Rebecca. One, two . . . three sizable holdalls and a vanity case. Yet she would be in Milan for only five days; how was she going to find time to wear it all?

What Annie didn't know, until Iona pointed it out, was that being one of the fashion industry's most senior editors at the Milan collections was a serious business, involving more outfit changes than Liz Hurley hosting an awards ceremony.

In the coming days their boss would be expected to wear Armani to Armani, Gucci to Gucci, and Prada to Prada. Not only that, but each had to be the right outfit, previously unseen and new season. Then there were additional changes for dinners and cocktails, plus Mariolina Mantolini's party in honor of Miranda Lawson, which would require something a little bit special.

At the thought of the trip to Lake Como, Annie grinned. She couldn't help it. For the first and, quite possibly, last time Annie Anderson would walk into a room full of beautiful people and know she looked the part. There would be no fail-safe jeans with "interesting" top for her. While *Handbag*'s fashion team had been charging around London as if the Jimmy Choo press office had asked for their shoes back, borrowing a sample here, picking up a VIP discount there for Rebecca's Milan trip, Annie had taken the back door, as usual.

It had been the work of minutes and the cost of a hot chocolate to befriend Suzi Quattro Junior, also known as the fashion assistant, and ask her advice.

Astonished that anyone as important as she believed Annie to be even knew she existed, let alone knew her name was Chloe, the girl had become Annie's personal stylist. Thanks to her, Annie would be sweeping into a room full of the world's most fashionable in a 1950s black lace vintage Dior (called in for the Megan Stroak cover, which would probably never see the light of day), paired with fuchsia satin heels. And for the first time in almost ten years Annie slipped comfortably into a size ten with room to spare. Starvation, insomnia, and raw nerves had to have some benefits.

You had to hand it to Rebecca, Annie thought. She looked every inch a woman who'd had her full eight hours and an army of styling elves to groom her before dawn. As she rapid-fired Italian into her mobile, oblivious to the fashion team who scurried around collecting her luggage, Rebecca looked immaculate. London to Milan wasn't exactly a long, tortuous flight, but *Handbag*'s editor in chief bore no sign of having breathed the same reconditioned air as everyone else. As if noting her for a profile, Annie ticked off the checklist.

Hair (sleek and unruffled).

Makeup (understated and immaculate).

Earl Jeans (Annie had never seen her boss do casual before but, inevitably, she looked fantastic).

Chanel jacket and white T-shirt (uncrumpled).

And loafers—and not just any loafers. Tod's loafers. Annie felt sick with envy, not because she was desperate to own a pair but because she'd have killed to have been able to carry them off without looking like some sad-sack granny. It was a skill that only the likes of Cindy Crawford, Elle Macpherson, and, typically, Rebecca possessed. The woman looked like something from a Calvin Klein fragrance ad, and Annie just knew her head would be as clear as her face. Rebecca was bound to have eschewed any liquid that wasn't Evian for the whole trip—champagne on flights was for those who still found the drink a novelty.

Snapping her Motorola shut, Rebecca waved in Annie's direction. "If it isn't my errant reporter! Where have you been? What's happening? Is Patty here yet? When are—" She stopped, her eyes drawn to the black bag slung over Annie's shoulder. It contained her precious tapes, laptop, and notes, but little else.

"Annie," Rebecca said sharply. "Where's your luggage?"

"Probably on the carousel."

"Annabel!" The befringed fashion editor snapped to attention at the sound of Rebecca's voice. "Do you have Annie's cases?"

"Case," Annie corrected Rebecca's back.

The girl shook her head. "Haven't seen it. Iona?"

"Nope, 'fraid not. Could be a problem." The fashion director indicated the conveyor belt.

Annie was horrified to see it was now still. And empty.

Rebecca's brow creased. "You *did* check it, didn't you?"

Annie unpacked her air-hostess smile; of course she'd bloody checked her case. She wasn't stupid.

"They've probably taken the remnants off and piled them up somewhere," said Annie. "I'll go and find out."

There was a sad little stack of cases, mostly black, lying beside baggage carousel G. In every airport Annie had ever passed through there was always a sad little pile of black cases lying abandoned beside a baggage carousel.

Dismantling the pile, Annie hefted the first case off the top, examining it before she heaved it aside and pulled down the next. Each was almost identical, some bigger some smaller, some heavy and some light, but none bore the marks of suffering that scarred her own case. By the time Annie reached the bottom there was nothing to see but beige faux marble tiles. Where the bloody hell was it?

"Found it?" Rebecca strode toward her, face full of concern. More concern, in fact, than most of the times Annie herself had gone missing.

"It was just my clothes," said Annie, feigning indifference. "I've got all my notes and everything in here."

Thank God for that, said the voice in her head. And thank God that her case—finally packed in five seconds flat, as her taxi driver leaned on his horn at 6 A.M. on a Saturday and infuriated neighbors she'd never spoken to and now never would—thank God, it had been almost impossible to shut, even without her notes. Thank God, she'd decided to bring another bag for her work rather than evict a few clothes.

"*Just* clothes?" Rebecca said, bestowing the same look on Annie that Annie had been treated to in front of the entire British fashion press at Marc Jacobs, the one that said, *You work for* Handbag *now. Start dressing like it.*

That was when Annie remembered the dress.

"Bollocks," she muttered. She'd only gone and mislaid a vintage Dior: and those beautiful, beautiful shoes. Annie had been harboring fantasies of losing them—at the back of her wardrobe. Triple bollocks.

"Can I help you ladies?" A portly Italian in pale blue shirtsleeves and navy suit trousers approached them smiling his best *uh-oh-tourists* smile.

"Yes pl—" Annie started. But Rebecca was already babbling fluently, gesticulating at Annie, at the pile, at the trolleys, and the man was nodding and smiling tensely, looking as intimidated as people usually felt on first encountering Rebecca Brooks in her native tongue. Iona and Annabel just looked bored, which seemed to be their default expression.

"He says he can't understand it," Rebecca informed Annie, although the man had barely uttered a word. "Apparently single cases hardly ever go missing. It's far more common for a whole batch to be loaded onto the wrong plane or for the ground staff to miss a trolleyful. Give him your details, flight number, hotel, address in London, the obvious, and when it turns up we'll send a driver to collect it. Meantime, I'm sure Annabel can borrow something for you to wear."

She looked Annie up and down and Annie shifted uncomfortably.

"You've lost weight," observed Rebecca, before adding, "Samples should be okay size-wise . . . I'm thinking Emporio, CK . . . And call Max and Company, I'm sure they'll be happy to help."

Annie just stood there like some kind of mannequin while Rebecca and Annabel sized her up and styled her up. Now she knew how models must feel, but at least they got paid for it.

It wasn't the loss of an irreplaceable designer frock, not to mention her Mantolini jacket, that bothered Annie so much as the fact that it was her case and her case alone that had gone missing. Lone cases almost never went missing, that's what the Italian had said. So why hers and why now? Out of a whole flight . . . A flight so overbooked there hadn't been a single empty seat, not even in business. A flight with a holdful of Vuitton suitcases stuffed with designer clothes and only her case, probably the dullest, cheapest, and least promising of the lot, had gone AWOL. Annie knew why; she had a creeping sense of discomfort and it had nothing to do with missing clothes. Something like this had happened once before, too recently for comfort.

In the last bleak days of the Kings Cross investigation Annie's previous bag had been stolen, and with it her diary and keys. After that the silent phone calls began, her flat was burgled, the boot of her old Mini crowbarred open. Annie still didn't know how they'd connected her to Irina. The point had been to save Irina and those like her, not land the girl in an early grave.

So what had gone wrong?

Annie was currently way off being a threat to anyone. All she had was a long list of suspicions and half clues. As of now, that meant she had more problems than her errant luggage. (1) They obviously thought she knew more than she did. (2) She didn't. Or if she did, she didn't yet know it. (3) She also didn't know who *they* were. (4) If she didn't know who *they* were, then how could she watch her own—or Patty's—back?

The others were way ahead of her now, through Customs and halfway across Arrivals, headed toward a chauffeur-driven Mercedes that waited patiently outside.

"Welcome to Milano," said an Italian police officer, waving her through. "Enjoy your stay."

Annie nodded, picking up most of what he'd just said.

You've spent too much time listening to Patty, she told herself. *You've lost all sense of perspective.* She had been last to check in, with the flight closing right behind her, so her case was probably still sitting at the Alitalia check-in, Heathrow terminal two, waiting for someone to notice it. That was the logical, nonparanoid, answer.

A small crowd waited outside Customs, a couple of taxi drivers chatted idly, large name boards hanging by their sides, a guy in blue overalls mopped an area of floor by the windows, and a gaggle of green-and-blue-clad Alitalia flight crew came out of baggage reclaim talking loudly. There was no sinister-looking man in a trench coat, collar upturned, pretending to read that morning's *La Stampa*. No one muttering darkly into a mobile—except Rebecca—and no one who looked like he had a sawed-off shotgun stuffed down his trousers.

"See," Annie told herself. "Why don't you just enjoy yourself."

She sounded like her mother.

chapter twenty-five

It was the roof gardens that struck Annie first, as *Handbag's* hired midnight-blue Mercedes E-class glided into northwest Milan. It was gray, it was cold, it was a Saturday afternoon in February. Milan was as gray as New York or London but still foliage spilled over roofs, softening the tops of austere stone buildings. Not in twee, English hanging-basket style, but robust, confident, statement making with evergreen plants and trees. Trees, for heaven's sake, on the roof!

And the buildings. Never having set foot in Italy before, Annie was entranced, gazing at the ornate, centuries-old palazzos that lined Milan's wide streets. Weather-beaten gray stone gave way to five-story confections of yellow, pink, and aquamarine, all faded by years of exposure to the smog for which Milanese summers were famous.

These sixteenth-century beauties rubbed shoulders with younger sisters, eighteenth- and nineteenth-century versions, occasionally interspersed by the kind of modern concrete blocks roundly condemned as architectural monstrosities.

Over the previous days Annie had zoned in and out as *Handbag's* fashion department bemoaned the next week's coming ugliness. "So urban, so gray, so industrial," had been the refrain.

So, are you blind? Annie wanted to yell, now confronted with Milan's austere elegance: If they wanted ugly they should try traveling home via the Westway. Okay, so Milan wasn't Rome or Florence, but it compared pretty favorably to Shepherds Bush.

Transfixed by an outbreak of rooftop greenery, Annie almost missed hearing the hum beneath her fade as the Mercedes slid to a halt outside a weathered palazzo, its façade lovingly carved from centuries-old gray stone. It was impressive. And not just because Annie knew what lay behind its imposing wooden doors.

"Frank will be collecting me at 4:30 for D & G," Rebecca told the others as her young Italian driver teleported from his seat to materialize beside Rebecca's door. It swung open, and she was up and out in one fluid movement.

"I've told him to collect you from your hotel at four to be with me in plenty of time." She was talking to Iona, although Annabel and Annie were undoubtedly included. "Make sure you're not late. I won't be kept waiting."

Hoisting her Birkin into the crook of her arm, Rebecca made as if to walk away and then stopped, spun on her heel, and stuck her head back through the open door.

"I shan't be needing him between now and then so, Annie—" She fixed her eyes on the backseat. "—if you need to use Frank to visit Patty—and I'm assuming you *will* be seeing Patty this afternoon—that will be fine."

There was nothing like being given a choice in the matter. Annie watched as her longed-for bath, head time, and maybe even an hour's sleep in the comparative safety of a locked hotel room sailed out of the Mercedes's window and off up the Corso Como.

"Remember," said Rebecca. "For the next week Frank works for *Handbag*. He won't be going anywhere we aren't and wherever we are he'll be waiting outside." And, with that, she marched into the darkened entrance, leaving a mini mountain of Louis Vuitton on the pavement beside the car.

"One ring on Frank's mobile will suffice," explained Iona. "He'll pick you up as arranged. Rebecca likes us to make sure the arrangements are precise. It's a very busy schedule this season," she added. "So there's no room for error."

Where do you lot think you are? Annie wanted to yell. *The upstairs bit of* Edwardian House? Fortunately Annie had long since learned to keep thoughts like that to herself, which didn't alter the fact that this was a twenty-first-century version of ringing a bell to summon a servant. It was probably lucky for Frank that he wasn't wearing a cap or he might be expected to doff it.

It was no big surprise that Rebecca was staying at 10 Corso Como, and Annie could hardly blame her. The lifestyle-compound-*cum*-shopping-emporium, and recently-launched-three-room-micro-hotel (aptly called three rooms), was fashion legend. To Annie it had sounded like an overpriced, overhyped, overrated B&B when she first heard the fashion department enthusing about it, but that was then. Now, although only the stone façade that protected the interior from prying eyes was visible, she could see what all the fuss was about. And she had a pretty good idea that she wouldn't be checking in anywhere even half so palatial.

"Isn't it amazing?" whispered Annabel, crammed between Annie and her fashion director boss in the backseat. Ignoring Iona's look of contempt, Annabel grinned. "It's incredible inside," she said, obviously having forgotten or forgiven the fact that her first job of the afternoon was to call in clothes for Annie. "Not that we'll get to see it," she added, "now that Rebecca's staying there. Her hotel is always strictly out of bounds in Milan. You know Rebecca, when she's on she's *on,* but when she's *off,* she's really off limits."

Surprise flickered across Annie's face. In her, admittedly limited, experience Rebecca Brooks was on twenty-four hours a day, seven days a week, and expected everyone else to be, too. The idea that her editor in chief had a life outside *Handbag* and the fashion industry, no matter how minimal, had never occurred to Annie.

"She does *off*?"

Annabel nodded. "Yeah, well, I guess you have to have some downtime when you've got a kid. Even if you're Rebecca."

Annie did a double take. A kid? "I had no idea . . ."

"Oh yeah," said Annabel. "Rupert, he's four. You remember that stuff about her marriage to the American guy? Ron, I think his name was. Ru's the result. Cute kid, apparently. Not that I've seen him. Iona has, though, haven't you? He was in the car that picked Rebecca up from Heathrow one time you flew back from New York."

Iona said nothing, her lips forming a line so thin they almost vanished. And then she turned pointedly to stare out of the car window.

"What does she do with the kid all week?" Annie asked. "I mean, when does she see him? She works all the time, day and night."

"But never weekends," Annabel pointed out. "Apart from, like now, during the shows. The rest of the time, Friday night through Monday mornings are sacred. *Rupert-time,* her old PA, Magda, called it. She used to say she wouldn't dare phone Rebecca after 6 P.M. on a Friday, even if the printers were burning down."

"Really?" Annie was about to probe further when Iona's head snapped away from the window. "For Christ's sake, Annabel," she snapped. "I don't think Rebecca really wants the whole world to know her business, do you?"

The deputy fell silent, and for a second Annie thought Annabel might cry.

"Tell me about the hotel," suggested Annie hastily, partly to spare the girl's embarrassment and partly because, well, you have to speculate to accumulate.

"Ten Corso Como?" Annabel perked up instantly. "It's fabulous," she said. "It's not just a shop, it's a . . . bazaar, more or less, full of clothes, furniture, *objets.* There's an art gallery, bookshop, café . . . Kind of like shopping in someone's home, assuming you know someone who lives in thirteen thousand square feet of Milanese palazzo full of Yohji and Prada and Arne Jacobsen. Rebecca was lucky to get a suite. Libby says it was booked for this season before *Handbag* even existed. Rebecca brought the booking with her from *Trend.*"

It seemed to Annie that Annabel was far more excited about this than Rebecca ever would be. To Rebecca, having the right seat at the right shows and staying at the right hotel was just part of the job.

Three rooms at 10 Corso Como was the ultimate *Handbag* hotel, hipper by far than the luxurious Four Seasons, Anna Wintour's habitual Fashion Week haunt in the heart of Milan's platinum-card shopping district, and far more sought-after than any other boutique hotel in the city. This season, it was *the* place to stay, and that Rebecca would stay there went without saying.

"The suites are something else." Annabel was still gushing. Annie just smiled. Mostly at Iona, who stared stonily through the window.

Ten minutes later they pulled up outside the Sheraton Diana. There was no trendily flaking stucco here. The place was immaculate. Its pristine cream walls and freshly scrubbed art deco balconies didn't just hint at refurbishment, they screamed it.

The Mercedes had barely slid to a halt before Frank was opening the back doors, summoning doormen, and unloading the remaining luggage from the boot.

"I'll check in later," said Annie as the others prepared to follow a procession of uniformed case carriers inside. "I have work to do."

Dare she put her feet on the seats? Annie gave her boots a cursory once-over. What the hell, she'd seen worse. Stretched across the full width of the Mercedes's backseat, she watched the curved façade of the Sheraton recede into the distance. It might be cold and damp outside but there would be no thirty-block hikes in subzero conditions for her this time, no more head-to-toe sludge baths courtesy of some sicko cabdriver.

Smiling to herself, Annie almost relaxed, then caught sight of Frank watching her in his rearview mirror and sat up straight, returning her feet to the floor.

"Dove ora?"

Presumably that was a request for directions, but where to start? Annie's Italian was just about on a par with her French, German, and Spanish. *Two beers please* was about the extent of it, and Annie wasn't even sure she could manage that now.

"Where to?" the driver asked, pulling up at some lights and turning to look over his elegantly suited shoulder. His English was near perfect, the merest hint of an accent.

"I—I thought you didn't speak English," stammered Annie, half appalled at the inanity of the conversation he'd been subjected to on the journey from Corso Como.

Nodding, Frank smiled, looking a touch too pleased with himself. "Francisco Giordano," he said and stretched out a hand to shake. "I study English at the university." He turned swiftly to pull away as the lights changed. "I drive during Fashion Week, the furniture fair, that kind of thing. It makes extra money and improves my English at the same time."

His English didn't seem in much need of improvement to Annie. Maybe he could boost his income giving backseat Italian lessons.

"I'm going to the Navigli district," she told him. "Via Tortona."

"Number?"

"Thirty-six." Annie watched him still watching her in the mirror. His gaze was beginning to unnerve her. Who was this guy anyway? Did all Milanese taxi drivers—Mercedes-chauffeuring ones—have English degrees and speak fluently with barely a trace of accent?

Snap out of it, Annie. "You drive Rebecca before?" she asked.

Frank shook his head. "First time."

"Ah . . ." Annie couldn't help wishing she hadn't told him the exact address, just let him drop her at the end of the street. He could easily have waited for her there. Waiting was part of his job, after all.

She risked another quick glance. Yes, he was still looking at her.

"So, you're going to the model village?" he asked.

Annie frowned, picturing a sort of Lilliputian Legoland.

Frank laughed, as if reading her mind. The thought made her twitchy.

"Where the models live," he said. "Via Tortona. The model agencies put the models there."

"Via Tortona. Is where all the models live," he repeated, his fluency fading with his confidence. "The model agencies. They put the models there."

A light went on in Annie's fogged brain. Of course, Patty had mentioned it, among other things. "Seriously? There's a village for models?"

"No, not really. It's just what locals call it because so many models live there. Via Tortona is full of apartments owned by the agencies. Thirty-six, where your friend is staying, is one of those."

Annie reran the conversation in her head. No, she definitely hadn't told Frank why she was going there. Instinctively she did a reccie of the back of the car. Kamikaze somersaults out of speeding vehicles weren't really her thing. Since the car was centrally locked, the question was probably immaterial.

"My friend? I didn't say I was going to see a friend."

"This Patty, she isn't a friend?" asked Frank, innocence and confusion written across his face, like a small boy who'd just yanked the cat's tail and didn't understand why he'd been slapped. "I'm sorry. Signora Brooks said you were going to see Patty. I assumed Patty was your friend."

Annie didn't believe him for one second.

chapter twenty-six

Milan's model village was about as far across town from the Sheraton as it was possible to get. That's if you went as the crow flies; if you opted to go as the chauffeur drives, it was substantially farther. The Mercedes pulled up outside green wooden double doors, flaking paint revealing ancient gray undercoat beneath. Annie practically flung herself from the car the second the engine lulled.

"Your friend is staying here," said Frank, pointing at the doors. He'd obviously recovered from his confusion. "I'll wait at the end of the road. More room to park there." As he spoke, his gaze swiveled 180 degrees. A group of young girls were walking past, rucksacks thrown over their shoulders, hair pulled back, faces scrubbed of makeup, tiny jeans hanging loose over child-like hips. They looked fifteen, at the most. Jailbait. Like Irina. Annie waited pointedly for Frank's head to swivel back in her direction.

"At the end of the road," she confirmed.

Indicating right, Frank slowed as he passed the group of girls on the corner. It didn't make him bad, just an unreconstructed Italian male, and, as yet, that wasn't any kind of criminal offense.

•   •   •

"Harry Potter," announced Patty, extracting the hefty paperback from where she'd wedged it under one armpit to free up a hand to open the door. Her other hand was clutching an unfamiliar white packet.

God forbid she should actually put her fags down for five minutes, Annie thought.

Catching Annie's glance, Patty smiled. "I know, I know," she said, speaking out of one side of her mouth. "Mark was always on at me to give up but, you know, one thing at a time . . ."

Wondering idly whether Patty had any Peroni in her fridge or a bottle of Chianti maybe, but all the while knowing the model was on a nicotine-only regime, Annie stepped through the front door and pushed it shut behind her, relaxing only when she'd heard the catch click shut.

"How are you doing?" Annie asked.

"Can't sleep. Figured I might as well do something with my time," said Patty. "So I'm reading this. It beats my own company."

Well, it wasn't exactly *War and Peace* but it wasn't the *National Enquirer,* either. Then Annie remembered: Patty refused to have the *National Enquirer* in the house, probably because she was one of their favorite subjects.

"Coffee?" Patty asked, tossing *Harry Potter and the Order of the Phoenix* onto the sofa.

Annie nodded. As stimulants went it would have to do.

The third-floor flat was small but less grim than Annie had expected, overlooking a courtyard where, should she want one, Patty had a good view of other models coming and going. The living area was almost cozy, with unexpected personal touches added by the dozens of models who'd stayed here over the years. A postcard tacked to the wall here, a tattered throw that looked like it had been picked up in Marrakech there. And books. A windowsill full of tattered paperbacks left by previous owners. Annie ran her finger along the small library, a few classics and plenty of trash, a mixture of A-level texts and impromptu airport purchases: *Tess of the d'Urbervilles, Jane Eyre, Valley of the Dolls, Bridget Jones's Diary, The Female Eunuch, Hollywood Wives, Memoirs of a Geisha,* a couple of crime

novels . . . It made for an interesting collective psychology of the flat's itinerant inhabitants. Interesting, too, that Patty had chosen Harry Potter—
not that Annie blamed her. Who needed Patricia Cornwell when you had
Patty's life?

Idly she reached for a crumpled cigarette packet, unconsciously straightening the cardboard. *Superleggera?* Rothmans? What happened to Patty's
Camels?

"Hey," said Annie, when the model reemerged bearing two enamel
cups of thick black liquid. *"Superleggera?"* Annie waved the packet at the
woman who stooped to hand her a cup and then took a seat opposite.
"You don't smoke *leggera,* let alone *superleggera.*"

"New city resolution." Patty smiled, took a slug of her coffee, and grimaced. "Figured if I couldn't give up I could at least cut back. I thought
it would be easier to trade quality than quantity. I picked those up at the
airport."

No wonder Patty had been dragging so hard on the phone the previous
night. Trying to get even half a Camel's worth out of those would take
some doing.

Now that Annie thought about it, Patty did look better. Less haggard.
The dark circles around her eyes were paler. She looked cleaner, too, her
straw-colored hair five shades lighter for having been reacquainted with
shampoo. A vast improvement on her appearance five days earlier, and
nothing like as rattled as she'd sounded on the phone before Annie caught
her flight. In fact, nothing at all like a woman who hadn't slept for a week.
Annie couldn't help wondering why.

"You getting on all right without, uh, anything?" Annie ventured.

"Yes, Mom," said Patty mildly, but Annie could see the hurt in her eyes.

"Sorry," she said. God, she'd be asking Patty if she was eating properly
and taking vitamins next. "I'm just worried," Annie explained apologetically. "You seemed, you know, pretty upset on the phone last night."

For a split second Patty seemed to glow, and Annie could see what had
made her a supermodel in the first place. Her entire face lit up and energy
sparked from her eyes. "I was," she said, springing up. "But now I see . . .
Now I see what it means, how important it is. I didn't before." She
sounded like she was about to announce she was born again.

Vanishing through a door that led off the main room, she was back in seconds, holding a crumpled newspaper clipping. "I found this." She shoved the tatty piece of paper into Annie's hand. "It was tucked into Mark's laptop case. In his pile of rubbish by the bed. I was gonna tell you about it last night but, I dunno . . . It just didn't feel safe to talk about."

POLICE BUST COUNTERFEITING RING!

It was a small piece, less than half a column. From a local paper probably, given the familiarity of its tone. Annie turned the clipping over, examining it. The paper was still white-ish, and the newsprint unfaded. That made it recent. Whoever cut the page—and she was assuming it was Mark—had cut so neatly that all trace of the publication's name had been removed and the date trimmed in half. At a guess the date looked like February 8; there was definitely a curved single digit, but equally it might have been a three.

Scanning down the article, it didn't take Annie long to discover the headline was wildly inaccurate. The police hadn't "bust counterfeiting ring" at all, they'd simply hauled in the New Jersey middleman who was taking delivery. Reading between the lines, a more accurate headline would have been *Local Cops Blow Counterfeiting Bust! Feds Furious!*

Still, she now knew it was a New Jersey paper, and there couldn't be too many of those. It would be the work of five minutes to find out who'd run this story and the date it ran, if only she had access to the Internet. Mentally crossing her fingers, Annie prayed Libby would have thought of that when she booked the hotel.

"You see," Patty said. "See what I mean?" She was standing next to Annie, reading it over her shoulder.

Annie stared at the clipping, rerunning every detail. This was what she did best, make connections, get under the skin of things. That was how she got to Irina. How she got her job on the *Post* in the first place.

Now that she looked at it, Annie could see some significance. The interest wasn't in some foot soldier who got busted taking delivery of fake goods to be shipped around the country. It was in the goods themselves. A list of Italian designer labels as long as Rebecca's new-season shopping list, which explained the reference to the European Anti-Counterfeiting Group. At the foot of the list, almost tagged onto the Pradas, the Armanis, and the Versaces, the household Italian brands the local paper's Jersey audience would know, came Fava, Mantolini, and the shoe label Borgias.

"I'm right, aren't I?" Patty said, patience snapping as she reached across to grab the slip of paper, rereading words she must already know by heart. "This has to do with why he was killed, doesn't it?"

"Maybe." That was when Annie decided they should take a walk, get out into the open air, and lose themselves in the noise of the streets.

"It's more difficult to bug people when they're moving," Annie said, then realized her attempt to reassure Patty had only made things worse. "Not that I think you're being bugged," she added. "It's just a precaution."

At nearly three in the afternoon the weak winter sunshine had long since given up its battle with the gray clouds that hung low over their heads. Annie had taken an instinctive left out of the courtyard, heading in the opposite direction from the one chosen by Frank and the Mercedes and straight into an oncoming February wind that roared down Via Tortona.

The street was almost deserted. Given the wind, the premature twilight, and the constant threat of rain, Annie wasn't surprised. Crossing over, they headed down a narrow alley that Patty assured Annie would lead to the Naviglio Grande and the canal district.

Whether Patty's sense of direction could be relied on Annie had no idea, but anything was better than walking Via Tortona in full view of anyone watching. And if the driver had been sent to keep an eye on her— and looked at rationally there was no reason to believe he had—Annie had no intention of letting him do so from the centrally heated comfort of his Mercedes. If Frank Giordano wanted to follow, he could freeze his arse off with the rest of them.

You're being paranoid, Annie told herself, but cut under an arch anyway, sidestepping between a building and a wall in what she hoped was the direction of the canal.

"Not you, too," said Patty crossly. "That's what Anya said. I figured at least you'd believe me."

"Anya's here?"

"No," said Patty. "She couldn't make it. Family stuff."

Annie sighed. She really needed to stop talking to herself.

The wind became harsher as they reached the banks of the Naviglio Grande and a line of cars parked next to buildings in various states of renovation. The place reminded Annie of Camden in London, north of the lock.

Thanks to a few stalwart tourists determined to see the sights regardless of the weather, the towpath was—if not exactly thronging—then crowded enough to hide them. A troop of teenage boys stamped past, followed by a young couple who loitered on the bank. Now it felt safe to talk.

"Can I bum a cigarette?" Annie asked.

"Hey lady," Patty mocked. "*You* want a cigarette? Don't you know they're addictive?" But she smiled all the same and offered Annie her packet.

"So," said Annie. "Let's take this from the top. You think Mark was murdered?"

Patty nodded.

"Why?"

"Because two-bit pieces of shit like Michael Watt don't kill people like Mark." Patty's voice was vehement. "It doesn't happen. Mark had friends. Connections."

Annie thought about that. "Surely that makes it more likely to be random, an accident?" She shrugged. "I mean, if he had *friends*." Annie wasn't sure how much emphasis to put on that last word.

"You're missing the point," said Patty. "That cop said Michael Watt had been one of Donnie Cassano's errand boys. You think an asshole like Watt didn't know The Elephant was protected?"

Okay, now Annie got it. *That* kind of protected.

"So," said Annie. "Who organized it?" Assuming anyone did, which was still a massive assumption in Annie's book.

"Mariolina Mantolini," Patty said decisively.

Taken aback, Annie stared at Patty, cigarette hanging forgotten from her hand. "Why would Mariolina Mantolini have Mark killed?"

"Because Mark was going to sign with her and changed his mind." Patty looked Annie straight in the eye. There was no hint of doubt.

"I think that's who the row was with," she added before Annie could interrupt. "He was thinking of going with Mariolina. I was surprised, you know, because I thought he'd go the other way. The Fava deal was more clear-cut. Baroni funded Mark's label and got the hip connection. It didn't seem to be any more complicated than that, and Mark liked to keep things simple. But Mariolina's father knew Guido so, you know, it wouldn't have been my choice, but Mark said he liked her, liked what House of Mantolini stood for, that history thing again, and thought he could work with her. They'd worked out a deal—you saw, on that letter I showed you—not a straightforward backing deal, more a mutual arrangement."

Annie nodded. "Well, it's a theory," she said.

"It's more than a theory. Something went wrong. Something changed. I think he found out something, something he didn't like. That argument on the roof, when he was on that cell phone, our fight afterward . . . Mark seemed, you know, well, scared." Patty hesitated, unsure whether to share something or not. "Scared enough to talk to a journalist." She paused, fixing her blue eyes on Annie. "You. Plus, after that call he said I couldn't do his show." Patty dropped the stub of her cigarette and ground it under the heel of her boot. "I wanted to, he said no. At the time I thought he was trying to hurt me, but now I see he was trying to protect me."

Annie struggled not to look skeptical. More likely Mark had been protecting Patty from herself and the paparazzi. Maybe even protecting his own reputation, on the cusp of a lucrative buyout, from yet another front-page scandal.

"Have you told anyone else about this? Guido? The police?"

Patty laughed. "Yeah, really."

For once Annie wished Patty had. Maybe this time they would have taken the model seriously. But right this second there were more immediate problems.

"You realize you can't go tomorrow, don't you?"

Patty frowned. "Why?"

"Why do you think?" Dropping her own cigarette on the cobbles, Annie was unable to suppress her exasperation. "You just told me you think Mariolina Mantolini had Mark killed and now you're planning to go to her party. Were you born stupid?"

Annie had gone too far. Pushing Patty to see what gave was one thing, but good cop–bad cop worked only when there were two of you. Trying it single-handed was a recipe for schizophrenia.

Patty was staring at her, eyes so hurt that Annie looked away, unable to hold her gaze.

"I'm not stupid," she said quietly, looking straight at Annie, daring her to talk back. "Mark was my husband. Someone killed him."

Annie nodded, shamed by the pale blue eyes that pierced hers. Taking Patty's arm, she walked to the edge of the water and pulled up in the shadow of a tree.

"I'm sorry, Patty," she said gently. "I didn't mean it, I'm just worried. You mustn't go to Villa Mantolini tomorrow. If you're wrong you'll embarrass yourself. If you're right—and I'm not saying you are—then you're putting yourself in danger. Don't do it."

"I'm sorry, too," said Patty. "But I'm going. That's why I came here. I have to know. And anyway Guido's already arranged the introduction."

Of course. She should have known Guido would be involved somewhere. "What has Guido arranged?" Annie asked, slipping her arm lightly around the taller woman's waist. Annie could feel ribs through Patty's peacoat. Not just through the coat, but through jumper, T-shirt, and even skin.

"I'm staying at Mariolina's," Patty said. "She's sending a car to collect me tomorrow afternoon and bring me back Monday morning."

Before Annie even had time to point out how bad an idea that was they were both startled by the sound of a mobile phone. "Yours," Patty said. "I left mine in the flat."

Rebecca probably, checking up.

Extracting the phone from a tangle of papers and wires, Annie pushed a button to illuminate the darkened screen. Not Rebecca . . . Annie didn't recognize the number at all and there was no name, so it wasn't in the phone's address book.

"Hello?"

"Miss Anderson." The voice was familiar. "It's time to go. Is four o'clock. We are already late to collect Signora Brooks. Where shall I pick you up?"

Annie frowned. Why would Frank assume he'd pick her up anywhere other than where he'd dropped her? Her mind swam with myriad, probably unfounded, suspicions that were draining her courage.

"You go ahead. Get Rebecca. Tell her I'm still with Patty. She knows who that is, she'll understand."

Although Annie wasn't as convinced as she sounded, Frank seemed to buy it.

"Okay, Miss Anderson. I won't be able to come back later, though. Signora Brooks needs me all evening."

"That's fine," Annie assured him. "I'll get a cab. You go and collect Rebecca and if you're late, blame me. She won't have any trouble believing that."

Happy to be free of the driver and the demands of her schedule, Annie tossed the Nokia back into her bag and stood beside Patty, following her gaze down to the unforgiving gray water. She didn't notice the man standing in the trees fifty yards behind her who snapped shut his phone and slipped it into the inside pocket of his suit, just below his shoulder holster, before turning to walk away.

Her missing suitcase had been waiting at the Sheraton Diana's reception when Annie finally made it back from Patty's flat—exhausted, frozen, and bedraggled from an insidious frizz-inducing drizzle that soaked into her as she walked from one side of Milan to the other. An hour's walk made worse by the hour she'd wasted hanging around on a variety of street corners in the futile hope of hailing a cab.

Why, in all the tidbits of advice contained in Rebecca's gospel (an e-mail of advice, instructions, and expectations sent before the ready-to-wear shows began), was there nothing about hailing cabs, and the futility of even contemplating it on the darkened streets of Milan? Because she'd never had to do it, that's why.

As for whoever thought it was a good idea to cloak the streets of Italy's fashion capital in cobbles, it had to have been a man, Annie decided as her spike heels finally regained solid ground and the pavements of Corso Venezia.

"When did this turn up?" she demanded, relinquishing her passport and company credit card to the young woman behind reception.

The desk clerk shrugged. Her hair, dyed a kind of orangey blond that Annie had already come to think of as Milanese ginger, stayed frozen in place, Elnetted to within an inch of its life.

"A man, he brought it. He said it had gone missing."

"Young guy, short dark hair, good suit, dark blue Mercedes."

To be fair, the description could have fit almost any of a dozen drivers stationed outside the hotels of central Milan awaiting a summons from their employer-for-the-week. The receptionist could be forgiven for not being able to put a name to a face.

"Si, uh yes, maybe . . . sorry, I, uh, not sure," said the receptionist. "You need help with your bags?"

Bag, corrected Annie automatically, and shook her head. There was no way she was letting this baby out of her sight again, even for the minute or so it might take to reach the third floor. "No thanks," she said. "I can carry it myself."

Dumping the case on the single bed, Annie gave her room a rapid once-over: windows, shut, no lock; wardrobe empty, too few hangers; bed hovering just inches from the rust carpet. And then, suddenly realizing she couldn't remember the last time she'd used the loo, Annie checked it out, went back to lock the bedroom door, and left the bathroom door open.

Hefting the case onto her knee, Annie examined every millimeter of its scuffed black surface for evidence of a forced entry. There was none, but there didn't need to be, because getting into the case would be simplicity itself. The padlock was gone. The question was, had it ever been there in the first place?

Annie couldn't remember. The only thing on her mind that morning had been catching the fashion bus. She had a clear image of herself charging from kitchen to bedroom, grabbing knickers from a cold tumble dryer, pulling socks out of drawers and hurling in bras, slowing only to lay the vintage Dior on top, carefully ensuring it didn't snag as she zipped her Samsonite shut. The result? A case that looked like it had been ransacked. And she still couldn't remember whether or not she'd locked it.

Every instinct told Annie she had and, until a few months ago, she would have bet her life on those instincts. Had, on more than one occasion. But now . . .

If all else fails, ransack the mini bar, she told herself, before systematically removing every single garment from her case. By the time she reached the bottom Annie was almost certain nothing had gone. She couldn't account for every last sock, but then while she'd counted them out, she hadn't counted them in.

A fashion thief might have recognized the vintage lace dress for the designer treasure it was and made off with it, but this wasn't the work of a fashion thief. A fashion thief would have opted for a more promising-looking case to start with. Whoever had intercepted Annie's case had been after a different sort of valuable altogether. The kind safely hidden in her bag in an overhead locker.

Not clever, Annie thought, not clever at all. They hadn't even relieved her of the adored Gina shoes that still lay at the bottom in all their pink satin glory. Surely if someone had wanted to make it look random they would at least have done that?

chapter twenty-seven

"*. . . Prada.*"

Annie turned to stare, in a manner she very much hoped was icy, at the woman sitting beside her in the back of the Mercedes.

"What?" she hissed. *Have you got against me?* she wanted to add, but kept the thought to herself. Anyway, she knew the answer. Iona believed it was Annie's intention to shove her off the "Rebecca's favorite" pedestal that had previously been her own. For all Annie cared, Iona could have her bloody plinth back! She didn't like it up there anyway, way too conspicuous and way too chilly. Not least because Rebecca was now furious, in a glacial sort of way.

"I said," Iona whispered—although, schooled by Rebecca, she'd acquired their boss's talent for pitching her whisper so it was anything but—"you missed Prada. *Prada.* I had to move Annabel forward to fill your seat in the *second* row so the PR wouldn't put you down as a no-show."

Annie didn't mind being in the doghouse but she preferred to have put herself there intentionally. D&G she could just about get away with missing. She should have known that Prada she couldn't. She *so* couldn't. The show had been twenty-four hours earlier and still Rebecca hadn't spoken a single word to her, not even communicating via a henchperson.

Watching the back of Frank's head, Annie tried to summon a suitably cutting response, one that was neither juvenile nor sycophantic. Something mature, appropriate, and sophisticated, like pulling the head off Iona's Sindy doll or sawing through the heel on her new Manolos. Frank appeared oblivious to the whole proceedings as he rode the white lines of autostrada nine at a solid 110 kilometers in the dark, steering the Mercedes in an elegant waltz from middle to fast lane and back without so much as a tap on the brakes. They were on their way to Lake Como, Mariolina Mantolini's party.

He wasn't as oblivious as he seemed. Annie knew that, and she wondered if anyone else in the car did—if Rebecca, so keen to demonstrate her fluent Italian, had the slightest inkling her driver's English was near perfect.

Forgetting Frank for a moment, Annie discarded cheap thoughts of revenge. She'd just worked out a far better way to piss Iona off.

"I'm sorry," Annie said, leaning toward Rebecca.

Her boss remained silent. Although the slightest tilt of her head signified that she might just be prepared to listen.

"I know I should have been at Prada last night," Annie said, "but I thought Patty was more important. I was wrong. I'm sorry if I've embarrassed the magazine or caused problems for you with Prada." As if.

There were so many hooks in the sticky bait of that apology that Rebecca barely knew where to begin.

"You were right," said Rebecca. "Patty *is* more important. And of course your absence won't cause me problems." Rebecca smiled, nodded to herself at the absurdity of the very suggestion. Problems? Rebecca Brooks?

"You must fill me in . . . We need to concentrate on Miranda Lawson tonight, so it'll have to be tomorrow morning. Why don't you come to Ten Corso Como for breakfast?"

"Of course," Annie said, while Iona simmered beside her.

"There should be plenty of time before MaxMara and Fava," Rebecca continued. "Which reminds me, have you spoken to their press office at all? Might make an interesting addition to the Mailer piece. After all, Ugo's still claiming the Mailer deal was his."

"They both are," Annie replied. " Mantolini, too. I'm waiting for both to get back to me."

High above the side of the lake a church bell tolled, calling the faithful to the Sunday-evening service. Birds swooped over the water's surface, hungry and hunting. And Annie sat in the backseat of Rebecca's Mercedes, considering whether taking the job at *Handbag* had been such a good move after all.

Breathtaking as the scenery had been ever since they'd left the autostrada to take a lakeside road northeast of Como, nothing could have prepared Annie for the sight that awaited her as the Mercedes turned off just before Bellagio. Appearing as if from nowhere in front of them as they rounded a bend, the Villa Mantolini loomed majestically above the bay. It was no happy accident. The villa was built to be seen, day or night, winter or summer, its ocher-and-cream stucco revealed by up-lighters from every angle. A statue of a mounted condottierei glared down at the Mercedes as Frank slowed to let his passengers appreciate the full grandeur of the house. Covering four floors with what looked like a hundred rooms, it oozed arrogant luxury from every window.

"We wait here for while," he said, killing the engine. Although the villa was clearly visible, they still seemed a horribly long way off. But then so was the long line of limousines in front of them, all waiting to be parked. The fash pack had come to Lake Como.

It took almost an hour to crawl the final three hundred paces to the foot of the stone staircase that led up to the villa's spectacular entrance, as long again as the trip from Milan. The stairs swept dramatically across the front of the villa and back again in four lavish upward swoops.

Annie half expected to see the steps adorned with the obligatory red carpet—not very fashion, but very Hollywood, and here the two seemed to combine. Instead, the steps were lined with enormous church candles almost as tall as Annie, interspersed with what could only be described as footmen, albeit footmen clad head-to-toe in Mantolini menswear.

One candle, three footmen, one candle, three footmen . . . Presumably the footmen came cheaper than the huge beeswax candles. And what footmen they were, perfect tens to a man. Each step was strewn with delicate white flowers that weren't faring well under the onslaught of heels raining down on them. From where Annie stood, next to Iona and behind Rebecca at the foot of the stairs, the flowers looked very much like . . .

"Daisies," said Iona, "Miranda Lawson's favorite, apparently," answering the question Annie hadn't asked, transparently delighted to have the opportunity to display her superior knowledge. "Sweet, isn't it?"

Oh yeah, thought Annie. About as sweet as Woolworth flip-flops and Wal-Mart vests on a New York front row in February. It reeked of creating conflict, defying expectations . . . It reeked of Christy, the über-stylist, self-proclaimed, real most-powerful-woman-in-Hollywood.

The crowd was thickening now, spilling from chauffeur-driven cars and sweeping slowly upward, carrying Annie up the steps in their wake. Ahead of her, feet strapped into shoes that doubled as works of architectural genius and had probably cost the national debt of Guatemala climbed steps and crushed daisies, while a sea of little black designer dresses and cleverly-cut-to-conceal-middle-aged-spread tuxedos rolled in waves up the steps to either side. So this was what the beautiful people did with their weekends . . .

The cream of the worlds of fashion and film ascended the stone staircase of Villa Mantolini, greeting and air-kissing, ticking names off their personal must-schmooze lists as they went. The paparazzi fought for pole position at the foot of the staircase, and the footmen stood beautifully to attention between the impossibly large candles the color of old ivory. And that was before you even considered the guests who were already inside and those who were yet to be released from the waiting limousines.

Unsure quite what she was meant to be looking for, Annie couldn't see it, couldn't see anything but the throng around her. It was a lost cause and

214 • SAM BAKER

she gave it up willingly, allowing herself to revel in the spectacle. The one time she'd attended a party approaching this glamorous had been in London, as a waitress, and even then she hadn't been legit. So she planned to enjoy actually being allowed through the front door. Which was just as well, because at the head of the staircase stood an imposing man, elderly but erect in a starched dinner jacket, flanked by three young women with caramel dresses bandaged around their curves, who collected the starched white invitations, spot-checking names against a guest list.

Behind her, an outbreak of hysteria from the papps told Annie someone who really was someone had arrived.

"*Signorina, prego! Prego!*"

"Miranda, over here, Miranda! Miranda!"

"Give us a smile, Miranda!"

"Let's see the frock, love!"

Although looking over your shoulder was strictly in breach of the gospel, Rebecca was now so far ahead—ticking off as many air kisses as possible—that Annie dared to turn and stare like the tourist she was: Miranda Lawson and Robert Dellavecchia, both head-to-toe in what, had it been a shade of paint, would definitely have been called daisy white. They'd climbed from a similarly hued limousine and were standing, hand in hand, smiling unseeing into a blaze of flashbulbs, temporarily blinded to everything but their own fame.

The crowds, the bay, the picturesquely lit villages nestled up the hill to one side, the centuries-old grandeur of the magnificent villa itself, all were burned into shadow by the harsh glow of tomorrow's front page.

Annie would willingly have bet her shoes and the Dior dress that la Lawson was a houseguest at the Villa Mantolini and had just taken the long drive from a side door to the foot of the stone steps to make her entrance.

The words of her boss rang in Annie's ears.

Always be seen to arrive.

chapter twenty-eight

The flickering light of a thousand candles greeted Annie. Traditional white candlesticks suspended on immense chandeliers hung from high ceilings. The human-sized pillars of wax that had adorned the stone steps also lined the entrance, and countless tea lights were borne aloft on silver trays. The effect was flattering, rendering bags, crow's-feet, and wrinkles instantly invisible. More candles led the way through the marble-floored hall toward gigantic cedar doors, pulled back to reveal a banqueting room even more colossal than the hall in which Annie still stood. Beyond that, huge French windows opened into two marquees of almost blinding whiteness.

For a second Annie felt she'd strayed into a fairy tale. Like Alice, if she stood on tiptoe, she didn't expect to be able to reach the door handles.

On the right of the entrance hall, an ornate Carrara marble staircase swept up to join an elaborate Romeo-and-Juliet-style balcony. A tiny, dark-haired woman stood dead center, surveying the noisy crowd below, a faint smile playing at her lips; whether with pride at the success of Mantolini's comeback or amusement at the ease with which she'd commanded the great and good to dance at her feet, it was impossible to tell.

Simply dressed in a high-necked champagne silk dress that on anyone else would have been unqualified frump, black hair coiled into an elegant chignon at the nape of her neck, and standing little over five feet tall, Mariolina Mantolini would have been passed over by any but the most observant eye. A person might have walked past her on a Milan street without a second glance, but as Annie took in the fierceness of her host's gaze she knew they never had.

Mariolina was one of those who could silence a room just by entering it, and not for the usual reasons. No fake class or manufactured cool, thought Annie. Unlike most of those Mariolina surveyed, many of whom could not deny they carried a little of the fraud about them. Miranda Lawson might fill the tabloids and the gossip columns but Mariolina Mantolini . . . She was hard news. Here was a woman who knew what she wanted for the House of Mantolini and was determined to have it. Wondering just how far Mariolina might be prepared to go to get it, Annie's thoughts returned to Patty and the more pressing issue of how to set about finding her in this sea of black.

Waiters moved among the crowds bearing golden platters. The champagne was gratefully received; the canapés remained largely untouched. Taking advantage of a prolonged separation from her boss, Annie took a glass of golden bubbles from a passing tray and stared around the room. *Just the one,* she warned herself, taking a sip. *You're on duty.* She didn't know the label, but she knew it was good. Since she'd started on *Handbag* she'd drunk more champagne in four weeks than in her entire twenty-eight years, weddings included, and this was unquestionably the best by far.

Half an hour later and two laps of four rooms—both tents, the entrance hall, and the banqueting hall—Annie felt as if she'd done a half-marathon, but still had seen no sign of Patty.

Another sip, another glass, and Annie's champagne was soured with a bitter aftertaste of guilt. What was she doing at Villa Mantolini, sipping champagne and rubbernecking, when her case study had gone AWOL in the heart of a prime suspect's lair? Rebecca would kill her if anything happened to Patty, which was nothing to what Ken Greenhouse would do if he could see her now.

Annie did another circuit: entrance hall and banqueting hall, marquee one, marquee two, orbiting large white-clothed tables where the fasherati compared seats and outfits and Mariolina Mantolini, now descended from her aerie, flitted from table to table holding court. At a table to Annie's right, Miranda Lawson listened politely to a minor European royal, while Rebecca Brooks stuck to her June cover star like glue. No über-VIP areas here. Signora Mantolini was wise enough to know that, in their own eyes at least, each of her glittering guests was an über-VIP.

As Patty was quite obviously absent from all of these rooms, Annie decided to try elsewhere. A couple of doors opened onto narrow stairwells that appeared to spiral belowground and a third had brought a footman running, begging leave to show the signorina the way to the bathroom. Even concealed by the throng, Annie's every move was soon attracting the attentions of one servant or another, bringing each one rushing down on her as if every door she opened tripped some sort of wire to their brains. Surely Mariolina's staff had better things to do, like serve champagne and prosciutto canapés to several hundred very high-maintenance guests?

But no.

Who knew that being loaded had its downside? The thought had never occurred to Annie before, but maybe privacy and freedom of movement were wealth's first casualties.

Much as it galled her, Annie had to confront the unpleasant fact that if she wanted to get more than ten yards without having her host's dogs set on her, she had no alternative but to ask. Annie wasn't into this above-board thing at all. Life was so much easier when you could use the trades-man's entrance.

"Scusi," she asked the next waiter who tried oh-so-politely to prevent her from opening a door she wasn't meant to open. "I'm looking for my friend. She's staying here, with Signora Mantolini."

"Signor*ina* Mantolini, she has very few houseguests," the waiter replied.

"Oh, she's definitely here," said Annie, more confidently than she felt. "Patty—Signorina Lang—she arrived this afternoon. Very tall, blond-ish, thin—very thin, big blue eyes. She's a model . . ." Annie's voice trailed off. That description could have fit any number of the women who roamed the rooms around her.

The waiter gave her a look, the look very busy staff give clients, customers, and guests they suspect are wasting their time. *"Una seconda,"* he said, brandishing his empty tray like a shield, and vanished into the crowd.

Within seconds he was back with the stern-faced man who'd taken Annie's ticket earlier.

"You say you are a friend of Signora Mailer?" he asked.

Signora *Mailer?* When did that happen? Annie did a double take while her face, ever mindful of appearances, smiled obligingly. What was Patty thinking? Announcing herself as Mark's widow? Did she have a death wish or something?

"Okay, Signorina. Signorina . . . ? "

"Anderson," said Annie, "Annie Anderson," and watched recognition flicker in his eyes. Damn this doing everything by the book.

"Ah yes," he twisted his mouth and shrugged, *why not?*

Through an arch cut into the wall, up some back stairs, and along corridor after corridor, Annie followed the old man, absorbing the contrasting décor. Marble floors in the public areas, uncarpeted stone stairs for servants' use, Murano glass mirrors in fantastic frames but speckled beneath the surface with age; the stark contrast of public ostentation and private poverty, or was it penny-pinching? From what she'd heard and read, until Mariolina Mantolini returned to the fold and took the family business in hand, the House of Mantolini had come precariously close to bankruptcy. When people wrote that, were they talking about the family or the firm?

With every step, the babble of voices and the distant jazz band grew fainter until they reached an area Annie guessed was toward the rear of the villa. The walls were painted a muted blue, and heavy oak doors led off on either side. Here the noise was so remote the party could have been several miles away, up the coast in Bellagio itself, subtly heard through an open window if the wind was in the right direction.

"Here." The elderly man stopped abruptly.

Annie overshot him.

"This begins the guest wing. It is very private up here. Signora Mailer, she is in the suite at the end." He waved a hand toward a far wall where a carved door faced them some fifteen or twenty paces away, then turned back the way he'd come. "Signora Mailer knows the way downstairs."

With the majordomo gone, the corridor was almost entirely silent. If there were other guests staying in the wing they weren't here now. Probably downstairs drinking champagne, Annie thought, wishing for a split second she was, too. Guiltily, Annie suppressed the thought.

"Patty?" She said the word aloud, although not loud enough for public consumption, as if testing it. "Are you there?"

There was no answer so Annie took a few more steps toward the door, heels ringing on the tiles. For some reason she hadn't noticed how loud they were when hers hadn't been the only ones.

"Patty?" Louder now, definitely loud enough for Patty to hear, even behind the thickest wooden door. Loud enough for Annie's voice to echo down the corridor behind her. *Patt-y-y-y.*

Still nothing.

At the door Annie stopped, aware that the buzz of voices she could now hear came not from the distant party two floors below but from behind the door in front of her. A television, of course, Patty's ubiquitous background companion.

"Patty!" Annie rapped on the door, feeling a dull thud as her knuckles hit ancient oak. "It's me, Annie!"

There was no answer.

A harder knock drew the same result. She was probably having a shower, reasoned Annie, sucking her knuckles. Patty would never be able to hear anyone call over the thunder of water.

Annie pushed at the door handle, more for something to do than because she expected it to open, but it did, swinging inward on recently oiled hinges.

The room was dim with no light but for the glow of an Italian soap playing to itself on the TV in one corner and a harsh yellow line spilling under a door in the far wall. A bathroom, it had to be, no other room would have such unflattering light. There was no sound of water draining from a bath, no loo flushing or shower running, and certainly no towel-draped supermodel stamping out to confront the trespasser.

Annie reached for a light switch, just as she would if returning to her room, but she pulled back her hand before it made contact. Instinct, cold and ugly, also told her not to touch anything unless absolutely necessary.

"Patty, you in here?" Annie's voice was higher-pitched than she intended, overlaid with concern as she took in Patty's unmade bed and the copy of Harry Potter lying facedown, broken-spined, on the carpet. At the foot, partly hidden by thrown-back blankets, lay a slash of purple satin, and on the floor beneath this, ready to step into, stood a pair of strappy Manolos, dyed purple to match the one-shoulder dress.

The room was a mess, though Annie had seen worse, Patty's flat for starters. This was the scene left by someone who'd decided to take a nap and woken two hours later, very, very late for a date.

Pushing the door shut behind her, Annie noticed a bottle of Stolichnaya almost half empty on a small walnut bedside cabinet. Next to it an ashtray overflowed with the bent and twisted white filters of Patty's Rothmans.

Stoli? Patty didn't drink vodka. She didn't drink anything. The woman was a recovering addict, for Christ's sake. Alcohol might not be her drug of first choice but it was still out of bounds. Had Patty hit the bottle? Or maybe someone else had been in here . . . Annie didn't know which was worse.

Propelled by a sense of hideous inevitability, Annie was across the room in a second, which was all it took to screen a number of possible nightmares in her head. Patty soaking in the bath, too drunk to get out; Patty ready to go but for her frock, staring frozen and tearful at her reflection as she tried to apply mascara; no Patty at all because she'd wandered inebriated and semi-naked out into Mariolina's party.

None of them greeted her.

Annie gave the bathroom door a push and it opened slightly to reveal an empty tub, not even the foamy scum of a bubble bath lining its bottom. So she pushed more and the door bounced back in her face.

Annie felt nausea rise inside her.

"No!" The voice was scarcely recognizable, though she'd heard it before. It came from somewhere deep inside, a groan crossed with a scream and bitten off into silence.

Forcing the door enough to squeeze through, Annie automatically stepped over the body in her way.

Patty lay awkwardly, head half propped against a wall, one arm twisted up behind her. At first glance, anyone might think she had slipped and fallen—but for the empty pot of Vicodin that had rolled away across smooth horsehair marble and lodged beneath a basin.

The vodka was beginning to make an ugly sort of sense.

"Shit." Annie sat on the side of the bath, still competent enough to notice that it was cold. No long hot bath had been had in here this evening.

Keep calm, she told herself. *You've seen it before, more than once. All the same . . .*

Annie didn't scream or even shout for help. Instead she crouched next to Patty's body, naked but for sheer mesh hipster knickers that stopped just below razor-sharp hip bones, feeling for a pulse.

"Not like this," Annie begged. "Please let her be all right, let her live." A prayer whispered in her head escaped through open lips.

"Thank you . . ."

There it was, distant and faint and growing fainter with each beat, but the pulse was still there.

Putting her hand under Patty's neck, Annie tilted her head back as far as possible, banging it against the marble floor as she did so.

"Sorry," said Annie automatically.

She prized open Patty's mouth with shaking fingers and checked the position of her tongue. It was clear, good.

Don't think, she told herself. *Don't worry about whether it's going to work. You can do it.*

Pinching Patty's nose with her free hand, Annie took a deep breath.

It took Annie three goes before it happened. Then Patty's ribs moved of their own accord, definitely. Hope soaring, Annie blew again, a fourth time, and was rewarded with a cough as Patty's body lurched of its own volition; air filling her lungs, choking her back to the life she had wanted to call time on.

Patty vomited, white froth splashing into Annie's face. The acrid smell of vodka and something else, stagnation and worse, filled the bathroom.

Translucent and veined, Patty's eyelids flickered. She was alive, but only just.

Annie forgot all caution. Forgot all about shock and recovery positions. In her haste to evict as much alcohol and barbiturate as possible from Patty's body, Annie heaved the model onto her knees and wrapped her arms around Patty's stomach from behind. Ignoring the brittle ribs she could feel under her hands Annie clutched Patty's distended stomach and pulled upward again and again until the model vomited.

Only when Patty knelt moaning in a pool of liquid that said her stomach had seen nothing recently but vodka, pills, and copious amounts of black Italian coffee did Annie allow herself to relax.

"Why did you do it?" Annie asked, knowing Patty was nowhere near being able to give her an answer. "Why did you give up?" Distractedly she lifted a handful of Patty's hair out of a puddle of vomit. As she did so something caught Annie's eye; old faded scars on the back of Patty's neck, nestling in the roots of her hair. Annie didn't need telling they were track marks. And the full scale of the model's past addiction hit her.

"I'll be right back," Annie promised.

White froth dripped from her black dress and trickled onto bare legs as she ran from the bathroom, kicking off her shoes before hurtling through the bedroom door and down the corridor.

"*Scusi!*" she shouted, hollow voice echoing from the walls. Not loud enough, the thick stone and heavy doors deadened her words, just as they muffled the sound of Mariolina's distant party.

"Help!" Annie was screaming now. "It's an emergency!"

The corridor seemed to grow as she ran along it, twisting handles and pushing at doors in the hope they might open onto the stairs she'd climbed just minutes earlier. All were locked.

Fuck it, thought Annie. What kind of fun house was this? The party sounded miles away and there was no hope of anyone down there hearing her above the music and noise of several hundred voices. All the same, there was no way she was going to be beaten by a bunch of locked doors, not now. One of the doors had let her in, so one could let her out.

Annie was nearing the end of a second corridor when she heard voices and the sound of feet pounding up wooden stairs behind a door just ahead of her. The old man who'd led her to Patty's suite was flanked by two waiters, both far younger than him but hardly fitter, it seemed, given the distance he'd just covered at speed and the fact the old man wasn't even out of breath.

"What?" he demanded. "What happened?"

"It's Patty . . . ," Annie whispered, reserves gone now that there was someone else to depend on. "She . . ." Did what? Tried to kill herself? Annie couldn't get the words out, couldn't bring herself to face all that the words implied. Bent forward, Annie inhaled deeply, like a runner struggling for breath.

"Signora Mailer," she began again.

But the man was gone, skidding up the corridor toward Patty's room and firing instructions over his shoulder that sent the waiters sprinting back the way they'd come.

When they reached Patty she was still exactly as Annie had left her, conscious but only just. The merest groan escaped her as the majordomo shifted her into the recovery position, opening her mouth to feel for her tongue and taking her pulse. It wasn't until he was satisfied his guest would survive that he led Annie back to the bedroom.

Had she been like that when Annie found her?

No, she'd been infinitely more dead when Annie found her.

How long was she unconscious?

How would Annie know? It couldn't have been long. At a guess, five minutes—maybe ten. Five minutes that went into her Top Five all-time worst five minutes ever. A record the model had the dubious honor of sharing with her dead husband.

Did you move her?

Yes, she'd done mouth-to-mouth and forced Patty to vomit.

Did she think Signora Mailer had taken the whole pot?

Yes, Annie did.

Was she sure?

No, but there were no spare pills lying around so it was an educated guess.

Did her friend drink often?

Annie had never seen Patty drink alcohol before.

He might have gone on all night if one of the waiters hadn't burst in with a youngish guest he introduced as *il dottore.*

The elderly man nodded to Annie before leading the doctor through to the bathroom. Even with the door half shut to obscure Annie's view—at least Annie assumed that was the reason—she could hear the majordomo talking rapidly, his tone growing more angry with every word.

Within a minute the second waiter returned, Mariolina Mantolini in his wake. A few minutes later the slapping of feet on tiles announced the arrival of paramedics bearing a stretcher. One by one, each vanished into the bathroom, barely glancing at Annie slumped on the floor with her back against Patty's bed.

The white Rorschach blot stain on Annie's dress had set to a crust. Annie wondered idly what it reminded her of. A flower? A face? No, none of those. It looked like nothing so much as a mess and a very big dry-cleaning bill.

The bathroom door had been opened wide to allow in the stretcher, the back half of which protruded out into the bedroom as Patty was lifted onto it.

"Where are you taking her?" Annie scrambled to her feet.

One of the paramedics glanced around, though the others took no notice.

"I'm coming with you," insisted Annie, picking up a single fuchsia shoe from where she'd kicked it, her eyes scanning the floor for the other one.

"It is best not." The hand on Annie's arm was light but firm. "You have done all you can. You need some rest now."

Annie hadn't noticed Mariolina Mantolini slip out of the bathroom to stand beside her. And she didn't know what she'd been expecting—a cartoon villainess, some kind of Margaret Thatcher/Cruella De Vil combo— but the eyes that smiled up at her were a soft brown, several shades darker than her dress but with lights that matched it exactly. The crinkles surrounding them exposed their owner as a Botox refusenik.

"Ciro tells me you saved Patty's life," said Mariolina without relinquishing her grip. "He says if not for you Signora Mailer would be dead.

You have done enough. Let the doctor take over now. He's good. Everything will be all right."

Annie showed no sign of agreeing.

"I must insist. Patty's in good hands now."

What was Annie supposed to say? *I can't leave her. She's not safe on her own? Someone's killed Patty's husband and they might try to kill her? Patty might try to kill herself and next time she might succeed? You might succeed?* That thought stopped Annie in her tracks; better to say nothing at all.

"Come."

Curiosity overcame Annie's instinctive suspicion. She retrieved her bag and hooked up her remaining shoe, then followed the woman whom Patty believed had ordered Mark Mailer's murder.

chapter twenty-nine

Always be seen to arrive. Strange how the same never seemed to apply to leaving.

Mariolina Mantolini was as practiced an exponent of the black art of being seen to be seen as the most famous of her guests. Within seconds of abandoning Annie on the back staircase, with a hand gesture that Annie realized with shock she'd last seen a lifetime ago in the *Post*'s newsroom on her last day, but which meant the same—*five minutes*—Mariolina was back in the throng.

Half an hour after following her host from the scene of Patty's near demise, Annie was watching as Mariolina Mantolini air-kissed and smiled her way through the rooms to a discreetly placed microphone in the first marquee and she clapped for silence. Her speech, of course, was perfect, modest not quite to a fault. Thanking her guests for their support, she invited the luminaries in their midst to admire her third collection—just a small one as ever, in this case largely evening wear—now being displayed so beautifully by the many models in attendance. And, of course, her delightful, famous, and talented guest of honor.

Patty Lang, too, had she ever made it to the actual party, Annie realized. Very clever; save the cost of a show, pick yourself a stellar audience, and get guaranteed coverage in every paper and magazine in the Western Hemisphere. Mariolina Mantolini was nobody's fool.

But the real coup was still to come.

"A toast," declared Signora Mantolini. "Not to me or the House of Mantolini, but to my beautiful, talented guest of honor, the woman of the hour, Miranda Lawson and her new fiancé—yes, *fiancé*—Robert Dellavecchia."

Champagne was drunk, canapés consumed, and more toasts made. Thus ensuring that everything was as it should be and no one would ever know how close the supermodel the tabloids loved to hate had come to her final fall.

The whole sorry drama had been enacted and cleared up as effectively as if someone had airbrushed it out of history, without ever imposing on Villa Mantolini's gold-plated guests or their gold-plated lives. Annie didn't know whether the thought sickened or reassured her. Both, probably, she decided as she slipped through the crowd near the front of the marquee, frock sponged and brain lubricated, in time to hear tributes being offered to Miranda Lawson who, judging from Rebecca's smile, was unquestionably the most coveted cover star of the moment.

Oh, how wonderful!

How romantic!

Congratulations!

Effusions fell like confetti and littered the floor in just the same tawdry and environmentally unsound way.

A peculiar sense of elation had overtaken Annie, and it wasn't just the vintage brandy straight from the Mantolini family cellars—a deep, dark VSOP. Patty was alive. Patty was not Irina all over again, and history had not repeated itself. Okay, so alive probably didn't feel that fantastic to Patty since she was currently at the Como hospital having her stomach pumped; but alive Patty was. And she was alive because of Annie.

Relieving a passing waiter of a pink champagne, Annie watched with amusement the undignified scrum surrounding Miranda Lawson and her magazine-magnate fiancé. The visiting fasherati were putting up a good fight, but she wouldn't even give them odds against Rebecca, who occupied a seat at Miranda's left, one hand casually on the arm of the actress's chair. Right now, Rebecca looked like even a trolley dash around Chanel wouldn't persuade her to give up her position.

Fashion, Hollywood, old money, new fame . . .

What made Mariolina Mantolini tick? Annie wondered. Was the older woman really a born-again black sheep returned to the fold, whose only interest was to restore the House of Mantolini to its former glory and secure her ten-year-old son Paola's inheritance? And all this was motivated by what? Maternal instinct? Interesting concept, not convincing, just interesting. Good-Catholic-but-divorced guilt more like.

Thirty minutes earlier Annie had been invited to Mariolina Mantolini's private suite of rooms on the third floor of Villa Mantolini. She watched as her prime suspect reclined in a chair that had apparently once belonged to Marie Antoinette. Mariolina was nursing a glass of vintage brandy and eyeing Annie with open interest.

"How do I know Patty's safe?" Annie said, not because she expected an answer or expected to believe whatever answer she did get.

"You could take my word for it," Mariolina said. "Alternatively, you can call the hospital and ask them. I have the number and you can use my telephone if you wish. There are many English speakers there, because of the tourists, you know . . ."

That would have been the easy option. Annie rejected it; she needed to be absolutely sure Patty was safe. "Do you have a telephone directory?" she asked, pointedly opening her bag and finding her own mobile.

Mariolina vanished through a door, all carved wood and gilding, and Annie heard her issue an instruction in rapid Italian. In less than a minute the elderly majordomo appeared bearing the local *pagine bianchi*. He flicked through until he found what he was looking for and placed the huge book on Annie's lap. "Here," Ciro said. "You see? Here is the number for the hospital at Como."

Having checked that he told the truth, Annie dialed. It took her a further five minutes to get connected to a man who told her tersely that Signora Mailer was as comfortable as could be expected given that she was currently having her stomach pumped. Annie should call again in forty-eight hours. Only then would they be able to assess whether or not Signora Mailer was well enough to be released.

"So," said Mariolina, when Annie slipped the Nokia back into her bag and let the bag drop to her feet. "Now you are satisfied, we talk."

It was more instruction than suggestion, but Annie nodded anyway. For all that Patty insisted Mariolina was behind Mark's death, there was no doubting that the woman who sat in front of Annie had indeed delivered Patty to hospital, just as she'd promised.

With every minute Annie spent in Mariolina Mantolini's company her grudging respect for the woman grew. If nothing else she reminded Annie of Rebecca: determined, forceful, smart. A woman with something to prove. And much as Annie wanted to suspect Mariolina, after years of reading between the lies of con artists and crooks she was more than half prepared to believe the woman was telling the truth.

For a start, Mariolina made no attempt to disguise the fact that she knew everything there was to know and plenty more besides. Patty's career suicide on the New York catwalk. Mark Mailer's unfortunate killing (as Mariolina put it). The fact that Annie was there when it happened. Also the fact that Annie had become so "attached" to the case that she appeared to have taken on Mark's role as Patty's protector. Mariolina even knew that Patty thought she'd ordered Mark's killing. So, Mariolina wanted to know, did Annie think Patty's attempted suicide at Villa Mantolini was intended to punish Mariolina, to slander her?

"We have a saying over here," Mariolina added. "Keep your friends close and your enemies closer. Nowhere is that more true than in this industry.

"Anyway, it's my business to know things," she added. "Ignorance does not necessarily equal innocence, you know. And this business we call fashion . . . It is not just a game of dressing young girls in pretty clothes and selling them to grown-ups who believe that they, too, can look this way. It is a very big business indeed. Do not underestimate the importance of the fashion business to Italy's economy."

Annie didn't. She should have known Mariolina would have her sources.

"Guido?"

The woman nodded. "To a degree, yes, Signor Brasco keeps me informed. You mistrust him and he you, but you are both wrong. He was a father to Mark and he hopes to protect Patty. That's why she was here, staying the night in my home."

Protect her from what? Annie wanted to ask but kept that thought to herself.

"He believed I could shelter Patty," said Mariolina, voice bitter. "But I could not even save the stupid girl from herself. Maybe no one can do that. Not Guido, not Mark, and not me or you . . ."

If it was an act it was an Oscar-winning one and, despite herself, Annie began to wonder if both she and Patty were wrong. Maybe Mark's death really was a tragic case of wrong place, wrong time.

"How do you know Guido?"

Mariolina smiled. At Annie's presumption probably.

"Guido and my father were friends for many years. Friends and business associates, but Guido is not my only contact. I have others, both here in Italy and in America. I am a businesswoman after all."

Annie didn't doubt that for a moment.

"You have to understand something," said Mariolina. "Mark represented the future for the House of Mantolini. My future, Paola's future, the future of the villa itself . . ." She shrugged. "I have some talent but I do not fool myself. I am not one of the greats. I am no Lagerfeld, no Galliano, no Mailer . . . So I was very upset—upset and, yes, angry—when Mark told me he was accepting an offer from another house."

"But he accepted yours . . . ," Annie started. "I saw the letter he sent you. A letter of intent, written January twenty-fifth. It was on his computer, Patty showed it to me."

"Really?" For the first time the woman opposite looked uncertain. "January twenty-fifth? Yes, that was the day after we talked. And certainly I believed we had reached an understanding but, I'm sad to say, we had no official agreement. This letter of which you speak, I don't believe he ever sent it, and certainly I never received it. Nothing was signed and so the fault is mine. I allowed myself to take Mark at his word when he said he wanted to tie his future to the House of Mantolini . . ."

Yes, Annie thought. After all, Annie had believed that, too. It was time to play another card, perhaps the last in her hand.

"So, you spoke to him when . . . ?" Annie asked. "A day or two before he died? Sunday evening, maybe nine or ten your time?"

"No." This time Signora Mantolini was emphatic. "You are wrong. I had not spoken to Mark for more than a week before he died. I'm sorry to say, my last words to Mark, they were not kind. He had made a promise and broken it. Something I would not have suspected of him."

"You accused him of betraying you?"

Mariolina Mantolini's face was bleak. "He did," she said. "He was going with Baroni. Ugo Baroni is a fake in every sense of the word. He cannot cut or design, he has no taste. Everything he has done is by someone else . . ."

Annie's face registered her surprise. Surprise that, contrary to Patty's belief, Mark had decided on the Fava deal, but surprise also that Mariolina would be so overt in her dislike of her rival. She'd thought the woman smarter than that.

"Do not quote me on this," Mariolina said firmly, standing up to indicate the interview was over. "Or any of the other things I have just told you, because I'll simply deny ever saying them."

She shrugged, listening to the sound of distant laughter. "Come. It's time I rejoined my guests."

This was the kind of party she liked, Annie decided, finishing her pink champagne and then taking another from a passing tray—flushed if not with happiness then with the contentment that came with knowing there was nothing else she should have been doing and she was free to roam.

Marquee number two was the smaller, set with circular marble tables and obviously intended to encourage conversation rather than schmoozing or grooving. It was quieter in here, just the distant sound of a jazz band in the banqueting hall, a low-level buzz of conversation, and the occasional burst of laughter at some shared private joke. The tables were spaced carefully, to create some semblance of privacy.

On the far side of the marquee, at a table surrounded by models and their sprawling hangers-on, a famous model and her film-star boyfriend exchanged saliva laconically, free of the ever-present plague of paparazzi and rubberneckers. So the gossip was wrong, they hadn't split up. Or maybe they were back together again. Who knew? Or cared, thought Annie, transferring her attention to a different table where a young British actor whom Annie had always thought better of was getting rather too intimate with a woman Annie was 110 percent certain was not his eight-months-pregnant wife. Behind them, one of Hollywood's most famous bachelors, gorgeously disheveled in DJ with bow tie slung loosely around his neck, listened with less than half an ear to an animated blonde.

Bang on cue, he gave his jeweled Rolex a shocked glance, muttered something apologetic, and the blonde smiled tautly as she watched him lope off.

This was more like it. This was what the boys on the *Post* had in mind when they'd conjured green-eyed, rose-tinted images of glamorous parties from their vantage point upstairs at The Swan.

Annie was so starving, she wanted to intercept the nearest waiter and ask if anyone actually planned to *cut* the five-story raspberry-and-chocolate "engagement torte" that stood on a large circular table in the center of the small marquee. Or whether it was just some kind of sadistic table decoration. She was horribly afraid it might be.

"I hope the waiters are hungry," said a voice. "I can't see this lot consuming that many calories in a year."

Annie spun around.

"Hey, Annie, it's okay." The man behind her raised his hands in mock self-defense. "I didn't mean to make you jump. You were just staring at that cake like you could eat it or something . . ." He paused. "You don't recognize me, do you?"

She looked again. That messy fair hair, the gray-blue eyes that crinkled at the edges when he smiled, the lanky body that could make even the best clothes look stylishly scruffy, cheekbones like wing mirrors. Still gorgeous, still much more her type than Lou's.

Of course she recognized him.

Through her own rose-tinted, alcoholic haze Annie heard a distant alarm bell ring and chose to ignore it.

"The Algonquin? Daffodils?"

"Much better than roses," said Annie.

And Chris smiled.

"Hate roses," they both said, and Annie felt an unexpected surge of human kindness. *Annie likes someone, shocker.*

"I'm sorry," Annie said. "I wasn't really all there last time we met."

"Not surprised." Chris shoved his hands in his pockets and immediately ruined the line of a beautifully cut black suit. He stared at the cake.

"What's the politics of that, then?" Annie asked, nodding at the gateau.

"Personal or public?"

"Take your pick. There's got to be some significance in having a ten-thousand-calorie cake mountain at a fashion party. Especially when all the canapés were thimble-sized or smaller."

"That's Mariolina for you," Chris said. "She's probably got CCTV cameras in the loos so she can play spot-the-bulimic!"

Annie grinned. Until then she hadn't realized quite how much she'd been missing Lou's black humor. And now that Lou was sulking, maybe Lou's friend could fill the gap. Annie sneaked another look at the guy. Yes, Lou's aim definitely was improving.

"We weren't properly introduced," Annie said, switching a now empty glass to her left hand and holding out her right. "I'm Annie Anderson."

"Chris Mahoney," he said, ruffling his hair self-consciously in a way that definitely suggested it was genuinely rather than artfully scruffy.

"Good to see you again," said Annie. "And thank you."

"For the flowers?"

Annie shook her head. "For leaving when you did. But the daffs weren't bad, either." There was a pause while they stared at each other.

"So, you know Mariolina?" asked Annie, abandoning all hope of locating, let alone demonstrating, her astonishing intellect.

"Only by reputation. I wasn't actually invited, but don't tell anyone." He smiled in a cute-little-boy way that a sane and sober Annie could have found as irritating as hell. As it was, she was feeling uncharacteristically tolerant.

"My boss was," said Chris. "Only he couldn't come, show tomorrow, final fittings to oversee, so I took his ticket."

234 • SAM BAKER

"They didn't notice at the door?"

"Oh yeah . . . Mariolina will have noticed. Everyone knows everyone here, it's like small-town England. You know, you go home, lock the door, close the curtains, turn out the light, sneeze, and the next day someone you've never met in your life asks your mother how your flu is!"

Annie knew, she'd grown up there. It was called Basingstoke.

"Well, that's what Milan's like, the fashion industry at least. And Mariolina, she might have ruffled a few feathers in the last few months but she still knows everyone."

Feathers? Ruffled?

Annie could see a couple of interesting lines of questioning opening up, she just couldn't be bothered to take them.

"Cake?" said Chris, nodding to a passing waiter without waiting for Annie's answer.

Was this man too good to be true? Quite probably, they usually were.

The gateau was every bit as delicious as it looked. Not too creamy, not too chocolaty, the tartness of fresh raspberries a perfect foil to the sweetness. It was so more-ish that Annie had her plate out for a second piece before she noticed a queue had formed.

"Models in eating shocker," she hissed.

"They'll be queuing again in about ten minutes . . . for the loo," he added, before Annie had time to look puzzled.

"So, you're with Rebecca?" Chris asked, after they'd both finished a second slice and retreated to the banqueting hall, via the bar, to mock the rhythmically challenged who'd dared brave the dance floor.

"Yes, she's over there—"

"No, I meant work-wise."

"Oh, yes, sorry. I started a month ago. What about you? Lou said you're based here . . . ?"

"Oh yeah, I've been in Milan for a few years. Started in London, but one of my clients took their UK representation back in house and offered me the job. Only hitch was I had to come here to do it. That was six years ago and I haven't really been back since. Well, you know, Christmas, family weddings, that's about it. Left that job after a year and went to Armani, stayed there for two. Great experience, but it wasn't really me. Fabulous clothes, though, still wear the suits." He grinned and indicated his lapel.

"So where are you now?"

"Oh, I've been with Ugo Baroni ever since."

"Fava?" Annie hoped her face was doing its very best impression of nothing very much. "That must be interesting."

The alarm bell, which she'd been busy ignoring for other reasons, went berserk in Annie's head.

This was not how it was meant to be. How could Lou do this to her? Fix her up with the very bastard who'd been busy ignoring her calls about Mark . . .

"So you're still doing their PR?" Annie's voice was a lot more casual than she felt.

"No, thank God."

Then he probably wasn't the one who'd been shielding Baroni, but, even so, if Chris worked for him then she'd already missed a few opportunities to grill him. Annie tried hard not to mind, and failed.

"I joined Fava as their European PR director, but I moved over to the advertising side. Now I'm director of international advertising, i.e., the whole world that's not Italy." He grinned. "Don't be fooled, it's not as important as it sounds. Still, I could tell you some stories."

Chris jerked his head toward Miranda Lawson's table. "Now, there's a guy who's fallen on his feet." He was talking about Robert Dellavecchia. "What a con artist."

Annie raised her eyebrows. Maybe she'd get a present for Mr. Gossip at the *Post,* if nothing else.

"A couple of years ago, when Dellavecchia had just started seeing Miranda, this fax turns up, beginning of the spring shows, saying he's just flown in from JFK via Charles de Gaulle and, somewhere in transit, the airline's lost his luggage. He's got wall-to-wall shows, dinners, cocktails, the works, and he hasn't got a thing to wear except for the clothes he traveled in and no one in their right minds would expect him to wear that for the rest of the week . . . Could we, you know, possibly have a couple of suits and some shirts sent to the Four Seasons to see him through, as a favor . . . He'd really appreciate it and, you know, he *is* dating Miranda Lawson and she'll be joining him tomorrow and he'll be photographed in all the front rows so, in return, obviously, there'd be a bit of publicity coming our way."

Annie smiled. She could see what was coming, but then she'd been hanging around con artists for much of her professional life.

"Seemed fair enough to me," said Chris. "I mean, what the hell, we scratch his back and maybe he'll scratch ours. So we send around a couple of suits from our new autumn/winter collection and wait for an avalanche of press. A couple of days later I'm in Cova on Via Montenapoleone, feeding some fashion journalist or other and she's got a pile of British papers and there's Miranda Lawson with Dellavecchia, outside some trendy restaurant or other, wearing . . . Gucci! Fucking Gucci!"

Annie was laughing now.

"So I call a girl I know in their press office and, yup, you guessed it. They had the same fax, same time, same day. I call Calvin Klein, Prada, Armani, even Brioni, same fucking deal. And more than half of us delivered. Can you believe the brass neck of the guy?"

Annie was just relaxing properly for what felt like the first time in days when she spotted a familiar caramel bob moving through the crowd and put down her champagne. The evening, which had been coasting along nicely, thank you, took a dive. As Rebecca reached the dance floor, the woman increased her pace as if dallying too long among the dancers might lead to contamination.

"Time to go," barked Rebecca. It didn't fall far short of an order. She glanced from Annie to the man who clearly didn't own a comb and had defied the dress code by wearing a suit. Annie was surprised to see a faint glimmer of curiosity. Surely the woman wasn't interested in anything so mundane as her staff's love life?

"Hello, Rebecca." Chris stood for the obligatory air kiss. Lucky for him, both fell an inch away from the cardinal sin of touching flesh. "I loved the teaser."

"Teaser?" Rebecca looked put out.

"In your editor's letter. Your team biked an advance copy over this morning."

"We biked copies to all our advertisers," Rebecca said dismissively.

"I don't doubt it. All the same, *The truth about Mark Mailer's death, next month, exclusive to* Handbag. You can imagine how interested we were."

Rebecca smiled before delivering her favorite put-down, the one that demonstrated exactly how high ad men came on her personal pecking order. "And you are . . . ?"

Only the very strong-stomached didn't crack at that, but Chris's digestion was clearly lead-lined. "Christian Mahoney," he said. "Head of international advertising at Fava. We have met—I'm surprised you don't remember—when *Handbag* came to pitch to us last year."

Ouch. One–all.

"I had no idea you worked with Annie." He was unable to refrain from capitalizing on his advantage.

Two–one.

"Annie works *for* me."

Sensing her disadvantage, Rebecca had transferred her attentions to an altogether softer target: Annie. "Although that appears to have escaped her notice and not for the first time."

"I was with Mariolina," said Annie, watching Rebecca blink. One to the umpire as well, if that was who Annie was meant to be in this contest. Unless she was one of those girls who ran around after tennis balls. That was more likely. "Perhaps we can discuss it later."

Chris smiled. "Good to see you again," he said to Annie.

The voice was soft and warm, his lips so close they almost touched her ear. It hit Annie somewhere near the pit of her stomach, a bit lower.

Bugger.

chapter thirty

God, she had been pissed.

Annie raised her head half an inch from her pillow, just enough to witness the devastation that doubled as her hotel room, and then let it crash back down.

Rolling over, she pressed her face hard into the pillow, as if trying to push it right through to the other side. The bright lights that strobed inside her eyelids cranked her headache up another couple of notches.

She never drank on the job, never. So why had she done it? The question was rhetorical. Twelve hours earlier, ricocheting between the euphoria of saving Patty and the horror of what Patty had almost achieved, alcohol had seemed like the answer. Well, *an* answer anyway. And Annie had never been able to come up with a better one.

"Never again. Nev. Er. Again."

She turned onto her back, eyes still screwed shut against the daylight, and put out her left hand, flapping it in the direction of the bedside cabinet in search of her watch. Not there. Which was when Annie realized she was still wearing the thing. Bringing it as close to her face as possible, Annie peered out of one eye. It was 8 A.M., she was meeting Rebecca in an hour, and, before that, Annie had to get her head together and try to remember enough of the previous evening to get it down on her laptop.

Opening her other eye, Annie sat up, threw back her hotel blankets, and made a dash for the bathroom. Christ it was cold, bloody freezing. So she wrapped her naked-but-for-yesterday's-bra-and-knickers body in a toweling robe and turned on the shower, leaving the water to warm up while she went back to investigate why the heating in her room didn't work.

It did. Her problem was the open window behind a pair of sodden curtains. From the puddle of rain on the windowsill and tide mark halfway up the curtain lining the window had been open for hours, if not all night.

Surely Annie, the security freak, the woman who locked and checked her door, windows, wardrobe, bed, and bathroom (and always in that order), hadn't been so trashed that she'd opened a window when she came in? It was just conceivable she'd been hammered enough to miss the fact that it was already open. After all, if she couldn't cope with taking off her watch, underwear, or makeup, she had to have been pretty far gone.

Annie pushed the window shut and twisted one of those metal handles that slid locking poles into place. Her room looked out onto fat ventilation pipes and a flat roof littered with half a dozen cigarette butts, a tissue that had all but biodegraded, and a couple of beer bottle tops. Half a dozen other windows overlooked it, too, none of them open. Someone had opened it and that someone definitely wasn't her. Ratted or not, Annie was allergic to fresh air—especially freezing-cold February air. Annie liked her life hermetically sealed.

She'd been burgled, all right. The only question was when.

Her borrowed Dior dress was discarded in a heap right next to the bed, where she'd stepped out of it. Hidden in its folds stood the pink shoes, surprisingly unbattered given what they'd lived through. And beside them, rammed into a six-inch gap between the bedstead and the matching bedside cabinet, was her black holdall, so tightly rammed that only someone who'd temporarily traded her brain cells for beer goggles could possibly have thought it a secure hiding place.

The hiding place reluctantly relinquished its hostage and Annie rummaged through the bag, checking off its contents, her relief increasing with each item she found. Everything was in there, exactly where she'd left it. So that answered *when*.

Someone had known she would be at Mariolina's party and come calling, looking for what? Whatever they hadn't found in her case, Annie thought. It had to be the Mailer tape. She had nothing else worth stealing.

Slowly Annie took in her room to confirm what she already knew: Some things weren't where they should be, and others were where they shouldn't. She'd packed her case in such a hurry it was impossible to tell if other hands had rifled through her possessions, but this was different. Strange, too. It seemed there was nothing like a bad hangover for keeping a lid on terror.

Too unnerved to enjoy her shower, Annie stripped off the robe and yesterday's underwear and stepped under the hot water, soaping herself rapidly and giving her hair a cursory whiff of shampoo. She must have been so tired when she'd returned from Villa Mantolini that she'd stepped straight over the chaos, stripped off her shoes and dress, and fallen straight into bed.

Classy, Annie.

Two hours before the Fava show was scheduled to start and already a crowd was beginning to build outside the white walls that fortressed the palazzo's courtyard off Via Bezzecca. Fashion students and freelance journos chancing it, Japanese snappers photographing anything that moved, even the pigeons—fashion tourists basically—jostled with paparazzi for space on the wrong side of sturdy metal railings. Beyond the crowd Annie noticed something she hadn't seen before at a fashion show— heavyweight camera crews. Not the usual blond presenter–pet cameraman combos, but network vans with various logos from the world's major broadcasters, CNN, NHK, Rai Uno, ABC, and even the BBC. The news corps had come to town.

It wasn't rocket science to work out that this was less about clothes than the money they made, more about the infamous, and possibly fictitious, Mark Mailer deal than Fava's new collection.

Persuading Rebecca that she needed to skip MaxMara, La Perla, and just about everything else her boss had planned for that morning hadn't been the chore Annie was expecting. Not that Annie was in possession of a backstage pass, but this had never stopped her in the past. Winging it was Annie's specialty and she was back on solid ground, feeling more comfortable with every step that took her away from a hotel room that she no longer considered her own.

Annie had an ace up her sleeve. One she hadn't even known she held until she started emptying her bag to ensure nothing had been stolen, and even then she'd nearly missed it.

CHRIS MAHONEY
Director of International Advertising
FAVA

Just when he'd slipped it into her bag Annie preferred not to contemplate, since the very idea she'd been so pissed that Chris or anyone else could open her precious bag without her noticing appalled Annie. And she still couldn't decide whether it was creepy or cute. Given who he worked for she was horribly afraid it might be the former.

Annie's initial instinct had been to dump the business card in a bin along with all the other junk she'd accumulated since arriving in Milan, but opportunism had stopped her. An inside contact at Fava was an inside contact at Fava, whichever way she cut it. She would use it only as an absolute last resort, Annie promised herself, banishing all thought of those cheekbones from her mind as she stashed it in her purse just in case that last resort arose in the imminent future.

Still glowing with self-congratulation at having sealed a deal with Miranda Lawson *single-handedly,* as she was at pains to point out, Rebecca had been surprisingly mellow over breakfast. So pleased had she been with the deal that it turned out she'd also partaken of a glass or three the night before and could barely remember separating Annie from Chris in the banqueting hall, never mind anything Annie might have said in the car while waiting for Rebecca to be dropped off at her hotel. In fact, Rebecca spent the whole of breakfast sipping gingerly at an espresso while making sympathetic noises from behind an enormous pair of pitch-black Chanel shades. It was a side of Rebecca that Annie had never seen before, and didn't expect to see again. Annie had the distinct impression that Rebecca Brooks with a hangover was a once-in-a-decade occurrence. Shame the same couldn't be said about Annie Anderson, for whom two Nurofen and a black coffee seemed to be rapidly becoming second nature.

Not that Rebecca had much choice but to sympathize. Even Rebecca Brooks wasn't tyrannical enough to berate one of her writers for saving the life of a supermodel, and Patty *was* safe. Annie had put in a call to the hospital in Como that morning only to be told that Signora Mailer was asleep and would not be signed out until tomorrow at the very earliest. So for Patty there would be no Enzo Cotta show tomorrow, and, for today at least, Annie wasn't required to babysit. She could concentrate on getting to Ugo Baroni.

Clearing a path through the fashion tourists was no problem for Annie— head up, eyes forward, march straight through. Unfortunately, Fava's sleekly coiffeured security guards were tougher nuts to crack. Picking off a different guard each time, Annie tried marching in confidently like a VIP with someplace she simply had to be, she tried joining the entourage of a makeup artist, she even tried sneaking around the side when their backs were turned, a move that screamed *amateur.* They'd seen it all before, times ten. Lou had been right, you did need armor here. It was all protocol and unspoken rules; New York had been a doddle compared to this.

"I have a seat," she said crossly, when she was stopped again by a guard.

"The show is not for two hours. You will be admitted as soon as we are ready."

This was standing-ticket-only treatment and Annie didn't like it at all. Already she was used to better.

Summoning thoughts of Rebecca at her most haughty, Annie pulled a small white card from her pocket and thrust it into the guard's face, so that he had to take a step back to read it. "I have an appointment with Christian Mahoney backstage," she lied, with an irritated glance at her watch. "*Had.* Twenty minutes ago. And now I'm even later. Thanks to you."

Suspicion meeting disbelief across his chiseled features, the guard took the card and turned it over, his expression doubtful. All the same, he took a matte silver something from his inside pocket and flipped it open. Annie couldn't tell if it was a state-of-the-art mobile or the latest in walkie-talkie technology; either way its appearance was not part of her plan.

The card was meant to act as some kind of magical open sesame. She'd produce it, security would wave her through, and every door she approached would spring open as she drew near. Maybe Chris had been telling the truth when he'd said his job wasn't as grand as it sounded. At the time she'd put this down to false modesty, but now it seemed horribly plausible that she'd just threatened security with the third producer's assistant's assistant. Damn it, thought Annie, why hadn't she run even a simple check.

Frantically Annie reformulated Plan B while the guard listened to a faint buzz of voices coming from the silver box glued to the side of his head. Nodding abruptly, he flipped it shut.

"My apologies. You can go through. Signor Mahoney, he is expecting you . . . Through the two doors then first left, he will meet you by the catwalk."

Shit, that wasn't how it was meant to be, either. Now she'd have to think of something to say to him. Annie made herself stand tall and aloof before turning to look him in the eye.

"*Grazie,*" she said, taking care to use a tone that demonstrated just how little she meant it.

"*Prego.*" The man was politely oblivious to her contempt, or maybe just used to it.

At first glance the space inside seemed deserted. To the left lay a darkened auditorium, to the right, a long unlit corridor. As Annie peered into the gloom a sudden blaze of spotlights flared up to reveal seating laid out five rows deep around a lozenge-shaped catwalk. From the corridor to her right came generic rap, voices, laughter, and shouting. Models trying to make themselves heard above the sporadic roar of hair dryers that fired into life and died down again as one after another had her long-suffering hair blasted into place.

Well, Annie was in, but what was she supposed to do now? Dive off down the corridor and hope nobody noticed? That wasn't her style. Act like you had a right to be there, that was always more effective in Annie's experience.

She might have been banking on Chris's business card opening all the right doors, but he was still the last person she wanted to see right now. She'd planned to merge into the background, see the models being made-up, and ask the occasional question about eyeliner or straightening irons, just as the beauty journalists did backstage at the Mark Mailer show. That way, she'd be able to catch Ugo Baroni off guard, watch him when he didn't know anyone was there to watch. Now Chris would think she was there to see him, less than twelve hours after they'd last met: In his position it would have set off every single stalker alarm Annie possessed.

She liked Chris, actually she liked him a lot; too much. He was funny and clever, dressed well, and had excellent taste in flowers and cake. But he worked for Baroni and, like it or not, that would have to be an end to it.

"Annie!"

Any hope she was still harboring of sneaking in unobserved was lost.

"What a surprise! I didn't expect to see you so . . . soon. In fact, you're lucky to catch me, I only came by a couple of minutes ago for a quick meeting with Ugo."

It was said in a rush, and a slightly embarrassed rush at that. *See,* Annie told herself, *he's still gorgeous, he still works for the enemy, and now he thinks you've got stalker tendencies.*

Two formal pecks and feat of superhuman willpower later, her dry lips skimming the air millimeters above his cheek, and Annie was back on top, her smile just slightly condescending, as if she found his embarrassment both touching and childish at the same time. "I was coming to the show," she said, "and I had some time to kill, so I thought I'd come backstage, get a sneak preview. Don't let me bother you if you're working."

"You're not . . . I mean, I'm not . . . working. Well, I am, but, nice to see you anyway. Did you get back all right last night? Obviously . . . Anyway, let me give you a guided tour before I go."

He was floundering. Annie felt a twinge of regret. She hadn't intended to put him down, just wrong-foot him a little. Chris Mahoney wasn't as self-confident as he looked, which might have been another plus point, if she was prepared to allow it.

"That would be kind," said Annie, and was rewarded with a half smile.

Pulling back the heavy blackout curtains, Chris stepped aside to allow Annie in front of him. The noise level tripled instantly and light from hundred-watt bulbs blazed into the dim corridor. Despite a slow-burn frenzy of activity, the preshow scene was altogether mellower than Annie had come to expect from seeing the after-show backstage charge. No melee of journalists or well-wishers bursting with congratulations, just a handful of professionals with a big job to do and a finite amount of time to do it.

A battalion of hairdressers worked alongside makeup artists all building the same 1960s sex kitten look. For their part, the models gazed vacantly at their own reflections in a there-but-not-there kind of way that reminded Annie of Patty. Maybe it wasn't trauma after all, maybe it was just the result of years of institutionalized boredom.

"I'll give you a sneak preview," said Chris. "But only if you promise not to tell."

Tell? She probably wouldn't even be able to remember it in half an hour's time. Annie was much more interested in getting a good look at the label's owner and creative chief. She nodded all the same and Chris led her to a far corner, boxed off by garment rails full of outfits. To one side a small blonde, one of a phalanx of assistants, manhandled a pair of impossibly skinny trousers onto an ironing board while a harassed-looking stylist barked a litany of instructions. The girl, apparently used to it, simply began to iron.

"Mel, this is Annie. Annie, Mel."

The stylist, one of those irritating gamine types who could dress like a ten-year-old—cropped jeans, Puma trainers, Aertex T-shirt, preppy V-neck, and bunches—and still look unutterably cool, waved distractedly, wrists heavy with plastic bangles and beads.

Annie could read her mind. It said, *Fuck off, can't you see I'm busy?*

Annie was happy to oblige, but Chris had other ideas.

"Mel's day job is with *Trend,* in her spare time she's creative consultant to Ugo."

Mel nodded some more, smile still tight.

"Annie works on *Handbag* . . . for *Rebecca.*" The emphasis was undoubtedly on the last word.

Recognition crept in, animating Mel's face. Ah, *that* Annie, Annie could see her thinking, though it was not what she said.

"God, you poor cow," the stylist said sympathetically. "Been there, done that. Right bitch, isn't she? I'm not surprised her ex took the opportunity to dump her when she came back to London. Glad to get rid of her probably, like the rest of New York."

That was harsh, thought Annie, though she didn't express it. "Really?" Annie said. "I haven't been there that long, so the worst is probably still to come."

While the stylist repetitively accessorized and unaccessorized each outfit, Chris led Annie toward the rails of clothes. "These are Marian's looks," he said, gesturing toward the nearest rail. "Ingrid's here, Kat's over here . . . There are twenty-six girls, two looks each except for Marian who's closing the show."

Any self-respecting fashion junkie would have been as happy as Imelda Marcos in a Jimmy Choo factory; rail after rail of garments hung in outfit order, adorned with beads, belts, or bags and identified by a sheet of A4 taped to the front, with a Polaroid of the wearer stapled in the bottom right-hand corner. Scrawled in pink felt pen at the top of each sheet was the look number, followed by the model's name, and finally a succession of random-looking notes in a different-colored ink.

Below the looks, on a shelf just above floor height, stood a sweet shop of rainbow-hued 1980s-style courts. Tempting as each pair was individually, they jarred badly with the outfits above, which were all vaguely '60s in mood. The critics were going to have a field day, but the people who really mattered, Fava's customers, wouldn't care less. Consequently nor would Baroni, once he recovered from the critical battering.

Accessories and fragrance were where the profit lay, and these were shoes for which Annie could imagine actually parting with her hard-earned cash. Shoes that could make jeans look dressy and turn a financial disaster into an improved profit margin. A couple of the bags worked, too, now that she really looked at them, big practical bags with lots of pockets, cut from soft leather in jelly-bean shades. Annie couldn't help thinking that they reminded her of something. And then she had it: Marc Jacobs a season ago.

The problem, to Annie's untrained eye, lay with the clothes. Even on women whose bodies could make the dullest outfits look stunning these clothes would be, well, ordinary at best. At worst, they were . . . Annie struggled to put her finger on it . . . cut without panache or, dare she think it, even skill. In line with the other shows Annie had seen, there was a definite 1960s undercurrent, and the colors were bright. Yet somehow that wasn't enough.

There was no getting away from it, these pieces were nothing but poor imitations. Fava had needed the association with Mark Mailer and needed it badly.

"What do you think?" Chris asked.

Annie tried to smile. "Interesting," she said.

"Yes." Chris nodded. "That's what I thought."

He was trying very hard to mean it. He smiled, looking directly at Annie. "Someone said this was your first time in Milan."

"That was me," said Annie. "Last night."

"How are you enjoying it?"

Annie looked at him. "I'd feel better," she said, "if my hotel room hadn't been burgled."

"Fuck," said Chris, face shocked. "When?"

"Probably," she said pointedly, "about the time I was talking to you."

Across the room, a picture of calm in the middle of preshow mayhem, stood a tall, slim man, silver hair cropped close to his head. Seemingly oblivious to the raised voices and rising hysteria around him, Ugo Baroni smiled indulgently as a young American in an I-mean-business suit talked at him earnestly.

The man was not what Annie had expected, although she'd seen him before, both from a distance in New York and in pictures. His skin was tanned just dark enough to escape the look of tooled leather and his clothes were immaculate, perfectly cut black suit trousers and a bright white shirt, its sleeves rolled back in a workman-like fashion to reveal the toned forearms of a younger man. As if to say, *Look, I'm busy, you can have only a minute of my valuable time.*

He was disconcertingly attractive, which irritated Annie. She'd have preferred him to look like the slimeball she suspected him to be: the type that owned a yacht, played polo, and boasted a mistress and a substantial wine cellar in each of his many palatial homes. Instead, from where she stood, Ugo Baroni looked very much like a man she could imagine liking, but only if she was displaying uncharacteristically good taste.

As the camera rolled, the reporter fired questions at Fava's head of everything. He answered, just as rapidly. With her limited Italian, Annie understood only two words and they were the words that brought the young American's interview to a close: *Mark Mailer.*

Annie didn't need to understand Italian to get the gist of his reply because Chris translated. It was said that Mark would have made a valuable addition to the Fava stable but Fava didn't need Mark Mailer. Fava was fine.

That went against everything Rebecca had said and everything Annie had heard from Lou. And yet, looking at Baroni's quiet confidence in the megawatt glare of the TV cameras, it didn't look like a lie.

Forty-five minutes after the scheduled start time, with the auditorium almost full and the conversation dropped to a low-level hum . . . at last the event was ready to begin and the standers who'd been lurking in the aisles in the hope of scoring a seat were being ushered forward to fill space left by the no-shows. Slipping through a door that led from backstage to front, Annie was just in time to see someone who wasn't anyone slide into a seat right behind Rebecca Brooks. Her seat. Once again, Annie had scored an official no-show with one of *Handbag's* biggest advertisers.

Maybe Rebecca would be more forgiving when she discovered that Annie had been backstage trying to question Ugo Baroni, or maybe not.

It had taken bullying, cajoling, and out-and-out bribery for Annie to persuade Chris to engineer an audience with his boss. But if he wanted to buy her dinner that night—and, apparently, he did—what choice did he have?

"A minute," she'd pleaded. "Five at most. And no difficult questions," she added, spotting the merest chink in his armor opening up.

Chris slid between the waiting camera crews surrounding his boss and spoke quickly into the ear farthest from the microphone that was pinned to Baroni's collar.

Annie watched Ugo Baroni's eyes narrow, small pouches appearing beneath them as he peered over to where she stood, half concealed behind a rail of clothes. Accommodatingly, she took a step sideways and instantly felt his gaze rake her body. The discomfort Annie felt was palpable. But she looked the man square in the face and forced her lips up at the edges until he finally looked away, still unsmiling.

"He'd love to but he's already agreed to five more interviews after this one and then there's his show . . . You're welcome to wait around and if he can fit you in he will."

Suspiciously Annie looked at Chris. "Really?" Baroni hadn't looked to be saying anything much at all.

"Okay." Chris grinned. "What he said, precisely, was 'Not definitely yes, but not definitely no.' You'll get used to it. It's Italian for, *Get in the queue if you can find the end of it.* That's life here, I'm afraid."

Managing a smile, Annie said, "And how long is the queuing likely to take?"

"How long have you got?" Chris smiled back. "It could take hours. You never know, you might get lucky. If I were you I'd take your seat and come back after the show."

It was good advice, shame she hadn't taken it. Instead she'd stuck around backstage and watched Baroni give interview after interview to the world's news networks, all the while feigning obliviousness to the female journalist waiting in the corner. Her advantage was lost, because there was no benefit in watching someone who was also watching you. When the models had finally started lining up, Annie had no choice but to accept that she'd moved no farther up the queue and give up. Picking up her holdall she had made for a side door and as she did so, the silver-haired man caught her eye and held up his hands.

What can I do? they seemed to say. *Is it my fault if the entire world's media is breaking down my door?*

chapter thirty-one

If there had been anywhere else for Patty Lang-Mailer to go, anywhere at all, she would have gone there. The model apartment, with its lonely air of impermanence and detritus of snatched lives, was the last place she wanted to be. But when she'd checked herself out of hospital in Como that lunchtime, too exhausted even to be properly scared, the absence of any real alternatives defeated her.

Dr. Tomasi had tried to stop her, but Patty ignored him. She was fed up with people telling her what to do.

"Then it's your responsibility," he'd said.

Of course it was. Who else's could it be? Mark was dead and there was no one else she could trust, not really. But she couldn't stay there. The hospital, her private room—financed very generously by Signora Mantolini, Dr. Tomasi had told her, his tone dripping disapproval—wasn't safe. Right now, nowhere felt safe. After last night's party at Villa Mantolini, Patty didn't think she'd ever feel safe again.

There were people she could have phoned. People she could have called to come and collect her, people who would give her shelter. The question Patty couldn't suppress was what else they might give her, so she didn't.

She could have gone back to Villa Mantolini, but right now just about anywhere seemed more welcoming. She hoped, in fact she prayed, she would never have to see that room, or that house, again.

L'Aeroporto di Malpensa, now that was a pretty attractive option. Patty pictured herself taking a train away from Milan, away from everything, and spending every last euro she didn't have on a one-way ticket out of here, back to Manhattan. Back to what? Back to another empty apartment, back to waiting for the scrape of Mark's key that would never come. Back to Cathie and Guido and her agent who wanted Patty to "embrace her newfound notoriety . . . Perhaps reconsider the whole *Maxim* thing." Six months ago, if anyone had told Patty that magazines—even men's magazines—would be fighting to have her on their cover she'd have laughed in their face, but now . . . Now, apparently, she was spoiled for choice. Who would have thought Mark's death would turn out to be such a boost for her career.

No, she would stay, until tomorrow at least. She'd come to Milan to do a job and that job still had to be done. It was a point of principle. By two o'clock tomorrow afternoon, when the Enzo Cotta show was over, she'd be free.

So instead Patty took a taxi to the station. Throat too raw even to whisper, she scribbled her destination on the back of an old Starbucks receipt from the bottom of her bag, waved it mutely at the driver, and boarded the first train back to the Stazione Centrale in Milan. Back to her future. Already resigned to whatever that might be.

Now she was here. In a ratty apartment full of hand-me-down scented candles and discarded paperbacks. A place that even her addled imagination couldn't make pass for home, not even for one night, not even for an ex-supermodel with nowhere else to go. Home was where Mark was. Only Mark wasn't anywhere now. She'd known home only briefly and right now it felt like she'd never find another.

Taking a long, painful drag, Patty inhaled, swallowed saliva, and winced; tears tried to seize their opportunity but she fought back and won. "No point crying," she told herself. "It won't change anything. And anyway, Mark wouldn't want to see you cry."

Every cigarette irritated her eyes more, but still she took another slow, excruciating drag, all too aware of the ludicrousness of self-inflicting pain when her body ached so much already. Her stomach was bruised from the inside out, her rib cage hurt whenever she moved, and her throat was raw. Evidence of enforced vomiting she could barely remember and a pipe into her stomach that she longed to forget. Pain so sharp it made smoking an even more perverse form of self-mutilation than usual.

She'd gone back to Camels. The others, the pointless empty white ones, were in a wastebasket outside Como station where they belonged.

Patty knew that walking the four or five miles from Stazione Centrale to the apartment wasn't one of her brighter ideas the moment she passed the station's taxi rank. And yet, even on a late afternoon during a damp Milan winter, with mist hanging low over the city and drizzle soaking into her jeans and jacket, she felt happier, relatively speaking.

Getting there had always been better by far than arriving. Christmas Eve was her favorite day of the year. You could keep Christmas Day itself, that was when family fights started. She'd always loved the anticipation of any vacation more than actually going. The getting ready for a big night out more than the night itself.

Her credibility was shot, Patty knew that. It had always been fragile, but now she was no longer just Patty Lang, the rehab yo-yo, she was Patty Lang-Mailer, the failed suicide. Look, they would all say, the woman can't even kill herself properly.

It was inspired, the perfect plan. And it would have worked if not for Annie Anderson. Who'd ever believe Patty hadn't OD'd? Crazy, addicted Patty, no friends or family to speak of, her partner—lover, spiritual healer, meal ticket, whatever they all thought Mark was to her—still lying in one of those macabre filing cabinets in the morgue. What did Patty have to live for?

She'd known better than to even try confiding in the medical staff who'd bustled in and out of her room. Most of them didn't speak much English anyway and those who did made it clear that they had little time to waste on a stupid girl who'd brought all this on herself. Annie was her best hope, only Annie wasn't answering her messages.

"Shit." Grinding a cigarette into wet cobbles, Patty scrolled down her cell phone's tiny screen and clicked to erase the text message she'd just written. I NEED TO TALK TO YOU, SOMEONE TRIED TO KILL ME sounded hysterical even to Patty, and she'd been there when rubber-gloved fingers began thrusting pill after pill down her throat.

Earlier, in a last attempt to reach Annie, Patty had stopped in the shadow of a church and dialed her direct, only to be thwarted by voice-mail instructing her to leave a message and Annie Anderson would get back to her, followed by an endless succession of bleeps. Aware that her rasped attempts to form the words would only scare the journalist witless, Patty had hung up.

All the same, there were things she needed Annie to know. So Patty would keep trying.

They had failed once, but they would not fail again and they could take as long as they wanted, because they knew where she was. But still she went there, returning to the empty apartment alone. She would greet them head-on; if nothing else she would make her husband proud. Patty Lang had been many things—addict, fallen supermodel, high school dropout—but she would not run. Although she had no problem with try-ing to hide.

She'd strained her already bruised stomach dragging a small but leaden two-seater sofa from its home in the center of the room to the back wall, so she could see every available exit—or entry, depending on how she looked at it. Yanking a blanket from an unused bed, Patty swathed herself in it, then huddled on the sofa with thick black coffee, sweet as runny tof-fee. Someone had once told her—someone's mom or grandma, since Patty didn't have those kind of relatives—that sweet things were good for trauma, sugar especially.

"Hey Mark," she whispered, voice hoarse, finally allowing her eyes to fill up. "Look, I've collected a whole new set of habits."

She laughed to herself, but she couldn't stop replaying in her mind the horror of what had happened at the Villa Mantolini.

The knock on the door of her room had woken her from a doze, her first few minutes of sleep for weeks. Why had she not called out or asked who was there? Because she'd been expecting . . . Someone else. Annie, probably. Or Mariolina. Mariolina whom Guido had sworn she could trust, had promised would protect her . . . Instead, half asleep and unsuspecting, Patty had opened her bedroom door to the shock of cold steel against her neck and a rubber hand pushed roughly over her mouth, thumb hard into the hollow of her jaw while another went over her eyes. Two men working as one, professionals.

They'd had her inside and flat on her back in one practiced movement. The hand over her face changing position to close off her nose, forcing her to breathe through her mouth. They wore black balaclavas made from what looked like silk.

Terror turned to confusion as vodka splashed onto her face. At first she fought back, spitting vodka at where she thought they might be, but then the blade reappeared against her throat.

"Filthy bitch."

The hand came away from her nose and somebody slapped her.

She fought some more but she'd already lost. Not to them, but to the Stolichnaya being poured down her throat.

Her body had betrayed her.

At the memory Patty felt her face flush with shame. She had missed the taste, yearned for it, and its longed-for fire had ensured her terror was shot through with a kind of homecoming as the alcohol hit her brain.

"Hey," said one of them. "She's enjoying it."

Until then the men had said little and, when they had, their southern accents meant Patty's limited Italian was worse than useless. What she knew she'd picked up during her years of working the Milanese catwalks or hanging around Guido's with Mark. The vodka pourer fired a volley of instructions at his partner and through the alcohol soaking her brain Patty felt herself being lifted. The sensation lasted no more than a few seconds and Patty couldn't remember if she'd kicked or fought. All she remembered was a change in the quality of the light and the smooth cold tiles against her legs.

The pills had been a shock. What was she expecting? What would she have done in their place? Razor blades, a swift vertical slash to each wrist and watch the blood splash over the bathroom floor? Too messy. Heroin, one quick shot might have done it, if the dose was high enough.

But for some reason, they chose pills. Not knowing she would never use pills. Those were what her stepmother took.

Tears fell now, trickling down the side of Patty's nose. Sometime in the last hour the apartment had grown cold.

"It's okay," Patty told herself, voice deceptively calm. "You're okay." It was a lie, of course. No problem, she had lied to herself, and just about everyone else, for years. Everyone, except Mark.

chapter thirty-two

The water looked as cold as Enzo Cotta's glare, a bottomless gray viscous mass, just a couple of degrees short of ice and an exact replica of the merciless gray sky hung low overhead; but somehow still welcoming, at least for Patty.

"You want us to get in there?" a young model shrieked, American, southern. "No way, no fucking way. Now I know why you didn't wanna runthrough beforehand."

Patty watched as Enzo Cotta shrugged, resigned to the ignorance of inexperienced models and all the others who were too shortsighted to understand his methods. "Your agent didn't tell you?"

The girl shook her head fiercely. "Whaddaya think?"

Patty could see that the model—a child, barely legal, not legal in many states—was crying, hot tears of fear and humiliation.

Although not exactly an old hand himself, in the two years he'd been showing at Milano Donna Moda, Enzo Cotta had acquired a reputation for interesting clothes that made just-thought-provoking-enough statements, mixed with ideas pushed to their very limits and, in some cases, quite a bit beyond. He'd had girls strut the catwalk dripping honey. He'd painted them silver and made them walk naked across a sea of insect car-casses. None had ever made this kind of fuss.

He was not very "Milan" at all. Consequently, the world's indie press loved him.

"I especially ask for girls who can swim. Not Olympics, just so you don't get in trouble out there. Your agent knew this."

The other models—five young women and two men, boys really, both still wearing the telltale pimples of late adolescence—watched from the relative warmth of the location vans that had delivered them to this bleak spot. They might not have known exactly what to expect, but they knew it would be unorthodox. They also knew Enzo Cotta was a career maker. They weren't about to complain about a bit of cold water if the result was a spread in *Nylon* or *Dazed and Confused*.

This, after all, was the man who did an entire show with five girls wear-ing nothing but tampon strings and endless rather beautiful variations on the same cropped jacket cut from transparent plastic.

"But we'll freeze to death!" the girl wailed. Patty's heart bled. She could remember her own first season in Milan, aged sixteen, not long out of Oklahoma City, isolated by language and upbringing. The life had seemed so unbearably glamorous then.

"It's going to be fine," she told the girl. "And when you see the pho-tographs in print you won't even remember how cold you were."

The girl summoned a doubtful smile.

"Ever the professional," Enzo said. "Patty, ah, you look fantastico!"

She didn't and she knew it, but Patty didn't call him on it. Given his reputation, there was every chance she actually *was* looking fantastico for his purposes. If, for Enzo Cotta, next season was all about that cutting-edge new shade of off-white, corpse gray.

"You okay, with everything? You close, of course. As you know we're doing just the one look. So put it on, lie on your back, and let the tide machine do the rest."

Patty nodded. Her throat still tightened in pain if she tried to speak and her voice, on the verge of returning the night before, had since been wrecked by hours spent croaking down a phone to Annie, who'd finally responded to her messages. A nod would have to do.

She wasn't much of a swimmer, a life lived landlocked until she moved to Manhattan and a healthy respect for water had put paid to that, but she didn't plan on complaining. She could float well enough and muster a respectable breaststroke if necessary. Anyway, she'd said she would deliver and she would. Mark had always kept his word and so would she.

In the hour it took the makeup artist to paint her naked body from chin to toe with a thin coating of flesh-colored latex intended to protect her skin from the worst of the cold, Patty chain-smoked and tried to conceal her shaking. Finishing her own pack, she consumed all of the makeup artist's Marlboros before gratefully accepting something Italian from a young guy, there to operate the tide machine that would wash the models downstream. In between her assorted high-tar nerve-steadiers, the star of Enzo Cotta's show downed thimble after thimble of thick black espresso. By the time her latex body stocking had set, Patty's mind was numbed by a lethal cocktail of nicotine, caffeine, and . . . something else.

"You okay?"

Patty nodded, then stood quite still.

The stylist was easing the white dress over Patty's head, draping and pinning the fine cashmere in folds around her thin body, when Patty first noticed the change. It was as if someone had taken a pen to the canal bank in front of her and drawn a light around the edges. All of the objects in front of her—dresses, tide machine, Enzo himself—had acquired a hard, sharp edge.

Cautiously she closed her eyes and forced herself to count: *one . . . two . . . three . . . four . . . five . . .* Reaching ten she opened her eyes again and smiled. Everything around her was clearer than it had been in a long time.

Razor-sharp.

"Shit," she muttered under her breath, reaching out for a chair behind her.

"Patty hon," mumbled the stylist through a mouthful of pins. "Do me a favor, don't sit down. It'll ruin the line." Pinning one last fold, the stylist spat the pins into her hand. "I know you've been on your feet for hours," she said. "But it's only a few more minutes. We need you to go straight from here to the steps, okay? So Enzo can see how the fabric flows when you're in the water."

Patty took a deep, slow breath and nodded. It was the last cigarette that did this, she was pretty sure of that. High tar, low tar, filtered, and plain. She'd smoked them all from boredom and the need to stay thin and steady her nerves, but this was the first time she'd known one to come ready-loaded with crack. Putting up her chin and throwing back her shoulders Patty began to walk toward the canal.

A small crowd had assembled along a muddy track, although most people were still huddled beside a trestle table bearing two large silver urns. The table, made of chipboard, reminded Annie of the kind her dad used for wallpapering. In their hands, Oliver Twist–style, the crowd of economy-class fashion tourists clasped tiny polystyrene cups of sweet espresso. The photographers had already taken up their position on the canal bank, some setting up tripods and surrounding themselves with camera bags to stake their territory.

Annie had seen some bleak venues in recent weeks, but this was in a class of its own. Behind her, on the horizon, lorries roared past. In front, a canal that would have been stagnant had this been a smog-ridden Milanese summer lay almost motionless, despite the wind gusting along it. There was no sign of any catwalk. No seating, front row or otherwise, which would go a long way toward explaining the absence of the familiar sequence of digits inscribed on her ticket.

Earlier, when she'd arrived late at Enzo Cotta's show, Annie had found that virtually everyone who mattered had not bothered to come at all. She was late not because she'd overslept after spending most of the wrong side of midnight on the phone to Patty, but because what Patty told Annie convinced her that the tapes were no longer safe with her.

"There were two of them," Patty had said. "They tried to kill me, make it look like I'd killed myself."

"Have you told the police?"

"Of course I haven't. Do you really think they'd believe me?"

"No." Annie didn't even have to think about her answer. Which was why she'd spent more than an hour before the Enzo Cotta show queuing in an *officio postale*. In her hand were three small white envelopes containing tapes—one Mark and two Patty—all bound for London where, Annie hoped, no one could reach them. Not even whoever wanted them badly enough to steal her case and ransack her room.

Annie had spent most of the previous afternoon and evening actually doing her job, following the fashion caravan from Fava to Gucci to Pucci and on. And when Rebecca finally departed in the Mercedes for the Gucci dinner, Annie took a taxi to All'Isola to meet Chris as agreed, negotiating his dinner invitation down to drinks on the basis that the promised interview with Ugo Baroni had never actually happened.

By eleven—and this was the bit Annie was really proud of—she was still sober and back at her hotel. Alone. All in all, Annie Anderson had been feeling pretty pleased with herself, until she dug her mobile from the bottom of her bag and discovered that her day had been built on a lie. Patty was not secure in a hospital in Como as she had believed. Patty had discharged herself and spent most of the afternoon and evening clogging Annie's mobile with text messages. Then the guilt had come crashing in, and with it a long night of listening as Patty told a story that would have traumatized the brothers Grimm.

"I'll come right over," Annie had offered, reluctant to leave her star witness alone for a second longer than she already had. "Reception will get me a cab."

But Patty had stood firm. "I'm fine," she said. "Really, I promise, don't worry. Nothing can happen to me now."

Neither Annie nor Patty believed that for a moment.

"Talk to me for a bit longer," said Patty, "and then we should get some sleep. You sound like you need it and if I don't I'll never get through tomorrow."

"Tomorrow?" asked Annie, half dreading the answer.

"Enzo's," said Patty. "I've still got to do Enzo Cotta before I can go . . . Mark would have wanted it."

Annie had begged and pleaded with Patty to pull out, to call in sick, to do anything, other than turn up for her one Milan showing, but Patty had refused.

"It will be fine" was all she would say, sounding to Annie's ears stubbornly like her dead husband.

The crowd along the canal had grown large enough to almost warrant that description, and Annie scanned the faces in vain for Lou. After all, this was her kind of thing, wasn't it? But Annie couldn't see Lou among the fifty, maybe even sixty, people who had now gathered. There were a few other familiar faces, standing stonily apart wondering what the fuck their editors were thinking sending them to this godforsaken hellhole. Annie was inclined to agree.

Standing on the towpath, one of the battered-denim Italian boys gesticulated frantically and a tiny vanguard of hard-core fans, instantly scenting excitement, began to move in his direction, speeding up before breaking into a run.

"It is the show," someone shouted in English. "The show is now."

Annie walked upstream with the sparse crowd, heels sinking into the mire with every step. *What show?* She couldn't see a damn thing. Then, as she neared a slight bend in the canal, it dawned on her. The water was moving; the canal had acquired a slight current, and carried on that current came a doll-like object. A second glance revealed not just one, but others behind it, growing larger.

Was the current enough? wondered Annie. Or were they being pulled along on some kind of string and, if so, who was doing the pulling?

Ranged along the southern bank of the canal, the crowd jostled for space. See, Annie thought wryly, no matter how hard you tried to fuck with hierarchies, there was *always* a front row.

Another yell went up, then another. Almost instantaneously some self-appointed interpreter shouted a translation.

"Look! Floating clothes!"

"No! It's mannequins!"

"Not mannequins, models!"

"Oh my God!"

Annie leaned as far over the railing as she could without losing her balance. The crowd was shifting now, elbows flailing in the struggle to be first to see the objects that drifted toward them, rising and falling on the cold gray water that lapped at the Naviglio Grande's concrete edge.

"Fantastico!"

"Oh my God!"

"Amazing!"

Hush descended and, in the awed silence, Annie heard the howl of the wind, the low-level roar of traffic behind, and something else, the throb of an industrial-scale pump that was drowned out as the crowd began to clap. Applause, uncertain at first, built in confidence until it exploded into a frenzy of wild cheering. "Enzo! Enzo! Fantastico! *Bravissimo!*"

The fan club was right. The objects that seemed almost to hover on the surface of the murky canal were models, apparently naked beneath their sheer Ophelia-like dresses. Eyes wide open and faces to the sky, they glided along their watery runway. Cleverly pinned on their bodies to float artfully around them was Enzo Cotta's autumn/winter collection.

Now Annie understood why Patty had been so determined to be a part of this. Okay, so it was pretentious even by fashion standards; deeply significant, too, no doubt. Although Annie was buggered if she knew what that significance was. But the clothes . . . they were astonishing. Structured dresses that wafted beneath fluid coats, in perfect autumnal shades of berry, rust, and neutrals, their unexpectedly flattering tones taken from nature accentuated by the bleak wasteland surroundings.

The first wave of models had drawn level with Annie now, sheer force of will separating the girl who'd been terrified earlier from hysteria, as if every muscle in her body was fighting to suppress a shriek. Her discomfort was only emphasized by the models who floated on either side. They were both pictures of serenity, the merest hint of smiles recalling mermaids and sirens, so certain were they of their physical impact. After them floated another five models, two men before three women, each one clad in ever-more-ethereal robes.

And behind them all an ethereal blonde, in a translucent gown that was almost white, but colder and more icy, with the slightest hint of blue. Gasps of appreciation echoed around Annie as she clasped a hand to her mouth. Patty was beautiful. She looked like . . . like a Rhine maiden, a water goddess.

And that was it. The show was over.

Nine outfits? Annie didn't know whether to be impressed or outraged. This enormous schlep, miles from the city center, as far as it was possible to get from all other venues, far beyond the outskirts of Milan, to stand freezing on a muddy bit of wasteland beside a fetid canal for just nine looks.

But what pieces they'd been. You had to hand it to Enzo Cotta, the guy had pulled it off. You could count on one hand the international fashion press who'd been in attendance, and still this show would become legend. By this time next year a hundred more journalists would be claiming to have been among the few who had seen this audacious piece of iconoclasm with their own eyes.

Slowly the crowd dispersed, the legend already growing in grandeur as they stamped back toward the road. By the time most were drinking espresso on Via Montenapoleone, Enzo Cotta would be a Galliano in the making.

Only his most ardent admirers remained, and they followed the tableau's journey down the canal bank to where two location vans were parked. Annie trailed behind, wondering how easy it would be to take Patty back to the flat, pack her case, and get her out to the airport for the next flight home. Maybe *Handbag* would even pay for the taxi. Surely Rebecca would approve? And at least in New York Guido could look after her. That thought made Annie reconsider. The old man wasn't exactly her first choice given their last conversation. All the same, right now it was probably a question of any port that might offer protection to Patty in this deadly storm.

Fifty paces ahead, the first three models were being pulled from the canal, huge white towels flung around their waif-like bodies. Two of them were grinning through chattering teeth; the third, ashen with fear rather than cold, snatched the towel and burst into noisy tears.

"Is just water," one of the crew muttered, and the first two models' good humor drained from their faces.

"Bloody cold water," said one, turning her back on the men.

By the time Annie reached the vans the two boys were clambering up the bank and the final triumvirate of girls were sailing in, feet kicking to bring a speedy end to their hideous, if career-making, experience. Behind them floated Patty, looking more tranquil than Annie had thought possible.

"That was amazing!" Annie called.

"*Grazie,*" shouted Enzo Cotta.

There was no response from Patty, but Annie probably shouldn't have expected one. Probably Patty couldn't hear a thing with the pump running, the vans warming up, and her ears still underwater.

As she drew level with Patty, Annie knelt and reached down, offering Patty her hand.

"Patty . . ."

Annie leaned farther forward, but still Patty sailed on, no sign of recognition in her expression.

This was wrong, all wrong. Surely Patty could see Annie, even if she couldn't hear her?

"Patty?" Real fear surfacing, Annie shuffled along the towpath, mud caking her knees as she stretched out a hand.

"Please! Signora! Do not touch." A young man wearing jeans and a battered donkey jacket was tugging at Annie's coat, dragging her backward.

"Get off me!" Annie yelled, pushing him aside. He was easily ignored; one solid push and she'd have sent the boy onto his back. But by now she had hold of the sodden cashmere of Patty's dress and was pulling against the tide to drag Patty out of the water.

"*Signora!*"

Towels under their arms, the stylists bore down on Annie as Enzo Cotta detached himself from his disciples and joined them, his face a mixture of confusion and fury.

"*The clothes! What are you doing to the clothes!*"

"Please," begged the assistant, all too aware of the extent of Enzo's rage. "Do not touch the clothes. They are precious."

"Can't you see?" Annie gasped. "There's something wrong!" As she spoke, Annie yanked hard, using all her strength. There was no sound but the boy's wail as a seam gave, the gown ripped, and Patty's latexed shoulder was exposed beneath the cloudy water.

"Stop!" he begged. "Please stop."

"No," Annie cried, sheer fury overcoming her terror. "You stop! Get some help. Stop the tide. For fuck's sake, do something!"

Gripping Patty's dress with both hands now, she yanked again and Patty butted up against the canal wall, close enough for the crew, now clustered around the bank, to see clearly what Annie had seen several long seconds ago.

"Let me." Reaching past Annie, Frank lifted the model from the water. "Step back," he said. Frank was addressing Enzo Cotta. After one look at the bleakness in the other man's eyes, Cotta did as he was told.

Carefully Frank laid the body beside the path. Patty's blond hair had been turned dark by the water. Her year-round tan was gone and her face looked as pale as the wintry dress she wore, white with a hint of icy blue. In the midst of all that whiteness her lips, painted by the makeup artist's hand, shone out a startling, incongruous red.

The job was done, Annie realized. Patty had kept her promise.

"Patty . . . ," whispered Annie.

Patty didn't answer, would never answer. Her eyes were wide open, pupils staring straight through Annie, straight through Frank and Enzo, reflecting a steely sky that had closed in on Patty long before the canal gave up its victim.

chapter thirty-three

Even as she dialed Chris's number, every brain cell told Annie, *Not now!* She was in too much of a state—would seem too needy. What's more, she had no idea if she could trust him. But by then it was too late. The call was made.

She told him about Patty. She told him about the police. About not being believed and about feeling responsible. And then she cried down the phone at him for ten minutes. He listened quietly, then suggested they meet for a drink.

So now they were sitting at a tiny round aluminium table in the darkened corner of a crimson-lit bar in San Babila, two streets from Fava's studios. She hadn't said much in the last fifteen minutes.

Across the table, Chris's body language was not so much schizophrenic as a riot of multiple personalities. His posture said, *Hey, look how casual and relaxed I am.* His face told a different story entirely. The blue-gray eyes still crinkled but this time with concern not laughter. *Is it me she wants to talk to,* said his expression, *or has she called the first person who came to mind? Does she still want me here or would she prefer it if I fucked off?*

This and more had been in constant motion across his face ever since he'd slid his arm around her and moved in to kiss her hello twenty minutes earlier and Annie had burst into tears, leaving a dark damp patch of mascara on the shoulder of his shirt.

I know what you're thinking, she wanted to say, seeing in her mind's eye what he could see from where he sat across the table. A *Whatever Happened to Baby Jane* bad dream, mascara, eyeliner, and lipstick that would have gone awry even if it had not been applied through a blur of tears in the back of a police car. *You're thinking, "What a basket case? How the hell did I get into this?"*

The huge gulp she took of the house Bardolino soothed Annie so she took another, then another. A glass later she began to feel better, more coherent in a fuzzy kind of way. She was going to feel like shit tomorrow. Shit-er. Which was fine. She probably owed Patty that at least.

Chris watched as tears fell anew down her face. Lifting the carafe, he refilled her glass.

"Say something," Annie demanded.

"Okay." Chris smiled, leaned forward gingerly, and touched the top of her hand very gently with his fingers.

Annie couldn't help it, she flinched. She wanted to trust him, to fling herself at him and tell him everything, but if she did that anything might happen. Anything at all.

He shrugged, the hurt evident in his eyes. "Do you want to talk to me about Patty?"

She shook her head and dragged the back of her hand across her face, extending a mascara smear across her cheekbone.

"Why not?"

She shook her head again, dumb with pain.

"It's not your fault," he tried again.

Calm down, she told herself, *the poor bastard didn't ask for this. You inflicted yourself on him.*

"It is," said Annie, lifting her head to meet his gaze. "It *is* my fault. And this isn't the first time."

"What do you mean? Someone drowned before?"

Annie thought of Irina, a ring of bruises like a macabre choker around her neck, staring up from her faded yellow bedspread at a world that had finally overwhelmed her. "Yes," she said. "Sort of. Not drowned exactly, but I don't want to . . . can't . . . talk about it. Let's talk about something else. Something normal, something ordinary." She meant something that didn't hurt, something with no dark edges creeping in.

Chris took a sip, hesitated, and Annie, against all journalistic rules, filled the gap. "Why don't you tell me about your day?"

It came out all wrong, harsh and sarcastic, not the tone Annie had intended.

Chris winced. "Look," he said. "This doesn't seem like a good idea to me. Maybe I should just call you a cab."

"No," Annie said hurriedly, "no, I didn't mean it like that, don't go. Please . . . I just meant talk to me, you know, about normal things, anything, anything at all."

So he talked and she drank. It was a combination that worked for Annie, and he didn't seem to have a problem with it. At a guess, Chris drank one glass for every three of hers.

Who was counting? Certainly not Annie.

For a while, as the day-to-day gossip of Milan Fashion Week wafted around her . . . Ugo's fury at the hatchet jobs greeting yesterday's show . . . What a bitch this person was/what a slacker that one was . . . His problems with his Italian landlord . . . The ex-girlfriend who was the reason he hated roses . . . While all this flowed around her, Patty's death floated into the distance, carried away on a tide of personal trivia, petty rivalries, and the surface froth of a billion-dollar industry. That was one of the many things she liked about red wine, Annie thought. Just how much it helped you forget.

After the best part of another carafe, Annie reached her decision.

"Can we go now?" she asked abruptly.

"Of course," Chris said, brave enough now to squeeze her hand and hold it there, Annie just drunk enough to let him.

"I'll call you a cab," said Chris.

"Not yet."

"I don't think you're up for dinner, do you?"

"Who said anything about dinner?" said Annie, feeling a grim smile break through. "We'll walk."

"Where?"

As if he didn't know.

"Annie, I don't think . . ."

Annie grinned, using the hand he still held to tug him from his chair.

"I want to go to bed," she said, watching those blue-gray eyes give him away. "I'm afraid to go there alone. And I'd prefer to go with you."

He was good in bed. It was sickeningly inevitable. The man was kind, dressed well, looked okay without his clothes, and held her when she cried. He used her name and that was always a good sign, it meant he knew who he was in bed with. He was gentle without needing to be and rough when necessary. She wished she'd met him a long time ago.

There was good sex, there was bad sex, and there was the stuff in the middle, which was everything else. It came as something of a shock to Annie that she could even recognize the good stuff anymore.

Chris's head lay on her breast, his cheek slippery with sweat, his eyelashes fluttering against her soft skin as he kissed one nipple, sending tiny electric shocks down her stomach. In return she stroked his hair. It was naturally scruffy, she'd decided earlier, when her fingers meshed in it and found themselves without the obstruction of gel as she kissed him outside the bar, in the taxi, in the lift, and as she fumbled with the lock on her hotel door. Their clothes were off almost before the door shut and they fucked where they fell. Unwilling even to wait the four or five paces it would take to reach the bed.

There was none of the usual sex with a near-stranger stuff, clothes off, condom on, cock in, and ten minutes later you're wondering whether it was worth the carpet burns and knickers still around your ankles. But that didn't mean sex with Chris hadn't brought its own problems; it had, three.

For a start, she'd broken all her own rules. He wasn't a stranger, that was rule number one. She knew his name—both his first and second names— and it was conceivable that she'd want to see him again. So that was rule number two broken. Bad plan, sleeping with people you like. And the sex had been good, maybe even better than good. Embarrassing, sweaty, and bruisingly good, swollen lips, tangled legs, lipstick all over her face, forgetting to worry about whether she looked fat, moaning out loud because she'd momentarily mislaid the faculty that reminded her not to . . . The kind of sex that brought her right to the surface of her skin, so every millimeter tingled with even the slightest touch and each tiny sensation resonated in her brain, until she was right there, at the front of her eyes, looking out.

His body heat seeped into her flesh, his hands explored and stroked her arms, legs, and back, her stomach rising up to meet him. Right now Annie couldn't quite work out why she'd ever thought her rules were such a great idea in the first place.

Sensing her skin reawakening beneath him, Chris eased himself upward, kissing her breast a long, slow goodbye on the way past. That sensation joined the others, flickering down her body in little darts of pleasure. One of those faithless little groans escaped and Annie had to resist the urge to push his head back the way it had come.

Chris smiled, the secret kind of smile you see only on the face of someone whose body you've just shared, returning to kiss her other breast.

Seeing his face like that, in the half light that filtered in through Annie's still open curtains, she just wanted him all over again. The sex or Chris? Annie knew the answer.

Chris shifted, his face drawing level with her own, left hand sliding down her stomach to reach between her legs, stopping for the briefest moment to touch the soft skin of her inner thigh.

"Oh, fuck . . . Annie."

She didn't even mind him watching her face as he slid his fingers inside her.

"You didn't like that, did you?" The voice is soft with fake sincerity and concern; beneath it fault lines of sarcasm ran deep.

"Well, did you?" He rolls her over, lets his index finger trace idly down her spine. He enjoys the involuntary whimper that escapes her, she knows he does, *the shudder that could be a shiver, because the bathroom is cold and the floor colder still, but they both know it isn't.*

His parents are away for the weekend. Annie and Tony are meant to be somewhere else, at a party.

"Answer me." Tony's voice is harder, shades of triumphalism, colliding with the silence that suffocates the chill air around her.

She closes her eyes and tries to close her mind, to shut out the cold, his voice, the pain . . .

His hand travels lower, tracing each vertebra, each goose bump on her naked back with a lover's care. Reaching the base of her spine he stops, fingers poised, waiting.

She hurts. Just touching her there hurts.

"Answer me, Annie."

Fist still wadded in her mouth, Annie shakes her head, pressing her tears farther into a damp bath mat and feels the hard tiles of the floor beneath her ribs. Bright lights spin behind her lids.

"If you don't . . . ," he says, positioning himself over her.

Pain. Pain, sharp and deep and then darkness.

"I told you," he tells her, her body racked with silent sobs as the blackness recedes. His voice is soft as a parent, soft as a lover, full of sorrow. "I warned you not to make me do this."

She was sitting bolt upright, heart hammering in her chest, face and hair soaked, sweat and tears mingling. Woken by the memories and ghost of a pain so extreme it left her bruised and torn for weeks and haunted her a thousand times longer.

"Hey, are you all right?"

Annie froze, shocked. She was not alone.

"Are you okay?"

Oh God, she couldn't handle this anymore; how could this be happening? Then Annie remembered. She'd taken someone to bed.

Run screamed the memory, wide awake now. *Run.*

Where to? She was already home, or what passed for it. There was nowhere to run to.

Tony had been her first real boyfriend and her last.

"Yes," said Annie. "Yes, I'm fine. Bad dream."

"Bad dream?"

"Someone locked me into a bathroom."

Fingers came up to touch her face, wiping away tears. It was all she could do not to flinch.

"Bathrooms have locks on the inside," said Chris.

"Not this one." Annie shuddered. "Well, it did," she said, "but a chair was jammed under the outside handle. So I couldn't get free."

"Why the chair?" Chris asked, voice sleepy.

"I was hysterical," said Annie. "Look, it doesn't matter. I'm fine now, really. Sorry I woke you."

"I was only dozing anyway."

A lie but a kind lie, Annie recognized that.

"You sure you're okay?"

"Yes, honestly. It was just a bad dream. I'm fine. Go back to sleep."

"If you're sure."

"Sure."

Chris rolled over, not that there was far to roll on her single bed, his arm reaching across her hips. The casual intimacy of the move discomforted her. He was too close, his skin next to her skin, the warmth of his sleep-filled breath on her body. She wasn't used to this; Annie was normally long gone by now. A mistress of stealth dressing without the aid of light in unfamiliar surroundings.

Every second it took for his breath to slow seemed like ten. Come on, Annie begged, counting the ins and outs and fasts and shallows, listening as his breathing gradually grew deeper and quieter as the minutes passed. *Come on.*

And when there were no more snuffles and sighs, Annie muttered Chris's name, not loud enough to wake him if he slept, but loud enough for a change in the pattern of his breathing to give him away.

Silence. "Chris? You still awake?"

Easing herself from under the weight of his arm, Annie fought down her urge to fling back the covers and run.

She rolled from the bed and snatched at her clothes, locating boots and sweeping up a random armful. Creeping into the bathroom, she tapped the light switch as she passed, easing the door so it shut noiselessly behind her. A towel across the bottom prevented the sudden sliver of light leaking beneath the door to wake the man who slept in her bed.

Surveying the bundle of clothes in her arms, Annie sighed. That all the items weren't hers didn't matter, because the only item belonging to Chris was a black shirt and no one would notice that.

She knew why the dream was back. It was because she was afraid. And she knew why she was afraid. Patty had been murdered; Annie was certain of this. Whether it was one of the two men who'd attacked Patty at Villa Mantolini, both of them or someone new, Patty's drowning merely concluded what had been begun two nights before.

And if Patty had been murdered—and the makeup artist's protestations that she'd been stoned, under the influence of something far harder than nicotine, only confirmed that—then whoever had had Mark killed was behind it. And if that was true then Annie, the only person who still knew Mark had pulled out of a deal to sell to Baroni two days before he died, had to be next on their list.

"Fakes," said Annie, trying the word out for size. That was what the newspaper clipping was about. That was why Mark Mailer had pulled out of the Fava deal. Or was it why he pulled out of the Mantolini deal before he'd even put his acceptance in writing? Someone had killed Mark and then killed Patty. She had little doubt that they would try to kill her.

Annie didn't want to admit defeat but she needed help. She thought of Mariolina Mantolini, of Rebecca, even of Guido. She'd gone farther than this before in her work but never entirely on her own. There was no alternative.

Picking up the phone extension beside the toilet, she dialed nine for an outside line. Her hands were trembling as she punched in the familiar number. Across the miles she heard the line connect and a phone at the other end begin to buzz.

"Come on," she said, counting the rings. After five she put it down. *Just do it.*

Before she could argue herself out of redialing, Annie picked up the phone again and punched REDIAL. The connection was made in seconds, although she'd barely allowed the phone to ring once before cutting off the noise. She was shocked by how badly her hands were shaking.

"Get a grip, Annie," said the voice inside her head.

The reflection in the mirror showed a picture of chaos. Her hair was matted and what of her mascara hadn't been cried off was smudged across her cheeks; her eyes were bloodshot and dark-rimmed. Eyes that she'd seen before. Her mouth was red and puffy, sex lips. Annie felt the heat rise. Even now, in this state, her body was prepared to betray her.

Part of Annie yearned to ignore the nightmare once and for all, to turn back the clock just half an hour. Just long enough to nestle into the safety of Chris's arms and close her eyes. Assuming the arms of one of Ugo Baroni's senior staff was a safe place to be.

The thought made Annie retch, her eyes watering as she dry-heaved into the sink. How many times did she have to tell herself. The only thing more stupid than sleeping with a friend was choosing to sleep with an enemy.

Numbly, Annie picked up the receiver again. She let it ring three, four, and five times before hanging up and slipping from the bathroom, shutting off the light on her way out.

Five, one, five—it was a signal Ken would recognize at once, assuming he was there.

chapter thirty-four

The hotel corridor was as deserted as one would expect at five in the morning, just a Tunisian cleaner clocking on at the start of her shift and a *ping* in the distance to announce a lift reporting for duty. Reluctant to take the machine up on its offer, Annie crept to the end of the corridor and disappeared through a fire door.

Two flights down Annie paused, ears straining for the sound of feet above or below, a fire door creaking open then shut. All she could hear was the knocking of water pipes. Once certain that no one else was out of bed, Annie crouched and tipped the contents of her bag onto the floor, taking a rapid inventory as she tossed each item back in. Everything was there, exactly where she'd left it the morning before—everything except the tapes, and those were safely in the post.

That was another trick she'd learned from Ken Greenhouse. It was like hiding things in plain sight. Sometimes you had to trust to the notoriously unreliable because nobody else would.

"Bonjourno, signorina." The night porter greeted her as she attempted to slip from the stairwell unobserved. He leaned back in his chair at the

reception desk, last night's *Corriere della Sera* spread on the counter before him. "You are very early this morning. Too early for breakfast. Maybe I get you some coffee?"

Annie shook her head. "No, thanks, couldn't sleep." The quasi-whisper was fairly pointless, since the old man had just bellowed at her across the lobby, so she gave it up. "I thought I'd go for a walk, get some fresh air."

He shrugged and returned to his paper.

Darkness greeted Annie as she stepped from the hotel's brightly lit foyer and turned right under the shadow of scaffolding outside. It was cold and the air smelled of salt, which was strange for a city so far from the sea. This was a darkness she could handle, a predawn gloom that hugged the damp, chill street and promised the safety of daylight only a few small hours away. There had to be a café open somewhere, offering espresso, *torta sbrisolana,* and the comfort of strangers.

Annie leaned against the scaffold, out of sight of the hotel door. And, she hoped, out of sight of anyone else who might notice her checking the street. It was quiet, with that wonderful early-morning silence before man-made noise and nature come out of their corners fighting. The birds had yet to strike up their chatter; only the occasional crash of a rubbish truck announced that Lombardy's capital was about to wake up.

Annie shivered, pulling her Mantolini jacket tight around her. If she walked for an hour, maybe two, Chris might wake and, finding her gone, be gone himself when she returned.

Ugo Baroni? Mariolina Mantolini? One of them knew something. One of them had to . . . And Chris Mahoney? The man whose memory was now trickling down the inside of her thigh. Where did he fit into it? Which one was the fake?

At the end of Viale Piave, Annie crossed into the piazza. Without the frenzy of pigeons that normally populated the square, like an avian Mafioso terrorizing and extorting food from anyone reckless enough to buy a newspaper at the kiosk in the center, the piazza seemed strangely empty.

Pausing, Annie listened. Rubbish trucks, a distant scooter, and something else. The tread of feet on cobbles somewhere behind.

"Keep moving," she told herself. That was the extent of her plan. Not so great for a journalist used to thinking on her feet. Staying alive played a major part in her plan, too.

Turning a slow 360 degrees, Annie peered into the shadows lining the piazza. No one else was around so far as Annie could tell, but still she picked up speed, clattering across endless cobbles toward Corso Venezia and the *giardini pubblici*.

The gate stood open, the park's gloomy tree-lined paths deserted. Annie gave the empty street behind her one final glance to check that she was alone and stepped under a wrought-iron arch, between two low ornamental hedges in need of pruning.

Halting at a bench beneath a row of sycamore, Annie ran through what she knew.

"The trouble with Ugo is once you've worked for him, he thinks he owns you, you're his property," Chris had said the night before. Somewhere between Patty's death and the darkness had come her first real break, lurking in the bottom of a carafe of house red.

"*That's* what happened with Tom."

It took Annie a second to realize he meant Tom Li, the man whose talent and credibility Mark was meant to be replacing. The man who had called Mark just days before he died.

"Ugo discovered him, got him out of some counterfeiting racket in Hong Kong, and gave him his big break. So Ugo's always saying anyway. He thinks Tom betrayed him, like he should have stayed at Fava forever, letting Ugo take all the credit."

"That's why Ugo needed Mark's label?"

Chris had nodded, unwilling to commit himself out loud.

"So now he's buying Enzo Cotta instead?"

Chris looked shocked.

"That's what I heard," said Annie, too drunk to remember where.

"Ugo doesn't take betrayal lightly," said Chris, filling his own glass. "And he's not the kind of guy to take criticism lying down. Most of those journalists who slagged him off this morning will never get invited to a show again."

Yeah, but there was a big difference between knocking someone off your invitation list and killing them. So Annie had decided at the time, struggling to follow Chris's train of thought.

"Who did Tom Li make fakes for?" Annie asked.

Chris shrugged. "I don't know. I don't suppose anyone knows."

Annie very much doubted that was true. Mark had known, she decided, remembering the newspaper clipping. And what was it Mariolina had said about Baroni? "The man's a fake—in every sense of the word, but don't quote me on that because I'll deny ever saying it . . ."

The truth became clearer. It was not Mark's rejection that tipped the balance; it was his reasons. Honest to a fault, Mark had not just pulled out, he had told Ugo Baroni why; standing on a Manhattan rooftop at 3 A.M., three nights before he died.

Annie laid the facts out in front of her, shuffled them, and redealt. Tom Li had started out in Hong Kong where Baroni discovered him . . . that was the official story. What if the truth was different? How about Tom Li always worked for Baroni, only Ugo had him change jobs, brought him over to Milan, and made him legitimate . . . How far would Baroni go to make sure that piece of information never got out? A very long way, decided Annie. The trouble was she couldn't prove it, and facing Baroni down on instinct alone would be a hell of a bluff, maybe the biggest Annie had ever tried.

I KNOW WHY MARK MAILER DIED. Annie fed the message into her mobile, one letter at a time, then pressed OK to send the message to Rebecca. She could have written *I think I know . . .* but that wouldn't have grabbed Rebecca's attention in quite the same way and what she needed right now was Rebecca's undivided attention.

She had Baroni, Annie knew she did. For a moment she regretted not listening to the tapes one final time before dispatching them to safety. Mark had been telling her all along, Annie could see that now. Answering her unasked questions with oblique half-truths of his own. One in particular played over and over in her head. *Some people, you think they want to help you. They're the most dangerous of all.* Not Guido, not Guido Brasco at all.

At the time Annie had been too keen to blame the old tailor, but he'd also been scared, because he understood what Mark was embroiled in—

what he'd helped to embroil Mark in—and he was powerless to stop Mark being swallowed.

"Leave it," he'd told Annie, not warning her but begging.

The old man had been right to be worried. She'd let her nose for a story get in the way of common sense.

"Signorina Anderson?"

A crunch of gravel, the sound of shoes on a path. A voice so soft that Annie wondered if she'd imagined it.

"Who's there?" she asked.

"Me," said the voice, coming from a line of trees.

That was when Annie heard another set of footsteps to one side. She never heard the man who coshed her, he'd been walking on grass. She just felt something very heavy hit the back of her head.

chapter thirty-five

When the car's boot was finally raised and daylight flooded in, Annie was blinded. It took a full five seconds for Frank's features to come into focus. Annie fancied there was a hint of regret, even apology, in his look, although common sense suggested it was exactly that, mere fancy.

Francisco Giordano had not acted alone. A boy was disappearing through a door and an older man stood behind Frank. Not Ugo Baroni; this man was both taller and thinner, his expression displaying a range that stretched from total lack of interest to contempt and back again. He was older by some way than Frank, into his fifties, and there was something familiar about his face, though Annie couldn't place him. This man, in his immaculate suit and red tie, was not at one with the aging process, Annie decided.

"Annie Anderson," Annie said, introducing herself. "I'd offer to shake hands only they're tied."

It was stupid, it was glib, it was the kind of comment that used to land her in deep shit with Tony, but Annie couldn't resist it. She just wished her voice had sounded a little more confident.

The man said nothing, his icy stare piercing straight through her and beyond as if he was expecting to see something more interesting behind.

Frank said something in Italian and the man nodded. "Okay," said Frank, turning to her. "We're getting out."

Clutching her under her arms, Frank dragged Annie clumsily from the boot of the Mercedes, banging her hip and shin against the lip as he struggled to extract her. Annie didn't exactly help but she didn't kick out, either. There was no point. Her only protest was the toddler's stance of stubborn defiance, affecting legs as stiff as a board to make her transit as awkward as possible.

While Frank cursed and dragged Annie's deadweight across the tarmac of a deserted industrial estate, the elder man barked a series of orders. Annie didn't know whether Frank was paying any attention, but after one particularly sharp barrage he gave an audible sigh and hefted Annie over his shoulder, carrying her through a small door in a huge metal hangar.

If she didn't have enough of a headache before, she did now. The older man had lost patience with Annie's struggles when Frank began to tie her to a chair and had coshed her again with the blunt end of his gun. Instinctively she put up her fingers to feel blood and realized she couldn't move: Both wrists were now knotted to the frame of a folding metal chair, and so were her ankles. Not a very stable chair, though, and instinct told her the knots were amateurish, tied in haste.

Why go to all that trouble and then not bother to tie her up firmly? Unless, of course, they didn't care if she ran because there was nowhere for her to run? Or worse, because they were toying with her.

"Who's there?" Annie called.

All she got was an echo.

"No," she told herself. Now was not a good time to panic.

She shifted on the chair to get a better view of the room. An underground store, crudely walled in breezeblock and lit by a single bulb hanging on a bare flex from the ceiling. Judging by the scale of the building she'd seen from outside, this room took up a fraction of the hangar's floor space. It was, however, the kind of room that would be reasonably sound-proof. Ideal for masking the sound of a shot, or a scream.

Sometimes Annie wished she didn't have quite such an eye for detail. Apart from her metal chair there was no furniture except a folding table directly opposite. In the center of the table, like some bizarre trophy, was her battered holdall. And piled high against the wall behind the table were cardboard boxes stamped with sequential serial numbers. Stock from Hong Kong? Annie had a pretty good idea what she would find if she could only get inside. The thought chilled her, and she wondered at the psychology of the man who'd brought her here.

Annie had already worked out what this place was. A depot, the syndicate's Italian equivalent of New Jersey, where stock was stored on its arrival from the Far East before finding its way out into the Italian and European markets.

Baroni didn't care if she knew, Annie realized. He was not afraid of her, but he was going to make damn sure she was afraid of him.

Long after she should have heard Ugo Baroni's approach, Annie sensed him watching. Her discomfort turned slowly to fear, but still she would not turn her head or shift the chair to show him she was aware of his presence.

And so he waited until her stillness told him what he needed to know. And then, when he was absolutely certain unease had turned to fear, he made her wait a full minute more, lest Annie forget who had the upper hand.

"Ah, Signorina Anderson. So sorry I couldn't speak with you on Monday. So, you see, I make time to see you today. Two days is not so long to wait. For you, I empty my diary." Ugo Baroni smiled expansively.

He was still attractive, Annie thought, revolted. Charismatic, rich, and very sure of his own power. The kind of man who knew how to dress for every occasion, even this one. He wore black leather gloves and carried a pair of pliers. His shoes had been recently polished.

How much had it all cost? wondered Annie—his hair implants, the dental veneers, the Botox, the body; all designed to delude. All as fake as the man who wore them.

"So much digging . . . so many people. You have been busy. Mark, Patty, Cathie Olsen, that old fool Brasco, Mariolina . . . that was very clever of you. Even my international advertising director."

Ugo Baroni's smile was not kind.

"Christian tells me you have many questions you'd like to ask me. Questions about the deal I had struck with Mark Mailer, the kind of questions I thought might benefit from some privacy."

So she'd been right. Chris . . .

Annie tried to smile, said nothing.

"No?" Ugo Baroni shrugged, strolled casually across the small room, and upended Annie's bag. The entire contents rattled onto the table or rolled to the floor—chewing gum and tampons and loose change, her purse with its euros and dollars and pounds, tickets to shows she'd missed, an old photo of Annie with her sister when they were children and things were different. Baroni ignored the debris; he knew what he was looking for. Without hesitation he removed the tape from her Dictaphone and slipped it into his jacket pocket.

Annie tried to look stricken. The tape was blank, but he would find that out soon enough. A notebook earned Baroni's attention, but it didn't take him long to dismiss the rest.

"I think you know what I'm looking for . . . You have something I need, sentimental value, let's say. Where is it, Signorina Anderson? Where are the other tapes?"

"That's the only tape I have."

"Please," said Ugo Baroni. "Do not disappoint me by being stupid."

"I'm telling the truth."

His look didn't scare her. She understood the man standing in front of her now. The vanity, the charm . . . He was Tony Panton in better clothes, amoral and spoiled. Tony with a gun.

Her wrists hurt like fuck and her head was pounding, part hangover, but mostly bruising. Annie wouldn't let him know this any more than she could afford to let him know that what she said was true. She really didn't have the tapes.

"You're not going to be stupid, are you?" Baroni said. Behind him, the hawk-faced man muttered something and was rewarded with a shake of the head. "Not yet," said Ugo Baroni, and he said it in English so Annie could understand. Frank said nothing; he just stood beside the other man, unable to bring himself to meet Annie's eyes.

"You've searched her, of course?"

Ugo Baroni read the answer in the faces of the other two men.

"Fools."

Frank stepped forward before the hawk-faced man could move.

"Are you wearing a wire?" he demanded.

Annie shook her head.

The driver searched anyway. Running his fingers expertly across her back and stomach, under her breasts, and inside the band of her jeans. And then, almost apologetically, he undid the first two buttons of her shirt and put his hands in the valley between her breasts.

"No wire," he said, redoing the buttons before resuming his place.

Baroni sighed.

"You stupid bitch," he said, raising his hand.

The slap was hard and Annie got the feeling it was really intended for the other two.

"Fuck you," she replied.

And the next slap was harder.

"You left a message for Tom Li . . ."

She had? Annie vaguely remembered doing something like that shortly after Patty died. "I wanted to talk to him about how he got started."

Ugo Baroni looked amused. "Tom doesn't like to talk about that. He thinks it's a secret."

"Oh, *that,*" Annie said. "Everyone knows that. It's *your* dirty little secrets you need to worry about. What happened with Mark Mailer. Why he pulled out of the deal."

"I don't know what it is you think you know, Signorina Anderson, but I assure you I have nothing to worry about."

"So why kill Mark? And Patty, why her?"

Ice-blue eyes regarded Annie not in amazement or anger, but bemusement. "I was very sorry for the death of Mark Mailer," said Ugo Baroni, walking over to her chair and gently wiping blood from her lips. Annie had to steel herself not to pull away. "The whole world knows that no one was more sorry than I when Mark Mailer died. And with him my future hopes for our combined brilliance. Believe me, I had more to lose than anyone from Mark's death. So why would I, of all people, have Mark killed? Your logic defeats me. And as for his . . . girlfriend . . ."

"Wife," said Annie. It was a mistake.

"Really?" Baroni raised his eyebrows. "How interesting. Surely that makes it even more likely that poor Patty would be so distraught when her *husband* was killed that she would try to follow him, and keep trying if she did not at first succeed. After all, she'd been killing herself for years."

"How do you know she didn't?"

"Didn't what?"

"Succeed the first time. How do you know what happened at Mariolina's?"

The man scowled. "You insult me," he said. "I have my limits, and you are now over them. Tell me where the other tapes are and we can bring this to an end."

A knot of panic tightened in Annie's stomach. She couldn't allow this conversation to finish because that was when her troubles would really start.

"What tapes?" Even she thought that sounded ridiculous.

"Your interview with Mark Mailer," said Baroni. "And with his *wife*. Those tapes . . ."

Annie could continue the game of cat-and-mouse or she could play her hand. Suspecting he had all the time in the world and she, trussed to a chair at his discretion, did not, Annie tried to finesse her own cards.

Bluff, Ken Greenhouse always said. *When all else fails, bluff.*

"They're back at the hotel, in my safe. I thought it would be better to leave them there."

Ugo Baroni spun around, snarling something at Frank in Italian.

Whatever the driver said in reply sounded defensive.

"Idiots." Ugo Baroni's voice was more irritated than angry. He was too confident of his own brilliance to be upset for long. How could he expect other people to always get things right when they weren't him? Turning to Annie, he nodded toward the hawk-faced man. "I believe you've already met my financial director, Silvio Vianni?"

Of course, that was where Annie had seen the man before. His picture was on the article from the *Financial Times* back in her hotel room.

"Silvio is my adviser," said Baroni, "and he advises me that we really must edit your source material. So he will accompany you to your hotel to collect the tapes and then you and I can have another little chat."

chapter thirty-six

Annie knew she was a dead woman when Frank didn't bother to return her to the Mercedes's boot, just fixed her mouth, wrists, and ankles with clear tape and pushed her into the back.

"There," said Frank sarcastically. "Now you have the whole seat to yourself."

"If you make a fuss I will kill you," Silvio Vianni added, almost as an afterthought; his expression was grim. "If I had my way you'd be dead already, despite what Ugo says. We do not need you there to make sure the code is right; we can simply take the safe."

Even if Annie's mouth had not been taped shut, there wouldn't have been much of an answer to that.

Milan was in the midst of morning rush hour when the Mercedes pulled into a narrow side street behind the Sheraton Diana. At least Annie assumed that was where they'd parked. It was hard to be sure from her vantage point on the backseat. And it had taken all her effort just to maneuver herself from where she'd been thrown, into a position where she could at least see the walls, tiles, and a patch of sky.

"Now," said Frank, opening the door beside her head and ripping off the tape before Annie could twist away. "Stay quiet." He took out a knife and flipped open the blade, slicing the tape away from her wrists.

A door opened on the other side of the car and Silvio cut the tape binding from her ankles.

"Bastards," said Annie.

It wasn't worth it. Reaching into the car, Frank wrapped his hands in Annie's hair and dragged her out. Even Silvio looked slightly shocked. Tears sprang to Annie's eyes but she refused to cry out. Sore mouth and bleeding scalp paled before what would happen when they discovered there were no tapes. At least none that Annie could reach.

"You hold the bitch," said Frank. "While I let the boss know we're here." There was something unpleasantly sly in his voice. A sense that he was beginning to enjoy himself.

"Enough," Silvio Vianni spat, making no attempt to hide his contempt for the other man. "Now we will walk through the foyer. If the receptionist speaks to you, wave or say good morning, but do not go over. I already have your key and so if there is something at the desk for you to collect just say you will pick it up on your way out. Understand?"

He produced a pair of dark glasses from his pocket and put them on Annie. They were too large and hid not only her eyes but almost half her face. Maybe that was the point; either way, they made her look very *fashion.*

She'd been burgled, that was the answer. Annie tried it on for size, wondering if she could carry it off. Her room would be a mess, it always was. She'd been burgled. She was shocked. The tapes were gone. What then? How would that make things better?

"Go straight to the stairs and we will climb together. We do not need the added complication of waiting for a lift. Frank will meet us on the third floor outside your room. Number Three twenty-one, I believe? At the rear overlooking the roof of the kitchens: not a good room."

There'd been no question in Annie's mind that Silvio and Frank knew her room number and that a house call had been paid by one or the other when she was at Villa Mantolini, but this idle confirmation chilled her.

Silvio Vianni no longer cared how much she knew, because he didn't expect her to be around for much longer.

Unnerved, Annie swallowed. Silvio saw it, and smiled.

The receptionists barely glanced up as the elegant middle-aged man with thick dark hair walked Annie across the lobby, whispering sweet warnings in her ear, one arm locked through hers and the blade of a knife hidden in his other hand.

Damn it, thought Annie, keeping her eyes straight ahead. Where were they with their packages and their telephone messages and their *Bonjourno, signorinas* now?

The stairwell was similarly deserted.

Where were all the maids and the bellboys, the Lebanese guy from room service, all the hotel staff she usually encountered in the course of a day? The only sign of life was a maid's trolley on the third floor and that was abandoned, draped with the evidence of lives lived in transit, damp towels and used sheets, discarded breakfast trays and plastic bottles of mineral water, most empty and lidless. A mop in a bucket leaned against the wall five doors along from Annie's own, but there seemed to be no owner. And the only voices Annie could hear came with music, applause, and canned laughter. Someone somewhere was watching television because someone somewhere was always watching television. Annie didn't sag, not visibly, but the fight was leaching out of her. She had scarcely ever felt so alone.

Too late, way too late, Annie wished she'd bothered to phone her mother back after shouting at her for giving Tony her mobile number. And after all that the bastard had never called back. How typical.

"Now," said Silvio as he drew level with her bedroom door, "we will not be staying long. We go in, you collect the tapes, and we leave. In silence. It is very straightforward. Do not try anything because Frank has less scruples than I do."

"You better believe it."

Throwing a look at Frank, who was approaching them, Annie wasn't so sure. For all his bravado, he was beginning to look decidedly uneasy.

"You will open the door," Silvio said, pulling a keycard from his pocket and wiping it with a handkerchief. "Understand?"

Taking her key without touching the man's handkerchief, Annie slid the plastic card into the lock and waited for the light to turn green.

"You go first, I go next, Frank stays outside," Silvio said, pulling the knife from his sleeve. Annie saw a flash of sunlight and felt cold steel against her spine.

Turning the handle until she heard it click, Annie pushed at the door. The buzz of laughter became louder as she realized the television she'd heard playing was her own.

Annie stepped through the door, fingers reaching back, trying to find the edge of the door while she wondered whether she could slam it hard and fast enough to break Silvio's wrist, or at least his fingers.

And then she decided not to bother.

Chris was still there, handcuffed and bare-chested, sitting on her bed.

"No," said a voice, "do come in." It was very definitely talking to Silvio.

Behind her, there was a scuffle and then Silvio stumbled past Annie, followed by Frank, now holding the knife. Silvio was nursing his fingers, looking shocked and suddenly much less certain.

"Annie!" Rebecca was standing by the window, glowering. A thickset man with a paunch so large that even good tailoring couldn't hide it stood on the other side of the window; he was also glowering, although his anger seemed to be directed at Frank.

"At last," Rebecca said, relief evident in her voice. "Do you have any idea how much trouble you've caused?"

Annie ignored her. She couldn't deny she was indescribably relieved the woman had come through, but now her attention was on another man who was holding a gun. He wore a gray uniform that managed to look simultaneously austere and expensive, and his eyes were hidden behind tiny tinted glasses. He looked, and Annie realized how absurd this sounded, like a very expensive and rather dangerous cat.

"Signorina Anderson?" he said.

Annie nodded.

"Colonel Visconti of the carabinieri." The man clicked his heels and bowed very slightly. The gesture was self-mocking. "I believe you know Signor Bernardini?"

Annie shook her head.

"Ah, well . . . It seems he knows your boss and in Italy that is everything."

"So it seems," said Rebecca. "But *I'm* Annie's boss, and I've never met this man before in my life."

Signor Bernardini, of the paunch and the well-cut suit, seemed serenely happy to maintain that arrangement. In a flash, Annie knew. He meant Ken. Bernardini must be a newspaperman.

It was Chris, still cuffed, who broke the silence. "Will someone please tell me what the fuck is going on?" he demanded. "What is Silvio doing here? Where's Annie been? What's all this got to do with Ugo?"

"You should know," Annie spat, unable to bear the thought that she'd trusted him even for a moment. Turning her back, she marched all of three steps to where Frank stood, opposite Silvio Vianni, the other man's knife now held loosely in his hand.

"I'm sorry," said Frank, nodding at her bleeding scalp. "I had to make it convincing."

"It was," Annie said. "You want to tell me who the fuck you are? Given that you're not our driver and apparently you're not Baroni's hired thug, either."

"He works for me," said Signor Bernardini. "And Colonel Visconti and I are old friends." Something about the way he said this told Annie that friends were the last thing they were. Allies maybe, bound by past history or, more likely, by necessity.

Bernardini held out his hand and, after a second's surprise, Annie shook it. "Rafael Bernardini," he said. "Editor in chief of *Gazetta di Milano.* Ken Greenhouse and I started together on the *Croydon Herald.*"

Five rings, one ring, five rings . . . The signal for *Get me out of here,* their code for not waving but drowning. Ken had come through, too. He'd checked the number, picked up the phone, and called one of a thousand contacts, the right one. It was what made her boss what he was, one of the greats. A man who understood that sometimes you have to make up your own rules as you go along.

"Annie . . ." Rebecca's voice was impatient. "Do you think you could tell me what's going on now?"

Annie looked at the woman who thought she was Annie's boss, so different from the middle-aged man who really was and yet so similar. Tell Rebecca that until Mark Mailer died she and her magazine had been part of a *Post* story, an undercover investigation into the workings of the fashion industry? Annie didn't think so, not right now anyway. So she asked Rebecca a question of her own. One that seemed obvious in retrospect. "How did you know I meant you to come?"

Rebecca smiled, which was unnerving in itself. "I didn't at first," she said. "But when you texted me I telephoned and he answered." She pointed to Chris. "Since he couldn't tell me where you were, I called the police . . ."

"Who called me," said Colonel Visconti. "About ten minutes after Signor Bernardini called me. Which I thought was very interesting."

Annie's head hurt.

"One thing," Rebecca said, waiting until she had Annie's full attention. "Are you sure you're okay?"

Such unexpected kindness was the last thing Annie could cope with. She wasn't. For a start she was crying, but that didn't matter, because Annie realized she was still wearing Silvio Vianni's dark glasses.

chapter thirty-seven

Less than thirty minutes later a midnight-blue Mercedes E-class pulled up on a familiar stretch of tarmac outside an anonymous-looking hangar on an industrial estate to the northwest of Milan. A hundred yards behind it, a large black Fiat van pulled over to the side of the road and the driver got out to check his tires, tutting crossly.

It was the second time Annie had visited this particular building that February morning, but the circumstances could not have been more different. For a start, she could see where she was going and, although Frank still drove, this time he wasn't the enemy. Only Annie, Rafael Bernardini, and the carabiniere colonel got out of the car.

The local police had been doing the legwork, closing off roads in and out of the estate. Chris was still in custody, proclaiming both his innocence and total ignorance of any wrongdoing, and Rebecca had finally returned to her hotel on the understanding that she would get a full update from Annie, "As soon as that man has finished with her." She was talking about the colonel.

"What about . . ." Annie turned to where Frank sat in the driver's seat. It had come as a shock to discover that their driver was an Italian journalist working undercover on the same story as she was, and an even greater surprise to discover he'd been wearing a wire. The man who searched her for wires had been wearing one himself. That took some nerve. It was just a pity he'd been wired to a transmitter, not a tape. Ugo Baroni's cellar had been out of range.

"Francisco stays here," announced Colonel Visconti. "In case Signor Baroni is out and returns. He can tell Baroni that Signor Vianni has the tapes and is inside waiting."

As they headed for the small door through which Annie had been carried, one side of the entire end wall began to slide back, revealing a slim, elegantly dressed man who strode toward them, arms wide open.

"Colonel," he said, offering his hand. "I read about your promotion. I was so pleased."

The carabiniere officer seemed surprised.

Ugo Baroni smiled, the biggest smile Annie had ever seen on a man whose life was supposedly caving in around him.

"Come in, come in," he said, in English, presumably for Annie's benefit. He could have been welcoming a glossy magazine to his lovely home rather than a senior carabiniere officer to a warehouse full of incriminating stock. As an afterthought he added, "Signor Bernardini, delighted as always . . . Signorina Anderson, how lovely to see you again. I'm so sorry I wasn't able to give you that interview. I do hope you won't be holding it against Fava when you write your piece."

She had to hand it to the man, he was charm personified; but then Annie had always considered charm a very overrated virtue. One mostly used by the kind of men who need something to paper over the cracks in their personality. She looked at Visconti, waiting for him to make his move, but the man was carefully not looking her way.

Instead of insisting they take the concrete stairs down into the cellar, Colonel Visconti turned left and followed Baroni into an office that would have been perfectly functional had it not been stuffed with so much furniture it looked like just another storeroom. Three desks, three chairs, three filing cabinets jostled for space in a room barely adequate for one.

"My foreman's office," explained Baroni, his smile fixed as he took a seat behind the larger of the desks. "He allows me to use it when I visit."

Even the colonel raised his eyebrows at that.

"Now, what can I do for you? I've already had a call from police HQ to tell me Signorina Anderson has had a very distressing experience on my property. Unfortunately they were unable to tell me more."

"Bu—" Annie started, then caught Signor Bernardini's eye. His expression warned her to keep quiet and stay that way. As if anything she might say would be quoted back at her, quite possibly in print.

"We need to ask you some questions," announced Visconti.

"Of course." Gesturing to the colonel to take one of the two remaining seats, Baroni shrugged. "I apologize for my lack of hospitality. As you can see, this warehouse is not designed for receiving guests. I rarely come here myself and I'm only here now to meet you."

Rafael Bernardini's smile was tight as he nodded to a metal chair of a type Annie had seen before. "You sit," he said. "This will not take long and I am happy to stand."

Forcing herself to take the chair, Annie smiled nervously in Rafael Bernardini's direction. His face was tense, mouth set in a thin line, and he made no pretense of smiling. He knew something she didn't, realized Annie, and she wasn't going to like it.

"Colonel Visconti will explain your exact claims to Signor Baroni in Italian. I will translate for you where necessary. Those are the terms under which the colonel is allowing me to be present," said Bernardini, his face grim.

It was over before it had begun and it was almost as if Annie had always known that was how it would be.

As Colonel Visconti began to speak Ugo Baroni's face fell, his expression ranging through shock, outrage, and anger to shock again. And as the carabiniere talked on and on, detailing the allegations against the head of Fava, Signor Bernardini would intervene, translate, and interject, but the intervals became longer and the interjections briefer. When they finished, Ugo Baroni slumped back in his chair, his face a mask of horror.

And then, slowly, haltingly, he began to repeat one name over and over, his voice mirroring the shock written so crudely across his face.

Silvio Vianni.

Suddenly Baroni was on his feet and thumping the desk with one fist, so theatrically that Annie thought the others must know he was acting.

Instead Colonel Visconti rose from his seat and put one hand on Ugo Baroni's arm, as if trying to calm the man; but Baroni merely shook him off, before dropping into his chair, his head in his hands.

"Well?" hissed Annie.

"Signor Baroni is shocked, and appalled," Rafael Bernardini told her. "Shocked at these accusations. And appalled by . . . He has worked many years to build up his label into a successful international business and he cannot believe his finance director could do this to him. Signor Baroni deplores counterfeiting. It is the curse of the fashion industry and he would rather die than allow such things to happen under his roof."

"You mean . . . ?" It was so obvious, Annie couldn't believe she hadn't seen this coming.

"Of course." The newspaper editor nodded. "As usual, you and I have the wrong man. All this has nothing to do with Signor Baroni and he is the wounded party. His most trusted, most loyal member of staff has ruined not just Signor Baroni's reputation, but potentially his whole beloved company. That his own financial director should use Baroni's premises and his company as a cover to import counterfeited goods is a devastating blow. One from which Signor Baroni may never recover."

Annie felt sick.

"This place is full of fakes," she said.

"So Signor Baroni has discovered. He does not know how this can be possible unless his warehouse manager has also been corrupted. The carabinieri are obviously free to search the warehouse and arrest any of his staff."

"This is outrageous," said Annie.

"He agrees," said Rafael Bernardini, voice sour. "And he understands you are upset. All the same, he says Mark Mailer's murder was nothing more than a casual homicide, the American police have said so. As for your friend—Miss Lang—she was a junkie who made wild accusations before killing herself out of grief. It is sad, of course, but for anyone to accuse him of complicity in any of this . . . Well, it's slander, and if such allegations were repeated or, even worse, printed, then he would have no alternative but to sue. Signor Baroni cannot believe we would put him in that situation."

"She wasn't my friend," Annie started to say, and then realized that Patty was, that she had been. She didn't have time to wonder when that had happened.

"So you're going to let him get away with it?" Horrified, Annie looked from Bernardini to Visconti and saw what she'd expected to see: an acceptance that this was how life was.

When Annie opened her mouth to protest, Visconti glanced at Bernardini, and the man stood without a word and led Annie outside.

"The evidence is not on your side," said Bernardini. His voice was kind, but he might as well have been talking to a small child.

"But the tapes . . ."

"Do they really say Ugo Baroni was trying to have Mark Mailer killed?" Annie shook her head. "Not in so many words, but . . ."

"Do they say he was counterfeiting?"

"No."

The man shook his head. "Then they are not enough. You know this already. Ask your lawyers, if you must. They are secondary evidence, nothing more."

"But he's lying!" said Annie. "The cellar is full of fakes. I saw them with my own eyes this morning, Baroni knows that. He was there."

But her breath was wasted. With the sudden clarity of someone who finally realizes that something bigger is at stake than a couple of small, unimportant deaths, Annie knew she was wrong. Most of the counterfeit goods were probably no longer there and would never be again. In the space of an hour, Baroni and his backers had cleared as much as they dared off the premises.

"Even if the fakes are there," said Bernardini, "Signor Baroni swears he was not—and who will believe Vianni when he says he was?" His voice was low. "It will be your word against his and I assure you, the case will take years . . ."

"Years . . . ?"

"Maybe longer. This is how it is done. You know what *omerta* is?"

Of course Annie knew. She'd seen *The Godfather* three times.

Signor Bernardini took her silence as ignorance.

"Baroni will be investigated," he said, "and though these are serious allegations, nothing will be discovered. Still, his backers will lose millions of euros while Baroni calls a halt until everything has quieted down." He paused. "You are not listening properly, Signorina Anderson. If you were, you would not look so depressed."

"What d'you mean?"

"There is another kind of justice," he said patiently. "Ugo Baroni has been careless. His carelessness has proved expensive and will not be overlooked. In many ways you have helped to sign his death warrant. At the very least you can console yourself with the fact that Signor Baroni must spend the rest of his life looking over his shoulder. You see, just because a man escapes once, even twice, does not mean he will go unpunished forever."

It was a nice theory, decided Annie, watching police cars roar belatedly along a narrow road toward her with their sirens wailing. She could only hope it was true.

The wasteland was deserted, and the trestle table with its big silver urns was long gone. The only sign left of the small crowd that had cheered the coming of a new fashion messiah was underfoot, where the grass had been churned to a thick layer of mud by leather soles and the tread of tires.

Chris had parked his silver Alpha at the side of the main road and let Annie walk the three hundred paces to the towpath alone, her heart sinking with every step. She'd wanted to bring flowers, but hadn't been able to decide what Patty would have liked. It wasn't something she had ever known about the model. Her favorite brand of cigarettes, yes. Her taste in men, clothes, and cats.

It was Cathie who suggested snowdrops, Cathie who'd flown through the night to Milan to collect Patty's body.

Apparently Mark had bought Patty a pot of snowdrops in Union Square to put on the roof of their 30th Street apartment, and so far as Cathie knew the flowers were still up there.

"They should be blooming about now," she said.

Annie hoped so.

Mark's mother had ordered bulbs for their double grave. Their ashes would be interred together in New Jersey. MARK MAILER, FASHION DESIGNER AND BELOVED HUSBAND OF PATTY LANG-MAILER. The wife they never got to know, finally adopted, accepted into the Mailer family.

Snowdrops in Milan at almost no notice? Now there was a challenge Annie would never have been able to meet if not for Rebecca, who had asked no questions and expected no thanks. Annie didn't know how she'd done it, or why, but she had: Fashion journalists, too, had their contacts and their ways of pulling in favors. Rebecca hadn't even been angry about the lost May cover, although Annie was not off the hook; she still had to write the story, the tragic romance of Mark and Patty Mailer, and do it by Monday. And that was before she even started on her piece for the *Post*.

That Annie had signed a contract to work for *Handbag* while still employed by the *Post* was something *Handbag*'s editor had yet to comment on. Annie had no doubt she would be hauled over the coals by Rebecca as soon as she returned to London. Assuming Annie didn't just return to the *Post*.

It was warmer today. The wind that whipped along the bank two days earlier had died but the air still had the chill of late winter and the water was still the same unyielding steel gray.

Kneeling beside the canal, Annie stared down, looking as if through a grimy window for some clarity that she knew must exist just beyond her reach. Instead she saw a vision in white, dirty-blond hair turned dark by the water, blue eyes wide open to an unforgiving sky.

First one fragile blossom and then another, a small shower of white and green tumbled from Annie's fingers, each small ripple diminishing the reflection of her memories upon the water's surface. The confetti Patty never had for the wedding no one ever knew took place.

She didn't realize Chris had abandoned the car until she felt his arm around her shoulder. The man was kind, dressed well, looked okay without his clothes, and held her when she cried. He didn't even seem to mind that thanks to her he was now unemployed. Too good to be true? Maybe not this time.

"Write their story," he said.

Annie nodded, watching as the last of the snowdrops disappeared below the surface.

Cathie's plane and her cargo were gone, high above the Atlantic by now. Patty Lang-Mailer was on her way home.

epilogue

The rain stopped sometime before dawn, and the sky that greeted Annie as she pulled the curtain aside was a light, almost bright gray. It was not yet 8 A.M. and the streets of Milan's San Babila district where Chris lived were empty of cars. A church in the street behind was already ringing for Sunday-morning Mass, and below the window two old women scurried along the pavement, unaware of Annie's gaze.

She'd woken thinking not of Patty, or Irina, but of coffee. A large cafetiere of Colombian, the kind you could glug cup after cup, the kind an expat would have stashed in his fridge. Almost the only thing Chris kept there except Peroni and an ice monster.

Sleep hadn't been a big feature of the previous night. And after the sex Annie had talked. It hadn't been easy, but she owed it to Chris to try to make sense of the whole sorry mess.

"Listen," she said. "There are some things you need to know . . ."

When she started she'd intended to keep it to Irina, the girl's death, and Ken's suggestion that Annie spend a few months undercover researching the fashion industry from the inside. In the end Annie covered pretty much everything since she was seventeen. Everything: Tony, the rape, the dreams, failing her A's and falling out with her mother, the drunken one-night stands . . .

And she felt . . . okay. Better than okay, she felt good, like a pressure valve had been released. For the first time in years, Annie felt calm.

Chris said nothing. Just held her close and stroked her hair. He asked no questions, made no comments, merely listened.

"So now you know," Annie concluded. She meant, *Now you know what you're taking on. Now you understand why this is a bad idea. Why I won't be surprised if you walk away.*

The room was silent, just the sound of his breath and hers, the groan of pipes as central heating creaked to life somewhere far below. For a moment Annie wondered if he'd fallen asleep. And then he kissed her forehead very gently.

"It wasn't your fault," he said. The first time she'd heard a voice in the dark that hadn't made her want to cry. Or run. Or both.

"What wasn't?"

"Any of it. Irina, Patty, and especially not Tony. You were sixteen for fuck's sake."

"Seventeen."

"Whatever. It wasn't your fault. Nothing you did made him rape you. You don't have to spend the rest of your life trying to make amends."

"But Irina . . ."

"Annie . . ." Chris shifted himself onto one elbow, his free hand stroking damp hair out of her eyes. "Haven't you been listening to anything you've said?"

Well, no, she hadn't. She'd been the one talking.

"You exposed the man who brought Irina and a hundred like her to Britain, used and abused her and sold her into sexual slavery. Thanks to you, he's in jail, awaiting trial for murder. Yes, Irina's dead, but he killed her, you didn't. And you've saved many other girls who might have gone the same way."

As she lay in the dark and listened to Chris talk, Annie hoped his words were true. "And as for Patty . . . ," said Chris. "She was linked to Mark and Mark was already involved with Ugo long before you met him."

"So you believe me?" Annie said.

"Believe you?"

"That Mark was murdered, that it was a hit . . ."

"Of course I believe you. Mark found out about Baroni's counterfeiting operation from Tom Li and pulled out of the Fava deal. It cost him his life. But even without that Patty was never going to stay clean . . ."

"I know," said Annie. "But Patty was my friend . . ." She stopped, surprised to realize that she meant it. "Not at the beginning, in the beginning she was a case study," Annie admitted, "but she was a friend by the end."

"I know," said Chris. "Even Rebecca was shocked by how badly Patty's death hit you."

He'd talked to *Rebecca*?

"Look." Chris's face in the dim light was deadly serious. "It doesn't matter why you became a journalist in the first place. It's enough that you did and you want to keep doing it. Assuming you do?"

Not be a journalist? Annie sat up and Chris reached for the soft underside of one breast. She swatted his hand away.

"How could I not be a journalist?" Annie said. "I wouldn't be me."

"Well, that's an improvement," said Chris. "When I first met you I wouldn't have put money on you even knowing who *me* was."

The kitchen of Chris's apartment was small, modern, and utterly impenetrable, like the inside of Annie's handbag.

For some reason, the handbag made Annie think of Lou. She had Lou to thank for this. If not for Lou, Annie would never have met Chris, let alone woken up next to him. She'd call Lou and apologize for sulking the second she got back to London. She didn't exactly have best friends to spare.

"Kettle's in the cupboard." Spinning around, Annie found herself standing less than three inches from the man she'd left sleeping just minutes earlier.

"The kettle," he said, sliding his hands inside the dressing gown she'd lifted from the back of his bedroom door, "is in the cupboard."

"Of course it is." Annie wrapped the blue toweling around his back and felt his hip bones push against her. "Which cupboard?"

Chris shrugged.

"Sorry I woke you," Annie added.

"No problem," said Chris. " I was dreaming some woman was wandering around my kitchen half naked and thought I'd better investigate."

It was another hour before the search for Chris's kettle resumed; and this time Annie tossed Chris the dressing gown and left him to it.

"How come you've got such great clothes," she asked when he finally returned with a tray, two cups, and a plate of dry biscuits. "And your dressing gown is so crap?"

"Easy," said Chris, dumping the tray on the floor beside his futon. "My mum bought me this for Christmas years ago and I haven't gotten around to replacing it. Never worked for a designer who did dressing gowns. Talking of which . . ." His expression grew serious. "There's something I need to tell you."

Reaching for a mug, Annie took her coffee and tried to remember to breathe while she played out all the possible scenarios in her head. *I'm married, I've got four children, I'm gay and you were just a detour . . .*

"I've got a new job."

Phew! Annie smiled. "That's great," she said. "I felt so bad about the bust-up with Baroni, losing your job because of me . . ."

"It wasn't because of you. Ugo and I fell out months ago. That's why I was in New York. Looking for a new job, remember?"

Shit. Yes, of course she remembered. "Oh, you got it, that's . . . great." Annie took a sip of hot, dark liquid.

"Thing is," Chris said, "I'm not sure New York's such a good idea anymore."

"You should go." Those were the words that came out of Annie's mouth.

For a second Chris was silent. His face gave nothing away.

"We could still see each other," said Annie, too quickly. She searched for her air-hostess smile but she seemed to have left it on a plane. "I can visit."

"Is that what you want?"

Annie swallowed. She liked Chris, she trusted him, she thought she might even be in love. She knew she didn't want him three thousand miles away on the wrong side of the Atlantic. Milan was just two hours on a plane on Friday night; New York was something else.

"Is it?"

Slowly, Annie shook her head. "No . . . not really, but it's your career."

Chris smiled and began to unwrap the sheet Annie had pulled around her. "My career's fine," he said. "When people discover I'm on the market I'll be beating them off with a stick. I could stay here or go to Paris or even—" He eyed Annie nervously. "—move back to London."

He gave the sheet a final tug. "Of course, I'd need you to do me a deal . . ."

Annie wasn't sure she liked where this was going. She wasn't a deal kind of girl.

"What?"

"I want to meet your family."

The man was kind, dressed well, looked okay without his clothes, and held her when she cried. She'd always known there'd be a flaw and there was. Chris was clearly insane.

"You want to do *what*?"

"Come on," said Chris. "They can't be that bad. They produced you and—okay, I admit it, you're fucked up, but I've seen worse."

"Cheers." Annie thumped him. When she looked at him again, his gray eyes didn't waver. "You're for real, aren't you?"

He nodded. "If I turn that job down, I'm doing it for us. What about you?"

"Me?"

"What are you doing for us?"

Annie raised her eyebrows. There was an *us*, she couldn't, didn't want to pretend otherwise. All the same . . . "Go on then," she said finally. "Get my bag. It's next door, on the floor.

"You'll regret it," she added, upturning the contents onto the sheets. "Seriously, you'll rue the day you ever set foot in Basingstoke."

"Try me."

The phone, as always, was answered within three rings.

"Mum," Annie said. "It's me."

The anticipated onslaught didn't come. Instead, her mother sounded relieved just to hear the sound of Annie's voice.

"Yes," said Annie. "I am, I'm absolutely fine. I was wondering . . . You know I said I might meet someone in Italy. Well, actually it was New York . . ."

about the author

SAM BAKER has been a writer and editor for numerous British women's magazines, including *Red, New Woman, Chat,* and *Take a Break.* After successfully relaunching the seminal teenage magazine *Just Seventeen* as *J-17,* she became editor of the British young women's magazine *Company.* Now editor in chief of *Cosmopolitan* in the UK, she is a regular broadcaster on young women's issues. Although Sam has spent the last six years on the twice-yearly merry-go-round that is the seasonal ready-to-wear shows, she confesses she still hasn't learned to kick that "fashion feeling." Sam lives between Winchester, Hampshire, and London with her partner, the author Jon Courtenay Grimwood.

about the type

This book was set in Garamond, a typeface originally designed by the Parisian typecutter Claude Garamond (1480–1561). This version of Garamond was modeled on a 1592 specimen sheet from the Egenolff-Berner foundry, which was produced from types assumed to have been brought to Frankfurt by the punchcutter Jacques Sabon.

Claude Garamond's distinguished romans and italics first appeared in *Opera Ciceronis* in 1543–44. The Garamond types are clear, open, and elegant.